# Kate Glanville

# A PERFECT HOME

**ACCENT**

The right of Kate Glanville to be identified as the Author of
the Work has been asserted by her in accordance with the
Copyright, Designs and Patents Act 1988.

First published in Great Britain in 2014 by Accent Press

This edition published in 2023 by Headline Accent
An imprint of HEADLINE PUBLISHING GROUP

1

Cataloguing in Publication Data is available from the British Library

ISBN 978 1 4722 8032 9

Typeset in 10.5/13pt Bembo Std by Jouve (UK), Milton Keynes

Printed and bound in Great Britain by Clays Ltd, Elcograf S.p.A.

MIX
Paper from
responsible sources
FSC® C104740

Headline's policy is to use papers that are natural, renewable and recyclable
products and made from wood grown in well-managed forests and other
controlled sources. The logging and manufacturing processes are expected
to conform to the environmental regulations of the country of origin.

To Alex and all the other fabulous women who have inspired me to pursue my dreams.

# Chapter One

*'Years of hard work and imagination have created a stunning family home in the heart of the English countryside.'*

A butterfly settled briefly on the crisp, white washing, its wings quivering in the air. It looked so delicate, so exquisitely beautiful. Claire wanted to touch it, to feel the velvet fluttering in her palm. Unable to help herself, she reached out – but in that second it was gone. She looked around, shading her eyes with her hand against the late-afternoon sun. Then she saw it, flying in a haphazard zigzag across the flower beds, over the flagstones and towards the house. It looked as though it might fly through the open doors of the conservatory but, as if pulled by an invisible string, it suddenly ascended until it was high above the steep pitch of yellow thatch, a dot against the cornflower sky before it vanished completely.

Claire took a deep breath and carried on working her way along the washing line. The scent of sage and lavender and cut grass mingled on the warm breeze, which brushed her cotton skirt against her legs and blew through the long strands of hair escaping from a clasp at the back of her neck.

She felt unusually calm as she un-pegged the sheets and pillow-cases and folded them into the wicker basket at her feet. The children had been fed and homework completed, a fish pie was cooking in the Aga for William's supper, she had packed up ten appliquéd cushion covers and thirty lavender hearts to give to Sally for the gallery and the boxes of stock to take to the school

1

fête were already neatly stacked in the back of the car. Claire looked at her watch; it wasn't even six o'clock. The washing was now done and she had deadheaded the roses around the porch to try to get a second flush of flowers before the photo shoot for *Idyllic Homes* magazine in five weeks. All that was left was to make two dozen fairy cakes for the fête tomorrow and put the children to bed, then she could pour herself a large glass of chilled Chardonnay and relax. For once she was in control.

Claire walked through the living room with the washing basket. She stopped to look at a selection of cushions arranged on the leather sofa. Each one was appliquéd with a little patchwork house made of felt; lines of silk embroidery traced the doors and windows and the roofs were made from faded corduroy, the gardens were a colourful concoction of antique ribbon and lace with gingham trees and pearly button-headed flowers. Claire had arranged the cushions on the sofa to decide if she liked the design. With the washing basket in her arms, she looked at them for the umpteenth time that day, trying to visualise how they might look in the gallery in town where she had recently started selling her work. Sally, Claire's best friend who worked in the gallery part-time, had finally been entrusted to do the window display. Anna, the gallery owner, had come up with the theme of 'home' for the display and it had been Sally's idea that Claire should design a range of cushions that would be central to her design.

The little fabric houses were not unlike Claire's own: symmetrical and square at the front, a flower-covered central door. It was a child's idea of a house. A doll's house. A perfect house.

Claire's house had once been a farm, but the farmland was long gone, leaving only a garden and small orchard around the eighteenth-century building. Its neatly proportioned stone walls, painted in a rich buttermilk cream, sat beneath a dark, honey-coloured thatch. The roof arched around two dormer windows on the second floor which gave the effect of heavy-browed eyes staring out impassively.

In May, wisteria bloomed along the front in a blush of pink and from late June lipstick-red roses blazed around the thatched porch. The back of the house rambled in a hotchpotch of extensions added over the previous two hundred years. The thatch clung to the additions in smooth, undulating curves, blanketing them like royal icing on a cake. The biggest extension was the large kitchen that William had built the year Oliver was born, and next to it was his latest project, a Victorian-style conservatory.

'It's so charming,' visitors would enthuse when they first saw the house. But every time Claire pulled into the drive she never got rid of the sense that it was watching her, judging her, making her feel she didn't quite deserve to live there.

Claire wasn't sure about the cushions – too twee perhaps? Too fussy? Something behind the sofa caught her eye – something wet and red and out of place. Claire picked up the dripping box of defrosted red mush. Her heart sank when she saw the pool of liquid on the floorboards. What would William say?

'Emily, Oliver, Ben!' she shouted. 'Who's taken raspberries out of the freezer and left them on the new oak floor?'

'Not me,' said Oliver from the other end of the room, where he lay draped across a jacquard-covered armchair eating chocolate Hobnobs straight from the packet. He was wearing a battered fisherman's hat of his father's; it was much too big and fell lazily over his eyes. From underneath it he watched animated cyber-warriors showing off their martial-arts skills in the defence of the universe.

'Not me,' echoed Ben, sitting cross-legged much too close to the cyber-warriors, naked apart from a bulging nappy and a smearing of melted chocolate around his mouth.

'Oliver, please could you find a more suitable programme for Ben to watch?' Claire asked as she peeled a half-sucked biscuit from the floor. 'This will give him nightmares, and put those back in the cupboard.'

'But Mum,' Oliver protested. 'This is my favourite programme and I *need* these, I'm starving.'

'Ben did it.' Emily appeared in the French windows, a long

3

daisy and buttercup chain in her hands. 'He must have put the raspberries there after I gave them to him yesterday. He was meant to put them in the fridge to defrost and tell you that they were there so we could have them on our cereal for breakfast.'

'He's only two,' Claire sighed.

'Nearly three,' said Emily.

'Why were they out of the freezer in the first place?'

'The freezer was too full,' replied Emily, shrugging her shoulders as she wrapped the floral chain around her thin wrist.

'But the freezer has lots of room in it.'

'Not enough for the rose petal ice cream that I made.' Emily smiled at Claire, showing her missing front teeth. 'I made it for Daddy. Milk, sugar, margarine, chocolate sauce, orange juice, Ribena and flower petals all mixed up in a cake tin. It's frozen now; I thought Daddy could have it for tea when he gets home.'

'How many times have I told you, Emily, no cooking without me? And what am I going to do with the raspberries now? You've wasted a whole box of fruit.' She shook it to emphasize her point.

'Careful, Mummy,' Emily warned. 'You're dripping raspberry juice all over the washing.'

The phone rang. Claire thought about ignoring it. It was probably her mother, but it might be William telling her he was stopping off at Homebase to look for flathead screws or tile grout. Worst of all, it might be her mother-in-law. While she dithered, Emily jumped to answer it.

'It's a strange woman,' she said in a stage whisper.

A loud, gushing voice greeted Claire as she took the handset.

'Claire, darling, how are you?' The woman on the other end of the line gave no time for Claire to answer. 'Wonderful, wonderful . . .'

She realised it must be the journalist, Celia Howard, from the magazine. She took a tissue and mopped ineffectually at the stain on the floor as she held the receiver under her chin.

'Enjoying the sunshine in that lovely country home of yours? Not like us stuck here in stuffy London,' Celia was saying. '*Super.*

4

How lucky you are. Now, darling, about this photo shoot – we've been thinking about it in the office and we think your house would be just *perfect* for our Christmas issue. We're writing features for that now so if we just change you to a festive shoot it will fit in wonderfully.'

'So you're not coming to photograph it at the end of August?' asked Claire, relieved at the idea of a postponement. She could put off all that cleaning now.

'That's right, darling; that date's all off now. We work four months in advance and the Christmas issue comes out at the beginning of November so the timing for this is fabulous. I've arranged it all and we'll be with you on Thursday.'

Claire stifled a cry. It was Monday afternoon – and Thursday gave her only two days to get ready and she had the school fête the next day and Oliver's piano exam and Emily's ballet class and she had an appointment at the dentist and Ben wasn't booked into nursery and the plug on the Hoover was broken; her mind spiralled into panic.

'Celia, I don't think I can –'

'It's a two-day shoot so the photographer will be with you on Friday as well,' Celia interrupted. 'Unfortunately I'm up to my eyes this week so I can't come to do the actual interview until next week. Now, of course we'll need to decorate the house in festive style. If you could get out a few decorations; just your usual ones. I don't want you to go to any trouble.'

'You want me to put up Christmas decorations in July?'

'No, you don't have to put them up, dear. Leave that to the stylist,' said Celia. 'She'll bring a tree and decorate it herself.'

'A tree?'

'Yes, she'll bring a Christmas tree. Unless you can get a tree locally – a good bushy one. You know, a silver Scots Pine or something like that.'

'I think I'd better leave that to you.' Finding the perfect Christmas tree in July would be difficult. Finding a good one in December was hard enough.

5

'And could you make some beautiful Christmas stockings to hang on the mantelpiece, in your lovely Emily Love style?' Celia went on. 'Covered in your gorgeous pearly buttons? We could feature them as a reader offer – I'm sure you'll get lots of orders. Oh, and some mince pies would be lovely. We always have mince pies.'

'OK,' said Claire, though it really wasn't OK. She felt a tight knot of anxiety forming in her stomach. Where was she going to find the time?

'Now I told you about the *fabulous* photographer, Sienna Crabtree, that we were going to be using for the shoot?'

'Yes, she sounds great.' Claire desperately tried to rearrange all the things she was meant to be doing, in her mind.

'Sienna really is wonderful, but she isn't available now, so I'm sending a photographer called Stefan Kendrick. He's very good, recently back from working abroad. He's a *brilliant* photographer and a big hit with the female staff round here and some of the men are rather smitten too. You'll absolutely love him, darling.'

Claire made a face at the phone. She didn't care how gorgeous he was; she just wanted someone to help her tidy the house from top to bottom, wipe the jam-smeared doorknobs, scrub the kitchen floor, dust the Cornishware on the dresser and most of all someone to help her get the raspberry juice out of the floorboards before William came home.

'Must dash,' said Celia. 'A million and one things to do. I wish I had your life in the heavenly countryside – *totally* stressfree, I'm sure. Lots of love.'

Celia was gone before Claire had a chance to reply. She stayed squatting behind the sofa, staring at the soggy tissue and pink stain, trying to understand how she had suddenly found herself getting ready for Christmas during a July heatwave. She looked down at the bulge her stomach made above the waistband of her skirt and hoped she wouldn't be expected to be in the photographs. She'd felt fat and frumpy since Ben had been born; there never seemed to be the time to lose that extra stone or get a proper haircut.

She licked raspberry juice from her fingers and wished she'd never let Sally get her into this in the first place.

It had been a month since Sally had persuaded Claire to send the pictures to *Idyllic Homes* magazine.

'The most important thing for any e-commerce site is to get the images right,' said Sally's husband Gareth who was designing Claire a website for her new business, Emily Love. 'Then you can leave it to me to work my magic on everything else.'

Claire had photographed a selection of her designs around her house; the pale colours and antique furniture made a perfect back-drop for the cushions, bags, and aprons which Claire appliquéd with vintage fabric and decorated with embroidery, ribbons, lace, and buttons.

'These pictures are fab,' Sally enthused, looking over Gareth's shoulder as he and Claire sat at the computer in Sally and Gareth's cramped, chaotic study. They tried to ignore the screeches and screams coming from the rest of the tiny terraced cottage as the children rampaged from room to room. 'You should send them to a magazine and get some publicity for Emily Love.' Sally picked up a copy of *Idyllic Homes* from a jumbled pile of newspapers and catalogues in one corner. 'I've been drooling over the things in this one.'

'With a cup of coffee and a chocolate éclair no doubt,' muttered Gareth. 'While I'm out slaving hard at work.'

'You don't know what hard work is,' Sally scorned. 'You try getting those two hooligan sons of yours out of the door to school every morning then you wouldn't be begrudging me a quick sit down with a magazine before I leave for the gallery.' She flicked through the pages of the magazine and showed Claire a glossy two-page spread. *Swish into Summer with Our Top Ten Designs for Curtain Poles!* read the heading.

'You could try making the beds or washing up before you leave for work instead of fantasising about fancy curtain poles,' said Gareth.

'You could try repairing *our* curtain pole in the living room and then I might not need to fantasise,' Sally countered.

'I did repair it.'

'With gaffer tape! It's hardly stylish, is it?' Sally gave Gareth's long thin ponytail a tug, he yelped and gave her well-upholstered bottom a slap.

'Stop this right now!' Claire put on her best stern mother voice and laughed. 'No fighting. My mother-in-law always says it's vulgar to argue in front of others; she says you shouldn't display your dirty linen in public.'

'There's plenty of dirty linen on display on our bedroom floor,' Sally said with a huff as she folded her arms across her generous cleavage.

'Well, you could pick it up sometimes,' said Gareth.

'I could if I had a linen basket that hadn't lost its bottom when your two sons tried to use it as a Tardis.'

'They're your sons too. I'll mend the laundry basket tonight.'

'With what?'

'With gaffer tape!'

'I SAID STOP!' Claire had to shout above their raised voices but she was smiling, she was used to Sally and Gareth. One moment they'd be bickering like children and the next giggling together like love-struck teenagers.

Sally tossed her mane of long blonde hair and looked at Claire. 'It's all right for you living with Mr Perfect, king of home improvements. You have your immaculate home to go back to when you leave here while I just have to live in this squalor all the time.'

'I like your house,' said Claire. 'It feels cosy. Sometimes I wish our house was a bit more like this.' She gestured at the disarray around her. 'I think William gets fussier every day. I certainly don't dare leave my dirty linen lying around any more.'

'Quit moaning,' said Sally. 'You don't know how lucky you are.'

'Talking of dirty linen, let's get back to your website, Claire.'

'Don't be so cheeky, Gareth,' laughed Claire. 'It's not dirty linen, it's vintage fabric.'

'And it's uber fashionable at the moment,' added Sally. 'That's why you should get it in a magazine.'

Fifteen minutes later they'd made up a press release, attached a selection of pictures, and pinged it off to *Idyllic Homes*. Claire had practically forgotten all about it when Celia Howard, features editor for *Idyllic Homes*, phoned up two days later, saying her magazine adored the cushions ('recycling fabric is so *in* right now') but they also loved the look of the house.

'*Exquisite!*' Celia had gushed. 'We'd love to do a feature on your gorgeous house and your lovely little rural craft business. Our readers just adore that sort of thing.'

William seemed quite pleased with the idea of showing off his home.

'I'll have to finish grouting the tiles on the conservatory floor,' he had said. 'And then I'll have to re-paint the hall. It's covered in mucky handprints. You've got to stop the children touching the walls, Claire.'

He was keen to be there on the day of the shoot, though Claire suspected that this was because he wanted to make sure the stylist didn't damage any paintwork or scratch the floors.

'They're not going to bang nails into the beams, are they?' he asked, as he touched up the paint on the banisters. He carefully dipped his brush in and out of a pot of Farrow & Ball Shaded White, dabbing at dots of missing paint. 'There are enough holes and chips all over this house as it is.'

'I can't see any holes or chips,' said Claire, trying to squeeze past him with a pile of ironing. 'It looks fine to me.' She stroked his head affectionately as she passed; she liked the stubbly feel of his new haircut. He pushed her hand away.

'That's the trouble,' William answered. 'You just don't notice the state this house is getting into.'

Claire bit her lip. She couldn't face an argument when she still had the tea to make and the children to bath. She continued up the stairs counting each tread as she did so. By the time she reached the top her threatened tears had passed.

At last the shock of Celia Howard's phone call began to lessen and Claire moved out from behind the sofa. She feared the raspberry stain was there for good and pushed the sofa back to hide it. As she did so she revealed something grey and lumpy which could only have been regurgitated by Macavity the cat. She didn't know how long it had been there; it was encrusted onto the floor and in between the boards. On closer inspection it looked as though it contained at least half of what had once been a bat. Claire shuddered. She'd deal with it later, she thought, and moved the sofa at an angle to cover it.

As she picked up the basket to wash the juice-splashed washing all over again, she thought about Celia's last words. *Stress-free life*? She had no idea.

Claire looked at the large clock on the kitchen wall – half past nine. The fish pie looked sad and dry on top of the pale blue Aga.

Claire helped herself to a portion and ate it at the same time as writing a list of all the things she had to do before the magazine shoot. She contemplated having more wine but this would break her self-enforced rule of one glass a night. After a few minutes she poured an inch or two of Chardonnay into the large glass and mixed it with some soda water. Surely a spritzer didn't really count?

The table was half covered in fairy cakes. On reflection Claire thought it had probably been a mistake to throw the defrosted raspberries into the cake mixture, which made them look soggy and unappealingly pink.

The phone rang and Claire leapt up to answer it before it woke Ben. She knew it would be her mother, Elizabeth.

'I'm not disturbing you, am I? You sound like you're eating.'

'No, it's all right, Mum,' Claire said, trying not to sigh.

'William not home yet, then?'

'I'm sure he's on his way. Actually I'm in a bit of a rush; the house is being photographed –'

'He's just like your father used to be . . .'

Claire wished she'd just pretended William was there.

'. . . Coming in whenever it suited him, no thought to me waiting for him after a hard day at work and looking after you. In the seventies we thought the next generation would be better, but they're all the same. Men! Better off without them, if you ask me. Honestly, Claire, I don't know why you don't put your foot down. You've got to stand up to him. That's what I used to do.'

Claire could remember lying in bed with her hands over her ears, trying not to hear her parents shouting downstairs.

'Of course your father was usually with another woman,' her mother continued. 'I always suspected that. I knew deep down but always forgave him. And look what he did in the end. Look where I ended up: dumped in a bedsit while he gallivanted off to California with his teenage bride.'

Claire didn't dare remind her that the woman her father had finally left her for was nearly thirty. 'It's a two-bedroomed flat, Mum, not a bedsit. And it's been twenty-six years since he left. You could have moved house. You could have found someone else.'

'And let someone do it to me all over again? No, thank you, I'm not that stupid.' Claire closed her eyes. She was used to this. She'd listened to her mother's tirades since she was ten years old and her assault on marriage hadn't lessened when Claire became a bride herself.

Elizabeth had been baffled by her daughter's wish to get married, especially to an accountant. Since Claire's father had left, she'd brought her daughter up to believe that marriage was a pointless institution that could only fail.

Claire had been determined to prove her wrong. Her marriage, unlike her parents', would work. Happily ever after, just like in the fairy tales.

'I'll see you at the school fête tomorrow,' said Elizabeth.

'You don't need to come, Mum. William has promised to take the afternoon off to look after the children while I'm on my stall.'

'And you believe him?'

'Mum! I'm sure he'll try his best to be there.'

'Well, I'm coming anyway, Claire. I'm longing to see all your

11

things displayed on your stall. This will be a big day for you, the first time you've shown your work in public.'

'It's a primary school summer fair, Mum, not a major exhibition at the V&A.'

'It's important; three years at art college shouldn't be wasted on just being a housewife.'

'Yes, Mum,' said Claire, and she added *polish banisters* to her list.

'Nightmare evening,' William said, suddenly seeming to fill the kitchen. 'The train was late, then I went to get the wood for the living-room shelves but they didn't have the right thickness. Can you believe it? It's a standard measurement. So I had to go miles out of my way to bloody B&Q.' He handed a bunch of yellow carnations to Claire and pulled loose his tie.

'I'd better go, Mum, William's home.' Claire put down the phone and smiled up at her husband, wondering how she could incorporate the carnations into the Christmas decor. 'Thank you for the flowers. Glass of wine?'

William was already opening a bottle of red, twisting the corkscrew down hard, before pulling out the cork with a muffled pop. He poured himself a large glass.

'Let me guess,' he said, nodding towards the phone. 'Your mother – as usual.'

'She's lonely, especially since she retired from teaching.'

'I'm not surprised she's lonely.' He sniffed at the fish pie. 'Who'd want to be with someone so miserable?'

'Please don't be cruel, William,' she said, pouring water into a glass vase. 'She hasn't had it easy. It's not like it is for your parents. They've been lucky. They have each other and a lovely home and lots of things to keep them busy.'

'That's right; you wouldn't find my mother moping about finding fault with her life.'

Claire held back the desire to say she was too busy finding fault with everybody else's.

'Fish pie?' she asked, putting on her brightest smile.

'I'll have it later. What are these?' He picked up a fairy cake.

'Raspberry buns. Do you want one?'

He shook his head. 'I'm going to put the new shelves up.'

'It's nearly ten o'clock. Isn't it a bit late? You might wake the children.'

'It's all right for you at home all day, Claire, but I've got to get things done when I can if you want this house to look perfect.' He collected the keys for his tool shed and headed for the back door.

Claire wanted to say she didn't want it to be perfect, didn't *need* it to be perfect. She was happy with it how it was. If only William could sit back and enjoy it, enjoy his family. Enjoy her, like he used to before they had the children, before Jack had died. She started arranging the carnations in the vase. William stopped, his hand on the door handle, and turned to look at her, his eyes softening. He suddenly walked back across the room.

'Sorry, darling. I don't mean to sound so irritable. It's been a long hard day and having to go to B&Q was the final straw.'

Claire reached up to kiss his cheek and wrapped her arms around him; the muscles in his back felt tense.

'I could give you a massage,' she offered.

'Maybe later. Tell me how your day's been?'

'You won't believe what the magazine people want to do,' she said, her cheek still pressed against his pinstriped shirt. 'They're going to come on –'

'Isn't that a bit tall for those flowers?' he interrupted her mid flow. 'I imagined you would put them in that Moorcroft vase my mother gave you for your birthday.'

'I think I might need that for the holly.'

'Holly?' He disentangled himself from her embrace. 'Why would you have holly at this time of year?'

'I was just trying to tell you.' Claire bent down to search in the dresser cupboard for a tin to put the cakes into. 'The magazine people are coming to photograph the house on Thursday and they want it to be a Christmas shoot. Christmas in July! I'm worried we'll never get the house ready in time.'

She turned around to an empty room. The thought struck her that William didn't need to have an affair like her father had done – the house was already his mistress.

'Claire!'

William was back. His face had turned the sort of blotchy red that she always knew meant trouble.

'What the hell has been going on in the living room? Did you know that the cat's been sick and there's a huge stain on the floor?'

'Oh, that was an accident with Ben and some raspberries. And Macavity –'

'I've only just laid that floor – it took me weeks to sand and varnish. Now I'll have to do it all over again.'

Claire took a deep breath.

'The stain is behind the sofa. No one will notice,' she said.

'I'll notice. Every time I walk in there I'll know it's there.'

'I'm sure it will fade with time.' Claire tried to sound optimistic.

William ran his fingers through his close-cropped hair. 'Can't you just try to look after the place a bit more?'

'I do, I really do but . . .' Claire began, but he held up his hand to stop her like a policeman holding up a line of traffic. He picked up his wine glass and left the room.

A surge of rage welled up inside Claire and, picking up a fairy cake, she threw it towards the empty doorway. It fell short and rolled across the quarry tiles to where Macavity sat inelegantly licking his back leg. He sniffed it for a few seconds and wandered away towards the fish pie on the Aga.

Claire sat down as the rage turned into a familiar lethargy. After all these years the house was finished; William had made a beautiful home, and now Claire felt that he almost resented having to share it with his family.

She looked at the flowers on the table and thought of her grandmother's florist stall in the little northern mining town where she had lived. As a child, Claire would sit on a stool in the corner and watch her grandmother making up bouquets and wreaths in the freezing early-morning air of the market. *All the flowers have something to tell us*, she used to say. *They all have their own special message, their very own language.* Claire tried to remember – red carnations were for longing and white for faithfulness but what were yellow? She closed her eyes and could see the reels of shiny satin ribbon that her little fingers had longed to unravel and the rolls of pastel-coloured wrapping paper laid out on the trestle table. Her grandmother's soft northern accent filtered into her mind: *You don't ever want to be given yellow carnations, Claire. Only disappointment comes with those.*

She slowly put the fairy cakes, one by one, into the tin. Had she become a disappointment to William? Or was the disappointment life itself? Ever since Jack had died he seemed to have become obsessed with the house, shutting her out, burying himself in DIY. It had been years since they visited Jack's grave together, she couldn't remember the last time William had even mentioned his name.

After a few minutes she heard drilling coming from the living room and then the sound of Ben crying upstairs. Emily appeared in the doorway, her long toffee-coloured hair tangled, her sleepy eyes half closed.

'Ben's awake,' she mumbled.

'I know,' said Claire. 'I'll be up a minute. You go back to bed.'

'Did Daddy have his ice cream?' Emily walked up to the table. She looked at the cupcakes and then at Claire. 'Don't worry, Mummy. I won't tell anyone you made them.'

'I'm starving.' Oliver stood beside them in his rumpled stripy pyjamas, the fisherman's hat still on his head. 'Is there anything to eat?'

'You've brushed your teeth. You'll have to wait till breakfast. Now go to bed, please.'

'I'll brush them again, I promise. I'll never get back to sleep without some food.' Oliver collapsed onto a kitchen chair as if weak with hunger, despite having eaten two helpings of spaghetti bolognaise and a bowl of ice cream for tea.

'Have one of these, then,' she said, picking up a fairy cake.

15

'No, I mean proper food,' he said, wrinkling up his nose in disgust. 'You know, like from a shop.'

'Claire! There's chocolate all over the armchair. How did it get there?' William shouted from the living room. Claire looked up at the ceiling and tried to count to ten. She gave up at five. 'And there are crumbs. Has someone being eating biscuits in here?'

'Come on,' said Emily to her brother. 'Let's go.'

'I think I've trodden on a cake,' said Oliver, as he moved towards the door and flicked damp sponge off his bare foot in a spray of soggy cake crumbs. William stood in the doorway. The children squeezed past him.

'Is there no end to the mess you all create?' he called after them.

'They're children,' said Claire as she fetched the dustpan and brush. 'It's a family home, not a show house, can't you just try and lighten up a little?'

'Lighten up?' William looked incredulous. 'All I'm asking is that everyone sticks to the house rules. Do you think my mother would have let me eat a chocolate biscuit in the living room when I was a boy?'

'No, I'm sure she wouldn't.' Claire squatted on the floor sweeping up the cake crumbs. She resisted the urge to say that William's mother probably didn't let William or his father eat anything unless they were sitting at the dining table with damask napkins and wearing full evening dress.

William turned to go back in the living room then stopped.

'Those cushions on the chesterfield?'

'The new ones with the houses on them?'

'Yes.'

Claire sighed. 'Don't worry, William, they're not staying there, they're going to the gallery for Sally's window.'

'That's a shame.'

Claire looked up from her sweeping, surprised. 'Is it?'

'Yes. I like them. They're very good.' He smiled at her. 'Well done.'

# Chapter Two

*'Quirky vintage finds complement the classic furnishings
around this stylishly refurbished home.'*

William was late. Claire desperately scanned the playground to see if she could see him coming. A crowd of parents gathered around the school gates waiting for the children to come out of the classrooms and the fête to start.

'What a splendid display, Mrs Elliott,' Mrs Wenham stood in front of Claire's stall, her jowly face heavily made-up, her steely grey hair perfectly coiffed, hairspray glinting in the afternoon sun.

Claire smiled back at Oliver and Emily's headmistress and tried to stop Ben from climbing up the table and lying across her display.

'Thank you for giving me the opportunity to have a stall,' Claire said.

'Here at Oakwood Primary, we like to support our parents' endeavours, however small.' She picked up a leaflet that Claire had hastily printed on the computer in the early hours of the morning. 'I see you have a website. More professional than I thought.' Sally winked at Claire from her position on the cake stall next door. 'Maybe you'd like to come into school one day and do a little bit of sewing with the children?' Mrs Wenham gazed at the colourful array of cushions, aprons, shopping bags, and tea-cosies. Heart-shaped gingham lavender bags hung from a collection of twigs in a jar and strings of pretty pastel bunting fluttered against the wire fence behind the stall. In the middle of the fence Claire had strung a long calico banner spelling out Emily Love in spotty letters.

'Emily Love,' Mrs Wenham read out. 'How quaint.' She moved on to the cake stall where Sally was trying to disguise the fact that her mouth was full of chocolate brownie. Mrs Wenham peered at Sally's face.

'I think I'd better go and open the gates before you eat all the stock, Mrs Smith.' Mrs Wenham gave a little braying laugh and hurried away, her high heels clicking on the tarmac.

'Condescending old goat.' Sally glared at the head teacher's retreating back. 'She insisted that I go on this stall – what does she expect me to do, stand back and admire it? Surely she doesn't think I got to look like this on a diet of rice cakes and lettuce, it takes hard work. I'm like an elite athlete – they need to go to the gym all the time to maintain their physiques, I need to eat chocolate brownies and Tunnocks tea cakes to maintain mine.' With a wiggle of her hips Sally pushed up her cleavage and smoothed her bright red top over her generously rounded stomach.

'What do you think?' Claire had come round to look at her stall from the front. She balanced Ben on one hip as she surveyed it, her head tilted, a critical expression on her face. 'Maybe there are too many cushions on the right-hand side.'

'It looks fantastic – look out, Cath Kidston!'

Ben made a lunge for Sally's stall. Claire held on to him with a firm grip.

'I wish William would hurry up.'

'I'm sure he'll be here soon,' Sally reassured her. 'I expect he's caught in traffic. Does Ben want one of these raspberry buns? I don't imagine they'll be very popular. I just can't think who made them.'

'I can't think either,' said Claire. 'But at least they tried. I bet you haven't contributed a thing.' Sally pulled herself up tall and pointed proudly to a lemon drizzle loaf. 'Don't go casting aspersions about me, Claire Elliot, don't tell me I don't contribute.'

Claire's eyes widened in surprise. 'Wow, Sally, that looks

delicious. For someone who says they'd rather go through child-birth again than bake a cake, you've done really well.'

After a moment's pause Sally's pretty face creased into laughter.

'Do you really think I could have made a lemon cake? I can't even put a fish finger in a cold oven without burning it.'

Claire picked up the golden loaf and looked at it. 'But isn't that your handwriting on the label?'

Sally took it back from her and put it prominently in the centre of her stall. 'Oldest trick in The Bad Mother's Handbook – buy the cheapest cake you can find in Tesco, take it out of its pack-aging, bash it up a bit on top, wrap cling film around it, stick on a hand-written label, *et voilà* – instant brownie points. I made sure Mrs Wenham saw me produce four of those from my bag, she even asked me to put one by for her to give to Mr Wenham for his tea.'

Claire shook her head at her friend. 'I've known you for over ten years and you never cease to amaze me,' she said. 'How do you do it? I'd never get away with that scam; I'm hopeless at telling lies.'

'Are you?' Sally's eyebrows rose. 'What about those mushy raspberry things?'

Claire raised her hands in surrender. 'OK, they're mine.'

'I knew it.' Sally laughed. 'Only you would use such pretty cupcake cases.'

Mrs Wenham's haughty voice crackled through the tannoy and suddenly people were pouring into the school yard. Within seconds Claire's stall was surrounded by enthusiastic mothers exclaiming with *ooh*s and *aah*s of delight, snatching up items and clutching them possessively in case anyone else should get hold of them.

Claire still had Ben hoisted on her hip and with one hand she started slipping things into paper bags and taking money as a stream of sales began.

Emily appeared, begging to have her face painted, and Oliver sauntered over to tell Claire she owed the meat roast stall one pound for the burger he held in his greasy hands. Tomato sauce dripped from his bun onto a small tote bag that Claire had been particularly pleased with.

'Look what you've done, Oliver,' Claire cried.

'That's spoiled now,' said a mother from the reception class. 'Can I have it for half price?'

A gust of wind blew and the Emily Love banner fell down onto the dusty tarmac where Claire's eager customers trampled on it in their fervour to get to the stall.

*Where was William?*

'I'll take him off you now.' Elizabeth plucked Ben from Claire's arms. 'Come along, Emily, let's get this face of yours painted. Here's five pounds, Oliver, now get those mucky paws away from your mother's stall and go and throw a sponge at a teacher or something.'

'Thanks, Mum,' Claire called out with relief as her mother and the children disappeared into the crowd.

An hour later only three bags, an apron, and two cushions remained. Claire felt exhausted and hot as she sat down on the edge of a nearby sand pit.

'Wow.' Sally came across to see her. 'You were popular.'

'Hello, ladies.' William appeared beside them looking handsome in a pale grey suit and lilac tie. He gave Sally a kiss on the cheek. 'Looking lovely today, Mrs Smith.' Sally grinned at him, lapping up the compliment. 'Red is definitely your colour.'

'You're not looking so bad yourself,' Sally replied. 'Is that a new haircut, Mr Elliott?'

Claire rolled her eyes.

'When you two have finished admiring each other perhaps you could tell me where the hell you've been, William.'

He turned to Claire and gave her a kiss on her cheek. 'I am *so* sorry, darling. The traffic was terrible all the way.'

'Told you,' said Sally pointedly to Claire.

'And I just had to stop off and pick up that replacement part for the hedge cutter. I hope I've not missed too much.'

20

'You missed seeing my stall,' said Claire. 'Not to mention looking after the children.'

William turned to look at Claire's stall beside him.

'It looks wonderful,' he said. 'Very nice.'

'There's hardly anything on it now.'

'Claire has been a sensation,' Sally said. 'She's practically sold out.'

'Clever girl,' said William.

'Oh, Mr Elliott, how lovely to see you.' Mrs Wenham bustled up to William and put out her hand in greeting. William took it and then leant forward to give her a kiss. Mrs Wenham simpered and drifted off to collect the floats, her fingers fluttering to her face.

'Daddy!' Emily and Oliver ran up to their father; they had obviously forgiven him for his stern words the night before.

'What a pretty fairy,' said William to Emily, whose cheeks glittered with sparkly butterflies and flowers.

'I've got a skull tattoo.' Oliver rolled up his sleeve. 'And a can of custard from the tombola.'

'I see you're here at last.' Elizabeth glared at her son-in-law while she held on to a wriggling Ben; his tiger face was already smudged and in his chubby hand he clutched a melting ice lolly. William backed away from him a fraction. 'It's such a shame you missed seeing Claire's work on display. It looked very impressive.'

William stiffened. 'I would have been on time if the traffic hadn't been so awful – you don't expect it on a Wednesday afternoon.'

'Good job I got here then.' Elizabeth's tone was frosty. 'Luckily the roads were nearly empty coming from my direction.'

'At least William is here now.' Claire wondered why she always felt she had to act as peacemaker between her mother and her husband.

'Come on, gang.' William put his arm around Oliver and Emily's shoulders. 'Who wants to go to the café by the river? Crisps and lemonade all round.'

'No, William,' Claire protested. 'I need to get the children to bed early tonight. I've got so much to do before the photo shoot.'

'Don't be a spoil-sport, darling.' William beamed a smile down at the children's eager faces. 'It's a big treat for being so good at the fête. Come on – race you to the car – three, two, one, GO.'

'Wait for Ben,' Claire called as the toddler ran across the playground to catch up with his siblings and his father who were already far ahead.

'Isn't he great with the kids,' said Sally through a mouthful of raspberry bun.

'When he wants to be,' Elizabeth said. Her Yorkshire accent was always more pronounced when she felt annoyed. 'He soon leaves it all to you, Claire, when he thinks of some bit of titivating to do on the house.'

'I wish my husband would do a bit of titivating,' said Sally with a wink.

'The trouble with William is he just can't stop.' Elizabeth started folding up the cloth that Claire had used to cover her stall. 'There's got to be more to life than paint charts and fancy radiators but to hear him talk you'd think that the Screwfix catalogue is the holy bloody Bible itself.'

Claire and Sally burst out laughing.

'Come on, girls,' said Sally. 'I've got something much more exciting than crisps and lemonade.' She produced a bottle of Prosecco from under the cake stall. 'Look what I won on the tombola stall. Let's go back to mine and have a toast to the future of Emily Love.'

# Chapter Three

*'The pale blue Aga is the hub of Claire's domestic routine.'*

The day before the shoot, Claire stood barefoot at the table on the patio, making mince pies. The Aga made the kitchen too warm to work in on such a hot day. Ben sat under the table playing with his own piece of pastry, every now and then sneaking a little lump of it into his mouth. Macavity lay stretched out beside them in the shade of a large pot of calla lilies.

Claire felt strange to be swatting away wasps as the familiar smell of Christmas competed with the mingled summer smells of the garden.

She had stopped answering the phone. All morning she had had a constant stream of phone calls from Celia Howard asking for *'just one more minuscule request'* – find holly, put out candles, make a wreath for the door. She was waiting for Celia to ask if she could lay on snow and a special appearance from Father Christmas himself. For the hundredth time she felt like cancelling the whole thing, but the thought of free advertising for Emily Love kept her complying with all her requests. Her triumph at the school fête the day before made her determined to make her business a success. She remembered what Sally had said at the school gates earlier that morning: 'Just go for it, Claire. After all, what have you got to lose?'

The flagstones were hot on the soles of her feet. She meant to go and get her shoes but she was in a hurry to finish cooking so she could have lunch and hoover the house before picking up

Oliver and Emily. Cooking always made her hungry and she had to try very hard not to pick at the raw shortcrust pastry.

As she filled the pastry cases with mincemeat, topping each one with a fluted pastry lid, she could feel her white cotton blouse sticking to her back in the heat of the midday sun. She should have moved the table into the shade but it was too late now. She'd nearly finished.

Wiping a strand of hair away from her face with her flour-covered hand she straightened up to admire her tray of finished pies. She smiled down at Ben and began singing 'We Wish You a Merry Christmas'.

'Merry Christmas to you, too,' a voice said.

Claire jumped and turned to see a tall man standing just a little way away from her on the garden path.

'I'm so sorry,' he said. 'I didn't mean to frighten you. I've been knocking at the front, but there was no reply, so I came round the side. I'm sorry, you were so absorbed in what you were doing. I tried coughing but . . .' He stopped and shrugged.

He smiled in a half-polite, half-amused way that revealed laughter lines at the corners of his dark eyes.

'I'm Stefan Kendrick.' He stepped towards her and put out his hand. 'I'm going to photograph your house for the magazine article.'

'I'm sorry?'

'You are expecting us for a Christmas photo shoot, aren't you?' He laughed and nodded towards the baking tray on the table. 'Or do you always make mince pies in July?'

'I thought you were coming tomorrow?' Please, please don't let it be today.

'I am. I will be,' Stefan said. 'I was doing a small job for another magazine this morning. It was only a few miles away and I finished early. I thought I'd just come and take a look at your place, so I'd know what to expect. I did try to ring, but no one answered. I like your house.' He looked around him. 'I can see why Celia's keen to feature it.'

He smiled at her and she noticed how thickly lashed his eyes were.

'You've got flour on your face,' he said, touching his own cheek to indicate where it was on hers. Claire rubbed it with her hand.

'You've smudged it now.'

'It doesn't matter, does it?' Claire knew she sounded annoyed but she didn't like strange men scrutinising her face, even if they were attractive.

Stefan ran a hand through his dishevelled dark hair. 'I'm sorry. I feel like I've got off to a bad start. I shouldn't have just turned up like this.'

'It's OK,' she said. 'I just wasn't expecting anyone. I'm a bit hot, and busy and, to tell you the truth, embarrassed. I don't usually sing in front of people over the age of five.'

'I enjoyed it,' he said. 'You should expand your audience age range – I'm well over five and I liked it.'

Claire smiled, she couldn't help it.

'Look, Mummy,' said a voice from under the table. 'Look at my heart.'

Claire had completely forgotten about Ben in the last few minutes. He was still happily squatted on the flagstones, carefully rolling out his own chunk of pastry and cutting out shapes with a metal cutter, before squishing everything together to start again.

'Wow, that looks delicious,' said Stefan, as Ben rolled out his lump again. It was grey with bits of grit and moss flecked through it from the flagstones. Ben pressed his cutter down onto the pastry and lifting out a rather wonky heart shape, handed it to Stefan.

'Biscuit for you.'

'Thank you. I'll ask Mum to cook it in the oven for me, shall I?'

'No.' Ben looked indignant at the suggestion. 'Eat it. Now!'

'Come on, Ben, don't get cross,' said Claire squatting down beside Stefan. 'I'll take it and put it in the oven with the mince pies.'

Ben's bottom lip began to wobble. Stefan looked at Claire, shrugged his shoulders and quickly put the raw pastry into his mouth. He cautiously began chewing.

'Mmmm, very tasty,' he said, in between mouthfuls. 'You're a great cook.'

Ben smiled proudly back at him.

'You're very kind to humour him like that,' she said. 'But you know there were squashed ants in that pastry?'

'It was rather crunchy.' Stefan grimaced and ran his hand through his hair again. Claire noticed thin strands of grey at his temples, the only thing that could suggest his age.

'If you can wait for them to cook you can have a mince pie as well.' Claire picked up the baking tray and turned towards the kitchen door. Stefan picked up the nearly empty jar of mincemeat from the table.

'This looks suspiciously like a whole jar of squashed ants,' he said, peering through the glass at the dark, slimy contents. 'I think I might give the mince pies a miss – maybe wait till December like I usually do.'

'Coward,' Claire laughed. 'You obviously don't appreciate our local delicacy.'

'I'm afraid I'm more of a caramelised locust kind of man.'

'How unadventurous you are.' Claire disappeared into the kitchen and Stefan followed her in, carrying the rest of the things from the garden table.

'Actually, I have been known to be very adventurous.'

Macavity jumped up on the table between them. Stefan stroked the cat's orange back and Macavity purred, pushing himself against Stefan's hand.

'He doesn't usually like strangers. Do you have a cat?'

'No. Though I did as a child.' He made a soft clicking noise at Macavity who gazed up at him with round green eyes.

'You are beautiful,' Stefan said, softly, as he scratched Macavity under the chin. He looked up to meet Claire's eyes watching him. Feeling awkward, she quickly turned away.

'It's much too hot in here with the Aga on,' she said. 'We'll have a cup of tea in the garden and then I'll show you around.'

Ben came in and stood beside Stefan, holding up his favourite toy car.

Stefan took it from him, examining it closely. 'Wow, that's fantastic. I bet it goes really fast.' He bent down and made it skid across the quarry tiles.

Ben squealed with delight. 'Again, again.'

'You've got a friend for life, there,' Claire said. 'Do you have children?'

'No,' Stefan replied, picking up the car and making it zoom across the floor again.

'I bet you'd make a great father,' she said, immediately wanting to swallow her words. What a ridiculous thing to say – as if he might just go out and buy a ready-made family from his local Sainsbury's.

'I've just got to find the right woman.' He crouched down to retrieve the car from under the table.

'Don't look too closely at the floor,' Claire said. 'I haven't had time to clean properly.'

'Don't worry, it looks spotless to me. It's a beautiful house, really unique.'

'Thank you. Though all the credit should really go to my husband. He renovated it, and frankly never stops working on it.' She laughed rather too brightly.

'I think you're underestimating yourself.' Stefan looked around the sun-filled kitchen. 'I bet you chose these colours. They're so fresh and light.'

*How did he know?* She had chosen the colours, a long time ago, before the twins were born, before Claire had lost all enthusiasm for paint colours and cupboard doors. The kitchen was the one room in the house that she really felt at home in.

'Celia showed me pictures of the things you make, I love them, although they're a bit too pretty for my bachelor flat; not quite the macho look I'm after!' He laughed. 'Not that I haven't got a feminine side to get in touch with as well.'

Claire smiled and hesitated over which mugs to use: floral ones, ones with hearts? No, the spotty ones would do. She dragged the kettle from the Aga as a splash of water hissed on the surface, almost scalding her.

'Your things are great; they have such a sense of fun about them,' Stefan went on. 'Fantastic mixture of vintage and contemporary – I've really been looking forward to seeing your house.'

'I hope it all lives up to your expectations,' said Claire, ineptly opening a milk carton, the praise making her feel self-conscious.

'It's all lovely so far,' he replied, with a smile. 'It will make a fantastic feature for the magazine. A shame it's going to be a Christmas issue, and we can't use the garden – it's beautiful. Who's responsible for that?'

'I'm responsible for trying to keep the flowers alive and my husband is responsible for the very short grass.'

A mobile rang, the sound breaking the few seconds' silence that had settled between them. Stefan took a phone from his pocket and answered it. After a brief conversation, he snapped it shut.

'Unfortunately, I've got to go. I'd arranged to meet up with a friend for lunch nearby. I'm late and she's wondering where I am. I'd completely forgotten the time since I've been here.' He handed back the car to Ben. Ben beamed back up at him.

'Sorry about the cup of tea,' he said to Claire. 'I'd better rush or I'll be in trouble. See you in the morning.'

He gave Macavity one last stroke and stepped out of the door into the sunshine. Claire could hear him whistling 'We Wish You a Merry Christmas' as he disappeared down the path to the front of the house. A minute later she heard the crunch of wheels on gravel as a car pulled away from the drive.

'I'm hungry,' said Ben, pulling at Claire's skirt.

Absentmindedly, she made him a Nutella sandwich and tried not to wonder who Stefan was having lunch with. She made herself a Nutella sandwich too, but as she sat down beside Ben at the table she found she wasn't very hungry after all.

# Chapter Four

*'Claire fell in love with the picturesque property the
first time she saw it. Although in need of some
repair she was quick to realise its potential.'*

'The photographer came today,' Claire said, mixing salad dressing
in a small blue jug as William went through the post. He'd loos-
ened his tie and undone the top buttons of his shirt.

'It's still so bloody hot, even at this time of night,' he said.
'Have we got any cold beer?'

'Yes. Can you get it yourself? I've still got loads to do after supper if I'm going to be ready for tomorrow.' As William bent down
to peer into the fridge, she noticed dark patches of sweat stained
his back and armpits. Claire looked away and began chopping a
cucumber.

'The photographer liked the house.'

'What photographer?' he asked, still searching in the fridge.
'There's something slimy on the bottom shelf in here.'

'The photographer who's photographing the house tomorrow,'
she replied. 'You haven't forgotten the photo shoot, have you? You
did say yesterday that you'd arranged time off to be there.'

William stood up holding a dripping pot of Petit Filous and
sniffed it. 'Ugh! It smells ancient. How long has it been in there?'

'I don't know, can't you just wipe it up?' Claire gave the end of
the cucumber one final loud chop.

William backed towards the dustbin. 'No need to attack the cucumber, Claire. I was just about to clear it up anyway.'

They were silent while he found a cloth and a bottle of kitchen cleaner. Claire got on with preparing the salad for their supper. Looking up she found William taking everything out of the fridge and putting half of it into a plastic bag.

'What are you doing?' she asked.

'Checking sell-by dates,' he replied. 'Did you realise how much of this stuff is out of date?'

'William!' she said in exasperation. 'There is so much to do. If you really want to help couldn't you go and put a new plug on the Hoover like I asked you to last night?'

'This needs defrosting too,' said William, poking at a thick layer of ice descending from the roof of the freezer. 'If you move all this stuff into the freezer in the garage I'll do it now.'

Claire thought of Sally, who would be trying to get her hyper-active boys into bed while Gareth lay on the sofa watching football on the enormous television he'd bought for Sally's Christmas present last year. Claire knew she was lucky to have William, she really did. But sometimes . . .

'I'll sort out the fridge *and* the freezer over the weekend,' she said, with strained patience. 'After the magazine people have gone. It's just that it would be so helpful if you could do something that really needs doing right now.'

'I had thought I might mow the grass after I've eaten. Before the light goes.'

'William!' Claire tried not to raise her voice.

'What?'

'I've told you, it's supposed to be Christmas here. They're not going to photograph the garden, mowing the grass is not a . . .'

'Don't shout, Claire.' His interruption made her jump. 'I've had one hell of a day at work to get things sorted so that I can be here tomorrow. I only want things to look smart when they come. It's just the same as you wanting your cushions and stuff to look nice in the pictures, I want the grass to look tidy for the pictures.'

'The grass won't be in the pictures.'

'It will show through the windows.'

He took a bottle of beer from the fridge and took a long swig before pouring the rest into a glass. Claire watched him for a few seconds, trying to decide whether it was worth continuing the argument. She decided she didn't have the time.

'He was nice,' she said after a little while.

'Who?'

'The photographer. He was lovely with Ben.'

William muttered inaudibly and started opening the post.

'This is the one,' he exclaimed, suddenly enthusiastic. He thrust his latest copy of *Home Build* magazine in between Claire and the chopping board. 'This is what I'm going to make for us.' He pointed at a picture of a wooden building, made up of tongue and groove, painted moss green, with a long veranda and a shingled roof. 'What do you think?'

'A shed?' asked Claire. 'Do we need another shed?'

'It's not a shed. It's a summer house.'

'Do we need a summer house?'

'Every English garden needs a summer house, Claire. Imagine – we could sit in it and drink wine in the evenings, read books, listen to music. We could have visitors to stay in it if we put in electricity, a little log burner in the corner. You and Sally could sit and drink coffee all day, or whatever it is you do together. Mix up witches' brew in a cauldron.' He laughed.

Claire ignored his remark. She took the magazine from him and looked at the picture again. It was charming. It looked like something from the Scandinavian woods. An idea sprang into her mind. It certainly looked spacious enough.

'I could use it as a studio and then I wouldn't need to use the spare room any more,' Claire said, feeling a charge of excitement at the thought. A studio in the garden would be lovely. A space of her own for sewing and designing; perhaps a little showroom area to display her latest designs for customers to come and visit. A shop; she'd always wanted to have a shop. If they built it at the side of the drive people could easily come and go. In her mind she already saw the Emily Love sign across the doorway; inside, a sofa scattered with her cushions, bunting strewn across the ceiling, aprons hanging from hooks on the wall, a dresser piled high with stock. The other half could be her work area – a large table for cutting out patterns, glass bottles full of buttons and beads and rolls of multi-coloured ribbon on long shelves around the walls, cupboards full of fabrics. She smiled at William. 'I'd love that – my own studio in the garden and a little shop. It would be wonderful.'

He took the magazine out of her hands. 'I'm not sure it would be suitable for that. Perhaps if your business gets off the ground we could think about converting the old woodshed for you.'

Claire turned back to the chopping board and sliced a yellow pepper very thinly and then chopped it up fast, into little tiny pieces.

'I thought I'd build it at the bottom of the garden, cut down some of those old yew trees,' William went on. 'At the back it will look out over the hills to the sea.'

'Can we afford it? Won't it take ages to build?' She didn't like the idea of cutting down the yew trees either. Wasn't that meant to be unlucky?

'No, it won't take long at all. A few months of weekends and evenings. I'll put a patio area in front, looking out over the valley. Use up those extra flag stones we found in the corner of the orchard. Maybe you could make a couple of little flower beds beside it? Some lavender, a few hollyhocks – what do you think, darling?' He walked over to Claire and gave her a hug. Claire leant into him and felt her anger seeping away.

He looked down into her face; his blue eyes sparkling, a familiar flush of DIY fervour colouring his cheeks.

'You'll love it, Claire. Wonder how we ever lived without it.'

'It could be nice, I suppose,' she said.

'That's my girl.' He squeezed her just a little bit too tightly before untangling himself from her arms and picking up the magazine again to look at the picture of the summer house.

'Maybe your parents could stay in it when they come to visit?' said Claire.

'Oh no,' he said dismissively. 'I wasn't thinking about it for my parents. They like to be on hand to help you with the children. I was thinking of our friends from London.'

'We don't have many weekend guests these days – apart from your parents,' she sighed, as she laid thickly sliced, home-cured ham on two plates. 'You're always too busy when people ask if they can come.'

'Don't get grumpy, Claire.' William started sorting through the rest of the post, ripping open the envelopes with a small, sharp knife. 'And if you're trying to have a go at my parents, just remember how good they've been to us. We wouldn't have this house at all if it hadn't been for them.'

Claire took a deep breath and counted to three in her head.

'I'm not having a go at your parents,' she said, trying to keep her voice calm. 'I know how grateful we are to them. They have been very kind.' She forced a smile and he seemed to relax a little.

Claire could never forget how grateful she had to be to William's parents; she was never allowed to forget. It had been William's mother who found the advertisement for the semiderelict Somerset farmhouse in the *Telegraph*'s property pages, William's parents who had given them a large financial gift for the deposit.

'I'll make it beautiful for you,' William had said as they stood for the first time, on the overgrown driveway, while his mother rushed ahead enthusing about potential and rustic charm. William had taken Claire's face between his hands and looked into her eyes. 'It will be the house of our dreams. The house of your dreams. I promise.'

Claire had sighed. She didn't have a house she dreamed about. William was her dream. He was all she needed to be happy.

She had stared at the cracked grey rendering, the sagging thatch, and tried very hard to imagine how it could be. If it was painted, if the garden was cleared, maybe it could be tolerable.

Maybe it could even be nice. A garden would be a novelty – she could plant vegetables, grow strawberries, have chickens, dogs, cats, even a goat or pigs. She could make jam for village fêtes, wear an apron, make bread. She suddenly had a picture in her head of lots of children running amongst wild flowers in the sun, golden-limbed with blond curls, like William's. Their children. The thought had felt nice.

'If this is what you really want,' Claire had said to William, 'maybe I'll get used to living in the country.'

Claire poured the thick yellow dressing onto the salad. 'I suppose we could think about building a summer house next year.'

'No, not next year, darling,' said William. 'I want to do it this year. This summer. In fact, I'll go and phone that tree surgeon in the village now. As soon as he's cut down the yews I can start to level the site and lay a concrete base.' He started to walk out of the kitchen.

'I thought you said you'd be busy with other jobs on the house this summer?' Claire called after him. 'And the supper is ready now.'

There was no answer; only the sound of the latch on the study door clicking closed. Claire stood in the middle of the kitchen and resisted the urge to throw the ham and salad all over the room. She had to keep it clean for the morning.

Sitting down at the table she ate three of the mince pies that she had made earlier on. She remembered Stefan joking about squashed ants in the mincemeat and smiled to herself.

The cat jumped onto the table with a soft thud and began to lick the ham on William's plate. She reached across and stroked the thick ginger fur. He arched his back and purred, dribbling onto the salad. Claire stroked him some more.

'Did you say dinner was ready?' asked William, coming back into the room.

# Chapter Five

*'In her blissful attic bathroom, Claire can relax in
her reclaimed 'Victorian-style' roll-top bath and
enjoy an uninterrupted view of the sea.'*

Claire woke up at dawn. It was already humid; no breeze blew
through the wooden shutters of the bedroom window. There was
no sound of birdsong; it seemed that even the birds were too hot
to sing. The house was still and silent. Her cotton nightdress clung
to her uncomfortably as she got out of bed and walked towards the
shower.

As she let the cool water wash away the stickiness of the night,
she thought about all the things she had to do before Stefan and
the stylist arrived at nine. She felt nervous but strangely excited
about the photo shoot; she was looking forward to it now. Stepping out of the shower cubicle she reached for the large towelling
dressing gown she usually put on as quickly as possible to hide the
little rolls of fat and stretch marks she didn't want to be reminded
of. Suddenly she let the dressing gown fall to the floor; she had an
urge to be naked in the warm air.

Standing at the window she wound her long, dark, dripping
hair into a towel. From up here she could see the woods at the
bottom of the valley and fields and, far away in the distance, the
sea. No need for frosted glass or curtains; there were no roads or
houses, no one to see you for miles.

The sun was already flooding the room with soft yellow light.

She could remember when this room was cold and dark, the walls tiled in mouldy cork and the floor covered in rotting carpet tiles. A chocolate-coloured plastic bath had been squeezed into one corner, a thick white ring of scale permanently encrusted around it. Claire had hated that bath, she had dipped in and out of it as quickly as possible when they finally had hot water. She still remembered her happiness at seeing it disappear down the lane on the top of a skip.

The bathroom was lovely now with its cast-iron bath standing, claw-footed, on the black and white chequered tiles. The white walls were half-panelled in Nile green tongue and groove; soft towels were piled high on a small pine table beside a ceramic bowl of smooth pink shells.

The shells reminded Claire of the holiday on a little Greek island the summer before they were married. She had collected them on the beach below their pretty villa on the edge of a fishing village. She and William had spent long lazy mornings in bed and afternoons swimming in the sea, exploring the hidden coves along the coast. Often they were the only people on the isolated beaches and more than once they had made love on the soft, white sand with the hot Mediterranean sun shining down on their entangled limbs.

That seemed like another life to Claire. It seemed like another man.

Claire and William had first met at a Christmas party hosted by the City accountancy firm he had worked for. It had been held in a fairy-lit, glass-fronted restaurant overlooking the Thames. A jazz band had played as the guests enjoyed the easy-flowing champagne and a five-course dinner.

The week before, Claire had signed up as a waitress for a catering agency. In her final year of art college, she was trying to make some sort of dent in her overdraft. She already worked weekends in a shoe shop on Kensington High Street, but had found herself with more shoes than actual cash.

Her first job as a waitress had been for a television production company's launch party, serving canapés while dressed as a Tyrolean mountain girl with tiny lederhosen and a low-cut frilly blouse – on roller skates. *Nothing could be harder or more humiliating than that*, she had told herself, as she queued up to put the cheque into her bank.

'This next one's silver service,' the boss had told her over the phone. 'You're fine with that, aren't you?'

'Oh yeah. No problem.'

Putting down the phone, Claire had turned to her flatmate, Zoë.

'Help! What's silver service?'

'It's a bit like using chopsticks but with a large spoon and fork,' Zoë had replied. 'I once had a boyfriend who was trained in it. He used to serve me baked beans that way and expect me to be impressed enough to sleep with him.'

'And were you?'

'No, I was more impressed by his brother who was in a band, so I slept with him instead. Anyway, silver service looked easy to me. You'll be fine, Claire. Just practise on me for a few days before the job.'

'I haven't got a few days,' she had said, sighing. 'The job's tonight.'

As Claire served the first course to a raucous table of men and women she soon realised that silver service was not easy at all. The large, shiny spoons and forks refused to co-operate in her inexperienced hands. Smoked salmon terrine slipped awkwardly back onto the serving platter and then slid onto the floor. The main course was worse. Miniature sweetcorn and mangetout skittered out of her grasp and onto the table. Claire ended up inelegantly shoving slivers of roast beef and potatoes dauphines onto the plates of increasingly drunken customers.

The men were loud and crude. They threw bread rolls at one another and downed champagne as though they were drinking pints in a beer tent. Their girlfriends giggled and simpered at their partners' juvenile behaviour as they sipped their drinks in black dresses and pearls. Claire wished she was somewhere else, where she didn't have to pretend to be polite to vulgar, spoilt, rich people, and where she didn't have to wrestle with over-sized serving utensils.

Profiteroles for the dessert course seemed like the last straw. Claire emerged from the kitchen laden with a pyramid of golden pastry balls. As she approached her table she could hear some of the men loudly debating the colour of her bra beneath her white shirt. With a shaking hand and immense concentration, Claire successfully managed to pick up two profiteroles between the spoon and fork. She started to transfer them to one of the accountants' waiting plate. As her hand hovered above it, the accountant suddenly slapped Claire's bottom and the spoon and fork skidded apart, sending the profiteroles flying through the air and onto his lap. They rolled slowly down the inside of the man's thighs and nestled neatly in his crotch. He began to laugh lewdly, drawing the attention of the rest of the table. Leaning back in his chair he demanded that Claire remove them herself – with her teeth. She heard laughter around her, and saw a woman watching her with a contemptuous smirk on her beautifully made-up face. Claire flushed red with humiliation and embarrassment, but then she felt anger taking over inside. She managed to smile calmly at the man who looked at her with an expectant grin on his pink, puffy face.

'Yes, of course I will, sir. But I prefer chocolate sauce with my profiteroles.'

She picked up an accompanying jug of hot sauce from the table and swiftly poured it into his lap. He immediately leapt up from his chair, thick, scalding chocolate dripping down his expensive trousers.

Claire didn't wait to listen to the string of insults he shouted at her, just threw the rest of her pile of profiteroles into the middle of the table, from where they bounced and rolled onto the laps of the other diners. She quickly marched across the room, into the kitchen, picked up her bag and coat, and left through the back door, before any of the other waiters, or her boss, had a chance to realise what had happened.

Once outside in the freezing night, Claire walked around the corner and, leaning against a railing by the river, lit a cigarette.

'I'm so sorry about what happened in there.'

Claire turned to see a tall, fair-haired man whom she recognised as one of the more civilised guests from the table.

'Sebastian was being his usual obnoxious self. He always gets like that when he's drunk. He deserved what you did to him. Well done.'

He grinned at her and she noticed how white and straight his teeth were, his square-jawed face clean shaven and lightly tanned. He looked older than Claire and handsome in a Nordic, clean-cut sort of way – not Claire's type at all.

Claire said nothing but, blowing out a cloud of smoke, stared at the man through narrowed eyes. She wished he would go away. He leant against the railing beside her.

'Someone should have told him he was going too far,' he continued. 'We should have stopped him.'

Claire looked at his pale, neatly cut hair. Tiny kinks in it suggested it would have been curly if he let it grow.

'I should have said something, stopped him myself.'

Claire still said nothing, but looked away, down into the oily water where she threw her cigarette end. It was cold. She shivered and wrapped her thin coat tightly around her.

'It's a freezing night,' said the man in his perfect English accent. 'Can I buy you a drink as an apology?'

Claire really didn't want to spend any more time with him, and didn't think he was the one who should be apologising, but the thought of a drink was tempting. She had only enough money in her purse for her tube fare home. The cashpoint machines had stopped giving her anything from her account and she knew she had little chance of ever getting paid for the night's work.

'OK.'

The man smiled. Tiny lines fanned out from ice-blue eyes. 'I know a little bar near here that's one of my favourites. My name's William, by the way.'

Claire let herself be led across the road and down a small flight of steps into a warm, red room thick with smoke, people, and the smell of warm beer. Worn velvet sofas lined the room with black and white mosaic tables in front of them. The walls were covered in bright pictures of bullfighters and dark-eyed women posing with castanets.

'I think it has a rather bohemian atmosphere,' William said, his face close to her ear. It was hard to hear above the guitar music coming from the band in the corner. 'It doesn't even have a name outside but it's generally known as The Spanish Bar.'

'I thought there might be a theme,' she replied, still reluctant to be in his company but longing for a drink. She liked to drink lager, but if someone else was paying . . .

'A double whisky,' she said, as William left her at a table and started pushing his way to the bar. He raised his eyebrows. Claire smiled at him and lit another cigarette.

The whisky and the womb-like room warmed her. The band in the corner stopped and were replaced with softer Cuban music. William sat beside her and started to talk. He talked about his job, a new firm of accountants he was moving to, his flat, and his family in some village that William said she really must visit one day and that Claire thought sounded deadly dull. She wasn't really listening to most of what he said. She was enjoying the warmth, the whisky, the music, and watching the other people coming and going. She took more notice when he started to talk about the girl he'd been engaged to. They had recently split up.

'Irreconcilable differences,' he explained when Claire asked what had gone wrong.

'Like what?'

'Like she wanted to take the job she'd been offered in New York and I didn't want to go with her. I'm happy living in England.'

Then he started asking her questions about her life. At first she was reluctant to tell him anything but lulled by the mixture of alcohol and intimate surroundings she found herself confiding in him. She told him things she hadn't talked to anyone about for years – about her father walking out on her tenth birthday, her mother's depression, her ambition to set up her own textile business printing scarves when she left college, and her recent break-up with her boyfriend Liam – a wild-haired Irish sculpture student who filled his days with sleeping and his nights with drinking and climbing up the tallest structure he could find (usually a crane).

William seemed genuinely interested about her life. He asked more, probed deeper.

The guitar trio came back and started to play a furious song. A couple got up to dance in the tiny space in front of the stage; they were soon joined by another couple and a girl who danced on top of one of the mosaic tables.

Claire had had enough of talking.

'Come on,' she said, pulling William up and leading him to the dance floor. She pulled her white waitress's shirt loose from her short black skirt and tied it tight at her midriff, exposing a flat expanse of stomach. She saw shock and surprise in William's eyes; she'd had three double whiskies in a row and didn't care. Raising her hands above her head she began to dance, slowly and rhythmically in time to the music, speeding up when the beat quickened. Twirling around William, she took his hand and made him spin her away and then back towards him.

'I don't usually dance,' he shouted into her ear above the noise of the band.

'I do,' she said.

Another man approached and cut in, whisking her away from William, taking her in his arms in an improvised tango. He dipped her backwards. Claire laughed. Her hair was falling out of the neat ponytail she'd tied it in for work. She was upright again and the stranger spun her around and around. She felt dizzy; her feet were slipping on the beer-soaked floor. The stranger let her go. She thought she would fall but someone caught her. It was William.

'I think you need to sit down,' he said, guiding her back to their table.

He bought her a glass of water and she began to think how nice his eyes were and that she liked the little dimple in his chin. It crossed her mind to ask him home with her and then she knew it was time to leave – alone.

She tried to persuade him that she would be fine getting the Tube, but William insisted on hailing a black cab and asking her address so that he could pay the driver in advance. He hadn't asked her to come home with him or made any attempt to even kiss her. Claire was surprised; most men wanted something for the cost of a few drinks and even more for the cost of a cab.

He waved at her as the taxi pulled away. Claire sat back and began thinking about what she'd wear to a party she had been invited to the next night, and how she was going to get through another bleak, grey Christmas Day with her mother and a small roast chicken in her lonely basement flat.

'The hall is full of roses,' said Claire groggily, as she shuffled into the tiny kitchen of their Clapham flat the next morning. The smell of stale cooking fat wafted up from the takeaway kebab shop beneath them.

'And they're all for you,' said Zoë, sounding disgruntled.

Three dozen pink roses and a note.

*I enjoyed our drink and dance, would you like to do it again? William x*

And then a phone number.

Claire phoned him to say thank you. They met for dinner in a small French restaurant off the Strand; afterwards Claire took him to a club in Soho. The following weekend they had another dinner in Chinatown, and then a visit to the theatre, and then a Sunday drive to Lewes for lunch beside a log fire in a pub. He constantly sent flowers.

'It's like living in a bloody florist's,' said Zoë, peering at Claire through a vase of gladioli on the Formica kitchen table.

★

For Christmas he gave her a charm bracelet with one tiny silver heart hanging from it.

After a lingering Valentine's Day meal on the King's Road, they walked over the Albert Bridge as snow began to fall. Surrounded by the glittering lights and the swirling snow, William took Claire in his arms and told her that he loved her. Claire told him that she loved him too and then, seized with the sudden joy at being alive, she had run over the bridge and shown him how to make snow angels in the park. Later he took her back to his pristine flat, undressed her very slowly, and took her to his bed. She'd been as impressed by his clean white sheets and matching pillowcases as she was by his love making. She'd been used to Liam's grey bedding that had been strewn across a mattress on the floor of his bedsit; he would no more have thought to neatly pull his duvet up each morning than actually wash it.

In the morning William woke her up with croissants and real coffee and the Sunday papers. Later she lay, stretched out, along his brand new sofa, naked except for a neatly ironed, pinstriped shirt she'd borrowed from his immaculately tidy wardrobe. Her head nestled in his lap as he read the Sunday supplements and she marvelled at the warmth and cleanliness around her.

'It's nice here,' she said, looking up into his handsome face.

'It's just a place I've lived in since Vanessa and I split up, a box I come back to after work,' he wound his fingers around her tangled auburn hair and smiled. 'Move in. Come and live with me and we'll make it into a home.'

Within a week she had moved all her things into the bright top-floor rooms of the red-brick mansion block. She set about transforming it with 1950s vases, chintz cushions, fairy lights, and old furniture that she found in skips and junk shops. She painted a mural of mermaids on the tiny bathroom wall. In the evenings Claire cooked invented meals made from ingredients she found in the Turkish supermarket on the Fulham Road, played him Leonard Cohen, and took him to her favourite club in Brixton. William seemed constantly amazed and entranced by what he saw as her lack of inhibitions and unconventional attitude to life.

'My beautiful bohemian girl,' he called her.

He seemed to find Claire's comprehensive school and art college education exotic; it was so different from his own conventional public school experience. She made him laugh and he made her feel safe and secure. He was seven years older than her and seemed so sensible, so grown up.

He took her away for long romantic weekends to Prague and Barcelona; walking hand in hand through the ancient streets, lingering over long meals and even longer mornings in bed. They spent Easter in Crete and a May bank holiday in Paris. Over thick black coffee on the Boulevard Saint-Germain, William asked her to marry him.

Claire couldn't remember ever feeling so happy. 'Yes,' she said.

They bought a ring from a small jewellers on Rue des Francs-Bourgeois and afterwards Claire persuaded William to climb the Eiffel Tower with her. With Paris laid out beneath her Claire felt as though she was flying, as if, with William, anything would be possible.

# Chapter Six

*'It's the perfect home for celebrating an idyllic Christmas.
Candles, holly, and warm mince pies around a blazing
fire; what better way to keep out the winter chill?'*

Claire had wiped the last handprints and pencil scribbles off the
walls and scraped out all the bits of Play-Doh from in between the
floorboards. The house was unnaturally clean and tidy.

The children had the day off school and were eating a breakfast
of brown bread and chocolate spread on the patio steps. Behind
them, William mowed the grass. It had got too late the night
before.

Claire hastily scattered as many Emily Love cushions as she
could around the living room and strung some of her bunting
across the kitchen beams. Looking in the hallway mirror she
checked for lipstick on her teeth and smoothed down her hair. She
had left it loose today and, newly washed, it shone as it fell onto
her shoulders. If she'd had more time she would have bought a
new outfit but the linen dress from last year's Boden sale looked
pretty, complimenting the curves she usually hated. Her arms
were brown and her summer freckles hardly noticeable at all.
Claire smiled at her reflection; for once she thought she looked
quite nice.

At nine o'clock exactly, a small bright orange hatchback pulled
up on the drive. The back windows were obscured by green foliage. A skinny young woman with a mass of curly hair, dyed a

shade of red that clashed dramatically with the car, jumped out of the driver's seat. She wore tiny denim shorts and a pink halter-neck top.

'Hi, I'm Babette. The stylist.' Her accent was Scottish. 'You must be Claire. Is Stefan here yet? He's always late. I'll never get this tree out by myself. Christmas shoots are always crazy.' She spoke with a very high, very fast voice; Claire could only just understand what she was saying.

'Love your house,' Babette went on. 'I love the oldie-worldy ones, but my flat is very modern. Sometimes I think I'd like to buy a cottage in the country like this, but I'd miss proper shops and I love my sushi bars and take-out coffees too much. Do you know what I mean?'

'I think so,' said Claire.

'And I don't suppose there's much chance of getting a good spray-tan in a twenty-mile radius of here?'

Babette opened the back of her car and Christmas tree branches started springing out in all directions. She pulled ineffectively at a few bits of tree.

'It's stuck. I'll have to wait for Stefan. I knew he'd be late. Could you get the box on the front seat? It's got the fairy lights and some dried-orange decorations. I make them myself. It's very effective for old-style shoots like this one. I have a fake pink tree at home, but obviously that's not what would look good here. My boyfriend hates it.'

Claire started to feel quite exhausted by Babette's incessant talking. Two days of this was going to be hard work. She took a large cardboard box from the passenger seat and asked Babette if she'd like a cup of tea.

'Do you have peppermint?'

'Yes, I'm sure I have.'

Claire led Babette around the side of the house to the back garden.

'Actually, I'll have coffee,' said Babette. 'Strong and black with two sugars. Oh, look at your children, aren't they gorgeous! I'd love to have children but my boyfriend's not so sure. We've only been together for eight months. Hi, you guys, are you going to be in some pictures?'

She waved energetically at the little group on the lawn.

The children stared, amazed by this lively newcomer. Ben's face was smeared in chocolate spread. He grinned widely.

'Is it Christmas now?' he asked.

'Looks like it,' said Babette. 'Are you excited?' She crouched down between the children. 'I'm going to decorate your house with a tree and lights and I've got wrapped-up boxes in my car that are like presents, but they're actually just empty boxes.'

'Oh!' the children groaned collectively.

'But,' Babette went on, 'I'll let you into a secret: some of them have actually got tiny wee presents inside, so when we're all finished maybe we'll open them and see if we can find anything for you?'

The children cheered, already enchanted.

'Who's going to show me their bedrooms?' asked Babette, jumping up from the grass. 'Let me guess. I bet you've got a pink one,' she said to Emily. 'Pink is my favourite colour.'

'Do you like fossils?' asked Oliver.

'I love them,' Babette said. 'My boyfriend has an ammonite he once found on a beach.'

'I've got nappies in my bedroom,' said Ben.

'Bet you do,' Babette said cheerily, as Ben and Emily took her hands and led her inside, closely followed by Oliver.

'Which are your favourite kinds of fossils?' he asked as they climbed the stairs. 'I've got ammonites and trilobites and a scorpion fossil from a desert in South America.'

Claire left them to it; Babette was obviously a big hit.

She was just filling up the kettle when she heard footsteps.

'Hello again.'

Stefan stood in the kitchen doorway. He wore a loose pale blue shirt which complimented his tanned skin and dark brown hair. He was carrying a small box of vegetables.

'I met a man in a van who gave me these,' he said, smiling, as he put the box on the kitchen table.

'Oh,' said Claire, feeling inexplicably flustered. 'It's our organic veg box. I thought it was coming tomorrow.' She reached out to pull the box towards her, knocking a bag of tomatoes onto the floor. Yellow, orange and red tomatoes in assorted shapes and sizes rolled across the kitchen in all directions. Claire bent down and started to pick them up.

'Is that your husband on the ride-on lawn mower?'

Claire looked up to find Stefan just a few inches away from her, collecting up stray tomatoes too.

Their eyes met and a half smile played across Stefan's lips.

'Yes,' she said. 'That's William.'

Claire thought of William chugging across the green expanse of grass and suddenly felt guilty.

She stood up.

Stefan stood up too and the cat greeted him by entwining himself around his legs as though he remembered him from the day before. Stefan bent to stroke him.

'It all looks very tidy,' he said, glancing round the kitchen.

'I've tried my best,' said Claire, her hands still full of tomatoes. One fell onto the floor again but neither of them bent to pick it up. 'With three children, it's hard to keep it perfect. Try not to make a feature of any Nutella handprints on the walls.'

Stefan looked around him again. 'I like a bit of mess, personally. It adds character, makes a house a home. Sticky fingerprints, worn-out chair covers – it's all part of family life. William should see my sister's house; it's chaos but it's the loveliest home I've ever been in and in my job I've been inside a lot of homes.'

'Coffee?' she asked, suddenly remembering about Babette upstairs with the children.

'Tea would be lovely,' replied Stefan. 'I'll make it while you sort out your vegetables. What are you having? Tea? Coffee for Babette, I'm sure. I bet she asked for herbal first. She starts a new detox diet every day and stumbles at the first coffee hurdle each morning.'

As Claire put away the carrots and potatoes in the larder she caught a glimpse of her reflection in the large stainless steel flour bin and grimaced. Compared to the coltish Babette, Claire felt frumpy. The dress she'd thought looked pretty suddenly made her feel ancient, and she wished she'd made the time to go to get a proper haircut. She undid a second button on her dress and wondered why she never seemed to have a cleavage.

Back in the kitchen Claire found Stefan adding milk to mugs.

'Sugar?' he asked. She shook her head and he handed her a mug of tea. She felt like a guest; he seemed so comfortable and at home in her kitchen and it was Claire who felt slightly awkward and out of place. She glanced out of the window and saw a beautiful cream convertible parked on the drive. Its soft top was down, revealing dark red leather seats and a shining chrome and walnut dashboard.

'Is that gorgeous car yours?' she asked, opening the window and leaning out to get a better look.

'Yes,' he said, coming to stand beside her. 'It's German; made in the same year I was born; I love old cars.'

'My parents had a Morris Minor when I was a child and I had a boyfriend with a Triumph Herald when I was at college. It was duck-egg blue and he called it Penelope. I've forgotten why.'

'I call my car Claudia,' offered Stefan.

'Can I ask why?'

'I'll tell you another time,' he said, laughing.

'I hate the people carrier I have now. But it does the job of transporting three children, plus their friends and all the stuff that goes with them.'

'My car's not very practical; she's always breaking down. But I'm very fond of her. Maybe I could take you for a drive later? Once round the village?' He paused and then added. 'William too, if he'd like to.'

Claire felt flustered again. 'I don't expect we'll have time,' she muttered, busying herself with putting mince pies on a plate. She immediately wished she had sounded more enthusiastic.

Stefan turned away and, picking up Babette's mug of coffee, set off to start the shoot.

William and Stefan dragged the tree into the living room and the children helped Babette decorate it with her fairy lights and dried orange slices. It wasn't exactly as Claire would have decorated it herself (she liked to use a combination of spun glass balls and brightly coloured tin decorations) but she had to admit that it looked lovely. Large sprigs of holly adorned the fireplace and Babette hung the Emily Love stockings that Claire had made late the night before on the mantelpiece.

'Where do you get a Christmas tree in July?' asked Claire.

'I know a man who supplies me every year. I do about ten Christmas shoots for different publications in the summer,' Babette explained.

'The trick is no shots showing windows,' Stefan told them. 'Otherwise you'd see trees in leaf and blooming flower borders which would spoil that festive feel.'

Claire looked at William; she knew that mowing the grass had been a waste of time. He was busy sliding cork coasters underneath the feet of the Christmas tree stand so that they wouldn't scratch the wooden floor.

'Now we need to get you all dressed up,' said Babette. 'No bare arms, no bare legs and no feet. You've got to cover up.'

'But it's going to be eighty degrees by midday,' said Claire, already feeling uncomfortably hot in her thin dress. 'And I'm sure you don't need me in the pictures, do you?'

'Oh yes,' Babette grinned. 'You're the star. But we need you in something wintry but glam. What did you wear on Christmas day last year?' Babette asked Claire.

'I wore a blue silk shirt,' said Claire.

'She looked like Margaret Thatcher in her prime,' William said, laughing. 'It had a funny bow thing at the neck, very Tory party conference.'

Claire winced. At the time he'd said she looked like Grace Kelly.

Babette looked confused. 'I always get muddled up between Margaret Thatcher and Cilla Black.'

'What about the cashmere twin set I bought you for your birthday?' said William. 'You look nice in that.'

'Sounds perfect,' said Babette.

*Thanks, William,* thought Claire, her back already prickling at the thought of the hot scratchy wool, her frumpiness increasing by the second.

'I know putting on a jumper seems unbearable in this heat,' said Stefan as though he'd read her mind. 'But it's just for the pictures. We'll let you strip off completely in between shots if you want to.'

Claire laughed and felt herself blush.

'I'm sorry about this,' he said. 'It will be worth it in the end – I promise.'

'The children need to put on some jumpers, and some tights for Emily,' continued Babette. 'Celia said that the children would be in traditional pyjamas for some of the shots?'

'It was hard but I've managed to find two pairs of stripy winceyette pyjamas for the boys and I've made a Victorian-style nightdress for Emily out of an old petticoat. She looks gorgeous.'

'Fantastic. You're truly wonderful,' said Babette, giving Claire an unexpected hug. 'William, do you have a sweater you can pull on over your shirt? And perhaps a jacket on top?'

He looked unenthusiastic and Claire tried not to smile.

'Great,' Babette said encouragingly. 'You go and get changed but if you could just light the fire first, that would be fab.'

'Fire?' William asked incredulously.

'We'll need you sitting in front of a lovely cosy fire, opening your presents and looking happy,' explained Babette.

Claire glanced at her husband's face. He certainly didn't look happy. He looked fed up.

'I'd better go and bring some logs in, then,' he said.

'I'll come and give you a hand,' Stefan offered.

'Wait while I get the woodshed key,' William called over his shoulder, disappearing into the hall muttering, 'I can't believe all this pretence is really necessary.'

Stefan turned to Claire and smiled. 'I know it's a long hot day for you all, but it's going to look beautiful. When you see the finished pictures you'll forget the heat and the hassle. You'll have photographs you'll treasure forever.'

'We could use one for our Christmas card this year,' said Claire, laughing.

'Great idea,' said Stefan. 'Maybe I could Photoshop Santa hats onto you all?'

'Somewhere William has a Santa outfit he wore one Christmas when Oliver and Emily were tiny.' Claire felt uncharacteristically giggly. 'Shall I get it out?'

'Pretend to William that he has to wear it now.'

'I'd love to see his face,' she said.

Stefan laughed.

'Excuse me, Stefan,' cut in Babette. 'Could you stop chatting her up and get on with the shoot?' She winked at Claire. 'Watch him. He's a bit of a charmer.'

For the second time, Claire felt herself blush. It was ridiculous, she never blushed – it must be the heat.

The day passed quickly. It was more fun than Claire had imagined it would be. The children opened their empty boxes, squealing with delight when they found a sweet in each, two little bears for Ben and Emily, and a pack of Pokémon cards for Oliver. They smiled happily and obediently crept down the stairs in night clothes, peeping through the banisters as if in awe of the magical scene below. Ben sat on the old dappled rocking horse, smiling to order, and Oliver and Emily pretended to eat mince pies, which they usually hated, eyes wide with appreciation. Claire stood beside them in her Emily Love apron holding Emily Love oven gloves as if she had just taken the pies from her Aga. Even Macavity the cat joined in and obediently lay in front of the fire beside the children.

\*

52

Stefan was keen to concentrate a lot of shots in the kitchen despite William's protestations that it needed redecorating and was looking shabby.

'Don't you want to do more in the living room? It's just been redone; the floorboards are reclaimed American Oak.'

'I like the kitchen,' Stefan said cheerfully. 'It's got real charm and sets off Claire's work perfectly.'

At first Claire felt embarrassed posing in front of Stefan's lens, but he and Babette were so friendly and funny that she soon relaxed and got used to the constant clicking. Even William seemed to be enjoying himself. Claire couldn't remember when they'd last spent so much time together as a family.

'You could all be top-class models,' Babette told the children at the end of the afternoon. 'You'd make a fortune.'

'Oh, could I, Mummy?' said Emily excitedly. 'Could I be a real model?'

Claire shook her head firmly. 'Definitely not. This is as far as your modelling career goes.'

'These are fantastic,' said Stefan, as he looked back at the shots he'd taken on his camera. 'The house looks great. What else are we doing today, Babette? Is that it?'

'I think we've got everything with the children and the tree, and we've done the kitchen from all the angles I can think of,' she said. 'We still need some pictures of Claire in her studio and the empty room shots but they can be done tomorrow. You won't need me for those.'

'Where are you going?' he asked. 'I thought you were booked into the hotel in town with me.'

'Didn't I say? I've got to get back to London tonight,' she said, taking orange slices off the tree. 'I'm doing a shoot on a houseboat in Putney tomorrow first thing, but you don't need me any more. I'd better get going because I've got a birthday dinner party at my boyfriend's best friend's girlfriend's flat tonight. It's an eighties fancy-dress do and I think it's going to be retro nouvelle cuisine; I need to get home to grab myself a piece of toast and a bag of nachos before I go, otherwise I won't get enough to eat and I'll get so drunk I'll never get up for Putney tomorrow.'

Babette unwrapped the lights from the tree, kissed and hugged the children as if she were their favourite aunt, and drove away in her orange car while Claire, the children, and Stefan stood at the front door waving happily. William had already left them and was busy measuring the space where the summer house would stand.

'Iced lemonade on the lawn?' Claire asked Stefan, after she had put out the fire in the living room and he had packed away his cameras and lights. The heat was almost unbearable, even now at five o'clock.

'Perfect. I think that's enough hard work for today for everyone and we'll get a bit of peace and quiet now that Babette has gone.'

'I don't think we'll get much peace and quiet with these three around,' Claire laughed, as the children suddenly appeared dressed in swimsuits. Emily had dressed Ben in an old pink shiny one of hers with a red and white frilly skirt. He was wearing it back to front and looked like an effeminate wrestler.

'Paddling pool, paddling pool!' they shouted together, hopping around her.

'We're so hot, I'm melting,' said Oliver. 'I'll soon be just a big wet blob.'

'Wait till Daddy finishes what he's doing and then he'll put water in the paddling pool,' said Claire, trying to get the jug of lemonade from the fridge as Ben pulled at her arm.

'Show me where everything is and we'll fill it up while your mum gets us all a drink,' said Stefan to the children, shepherding them into the garden.

Five minutes later the children were happily splashing in the cool water and eating ice lollies. Meanwhile, Claire and Stefan sat a safe distance away on wrought-iron chairs. On the table a large glass jug of lemonade sparkled in the sunlight.

'I can't believe we've just had Christmas Day,' said Claire, now happily changed back into her summer dress, her shoes kicked off, feet bare on the rough, dry grass.

'This is what it's like in Australia at Christmas,' said Stefan.

'Have you ever been there?'

'I lived there for a few years a while ago. I spent a few Christmases on the beach. Barbequed turkey drumsticks followed by an afternoon of surfing. It was fantastic.'

'What brought you back?'

'I don't know really,' he said, staring across the valley. 'I've never really settled anywhere for long, but in Australia I missed frosty winter mornings and the snow, and a relationship didn't work out.' He shrugged. 'The job with *Idyllic Homes* came up at the right time so I came back.' He was silent for a few seconds. Then he smiled at Claire, his dark eyes twinkling. 'Maybe I just missed a good cup of tea and a Marmite sandwich.'

'I thought you had Vegemite in Australia,' said Claire. 'Isn't that the same as Marmite?' She longed to ask about the relationship.

'No, it's not the same.'

'So a sandwich brought you back to the rain and cold and congestion?'

'Do you know, I don't think I've had a Marmite sandwich since I've been back?' Stefan laughed, but then was serious. 'I think I missed the British countryside. I'd like a life like this – old farmhouse, big garden, roses round the door, vegetable patch.'

'Dog.'

'Chickens,' Stefan added.

Ben came over, arms outstretched, dripping with water and melted ice lolly. He gave Claire a hug and a kiss before running back and belly-flopping into the pool.

'You've got sticky stuff on your skirt now,' said Stefan. 'Do you want me to get a cloth to wipe it?'

'You really don't have children, do you?' said Claire, laughing. 'If you did you'd know that after a while you don't care about the sticky stuff all over you. It all goes in the wash at the end of the day. Though William struggles with the messier side of parenthood, he'd definitely be getting a cloth right now.' She bit her lip.

'I always wanted to have children,' Stefan went on. 'But I think I'm getting a bit old now.'

'You don't look too old,' she argued.

'How old are you?' Stefan asked, taking a sip of lemonade.

'I don't think you're meant to ask ladies their age.'

'Sorry, I forgot. How rude of me.' He grinned at her.

After a brief pause she said, 'I was thirty-five last Guy Fawkes night.'

'Wow, fireworks on your birthday, what a celebration every year! But actually I thought you were older.'

'Thanks!'

'No, sorry. I didn't mean you look older; you look years younger, of course.' He flashed a smile that immediately made Claire forgive him. 'It's just you have so much, have achieved so much, when I feel I've hardly started. I've concentrated on my work and travelled for so long, but sometimes I look round at my life and wonder what I've really achieved. What have I got to show for it all? Most of my friends are part of couples, some of them even on second marriages. Most of them have children, nice houses, gardens – like you. For some reason I've never really settled down, I've never really made a home.'

'Don't you have a girlfriend?' Inexplicably she had found it very hard to ask that question but also impossible not to.

'No. Not really,' he replied, then after a few seconds added, 'well, I'm sort of at the end of something casual that hasn't worked from the start.'

Claire looked at him from the corner of her eye. Babette's comment about him being 'a bit of a charmer' echoed in her head. He looked at her and she realised she'd been staring.

A silence fell between them; the sounds of the children shrieking with laughter in the water filled the gap. Macavity jumped up onto Claire's knee and Stefan reached across to stroke his head.

William suddenly appeared with his notebook and tape measure. Claire felt a jolt of surprise. She'd forgotten that he was around. Stefan took his hand away from Macavity's head.

'I think the summer house is going to fit perfectly down there once the trees have gone,' said William. 'Any lemonade for me, darling?'

Claire realised she had forgotten to bring out a third glass.

'I think I ought to go to the hotel now,' said Stefan, standing up. 'I've got calls to make and emails to send. Can you recommend somewhere to eat in town?'

'There's a nice new little Italian on the High Street,' said William.

'Come back and have supper with us,' offered Claire, on an impulse. She felt her husband glaring at her.

'That would be great. If it's not too much trouble.' He turned to William. 'You can tell me all about the work you must have done to this place to make it so lovely.' Claire thought she could see William's chest visibly expand with pride, his annoyance melting.

'I'll show you pictures of how it was when we first moved here,' he said. 'I'm sure you'll hardly recognise it. I took pictures of work in progress too. Every stage has been documented – seven albums so far.'

'I'll look forward to seeing them later,' said Stefan.

Claire pushed the cat from her lap and stood up to walk Stefan to his car.

'Don't worry,' he said. 'I'll see myself out. You go and get William his glass of lemonade.'

# Chapter Seven

*'There is nothing Claire enjoys more than entertaining
family and friends with a selection of deliciously
tempting meals from her beloved Aga.'*

Stefan arrived on time, bearing wine and a bunch of red
chrysanthemums.

'They're from the petrol station, I'm afraid,' he said apologeti-
cally. 'The only place that was open.'

'No twenty-four-hour shopping here,' said William as he
opened the wine. 'It's the one drawback of living the rural dream.'

'There's something I forgot to do today,' said Stefan, bending
down to pick up one of Ben's toy cars that he had just been about
to step on. 'The magazine needs a picture of both of you. It'll go
in a small box in the corner of the article with some basic information about you. I'm sure you've seen the sort of thing I mean.
Can we do it tomorrow?'

'I'll be at work,' William put in quickly.

'That's what I was worried about,' Stefan said. 'We'd better do
it now, then.'

He posed Claire and William on the sofa in the living room.

'Could you put your arm around Claire's shoulder?' he asked.
William dutifully obeyed. Claire felt embarrassed. She had lost
the relaxed feel she had had earlier on in the day.

'OK, maybe one without your arm round her. Just sit side by
side. And could you both try to smile a little bit?'

Claire tried; her face felt stiff. Beside her William sat upright, perched on the edge of the sofa.

'I think that will be fine,' said Stefan after a few minutes. He quickly packed the camera back into its case and smiled at William. 'So, tell me about the house.'

While Stefan looked through William's endless renovation photographs, Claire made dinner. She hastily put together a pasta dish of wild rocket from the garden, feta and pine nuts and searched in the freezer for some leftover lemon ice cream she had made for a lunch party the month before. William's voice blurred into a gentle drone as Claire cooked. Occasionally a sentence would pierce her consciousness.

'And that was before I dug out the soak-away for the septic tank . . . Of course, I had to paint the rotten timbers with wood hardener . . . Bats in the attic were the biggest problem.'

She felt sure that Stefan must be bored. At one point he caught her eye. She dropped the packet she had in her hand and a shower of pine nuts bounced and rolled across the floor.

'Careful, Claire,' said William, before turning back to the photograph album. 'This one shows the stud partition wall I took down to make the dining room bigger.'

They ate outside in the warm evening air.

'This is delicious,' said Stefan, tucking into his dish of pasta.

'Yes, it's very nice, darling,' said William after tasting his first mouthful, then after a few seconds, 'Have you put any salt it?'

'Yes, of course,' Claire replied.

'I think it needs a touch more.' William took another mouthful. 'Yes, it definitely needs more salt. I'll go and get some.' He got up and left the table. Claire stared hard at her plate of tagliatelle, stirring it round and round with her fork, her appetite had vanished. Glancing up she found Stefan watching her. He smiled.

'The salt mill's nearly empty,' called William from the kitchen. 'And there's no more rock salt in the cupboard.' Stefan raised his eyebrows slightly and Claire felt a little better.

'I'll put it on the shopping list for tomorrow,' she called back to William. He returned and immediately embarked on a long discourse about house prices.

Claire sat back in her chair, not feeling much like eating. She sipped her wine and watched the sun setting at the end of the valley. The sky changed from pink to orange to red and finally to navy. Moths came back and forth to the lights of the patio; the air was thick and perfectly still. Claire stretched out her bare arms on her lap. They looked smooth; fine golden hairs glistening in the light of a candle. She felt unusually aware of her body. Her skin seemed to tingle as if the night was softly stroking her. She tried not to look at Stefan.

As she cleared away the ice cream bowls, William unexpectedly took her hand and kissed it. She saw Stefan quickly look away.

Claire took the bowls into the kitchen and started loading the dishwasher.

'Shall I wash up these saucepans?'

She turned to see Stefan already standing at the Belfast sink turning on the taps.

'Do I use this?' he asked, holding up the dishwashing brush.

'No, that's for the cat's plate,' she said, handing him another brush.

'You're a very good cook.' He squeezed washing-up liquid into the sink. 'That was a delicious meal. I thought the salt content was perfect.'

'Thank you,' said Claire gratefully. 'Not all my culinary efforts turn out well. I'm a bit hit and miss, with the emphasis usually on *miss*. Do you like cooking?'

'I love it! I'm renowned for my Moroccan tagine amongst my friends.'

'How exotic,' said Claire. 'I'm more of a roast chicken and fairy cake kind of a girl.'

'That sounds good. I'm never happier than with a nice cup of tea and a fairy cake.'

'I thought you'd be too macho for fairy cakes,' she teased.

'I like to get in touch with my feminine side from time to time,' he replied. 'I told you that yesterday.' He turned to grin at Claire over his shoulder, his hands deep in soapy bubbles.

She was putting knives away in the cutlery drawer; neat lines of wedding-present silver glinted up at her. Suddenly Stefan was standing beside her. She turned; only a few inches of space separated them. She desperately wanted to touch him, just to put out her hand and touch his arm, his chest, his face, to see what he felt like. She took a step back to stop herself.

'Is this where you keep your tea towels?' He pointed to the drawer below the cutlery drawer.

'Good guess,' Claire said, opening the drawer and handing him a chequered cloth.

There was a silence. She looked away from him, and when she turned back he was beside the sink again, drying the saucepan.

'Any coffee yet, darling?'

William stood in the doorway. Claire wondered how long he'd been there.

'I'll put the kettle on,' she said feeling annoyed. Why couldn't he get it himself?

'I'd better be going,' said Stefan. 'I think I'm all done here.' He hung the saucepan up above the Aga and folded the tea towel neatly over the oven rail.

'What time will you be back in the morning?' asked Claire.

'Nine thirty OK? I've only got to get a shot of you in your studio and a few more room shots. It should only take an hour or two at most, then I'll be out of your hair for good.'

Claire closed the front door after Stefan had gone and locked and bolted it for the night.

'Thank goodness for that,' said William, taking off his shoes in the hall.

'Thank goodness for what?'

'Thank goodness he's gone. I thought he'd never leave.'

'I thought you liked him,' she said, surprised by William's sudden irritable tone.

'Thinks a bit too much of himself, if you ask me.' He was pulling papers from his briefcase, looking for something.

'He was very helpful in the kitchen.'

'I suppose you're going to start on me now, about how I should have washed up?' he said gruffly, as he found the document he was looking for.

Claire ignored his remark. 'I thought you wanted coffee. I've just started making it.'

'Changed my mind. It's too hot for coffee anyway. I'm going to bed to read this report for tomorrow.'

William disappeared up the stairs. Claire sighed. He had seemed relaxed and cheerful, even affectionate earlier on, but now they were on their own he was suddenly irritable and cross.

She went into the garden to clear the last of the glasses from the patio table and thought how nice it would have been to have sat out in the moonlight for a little while, drinking coffee with William. Years ago they would have done just that and talked for hours before going to bed. Now William always seemed to have something more important to do.

Claire heard a noise and Ben appeared in the doorway, red-cheeked, his yellow curls damp on his forehead. He had taken off his pyjama bottoms and his nappy sagged between his chubby knees. He held up his arms and she picked him up, hugging his warm body close to her. She took him up to change him and as soon as she put him back in his bed he was asleep again.

She began to pick up toys from the floor of his room – wooden train track, farmyard animals, and knights stolen from Oliver's castle. As she turned to put them in the wicker toy basket, a sudden image of Stefan flashed into her mind. She froze in the middle of the room, her hands full of brightly coloured medieval men.

She wondered what would have happened if she really had touched him when he had stood so close beside her in the kitchen. A series of possibilities flickered through her head: Stefan taking her in his arms, leaning down to touch her lips with his. A gentle kiss at first, then harder. Claire breathed in quickly. She was shocked at her thoughts – it was the heat, too much wine, she was tired – but as she went downstairs to turn out the lights she could still feel the imagined pressure of his kiss on her lips.

Their bedroom was pitch black. She lay on her side of the bed facing William's back; it radiated fiery heat. Remembering his affectionate kiss at dinner, she reached out and touched his bare skin, running her fingers lightly over his shoulder.

'It's too hot,' he said, shifting away from her in the darkness. The window was open but there was no breeze.

Claire couldn't sleep, but it wasn't the heat. Something inside her ached. She turned over and over, wanting the dull pain to go away. She longed to sleep, but every time she let herself relax she saw the image of Stefan again, beside her, bending down to kiss her lips. Claire pushed her hands on to her closed eyes. What was wrong with her?

She must have slept at some point because she woke up to the sound of a bird singing outside. It was still hot, she was damp with sweat, and her head ached. She really must have had too much wine.

# Chapter Eight

*'Claire has always been creative. After the birth of her third child
she made her hobby into a successful career, turning piles of hoarded
vintage fabrics into gorgeous cushion covers, tea cosies, and aprons.'*

'Did you get a good night's sleep?' asked Stefan when he reappeared the next morning.

'Yes, thank you,' Claire lied as she cleared away breakfast. 'How about you? Did you sleep well?' She peeled a half-eaten slice of toast from the kitchen floor.

'No, not really.' He picked up a pot of jam and screwed the lid back on.

'I expect it was the heat and a strange hotel room,' said Claire. She felt shy and self-conscious in his presence now, though he had made her feel so relaxed the day before.

'I've got a present for you.'

'Oh?'

'Well, it's for both of us, really,' he said, delving into the brown paper bag he had been carrying. 'To share with a cup of tea.'

He held out a small square cardboard box. It was tied with a mass of twirling ribbons and through its cellophane lid Claire saw four fairy cakes exquisitely iced with pastel-coloured swirls and flowers.

'Where did you get these?'

'That lovely little patisserie shop you've got in town. I thought they might appeal to you.'

'I'll put the kettle on,' she said, beginning to feel a little better.

'Let me give you a hand.' Stefan lifted down two striped mugs from hooks which ran along the dresser shelves.

'I think your present calls for something more refined than mugs,' said Claire, taking two cups and saucers from a glass-fronted cupboard on the wall. Delicate pink camellias decorated the fine white bone china, gold lustre glinted on the cup rims and handles.

They sat once more on the wrought-iron chairs at the table in the garden, drinking tea and eating the iced cakes. Claire had put the phone to answer machine, the children were at school, and Ben was at nursery till lunchtime.

It was even hotter than the previous day. The air was heavy and still. Pale grey clouds started to bubble up on the horizon in front of them.

'I enjoyed last night,' said Stefan, slowly unpeeling the paper cover from his second cake. Claire watched his long, sun-browned fingers. His hands were large; they looked strong. 'William seems very proud of his home.'

'Yes,' Claire said, picking off a small corner of sponge and icing. 'He is.'

'I envy you both. You've got it all here.'

'Have we?'

'The house in the country, the lovely children, the beautiful garden.'

After a few seconds' pause, he added, 'The perfect family.'

Claire wasn't sure if he meant it as a question or not. She didn't answer.

They were silent for a moment. Claire took the last bite of her cake. Suddenly it tasted horrible, the pretty icing too sweet, the cloying sponge too difficult to swallow. She took a sip of tea to wash it away.

'Let's get on with the pictures, shall we?' she said, putting the cup back on its saucer. She moved too quickly, the cup tipped onto

65

its side; she tried to right it and instead it toppled onto the stone flagstones with a heart-breaking smash. The sound seemed to echo out across the quiet valley. For a second Claire couldn't move.

Stefan bent down. 'Maybe it can be mended.' He started picking up the pieces. 'Or maybe you can replace it?'

'I don't think that would be possible. It was my grandmother's,' Claire said, taking a tiny shard of painted flower petal from his hand. 'It was part of her favourite tea set. She was given it by a cousin who was a china decorator in Stoke-on-Trent; she painted it especially for my grandmother's wedding because camellias were her favourite flowers – it's unique, a one-off, I'll never get another.'

She felt so sad, as if a heavy weight had descended on top of her. Why was she always ruining things?

'The tea set is the only thing I have that was my granny's, and until now it was complete.'

Stefan gently touched her arm. 'I'm sorry,' he said. 'I wish there was something I could do.'

'Don't worry. I'm being too sentimental. It's just a cup.' She took a deep breath and threw the shard into the flower bed. 'Let's get these pictures taken, shall we?'

'I'll get my camera,' Stefan said. 'I've left it in Claudia. And I'd better put her roof up, it looks like rain.'

'Are you going to tell me why you call your car Claudia?' Claire said, trying to sound more cheerful.

Stefan smiled. 'No. You'll have to wait for that.'

Stefan was taking pictures of Claire and William's bedroom. He worked quickly, moving easily around the room, taking pictures from as many different angles as possible. Claire watched him from the doorway.

He finished and looked back through the shots. 'Come and have a look.'

Standing beside him she could smell sandalwood and lemons. She had a sudden desire to press her face against his chest, to breathe him in, to keep that smell inside her forever. She moved away slightly and peered at the screen on his camera.

'It looks good. That wooden sleigh bed is impressive.'

Claire looked at the king-size mahogany bed that dominated the room. She'd always hated it.

'It was a present from William's mother when . . .' She paused, she had a sudden urge to tell him about Jack; she decided not to. 'When Oliver was born.'

Stefan waited as though expecting her to tell him more, then he turned away and started looking through his camera lens. 'I'll just take a few close-ups of your cushions on the bed and then I'll be done in here. Any chance of another cup of tea?'

When Claire came back from the kitchen she found Stefan looking at the photographs on top of the chest of drawers. He held a picture of her wedding day in his hands.

'How long ago?' he asked.

'Eleven years,' she replied. 'Just before we moved here.'

'You looked very pretty.'

'I looked awful.'

She took it from him. Claire hadn't looked at it properly for years. It was a family group. From behind the glass her mother-in-law stared back at her, tight-lipped and straight-backed, in a huge feather-trimmed hat that looked as ridiculous as Claire's dress. She was standing too close to her only son, her head inclined proprietarily towards his shoulder. Next to her, William's father laughed his usual jolly laugh towards the camera, as if oblivious to his sour-faced wife.

Claire's own mother stood slightly apart from the group, husbandless, hatless, and looking dazed in an ill-fitting knitted suit. Claire was clinging on to William's arm as if she might collapse into her huge, white, puffy skirt. Her face looked pale, her smile forced. She remembered how firmly William's mother had laced her into the tight satin corset.

'I hated that dress. I could hardly move in all that net and chiffon,' Claire told Stefan.

'Not your choice?'

'I had bought a red crochet shift dress in Portobello market – a Mary Quant original,' she said, sighing. 'I imagined I'd be wearing that and we'd get married in the Chelsea Register Office with a handful of friends.'

'Very sixties rock chick,' Stefan laughed. 'I like it. I can imagine that wedding picture. You on the steps outside looking glamorous; your groom in a white linen suit and dark glasses.'

'Your car would be perfect for going away in'

'I can see the photographs now, they'd be fantastic.'

'Unfortunately William had other ideas. Or rather his mother did.'

For a start it had to be a church wedding, and not just their local Battersea church, or the red-brick church of her mother's suburban parish, but a pretty country church like the one in the Cotswold village that William had been brought up in. It had to be a traditional wedding – as many guests as possible, champagne, a five-course meal, three-tiered cake, morning dress for all the men, a picturesque setting for the photographs.

So in the end, of course, it was held in William's parents' village, the ceremony taking place in the ancient church where he had been christened, and a marquee on his parents' lawn for the reception.

William's mother had put herself in charge of everything from the guest list to the flowers in Claire's hair, rendering her new daughter-in-law redundant. On the day Claire had felt like an over-dressed guest instead of the bride.

She made a face at the picture in her hands.

Stefan laughed. 'I take it you have a formidable mother-in-law.'

'That's one way to describe her. I didn't know how to stand up to her. I'd always considered myself quite feisty, but somehow she just seemed to drain the spirit out of me. It was definitely not the kind of wedding I wanted.'

'Oh well,' said Stefan shrugging his shoulders. 'There's always next time.'

Claire looked at him and he grinned back at her and then they both burst out laughing.

All that was left to do were the pictures of Claire working. Stefan asked her to put on one of her Emily Love aprons – red gingham appliquéd with a bird whose wings were made of pearly buttons. He photographed her as if she was hard at work at the table in her makeshift workshop. He positioned piles of her vintage fabrics behind her so that the spare bed wasn't visible and asked her to look as if she was cutting out heart shapes with her big steel scissors. He put brightly coloured reels of thread in front of her, draped ribbon across the table, and sprinkled buttons in between. Without the children and Babette, Claire felt silly posing for the camera.

'Can you relax a little?' asked Stefan as he looked through his lens. 'As though I'm not here.'

'I can't. I can see you. You're definitely here. I feel ridiculous pretending to work.'

'Talk to me then,' he said. 'Tell me about Emily Love. Where did the name come from?'

'I'd just started the business when I answered the phone one day in the middle of telling Emily to turn the television down. It turned out to be someone who wanted to order a cushion. When I answered the first thing they heard me saying was "Emily, love" so they thought that was my business name and it just sort of stuck.'

'So it could just as easily have been called Turn That Bloody Racket Off?' said Stefan, looking at her through the lens.

Claire laughed and Stefan clicked and clicked.

'That's better,' he said. 'Now tell me where you get your vintage fabrics from.'

'Oh, all over the place. I buy bundles from local auctions, cut up old clothes and curtains from charity shops; friends send me bits they find.'

All the time he took pictures: from the side, from the front, moving to the other side of her.

'Now let me think. What else can I ask you?'

*Would you like to kiss me?* The words popped into Claire's head.

'Would you like . . .' Stefan began.

*Yes, please,* said Bad Claire in her head, *I'll just take my apron off and I'm yours for the rest of the day.*

'Would you like to move somewhere else in the future, or would it be too difficult to leave such a lovely home?'

For a second Claire found it hard to process what he'd asked. She felt sure he'd notice a sudden flush on her cheeks and the disappointment in her expression.

'William would never want to leave,' she managed to say, trying to banish Bad Claire to the outer reaches of her thoughts. 'He adores the house.'

'I'd imagine you could feel a little jealous,' Stefan said.

'Of what?'

'Of the house.'

She felt surprised and slightly annoyed by his comment. 'William's put in a huge amount of work to make us somewhere so beautiful to live. I'm very lucky.'

Stefan started to look back through the shots he'd taken. 'You're also very photogenic.'

'I bet you say that to all the housewives you photograph.'

'No,' he said, 'I don't. You also have a very photogenic house and I think there's a lot more of your hard work and talent in this house than you give yourself credit for.'

Claire could feel him looking directly at her, even though she had her back to him as she took off her apron.

'The little touches; ornaments, flowers, the general welcoming atmosphere – they are all you. They're the things that make it such a special home. Not the holes drilled for the damp-proof course or the varnish on the hardwood floors or the monumental bed.'

Claire turned around and was struck all over again by how beautiful he was with his strong features and sun-tanned skin. There were laughter lines around his chocolate-brown eyes but also a deep groove between his eyebrows that she hadn't noticed until now.

'I'm sure you could make anywhere you lived lovely.'

Claire didn't say anything but started tidying the table. She took a piece of scarlet ribbon and wound it round and round her fingers.

'It must be fantastic for your children growing up here,' said Stefan. 'The sort of home all children should have.'

'I think it's important to give them a nice environment to live in.' She slipped the ribbon from her hand and put it neatly into a drawer. 'And as much stability as possible.'

'Yes, you're right,' he said, slowly packing away his camera equipment. 'My father left when I was five. I came home from my first day at school and he was gone. I didn't see him again for years. The house we lived in, the house I'd been born in, was sold; my mother married again and again and again – we lived in a series of houses; my sister and I got used to moving schools and having a succession of different step-brothers and sisters. I always knew there was no point settling down anywhere; before long we'd be off. I used to be angry with my mother for giving us such an erratic childhood; why couldn't we ever have stayed in one place? Why did she have to make everything change all the time? But now I realise it must have been hard for her, she had a difficult life.'

'What about your father?' asked Claire.

'He decided to relive his youth in a series of bachelor pads, with a series of very young, blonde girlfriends, so no time for us. He even bought himself a two-seater sports car, so no room to take us out either. Both my parents are dead now. My dad crashed his sports car into an articulated lorry on the M50 and my mother died when I was eighteen.'

He looked away out of the window. Outside it was beginning to rain. Drops of water ran down the windowpane.

'My dad left when I was ten,' she said. 'Suddenly everything I thought I knew had changed as well. He went to live in America with his new wife, got a job as a lecturer in European History at a college out there. I thought I'd be having long summer holidays in California but apart from a few initial birthday cards I never heard from him again.'

71

'That must have been very hard for you.' Stefan had turned to face her.

'It was hard for my mum; she was devastated at the time, depressed for ages. We had to move to a basement flat with no garden and an awful lot of maroon paint. My mother could never be bothered to decorate it; my bedroom looked out onto a brick wall. It was a grim sort of place for a child.'

'But you haven't let your mother's experiences or your childhood put you off marriage or having your own family. That shows how strong you must be – how resilient.'

Claire shrugged. She'd never thought of herself like that before.

'In lots of ways my parents' divorce put me off getting married,' Stefan continued. 'I worry that history will repeat itself and I'll make a mess of it.'

'Commitment phobic?'

Stefan looked sharply at Claire in the pause that followed; she wondered if she shouldn't have been so direct.

'No. Just frightened of hurting other people. Frightened of being hurt.'

Stefan's eyes were focused on hers, his face serious, the groove in his forehead deeper. Claire knew she should look away but she couldn't let go of his gaze. He turned away and picked up his camera bag.

'My sister is the opposite of me,' he said. 'She's married to a lovely bloke and they have a nice house with two great kids. She's made the family home my mother never managed to, while I've made a career of looking at other people's homes through a camera lens rather than making my own – it just feels safer for me that way.' He laughed. 'Listen to me analysing myself, it must be the effect you have on me. You're so easy to talk to, have you ever thought about being a therapist?'

'I'll be sending you the bill later.'

'Maybe I need more than one session.' He looked at her and smiled.

Claire felt suddenly flustered and looked away. 'It's always sad to see the effect of someone's home breaking up. It's the children who always seem to suffer.' She folded up a length of paisley cotton and put it in a wooden chest.

'You'd never do that to your children,' he said, as though it was a fact. 'You'd never mess up their lives; spoil everything you and William have.'

'No,' she said slowly. 'I'd never do that. Making them a happy home is the most important thing for me – I'd hate my children to have the sort of childhood I had.'

Stefan stood up. 'I'd better go; let you get on with your life.'

As they started descending the stairs, Claire felt as if she was losing something with every step. Hope perhaps. But hope of what?

'Maybe you should stay until this rain stops,' she suggested. 'I could give you lunch. A Marmite sandwich if you like?'

'Thanks, but I'll be all right,' said Stefan. 'I've got to get back. I promised I wouldn't be late.' Who had he promised?

At the bottom of the stairs he turned to Claire and smiled.

'It's been a lovely couple of days. Thank you.' He said it with a formality that made her want to shake him. 'It was nice to meet you.'

In her head Bad Claire screamed, *Don't leave me here; take me with you.* Good Claire was horrified that she was capable of thinking any such thing.

'It's been lovely meeting you too. I'll look forward to seeing the pictures in the magazine.'

He leant forward and kissed her cheek, a light brush with his lips, and then he opened the front door and went out into the rain. Claire stood in the doorway unable to move. She wanted to run out, run out to him and say . . . say what?

He was getting into his car, waving through the rain. He had turned on the lights and windscreen wipers. Claire stood and watched, waiting for the crunch of the wheels on the gravel, but suddenly he was out of the car again, lights and wipers still left on, but he was running back.

'I just thought,' he said, standing dripping in the rain in front of her. 'It's my sister's birthday next month. I think she'd love one of your aprons – like the one with the bird and buttons you had on today. She's been very good to me since I came back to London. I'd like to thank her for all the Sunday lunches and dinners she's made me. I always call her the domestic goddess so an apron would be very appropriate.'

'OK. But I don't know your address or even your phone number.'

'I'll email you,' he said. 'I'll email you through your website.'

He leant forward and kissed her cheek again and ran back to the car. The sky lit up with a flash of lightning closely followed by thunder, then she heard the gravel crunch of wheels on stones, and the air filled with the smell of wet lavender as his car brushed by the bushes on the edge of the drive.

Claire stood in the doorway, staring at the empty drive, unable to move, the sensation of his kiss still on her cheek. At last she took a deep breath and looked at the watch on her wrist. Ben! She was late for Ben! She rushed into the house and ran around collecting keys, her purse, a raincoat from under the stairs, a raincoat for Ben.

In the car, she couldn't remember which pedal the clutch was. Her brain refused to work. It was as if she was trying so hard not to think of him that she couldn't think at all.

Somehow she managed to drive through the heavy rain to the nursery and to look interested while the nursery assistant read out a list of Ben's morning activities.

'Making sand pictures, song and dance, toast and fruit at snack time; he only ate the toast again, I'm afraid. Two number ones in the toilet and one in his pants.'

'How lovely,' said Claire.

# Chapter Nine

*'Wooden toys and games mix happily with antique furniture and junk-shop finds. The children's brightly coloured artwork lines the walls alongside Victorian paintings and contemporary prints.'*

After picking up Ben, Claire went into town and bought sliced ham and cheese at the delicatessen, fruit from the greengrocers, and two loaves of olive bread from the bakery. She didn't feel capable of cooking that day.

She noticed that the Women's Institute market was on in the town hall and wondered if they had the strawberry jam the children liked for sale.

'Coo-ee, Claire.'

Claire heard her name being called out. Sally's grandma, was sitting beside a table that was covered in patchwork quilts and knitted baby clothes. It was obviously her week to man the W.I. handicraft stall. Sally's grandma's name was Mrs Needles (Nana Needles to Sally and her great grandsons). Claire always thought it was a wonderful name, most suitable for Mrs Needles because she spent every minute of her spare time knitting or sewing or quilting or embroidering some item or garment of clothing. Claire looked down at Mrs Needles' lap and saw that she was in the final stages of a cross-stitch version of Van Gogh's *Sunflowers*.

'How was the photo shoot?' Mrs Needles asked. 'Sally told me that you're going to be famous in a magazine.'

'Not famous exactly, but hopefully it will bring in more business for Emily Love.'

'Well, I keep telling you, Claire, you need to join the W.I. and get yourself a stall here on a Friday. We've done really well today; two quilted dog blankets, a book mark, and a baby's matinee jacket. I'd make sure you got a nice table away from the draught next to me, we could have a really good natter and I'd teach you how to crochet.'

'I'll think about it, Mrs Needles,' Claire said, putting back a knitted toilet-roll cover that Ben had put on his head.

'Are you all right today, dear?' asked Mrs Needles. 'You seem a bit distracted.'

'Just a little tired. I'd better get Ben out of here before he destroys the place.'

As she walked back to the car park along the High Street, Claire passed the patisserie where Stefan had bought the fairy cakes. She had always loved the little crooked shop with its mullioned bow window piled high with pyramids of meringues and chocolate brownies and multi-coloured macaroons. A painted sign swung from a cast-iron bracket, *Patisserie Tremond* it read; the name was an amalgamation of Trevor and Edmond, the two men who owned the shop. Claire stopped and turned around and walked in through the pretty etched-glass door. A brass bell tinkled and Trevor looked up from behind an old-fashioned till to welcome her with a smile.

She could see the last few remaining fairy cakes underneath a glass dome on the counter.

'I'll have all of those,' she said to Trevor, pointing to the cakes.

'Aren't they just to die for,' said Trevor. 'We get them iced by a lovely lady that Edmond's mother knows, she's a real whiz with her icing bag and nozzle.' Then in an aside, 'Not too good with a paint brush, she gave us a watercolour painting of the shop for Christmas; we've had to put it away in the back of a drawer.'

'Want one now,' cried Ben, jumping up for the cakes as Trevor took off the dome.

'You're a right little monkey,' laughed Trevor. 'I bet you wear your poor mum out. She certainly looks as though she's in a dream today.'

'Sorry?' Claire had been thinking of Stefan's fingers peeling off the paper cake case. 'Did you say something?'

'I said, enjoy your cakes and come back soon.' Trevor winked at Ben and handed her two ribbon-tied boxes. Looking at the boxes she felt as though she was prolonging something, holding on to a tiny part of the last two days.

The rain had stopped; the sky had cleared and was now a bright Wedgwood blue. The air felt cool and fresh for the first time in weeks. When Claire arrived home she got Ben settled in front of the television, letting him watch any DVD he wanted. He chose one of Oliver's *Harry Potter* films, unable to believe his luck. She just wanted him to be quiet so that she could have some time to think.

What was happening to her? She felt as if she'd come down with some terrible illness: she couldn't concentrate, her heart was beating too fast, her stomach lurched, she kept forgetting to breathe, and, above all, she couldn't get the image of Stefan's face out of her head. The desire to see him again was almost overwhelming. She felt as though she was falling, actually physically falling. She tried to think about other things.

*I have a lovely husband and a beautiful home*, it went round and round in her head like a mantra.

'Who are you talking to, Mummy?'

Ben stood naked beside her in the kitchen. She hadn't realised that she was speaking out loud.

'Oh, no one, darling. Where are your clothes?'

She bent down and hugged him. How could she have feelings for anyone who was not the father of her children?

'I want one,' said Ben, pointing to the box of cakes above him on the table.

'All right,' she said, absent-mindedly untying a box and handing Ben a cake before remembering that she hadn't given him any lunch. He quickly snatched the bun from her and immediately started licking off the pastel-coloured icing, not bothering with the cake itself. As Ben trotted back to the living room with his prize, Claire made herself a cup of tea and wondered how she could have turned into the kind of mother who sat her naked three-year-old in front of unsuitable DVDs, with only yellow icing for lunch. She started to make him a hummus sandwich and cut up an apple, but she knew he'd never eat it – not now that he had had a taste of highly coloured sugar.

She didn't want anything to eat herself; her appetite had disappeared. She ought to be unloading the dishwasher and putting washing away, or sitting watching *Harry Potter* with Ben to make sure he wasn't getting scared by the CGI monsters, but she felt unable to do anything but lean against the work surface, paralysed by the thought of Stefan.

Ben appeared with the phone in his hand – still naked but with a purple feather boa of Emily's draped around his shoulders.

'Grandma,' he said solemnly, handing the phone to Claire. She hadn't even heard it ring. She really had to pull herself together.

'Claire?' the clipped voice said curtly. It was William's mother. Claire sat down on a chair, suddenly feeling exhausted. 'We'll come a little earlier this evening. My tennis tournament's been called off because of the storms so we'll be with you by six, if not before.'

'Today?' Claire was confused. She had no recollection of any plans for this weekend.

'Yes, of course today. You are expecting us, aren't you? William said you were looking forward to seeing us.'

'No. I mean yes, yes of course I am. Lovely.' Claire felt herself drooping at the thought of yet another weekend with William's parents.

'We were thrilled when William phoned us yesterday and asked us to come and see what he has planned for your new summer house,' she went on. 'A summer house, what fun! I've seen some lovely rattan furniture that I'm sure would be just right for it, I'll show you the catalogue it's in tonight.'

Claire tried to disguise a sigh. 'I'll look forward to that.'

'And we haven't seen the children for so long. I expect they'll have grown.'

She wanted to shout: *It's only been two weeks since you were last here; they haven't changed at all!* But she resisted and said, 'Yes, I'm sure you'll hardly recognise them.'

Claire hung up as soon as she politely could and rubbed her eyes until she remembered she was wearing mascara and now probably looked like a panda. Why couldn't William have mentioned that his parents were coming to stay when he came home last night or as he left for work in the morning? No wonder he had been so keen on mowing the grass.

Gradually Claire's angry thoughts subsided. *Stefan.* Would he be back in London by now? She looked at the large round kitchen clock on the wall. She thought he could be. Maybe he'd sent her an email about the apron for his sister already.

She went into the study to check, turning on the computer, aching with anticipation. She waited for it to hum into life. Nothing happened. It was dead. *The lightning,* she thought. The lightning flash as Stefan was leaving, it had knocked out the computer. The modem must have gone. *Of all the times for this to happen.* Claire wanted to wail. It would be Monday by the time she could get their local computer repairman round to mend it. There would be a whole weekend of not knowing if Stefan was trying to get in touch. Claire put her head in her hands.

What was she doing? What did it matter if he got in touch or not? He was just a man she had briefly met. She knew very little about him. He had been kind to her, but to him she was probably just another woman with a nice home that he was being paid to photograph. Just another lonely housewife dissatisfied with her lovely life.

Claire went into the living room and sat on the sofa in front of the television. She should have been clearing all her fabrics, sketches, and the sewing machine out of the spare room for her parents-in-law to sleep in. She should have been putting Ben into the car for a desperate rush to the supermarket – bread, cheese, and fairy cakes for supper would not be good enough for William's mother. Instead she pulled Ben onto her lap and cuddled him tightly. He smelled of Very Cherry shampoo and toast. She sighed.

'Why are you doing big breathing?' he asked from beneath her embrace.

'Just sighing, sweetheart.'

'Silly sighing,' said Ben. 'Silly Mummy sighing.'

'You are so right. Silly Mummy,' she said and Ben twisted round and put his arms around her neck.

'I kiss you all over,' he said, planting big wet kisses over her face again and again and again.

*This is what matters*, she thought. *My little boy, my children, my family.*

# Chapter Ten

*'Scrubbed wooden floorboards, quarry tiles and slate flagstones
create a naturally rustic feel around the house.'*

The weekend passed in a daze of loading and unloading the dishwasher and running around servicing her parents-in-law's many
needs.

'Are you all right, dear?' her mother-in-law asked her on
Sunday morning. 'You seem a bit distracted.'

'Just tired,' replied Claire, who had just burned a batch of croissants in the Aga.

'Maybe that little sewing business of yours is too much for you.
You have got three children and a house to look after as well.'

'I think I'm managing all right, thank you,' said Claire, trying
not to sound defensive. 'Emily Love is doing very well, I practically sold out at the school fête and I've had an email from a
local kitchenware shop asking if they can stock my aprons and
tea cosies.'

'It's a good thing that William has such a well-paid job he can
support you all,' the older woman droned on. 'And he's so good
around the house – a real "new man". I always knew he'd make a
lovely husband, even when he was a little boy.'

'Did you?' asked Claire, turning on the juicer and drowning
out her mother-in-law's voice.

William appeared in the kitchen in a striped dressing gown,
fresh from the shower.

'Ben is on the sofa rubbing toast and jam all over the cushions.'

'Could you take it from him and clean his hands?' she asked, pouring orange juice into a glass jug and giving William's father's porridge a stir.

'The poor boy has only just got up,' said William's mother, patting her son affectionately on the shoulder. 'Don't worry, darling. You have your coffee, I'll deal with Ben. I don't know why you let the children eat in the living room anyway.'

'That's just what I always say to Claire,' said William, joining his silent father at the table and sorting through a thick pile of Sunday papers. His mother returned to the kitchen carrying a very sticky Ben who was wrestling in her grasp and resisting all attempts to wipe his hands and face.

'I want Scooby Doo.' His voice was muffled by a damp cloth.

'Ben! Behave,' William barked from behind a giant wall of newspaper.

'Television at breakfast time can't be good for children,' her mother-in-law observed as Ben escaped back into the living room. 'William never saw any television before teatime when he was a child, let alone as soon as he got up.'

'That's what I always say,' said William.

'There *was* no television before teatime when William was a child,' his father said dryly, from behind his own wall of newsprint.

His wife ignored him. 'The children should be having breakfast with us, not glued to those terrible Technicolor American cartoons.'

'They will be having breakfast with us,' said Claire, through gritted teeth. 'As soon as I can get these croissants cooked and the table laid in the dining room.'

'I hope the magazine photographer got some nice pictures of the dining room.' William's mother leant against the Aga as she drank her coffee. 'I've always loved the curtains, I knew the taupe linen would work so much better than those second-hand

Sanderson ones you found and that oak dining table was one of my best finds. What fun it must have been to pretend to have your Christmas dinner in there.'

Claire didn't mention that Stefan had decided they should do the Christmas dinner shots in the kitchen, *It's got more of that lovely informal feel that we're trying to get across in this shoot.*

'I've told all my friends in the tennis club to look out for the article when it comes out,' William's mother continued. 'Though I've always thought there's something a little vulgar about showing off your home in public.'

Claire looked briefly out of the kitchen window and thought of Stefan standing in the rain. Suddenly everything felt much better.

At lunchtime the tree surgeon came and by teatime the space where the yew trees had been was a clear view to the smudged horizon above the sea.

'That's better,' said William's mother, looking up from a Sunday supplement magazine. 'Those trees always gave me the shivers.'

'I'll miss them,' said Claire, putting a cup of coffee down beside her. 'They were as old as the house, if not older. I've got a feeling the house won't be the same without them. Cutting down yew trees is supposed to bring bad luck.'

Claire could see her mother-in-law's plucked eyebrows rising above her large black sunglasses. The cat jumped up onto her lap and was immediately pushed away.

'I hope you're not being superstitious, Claire. I can't stand superstition; it makes no sense at all. I usually find it's a sign of ignorance.'

Claire glanced at the four-leaved clover pendant hanging from her mother-in-law's neck and said nothing.

The first time Claire met William's mother, Claire had immediately realised that she wasn't the sort of girl that William was meant to marry. It was obvious from the way his mother pursed her thin lips together when she looked at her and wrinkled up her nose as if finding her distasteful, like a nasty smell. She constantly asked questions about Claire's background – her parents, her grandparents, her childhood home – as if searching for something suitable about her. Or trying to find something bad enough to persuade her only son to give Claire up.

'I've never met anyone related to a miner,' she said when Claire had told her what her mother's father had done for a living.

Their upbringings couldn't have been more different. Life had treated William kindly. He had grown up in a big house in a postcard-pretty village. His father, also an accountant, played golf and his mother had been secretary of the local tennis club for over twenty years. Prep school, public school, university, and then into a safe and well-paid job. For four years he had been engaged to Vanessa, the daughter of his parents' next-door neighbour. Vanessa had been everything Claire's mother-in-law had ever wanted in a wife for her son; blonde and jolly with long tanned legs and the best backhand in the county. William's mother could never forgive Claire for breaking up the 'perfect match' despite the fact the relationship had ended before Claire and William met.

'If that girl hadn't snared him so fast I just know that William and Vanessa would have got back together.'

Claire had overheard her mother-in-law talking to a relative in the toilets at her wedding reception.

'They really were just right for each other. Vanessa understood William; this should have been their day.'

Claire resisted the urge to tear off her ridiculous dress and walk away from the marquee and the whole charade of a day; instead she had squeezed her voluminous skirts out of the small cubicle, smiled brightly at her pink-faced mother-in-law and the elderly aunt, commented on the rain that had started to fall and returned to her new husband for the first dance.

For a long time Claire half-envied and half-despised William's background. It stood for so much she had been brought up to dis-approve of by her mother.

84

Claire's mother had fought her way from a red-brick two-up two-down terraced house in a colliery town to university where she fervently threw herself into left-wing politics and CND marches. She studied French and had a passion for Simone de Beauvoir and a longing to write novels herself. In 1968 she had travelled to Paris on the back of a moped with a bearded history student to join the riots in the burning streets.

Somewhere between her subsequent marriage to the bearded history student (who had become a history lecturer in a newly built polytechnic) and moving into the small, dark, two-bedroomed flat as a struggling single mother, the fight had left her. A brief stint at Greenham Common (accompanied by a reluctant teenage Claire) had briefly reignited her passions, but the reality of the day-to-day lonely drudge of life left her despondent and depressed. She found a job teaching French to the uninterested pupils of an inner-city comprehensive and her dreams of living in France and writing novels faded away.

Claire knew she had been a disappointment to her mother. After a wasted youth snogging boys and mooching around in Top Shop, she had failed to shine academically, failed to find a worthy cause to fight for, and then failed to lead the independent, high-flying life her mother had hoped for.

Sometimes, in her darker moments, when she wondered why she had married William, she thought that he had been her act of rebellion, just as she had been his. His background seemed so tantalisingly different to Claire's – so middle class, so comfortable, so normal. She had been determined to show her mother how it should be done, show her that you could live happily ever after in the domestic dream.

*Look at me now*, Claire often thought – cooking, cleaning, school runs, planting flowers, making pretty things to sell in pretty shops, dinner on the table, matching socks neatly folded together in the drawers. *Isn't this what I've always wanted?* But sometimes it all felt so ridiculous she wanted to laugh – or was it scream?

The one person she suspected could see right through her was

William's mother. She knew that underneath their politely strained exchanges her mother-in-law was just waiting for her to fail.

At last it was Monday morning and everyone was gone. The computer man had promised to come and put a new modem in by lunchtime. Claire felt tight with nerves and anticipation. Would Stefan's email be there?

Until then she had to cut out fabric for a dozen aprons and decorate them with appliqué hearts and daisies. She found it very hard to concentrate on choosing the mixture of fabrics. Flowers, checks, spots, and paisleys swam and blurred in front of her. The choices she made were random rather than considered as she cut and pinned each one together.

All the time she could feel her heart beating beneath her blouse and her stomach ached. Repeatedly, she glanced to the window to see if she could spot the computer man's van coming down the lane.

The phone rang, a seaside gift shop wanted cushions with sailing boats on them; it rang again, someone wanted thirty metres of bunting for a wedding.

It was time to pick up Ben and the computer man still hadn't arrived. She had to go. Leaving the half-finished cushions she went downstairs and picked up her car keys. She thought about leaving a note for the computer man and the door unlocked but an image of William's face as she explained to him why the house had been burgled stopped her and she locked up and left.

The car was hot from the heat of the midday sun and she opened the windows to let the breeze blow in on her face. The smell of fresh-cut hay and honeysuckle swirled about her as she drove down the country roads and every song on the radio seemed to be about falling in love. She felt she could keep on driving and dreaming all day.

Ben collected, she retraced her drive home. As she came up the hill she could see the computer man's small blue van turning out of her drive and pulling away. She speeded up dangerously, beeping her horn and flashing her lights until she was only a few feet behind him, desperate to get him to stop. At last he indicated to pull over and she drove up alongside him in the narrow lane.

'I'm sorry,' she said through her open window. 'I had to go and collect my son. I thought you were coming earlier.'

'Running late,' said the large bearded man gruffly. 'I waited ten minutes for you. I've still got nine damaged modems to repair by five. That thunderstorm knocked out half your village.'

'Please come back,' she begged. 'I'm trying to run a business and I really need to collect my emails today.'

'I've got to get on. I can come back tomorrow morning,' he said.

Claire could hardly bear it; she'd never be able to wait until tomorrow.

'Please,' she begged. 'I'll pay extra. I'll pay double.'

'Well,' he said dubiously. 'And a cup of tea. Two sugars?'

'Yes. And biscuits – home-made.'

'You're on.'

'Fixed,' said the computer man, emerging from the study twenty minutes later. 'You did say double pay, didn't you?'

'Yes,' said Claire. 'Cheque OK?'

'Fine. All your emails are downloaded now and your internet's back on. Any chance of another one of those biscuits?'

'Yes, all right,' she said. 'Money, biscuit – there you are. Thank you so, so much.'

He left, munching loudly. Claire tried to sit down calmly in front of the computer.

'I want to play a game,' said Ben, his own biscuit in his hand, half sucked and soggy.

'In a minute, darling,' she replied absentmindedly as she scrolled down the list of emails. There were over a hundred. A handful of orders from her website, a few for William, an awful lot offering her penis extensions, Viagra, or fantastic financial opportunities involving large deposits into foreign bank accounts.

87

She quickly scanned the email addresses and titles. Nothing. She checked one more time – definitely nothing.

With a sigh she hoisted Ben on to her knee and clicked on to the CBeebies website.

Over and over again they made penguins hop over rivers on icebergs and flew a brightly spotted aeroplane through clouds avoiding balloons. Claire felt rather like a deflated balloon herself. She had been so sure Stefan would have contacted her over the weekend.

*Stupid woman, stupid woman.* Of course he wouldn't have been in touch. He'd probably forgotten her by now.

As she drove through the hot dry lanes to pick up Oliver and Emily from school, she tried to work out what she had hoped for anyway. Some declaration of undying love? An offer of an exciting new life, of endless adoration and affection? *Of course not*, she told herself, that would have terrified her. A small acknowledgement that he had liked her, thought of her, enjoyed their time together? Or an apron order? Just a gift for his sister? That would be enough.

She turned a sharp bend and in the distance she could see the spire of the little yellow church where Jack was buried. It had been ages since she'd been to visit his grave. She looked at the clock on the dashboard in front of her – still half an hour before the children would be coming out of school, and Ben had fallen asleep in the back of the car and would probably continue sleeping if she left him for five minutes.

Turning up the lane that led to the church, she parked her car outside a lichen-covered wall. The wrought-iron gate creaked as she pushed it open. The air felt hot and heavy and everything was silent as she walked towards the little granite headstone. Crouching down she pushed long grass and buttercups away to reveal Jack's name; two dates, picked out in gold, showed the heartbreakingly short time he had been alive.

Three weeks – just twenty-one days – and in that time Claire hadn't been allowed to hold him until he had given up his fight to live. The nurse had lain him gently in Claire's arms and she held his tiny body; still warm but lifeless as a child's rag doll. Claire had looked down on his perfect features and thought her heart would break in two.

Everyone had told her she was lucky to still have Oliver. She could have lost them both, but the pain refused to go away.

When she finally brought Oliver home, the lemon yellow nursery that she and William had decorated with such excitement seemed too big with just one cot, and no one had thought to put the duplicates of all the baby clothes away.

Claire took Oliver into the massive bed, which had appeared in the bedroom while Claire had been in hospital, and they spent long empty days huddled in it. Claire had felt like they were lying in some oversized wooden coffin that symbolised the part of her that had died with her tiny son. She couldn't sleep because she constantly had to check Oliver's breathing.

Around her she could hear the constant banging, sawing, and drilling of William working on the house; he seemed to be channelling his grief into walls and shelves and the large black slates he decided to lay on the hallway floor instead of the limestone tiles they had chosen together.

'I'll make a perfect home for you and our son, I promise,' William whispered as he cradled Claire in his arms late at night.

Claire didn't care, she no longer had any interest in her home or the renovations she and William had planned together – everything was Oliver, everything was keeping him safe and tending to his needs. He cried a lot. 'Colic' said the health visitor; *grief for his lost brother*, thought Claire.

It seemed so futile to be thinking about paint or fabric or window latches. By the time Claire felt her grey fog of misery lift, so many decisions had been made without her that she felt an odd detachment from her home. Before she found the strength to participate or protest she was pregnant again and filled with a new set of fears and anxieties about the unborn baby. Now *they* consumed her every minute.

Claire stroked the smooth curve of the headstone and wondered how different she and William would have been if Jack had lived.

She stood up. That had been so long ago; Oliver and Emily were strong and healthy and Ben had been an unexpected gift that in her mind went someway to making up for losing Jack.

William had been true to his word and given her a lovely home, how could she not appreciate what she had? How could she let a stranger make her want anything else?

# Chapter Eleven

*'Balancing motherhood and being a businesswoman*
*comes so naturally to Claire.'*

The house seemed to glow in the late-afternoon sunlight. Claire and the children sat on a red chequered cloth on the lawn, eating a picnic tea. Macavity sat beside them, hopeful for any sandwich scraps. Claire stroked his head and remembered Stefan doing the same. She stood up quickly and in her head reproached herself; she'd spent the whole week trying to forget Stefan and now she was letting herself think of him again. She cleared away the last of the empty plates and went into the kitchen, promising to return with pudding.

Nine days had passed since she last saw Stefan. Claire kept busy making lavender hearts as favours for a christening and shopping bags for her first London stockist. The website was taking off and bringing in a lot more orders. She methodically went through the routine of the days – breakfast, school run, shopping, sewing, school run – her mind only half engaged.

Standing at the kitchen table chopping strawberries she heard the ping of a new email from the computer in the study. She tried to ignore it and started mixing the strawberries with cream and crushed meringue. Maybe she ought to check her emails; it might have been an important order.

She sat down in the study.

Celia Howard: Re: article.

It took Claire a few seconds to recognise the journalist's name.

*Dear Claire,*

*Stefan has shown me the pictures; they look fabulous. I need to come and interview you for the article. I have a very busy schedule but can come down on Wednesday about 1.00 p.m. Please send directions.*

*Celia.*

As she walked back into the garden with her bowl of Eton mess, Claire tried to ignore the little flutter of excitement she felt developing inside.

The children's bedtime was the usual riot of squabbles, toothpaste, tears, and a vast array of excuses for not staying in bed.

Claire lay on Emily's paisley quilt reading her *What Katy Did*. She was finding it hard to keep track of what was going on in nineteenth-century small-town America. Katy didn't seem to actually do anything very much.

'Isn't there another book you'd like me to read?' she asked Emily.

'No, I like this story. Granny gave it to me.'

Suddenly Claire remembered her mother. She hadn't heard from her for days. Somehow she had failed to notice the lack of her usual phone calls. Images of her mother lying unconscious (or worse) in her flat flashed through her mind. Maybe she'd had a fall, a stroke, a heart attack – all three! Claire immediately picked up the nearest phone and dialled Elizabeth's number.

'You haven't listened to me read yet,' said Oliver, appearing with his school book.

'Cuddle!' demanded Ben from his room.

'What about Katy?' Emily was out of bed and tugging at Claire's arm.

The phone rang and rang. Claire quickly made a plan in her head. She'd have to put the children into the car and drive the fifty miles to her mother's. Should she call an ambulance first? Should she call the police?

'Hello,' said Elizabeth.

'Thank goodness,' said Claire, 'I thought something terrible had happened. I was worried about you.'

'Why would you be worried about me?'

'You haven't phoned for ages.'

'I can't be phoning you all the time, Claire. I have got a life to lead, you know.'

'Oh.' Claire was surprised by her indignant tone.

'Anyway, you haven't answered any of my texts.'

'You've sent texts?'

'Lots of them,' replied Elizabeth, 'and you haven't answered a single one.'

'I didn't know you had a mobile phone.' Her mother always shunned the idea whenever Claire had suggested it might be useful for her to have one.

'I bought it last week. I don't live in the dark ages, you know.'

'Oh,' said Claire again. 'I haven't looked at my mobile for days. It needs charging and I haven't got round to it.'

'Sounds like you're the one living in the dark ages, Claire!'

'Are you all right?' she asked.

Her mother sounded different. Unusually animated.

'I had a little accident in the car but everything is sorted out now,' said Elizabeth.

'An accident? Are you OK?'

'Absolutely fine. Look, darling, I'm just going out so I can't talk for long.'

Claire wondered where she could be going; she never went out in the evenings.

'I texted you to ask if you would like to join me for a week in a cottage in Cornwall at the end of next month.'

'Well,' said Claire dubiously, 'William is very busy. I don't think he'll have time to get away.'

'When is William not busy?' said her mother blithely. 'I mean you and the children. I've booked a lovely cottage online and I'll be going anyway.'

93

'You've booked it online?' Elizabeth had always refused to have anything to do with computers; just another instrument of the capitalist male, she said.

'No need to sound so amazed. I bought a laptop when I got my new phone. It's wonderful. I've been surfing all over the web. I'll send you an email with the details. You can Googlemap it. Email me back if you want to come. I must go now or I'll be late.'

'Late for what?' she asked, but Elizabeth had already gone.

Claire stood looking into the receiver. What had happened to her mother? She didn't sound herself at all – she sounded happy.

# Chapter Twelve

*'Colourful hand-made cushions and woven wool throws casually adorn an abundance of comfortable sofas and armchairs.'*

'Oh, my dear, don't you live in the back of beyond. *Lovely* roses. Shame we couldn't have had a shot of them around the door, but it's not very Christmassy, is it?'

Celia Howard wafted into the hallway. Cool, white linen draped itself elegantly around her long limbs, large amber beads emphasised her slender neck. She seemed to tower above Claire despite her flat shoes. Her hair was a thick swirl of blonde, effortlessly pinned up on her head. Claire noted with envy her high cheekbones. It was hard to determine her age. Maybe in her late forties? Probably older.

'*Lovely, lovely, lovely,*' she exclaimed, following Claire and Ben through to the kitchen. 'Stefan has captured its charm *so* perfectly. Oh, look at all the Emily Love cushions on the chairs. *Absolutely divine.*'

'Tea? Coffee?'

'Camomile is perfect for me. Now we need to be quick. As I said, I'm on such a tight schedule.'

Sunlight poured into the conservatory as Celia perched on a white wicker chair beside a pot of white geraniums. Claire served the camomile tea in porcelain cups with slabs of lemon cake.

Celia got out her tape machine. 'I want you to tell me your story: how you found the house, what it was like, what you have done to it, where you've sourced your furnishings and paint et cetera, and a little bit about Emily Love and how you got started.'

She turned on the recorder and Claire began hesitantly. As she talked, she began to feel as though she were telling a made-up story, some sort of renovation fairy tale.

*Had it really happened?* Claire wondered as she told Celia about moving into the house on a stormy winter's day and waking up the following morning to find a small stream flowing through the living room and that the porch had been blown away in the night. She and William had lived in a single room for six months. Claire told Celia about the meals she cooked on a camping stove and the dishes she had to wash up in a bucket. As soon as they came home from work Claire and William would change into old jeans and jumpers and within minutes William would be up a ladder hacking or hammering and Claire would be wheeling rubble to a skip or sanding down skirting boards. They had been a team, working together to make a home. Claire's voice trailed off as she tried to remember when that had changed.

'It all sounds beautifully romantic,' Celia sighed. 'Just the kind of article our readers *love*. Young couple restore old falling-down house, fill it with gorgeous things and children, start a small successful business using reclaimed vintage fabric. So "in" right now, glamorous recycling. Perfect. Inspirational. *I love it*. Thank you so much again, you've been wonderful.'

'I think I've made it sound much more romantic than it really was. It has been hard work,' said Claire. 'Miserable sometimes, if I'm honest.'

'I'm sure it has been, but no one needs to know that.' Celia squeezed Claire's hand across the table. 'Lovely looking lemon cake but I just can't at the moment.' She patted her perfectly flat stomach.

Ben was sitting in the corner dressed only in a T-shirt, having removed his pants, shorts, and nappy. Lemon cake crumbs were scattered around him and he was happily driving a toy fire engine backwards and forwards across them.

'Isn't he adorable?' said Celia doubtfully. 'How do you manage to keep it clean?'

'The house?' asked Claire, not certain if she might have meant Ben. 'It's a never-ending challenge.'

'It really is heavenly. I can tell why Stefan was so enthusiastic.'

'Was he?' Claire felt her mouth go dry and her heart start to beat hard in her chest.

'Oh yes. He *loved* it and you certainly seemed to make quite an impression on him too.' A surge of excitement swept through Claire. Celia finished her tea. 'Such a *delicious* man. I can't keep track of his love life though. Different women all the time.' She laughed. 'Now I really must go.'

Claire's heart felt as though it had sunk into the floor. *Different women all the time?* She tried to pull herself together. So he had a complicated love life? He had all but said the same to her. She had made an impression on him – wasn't that what she'd wanted to hear? She should be happy. Why did she feel so flat?

Closing the door behind Celia, she leant against it, suddenly tired.

'Mummy.' Ben pulled her skirt.

Claire realised that Stefan probably never had any intention of getting in touch with her. Why would he when he had so many women to choose from?

'Wee wee on the floor.' Ben pulled harder.

How could she have been so naïve? Of course he would never be interested in a scatty housewife buried in the back of beyond.

'It's wet, Mummy.'

Anyway she was married to William. She was perfectly happy.

'And poo.'

It was time to forget Stefan. Move on. Get over it. What was Ben saying? She let him pull her back into the conservatory where she immediately saw the puddle and the poo and the cake crumbs, all nicely smeared together by a little hand.

'Ben!'

The phone rang. Claire went into the study to answer it.

'Hi, it's Sally.' She sounded as dejected as Claire felt.

'Are you OK?'

'I'm all right.' Sally didn't sound all right at all. 'I just wondered if you wanted to come back to mine for a cup of tea after we've picked up the children? I can only offer stale malted milk biscuits and I've run out of milk so it will have to be UHT.'

'You're not doing a very good job of selling it to me, Sally.'

'Stop being so fussy and tell me if you'll come round.'

'I can't,' Claire said. 'I've just remembered the wood for the summer house is being delivered at half past four.'

'Oh.' Sally sounded crestfallen.

'You come here.' Claire absentmindedly clicked on send and receive on the computer beside her. At the ping of new emails Claire looked down at the screen.

'Are you sure you're not too busy?' asked Sally.

*Dear Claire,*
*I'm sorry to have not been in touch sooner . . .*

'Not at all,' said Claire, excitement building as she spoke.

'To be honest, I've got myself into a bit of a state . . .' Claire tried to concentrate on what Sally was saying.

*. . . I was away for a few days.*

'. . . I just need to talk to someone . . .'

*Am I too late to order that apron for my sister? Can you send it or shall I pick it up?*

*Stefan*

'. . . I don't know what to do.'

*P.S. I thought you'd like to see the attached photographs from the shoot.*

98

'It's fine to come here, Sally. Could you do me a big favour and pick up Oliver and Emily as well? There's just something I need to do before you come.'

As she put down the phone she wanted to laugh out loud. She was suddenly ridiculously happy. She picked up Ben and danced him around the study. He squealed with delight. That was all she had wanted, wasn't it? Just an email; some indication that Stefan was thinking about her. Surely that was enough. What did it matter about the other women? It wasn't as if she wanted to have a relationship with him.

Something smelled horrible. Claire remembered the wee and poo in the conservatory. Ben's hand was covered in it and now it was all over her too. She quickly ran around collecting disinfectant and kitchen towels, washed Ben's hands, changed her clothes, and wiped up the mess. Then she went back into the study.

Taking a deep breath she clicked on the paperclip at the top of the message. A little gasp of delight escaped from her as the attachment opened. The pictures were beautiful, the colours so intense and warm that each room looked as if it were bathed in a rosy glow. There was a lovely picture of the three children around the Christmas tree, all of them looking pleased with their elaborately wrapped empty boxes; a gorgeous one of Emily eating mince pies at the kitchen table. No one would ever believe it wasn't really Christmas. Claire's favourite was a wide shot with the fire glowing in the fireplace in one corner and the children creeping down the stairs, the Emily Love stockings, bulging with brightly wrapped presents, hanging above the mantelpiece.

The last one was of Claire in her workshop bending over the fabric, pretending to cut it out. She hardly recognised herself. Her hair hung heavily over one shoulder and her skin looked clear and soft and radiant. Lips slightly smiling, eyes just glancing to one side. Looking at the photographer. Looking at Stefan. Claire usually hated seeing pictures of herself. She always looked pale, her cheeks too chubby, her smile too big, or not there at all, but in this picture even she thought she looked beautiful. Stefan had made her look beautiful.

Claire pressed reply.

*Dear Stefan,*

*Thank you for the pictures. They are wonderful. The apron could be ready by this weekend. I can send it or if you'd like to collect it you'd be very welcome.*

*Claire x*

She hesitated, took away the x, and then pressed send.

Minutes passed and Claire stared at the screen. Just as she was about to give up:

*I'll try and rearrange my plans this weekend. It would be lovely to see you again.*

*S.*

*Lovely* . . . She realised she was grinning to herself.

Just then, Oliver banged on the window in front of her. The freckled faces of Sally's boys peered over his shoulder. Claire leant forward and opened the window.

'When will tea be ready?' Oliver asked. 'We're starving.'

'Soon,' she said. She hadn't even thought about what to make for tea.

'Can we eat apples from the tree?'

'No, they're not ripe yet.'

'What will we do then?' he whined.

'There's lemon cake in the conservatory. Share it with the others. I just need to send an email.'

'Can we really eat cake?' he said, surprised. Claire was usually very strict about eating before tea.

'Yes, really.' She was already sitting back down at the computer.

'You're the best mum in the world,' he said, running off to get to the kitchen before she changed her mind.

'I love you too,' she called after him without looking up. She quickly pressed reply. She could hear Sally in the kitchen.

*Dear Stefan,*

*It would be lovely to see you too. I'll get the fairy cakes this time.*

*Claire*

She hoped she didn't sound too eager. She pressed send. Sally appeared in the doorway looking tired, face devoid of make-up, her wild cascade of hair unusually lank.

'Mission accomplished,' she said, flopping onto William's wooden swivel chair. 'Two children collected and delivered, apparently intact.'

'Thank you,' said Claire, swiftly turning the computer off and getting up. 'Let's go and get that cup of tea and you can tell me why you sounded so down on the phone.'

Sally didn't move. 'I think Gareth's having an affair.'

'What?' Claire sat back down. 'Are you sure? How do you know?'

'I don't know for sure.' Sally looked miserable. 'I only suspect that he is.'

'Why?'

'He's cut his ponytail off.'

'I thought you hated his ponytail?'

'I did, but I want it back now. I hardly recognise him. He's had a proper haircut – in a salon – not just at the barbers round the back of the fish and chip shop in town.'

'Maybe he wanted a change of image? Maybe he did it for you?' Claire suggested.

'No, he'd never bother doing it for me. I know this is for another woman. There have been other signs too. He bought a polo shirt last week and a pair of jeans. He never buys new clothes. He's happy to go to work in trousers with the crotch hanging out and his Iron Maiden T-shirt that he's had since 1987. I have to nag him to wear anything different, even if we're going to a wedding.'

'Who do you think would have an affair with him?' Claire tried not to sound as if the idea of anyone wanting to have an affair with Gareth was completely implausible – underneath his grungy exterior he was a lovely man and Sally had chosen to marry him, after all.

'That's the bit I can't work out,' Sally replied. 'It's not as if he works with any women in his IT department at work and he never goes out without me in the evenings.'

'I think you're getting this all out of proportion, Sally. Gareth wouldn't have an affair.'

'I know what you're thinking,' said Sally. 'Too lazy.'

'Well, no. I wasn't thinking that exactly.'

'I always thought so too, but now I'm not so sure.' Sally looked as though she was about to cry. 'I don't want to lose him, Claire. I love him.'

In all the years she had known her, she'd never heard Sally say anything good about Gareth, let alone declare her love for him, but Claire had never doubted that Sally adored her husband. Claire got up and came and put her arms around her and Sally let out a huge sob.

Claire itched to go and check her emails, and then mentally chastised herself for being such a terrible friend. She owed so much to Sally. In the bleak weeks after Jack had died it had been Sally who, heavily pregnant with her first baby, came to see her every day, bringing chocolate and cream cakes and she had held her hand while Claire quietly sobbed. Later it had been Sally who bundled Claire and Oliver into her little car and, together with her new baby boy, drove them to baby groups and tiny tots singing lessons and infant aqua classes – forcing Claire to get out and face the world. After all these years this was the first time Sally had ever turned to Claire for support herself.

'I think this calls for something a little stronger than tea,' Claire said. 'I've got a bottle of Jacob's Creek in the fridge.'

The sudden beeping of a lorry reversing up the drive heralded the arrival of the summer house.

The wine and two bare-chested lorry drivers unloading the timber helped distract Sally. By the time she'd had her fourth glass of wine and finished the lemon cake she started to smile again.

'I wouldn't mind them at the bottom of my garden,' she slurred slightly, holding her hand up against the glare of the evening sun so that she could see the men as they carried the massive planks of wood down to the cement base William had already laid.

'Better than fairies,' she said and doubled over laughing. 'Do you get it, Claire? Fairies at the bottom of the garden.'

Her wine sloshed over the table.

'You've got hunky men at the bottom of yours.'

'I think you've had enough now,' Claire said, putting the nearly empty bottle back in the fridge. 'Let's have a cup of coffee and wait for William to drive you and the boys home.'

Sally yawned. 'I feel much better now. I don't know why I thought Gareth was having an affair. Only horrible people have affairs and Gareth is not a horrible person.'

Claire felt suddenly cold. 'You're right, Sally. Only horrible people have affairs.'

'I've never understood how people could deceive their partners. I mean, if you're not happy with your marriage you either work it out or get out. You don't go off doing goodness-knows-what with other people behind everybody else's back, do you?' Sally hiccupped.

'No, you don't.' Guilt crept over her. It *was* only an email or two.

'Hello, girls.' William was home early. He kissed them both, filled with good humour at seeing his latest project taking shape. 'What are we drinking to? The summer house?' He started opening a bottle of red.

'Before you have a drink could you drive Sally and the boys home?' asked Claire.

'Of course,' he said. 'Come along, my chariot awaits.'

'Now, *you* are a very nice man,' giggled Sally, getting up unsteadily from her chair and pointing a finger at William. 'You would never have an affair, would you?'

'No, of course not. Why would I want to have an affair when I have such a lovely wife?' He smiled at Claire and guilt settled in her stomach like a dull ache.

He left with Sally swaying on his arm and the two boys wrestling each other across the drive and into the car. Claire knew she ought to get the tea. Instead she poured herself the last bit of wine from the bottle, went into the study, and turned on the computer.

*Dear Claire,*

*Glad you liked the pictures.*

*Stefan*

*P.S. Let me bring the cakes. Do you like chocolate?*

Claire pressed reply.

*I love chocolate!*

*Claire*

Send.
One minute later:

*I know a shop that sells the most delicious Devil's food cake – can I tempt you?*

*S*

Reply.

*Go ahead and lead me astray!*

C

Send.

*I'd love to!*

S

It was suddenly too much for Claire. Were they still talking about chocolate cake? She shut down the computer, went into the kitchen, and started to peel potatoes very fast.

'What's for tea?' asked Emily, coming in from the garden.

'I don't know,' she replied.

'It must be potatoes, but what else?' said Emily.

'Whatever you like.' Claire felt unable to think straight at all.

'Fish fingers?'

'Fine.'

'No broccoli,' said Emily hopefully. Claire always gave them broccoli as it was the one green vegetable they would all grudgingly agree to eat.

'OK. No broccoli.'

'Sally's going to have a sore head in the morning.' William walked into the kitchen. 'What's all this about Gareth?'

'Sally thinks he might be having an affair,' she whispered, checking Emily was out of earshot.

'I can imagine him doing that.' William poured his glass of wine.

'Can you?' said Claire, surprised.

'Oh yes. He seems the type who would.'

'Is there a type?'

'I think so. You can always tell the ones who will and the ones who won't.'

'Is that true for women too?' Claire carefully laid the fish fingers in two neat rows on the baking tray.

'Definitely. I could look at all the mothers in the school yard and tell you who would and wouldn't be unfaithful.'

'That seems a bit of a sweeping statement.'

William came up behind her as she slid the tray into the oven. 'Trust me, I can tell,' he said. He put his arms around her and kissed the back of her neck. 'And I know that you, my darling, are one of the ones who wouldn't even dream of it.'

# Chapter Thirteen

*'Colours flow tranquilly from room to room . . .'*

Claire had planned to show William the pictures that Stefan had sent but somehow there never seemed to be the time. He spent every evening with the summer house, steadily erecting it with the help of a retired builder from the village. To Claire, the pictures were like a precious gift from Stefan which she wanted to cherish and not share with anyone for a little while.

All week she felt jumpy and anxious. When she put on an old denim skirt on Thursday morning it slid down low on her hips and she realised how little she had been eating. Her thoughts were constantly drifting to Stefan. Her sleep became sporadic and she spent many hours lying awake listening for the dawn, thinking of him.

She spent a long time making the apron for Stefan's sister, making sure every stitch was perfect, every detail of appliqué and embroidery exactly right, the pearl buttons in just the right position. When she had finished she folded it carefully and slipped it into the cellophane packaging, positioning the Emily Love label in the middle. Perfect. It was ready. Now she just had to wait.

By Friday morning Claire could hardly bear to stay still. Anticipation, excitement, fear, guilt – a mass of contradictory emotions threatened to consume her. She longed for time to speed up. The weekend seemed to be taking forever to arrive.

It was impossible to concentrate on the twenty-five metres of bunting she was making for a customer's garden party. Her sewing was all over the place; she hoped it would be going up on a windy day so that no one would notice the crooked stitching. Suddenly she didn't feel sure she wanted to see Stefan at all. Their email exchange had been exhilarating, but now she was frightened. She hadn't heard from him for a few days.

Claire had let herself imagine that she knew him much better than she really did. She realised that she didn't know him at all. Who was he, really? Beyond his kind, friendly manner and attractive exterior maybe he was cruel-hearted, sadistic even, or maybe by night he became a crazed axe murderer or a bloodsucking vampire – Claire knew she was letting her imagination run away with her but Celia's words about the many women in his life kept nagging at the back of her mind.

In her more sensible moments she told herself that she was a happily married woman with three children and she had always vowed never to behave as her father had done. Adultery? No, she could never do that.

So what was the point of seeing him again, stoking the fire inside her, stirring up emotions she was determined not to express? But, try as she might, she couldn't help imagining what it might be like to be in his arms, to feel his limbs entwined with hers, to let herself melt into his kiss.

Somehow the bunting was finished and it was Friday afternoon. Through the open window in front of her, Claire could see white clouds puffing up from behind the bare timber shell of the summer house. Ben was asleep beside her on the study sofa. She was at the computer writing a reminder letter to the kitchen shop about their unpaid invoice, trying to keep her mind focused on business. Macavity sat purring beside her on the desk. She determinedly ignored the sound of a new email arriving until she had finished her letter and printed it out. As she searched for an envelope in a drawer with one hand, she clicked on to her emails with the other.

Claire,

*Sorry but something has come up and I can't come to collect the apron this weekend. Could you send it to the following address instead? Shall I send you a cheque or would you prefer cash? Let me know.*

Stefan

Claire felt her heart plummet. For all her fears about seeing him again she had somehow never imagined that he wouldn't come, and this email was more formal, colder than the others. She wondered if she should have been more complimentary about his photographs, expanded on how much she had enjoyed her time with him, but she hadn't wanted to appear too enthusiastic for fear he'd guess how she felt about him.

Claire tried to rationalise her thoughts. It was good that he wasn't coming. It would put an end to her ridiculous fantasies, an end to these feelings she had that were almost like an illness in their intensity. She would send the apron in the post and that would be the end of it.

As she slid the apron and an invoice into the padded envelope, she noticed her hands were shaking. Her head began to spin, the room tilting unnervingly. As she sat down on a chair, tears started to stream from her eyes. For a few minutes she gave in to the sobbing and the feeling of despair that filled her. She could feel a real, physical pain in her heart. *Heartbroken*, she thought.

Rain was drumming down hard on the roof of the conservatory. Claire imagined what it would feel like to put her hand out of the window and let it pour over her palm, so cool and soothing.

Suddenly she had the idea of taking the apron to Stefan herself.

*I could do that*, she thought. I could leave the children with Sally and go on the train tomorrow and find his flat. *And then what?* She closed her eyes tight to try to stop the images of him that still seemed to fill her mind. *This must stop*, she thought. *It's got to stop.*

She forced herself to take some very big deep breaths, stood up, and reached for a pen to write Stefan's address on the envelope. If she left now she'd catch the post office before she picked Oliver and Emily up from school.

# Chapter Fourteen

*'Family heirlooms add a personal touch.'*

A week passed. Oliver and Emily couldn't wait for the start of the summer holidays. Claire tried to keep busy – sorting out orders, gardening, cleaning, taking Ben swimming. She bought a pale green halter-neck dress in a sale and a pair of high-heeled sandals – thin green straps of soft suede that flattered her newly slim legs. The dress and sandals were an attempt to cheer herself up, but all she could think of was how much she'd like Stefan to see her wearing them.

The weather was cooler now. The heatwave of the last month seemed to have burned itself out, just in time for the school holidays. It made Claire sad; the intense heat had seemed like a reminder of Stefan, and now she felt as if the light breeze that had blown all week was blowing him further away from her. She heard nothing. No payment in the post. No email of thanks for the parcel.

A visit from her mother seemed like a welcome distraction. Claire determined to pull herself together and find out what was going on in her mother's life, rather than moping around dwelling on her own.

An informal lunch of sandwiches and jam tarts finished, the children were ensconced in front of the television, enchanted by an old Elvis film they'd found on TCM. Claire sat Elizabeth down at the kitchen table and handed her a mug of tea.

'Are you sure you're all right, Mum?'

'Of course. Why?'

'It's just you seem a bit different, not quite yourself.'

The sound of wheels on gravel made both women look out of the window. William's mother's car was standing on the drive.

'I've always thought you needed something better than that old bench at the bottom of the stairs,' William's mother said as she instructed Claire and Elizabeth to help her lug a heavy piece of furniture from the back of her 4x4. 'I found this lovely mahogany console table in a little shop in Tewksbury; it will be a surprise for William when he comes back. I think its early Georgian, just like the one we have in our hall at home.'

'And I always thought you didn't like second-hand things,' said Elizabeth as they manhandled the table through the front door.

'Antiques are not the same as second-hand.' William's mother's reply was curt.

'You could have fooled me! Surely they've passed through many hands. If this table's Georgian it's probably at least sixteenth- or seventeenth-hand by now.'

'One needs to have been brought up in the finer echelons of society to appreciate the joy that quality antiques can give.'

Elizabeth put her end of the table down with a thud. 'I thought you grew up above a bra shop in Bracknell.'

'It was a purveyor of superior undergarments for ladies. Princess Margaret came in one day, you know.'

'Was she lost and asking for directions?' Elizabeth muttered under her breath.

'Anyone for a cup of tea?' asked Claire brightly.

As the three women sat in the conservatory Claire poured out the tea from a spotted teapot.

'You're looking peaky, Claire,' said William's mother. 'Wearing yourself out with that little business of yours.'

'I'm hoping Claire will join me for a restful break in Cornwall in a few weeks' time,' said Elizabeth. 'I've rented a nice cottage by the sea, I found it on the internet.'

'We'll be going to visit our friends the Crawford-Campbells in their gorgeous barn conversion in Tuscany; we went last year and it was absolutely divine. They've just installed a hot tub and I can't wait to be sitting in it, drinking champagne and gazing out across those lovely rolling hills. Surely nothing could be better than that.'

Elizabeth glared at her but William's mother was oblivious.

'Oh, Claire, I've just had the most wonderful thought.' William's mother's heavy gold rings clicked together as she clapped her hands with excitement. 'What about a hot tub outside the summer house? Wouldn't that be such fun? I'll talk to William about it, I'm sure he'll love the idea.'

Elizabeth started to say something but Claire quickly intercepted her.

'I've designed a new range of peg bags with appliquéd socks and pants along a washing line on the front.'

'You'll have to show us,' said Elizabeth.

'Do people still use pegs?' said William's mother.

'I'd like to shove her in her Italian hot tub head first,' said Elizabeth as they waved goodbye to William's mother from the front door. 'Does she have any idea how real people live?'

'She can't help it.' Claire was still waving and smiling at the retreating car. 'She's just –'

'Stuck-up,' finished Elizabeth. She looked at her watch. 'I must go, I've loads to do.'

'Like what?'

'Like living my life to the full, Claire! I'll just say cheerio to the children, pick up my handbag, and be off.'

'But I was looking forward to a chat.'

Elizabeth smiled at her daughter. 'Come to Cornwall, we'll have all the time in the world to chat then.'

★

The last day of term was also Ben's third birthday. The red and blue gingham bunting Claire had made especially for the party flapped and twisted in the drizzly wind. A group of anxious mothers sipped tea, nibbled on home-made shortbread, and sheltered in the conservatory as their children jostled noisily on the bouncy castle on the lawn.

'Be careful, Oscar.'

'Please be gentle with Ralph. He's only little.'

'No, Tabitha. Don't do that. You'll hurt yourself, darling.'

Claire and Sally watched the other mothers through the kitchen window.

'I hope my boys aren't being too rough,' said Sally, as she poured crisps into a stripy plastic bowl.

'They're fine,' said Claire. 'Those mothers from the nursery are so neurotic. Wait till they have a few more children. They'll soon give up worrying, and poor little Ralph and Tabitha will have to fend for themselves.'

Sally picked up a glass from a tray of untouched glasses.

'I can't believe that none of them wanted Cava,' she said, taking a sip.

'That won't last long either,' said Claire, laughing. 'Give them a couple of years and they'll be downing sparkling rosé at lunchtime along with the rest of us.' She took a glass off the tray and drank it in one go as if to illustrate her point. She even picked up another glass, but could only manage the first quarter before she spluttered on the bubbles.

'Are you all right, Claire?' Sally checked. 'I thought I was the only afternoon binge-drinker round here.'

Claire shrugged. 'I can't quite match you yet. I feel sick now.'

'You haven't seemed quite yourself lately,' said Sally. 'I'm sure there's less of you than there used to be. Have you been going to Weight Watchers behind my back?'

'I'm fine.' She sliced up the obligatory cucumber and carrots.

'New dress?'

'I needed a little treat.'

114

Sally gently turned her around for a better look. 'Ooooh. Very Marilyn Monroe.'

'I've got new shoes too, but I can't walk more than a few yards in them.'

'Taxi shoes.'

'What?'

'Oh, you know. Shoes that are so uncomfortable you can only wear them from the taxi to the entrance of the party. And I don't mean children's parties.'

'They're the only kind of parties I get to go to these days,' sighed Claire. 'Is it sad to spend days planning what you're going to wear to sit in someone's living room watching Charlie Chuckles and his Dancing Chipmunk while you shovel cheesy balls down your throat?'

'Yes, Claire, that is sad,' Sally said, giving her arm a kindly stroke. 'We definitely need to get you out. Life does go on after CBeebies Bedtime Hour, you know.'

'What about you?' asked Claire. 'Are you still worried about Gareth?'

'Oh that,' Sally laughed. 'I don't know why I thought he was having an affair. Poor man, it turned out he was up for promotion at work and so he felt he'd better smarten up his appearance.'

'Did he get the promotion?'

'He hasn't heard yet. But you can imagine how guilty I felt. Poor Gareth. I didn't tell him that I was sure he had a bit on the side; he'd have thought I'd finally lost my mind. Anyway, I'm getting used to him without long hair. He looks quite sexy, actually.'

'Can we play on the computer, Mum?' asked Oliver, red-faced and panting in the doorway. Behind him, Sally's boys looked similarly bounced out.

'OK. I'll need to go and turn it on though. Wait a minute. Sally, can you arrange these cakes on the cake stand?' she asked, handing her a tin of miniature fairy cakes iced with ladybirds and bees. She'd made them the night before, staying up past midnight to postpone yet another sleepless night.

'Wow,' said Sally, opening the tin. 'You've surpassed yourself this time.'

'Just some little things I knocked up last night.'

'No need to show off,' called Sally from the kitchen.

Claire went into the study and turned on the computer. *A quick check of my emails whilst I'm here*, she thought. Through the open window she could hear the shrill squeals of children on the bouncy castle. Glancing up she saw that, as usual, Ben had taken all his clothes off, despite the weather. She skimmed through the junk mail and some new orders from her website and then suddenly she saw Stefan's name.

'Come on, Mum,' said Oliver behind her. 'Hurry up. We're waiting to play my new game.'

'Just a minute.' She could hear her heart beating. Hardly daring to breathe, she clicked on the email.

*Dear Claire,*

*Thank you so much for the beautiful apron. I gave it to my sister last night and she loved it – I knew she would.*

*I still need to pay you. You didn't say if you wanted a cheque or cash. Can I treat you to tea and cakes somewhere special to say thank you and I could pay you then? What about next Tuesday afternoon?*

*Stefan*

Claire wanted to leap on the bouncy castle and bounce up and down for joy. *Next Tuesday. Somewhere special.* (That would be innocent enough. Only tea and cakes with a friend; not exactly breaking any marital vows.)

'At last,' muttered Oliver as Claire turned round.

'It's all yours, boys,' she said, an irrepressible smile across her face.

Claire walked back into the kitchen as calmly as she could.

'What are you grinning about?' Sally asked, her mouth full.

She was leaning against a worktop, working her way through a bowl of popcorn that had yet to reach the tea table.

For a second, Claire thought she would tell Sally, but then she remembered her friend's views on adultery and decided she'd interpret an innocent afternoon tea in completely the wrong way.

'Oh nothing,' she said. 'I have a favour to ask. Can you look after my three next Tuesday afternoon?'

'Yes. Why?'

'Something's come up,' said Claire, busying herself with opening a pack of Thomas the Tank Engine paper plates that Ben had insisted on. 'I've got to see a customer.'

'Is it another shop? Is it local? I hope it's not competition for the gallery, remember Anna's asked you not to stock anywhere too close to her shop.'

'No, a private customer,' said Claire, avoiding eye contact.

Sally looked at her inquisitively. 'Another bulk order of bunting?'

'Something like that.'

*Dear Stefan,*

*I am so glad your sister liked her apron. Cheque or cash is fine with me. Tea and cakes on Tuesday sounds lovely. Where did you have in mind? I'll meet you there.*

*Claire*

*Dear Claire,*

*I thought you might like a ride in my car. I'll pick you up. 2ish. OK with you?*

*S*

*Dear Stefan,*

*Meet me in the car park in town. 2.30 p.m. is better for me.*

*C*

*Dear Claire,*

*Meeting in the car park sounds a bit illicit! I'll be there at 2.30.*

*S*

Claire thought about explaining to him that she would be in town anyway. It would be easier to meet him there – nothing illicit about it at all – but she knew this wouldn't be strictly true and so didn't answer, just waited for Tuesday. She would see him once, that was all. Just an innocent cup of tea.

# Chapter Fifteen

*'Soft and pretty . . . Embroidered muslin curtains
filter shafts of dappled sunlight.'*

'You look lovely,' said Sally, as Claire handed over the children. 'It must be an important customer.'

Claire couldn't look at her. She fumbled in her handbag for Ben's spare nappies and his favourite bear.

'Those new sandals really suit you.' Sally looked her up and down. 'And your hair looks fab. Have you been to the hairdresser's today?'

'No, I just spent a bit of time blow-drying it for once. I had to blackmail the children with chocolate and a new DVD to leave me alone long enough to do it.'

'And your make-up looks gorgeous. Is that eyeliner you're wearing? You really do look like a fifties film star.'

The green halterneck dress, worn with a short cropped jacket and her new strappy sandals, had made Claire feel glamorous as soon as she put them on.

'You look pretty,' Emily had said before they left the house. 'Like a princess. Daddy will like you when he comes home.' It had made Claire wince with a sudden stab of guilt.

'It's just an innocent cup of tea,' she told herself for the hundredth time.

'Thank you so much for having them.' Claire gave Sally a hug. 'I hope Ben behaves for you.'

'I'm sure he can't be as bad as my two.' Sally looked behind her into the cottage's chaotic hall; trainers, bags, and coats littered the small space. In the living room Ben could be glimpsed rolling on the sofa, laughing with glee as the twins and Oliver tried to tie him up. 'Anyway, the boys already seem to have him under control. I'd better go and stop them from strangling him.'

'I'll be back by six. I promise,' called Claire as she walked down the path to her car.

'Don't worry,' called back Sally. 'I hope it's a big order.'

A wave of guilt washed over Claire again; it was awful to lie to her best friend. She got into the car, determined to turn back up the hill, go home, tidy the house, do some washing, forget Stefan. Then she started the engine and, as though pulled by an irresistible force, she headed for town.

The day had started overcast. Dull clouds had hung low in the sky all morning, but as Claire drove through the town she realised the sky had changed and was now bright blue. The sun shone warmly through her car window. Temporary traffic lights on the high street brought Claire's car to a halt just outside the gallery where Sally worked. Sally's boss, Anna, was in the window arranging a display of brightly painted pottery and handmade baskets. Looking up, she waved through the glass. Claire moved off; Anna was still waving and Claire hoped she wouldn't notice her turning into the car park and wonder why she hadn't come in to say hello.

She was late. She saw the car already there, standing out amongst the muddy 4x4s and small, dusty hatchbacks. Its hood was up despite the warm afternoon. Claire was relieved; she would feel less exposed as they drove through town.

Stefan stood beside the car looking ridiculously glamorous in a white collarless shirt and dark blue jeans. He wore sunglasses and his unkempt wavy hair and summer tan made him look like a film star himself.

Self-consciously, Claire parked the car. Stefan watched her with a smile as she tried to negotiate the narrow space.

'I know it's not straight,' she said, as she climbed out.

'It looks fine to me.' He walked up to her and lightly kissed her cheek. 'I was worried that you wouldn't come,' he said, standing back.

'Children, tractors, small roads. We're always late round here,' said Claire. She felt shy and awkward.

'You look lovely.'

She shrugged and smiled, pleased and embarrassed by the compliment.

'Shall we go?'

He opened the door for her and she slid into the passenger seat. The smooth red leather was warm against the back of her bare legs. The mahogany and chrome dashboard glinted in the sunlight. The smell instantly reminded her of long journeys as a child. She had a sudden memory of her parents together, laughing in the front as she ate Tic Tacs in the back. Her father driving with one hand on her mother's knee. *Had they been happy then?* she wondered.

Stefan started to manoeuvre the car out of the car park.

'The only trouble with classic cars is,' he said, heaving round the steering wheel, 'no power-assisted steering. Still, I'm sure it keeps me fit. Now tell me what you've been up to lately.'

In her nervousness, Claire found herself telling him about the fool she'd made of herself at the Oakwood Primary School sports day by falling over in the mothers' race and revealing her very large and very ancient maternity pants to the entire mass of assembled parents and children. As the words came out she wished they hadn't. This was not the sort of captivating conversation she'd imagined herself making with Stefan.

He laughed. 'Sounds like you were the highlight of the whole event.'

'If only I'd known I was going to fall over, then I'd have worn some less substantial knickers with a bit of lace on,' Claire went on, wishing she could just shut up. 'I have a sparkly thong that Sally gave me as a joke once. Even that would have been better than my enormous Bridget Jones-style pair.'

121

'Stop!' He was laughing. 'I can't concentrate on my driving with you going on about lacy knickers and glitzy thongs.'

Claire felt herself blushing. 'Sorry.'

'No need to apologise,' Stefan said, flashing her a smile. 'It's just I'm not used to picking up women in car parks who then launch into descriptions of their underwear.'

She cringed. 'Sorry. Again. It's just I'm not used to being picked up in car parks and to tell you the truth I'm a bit nervous, and when I'm nervous I say the most ridiculous things.'

'Well, if we're both being honest, I've been nervous about seeing you again too. But now I'm with you it feels as comfortable as . . .' He paused while he thought of a description. 'As comfortable as putting on my favourite jumper.'

'Or a big old pair of pants?' she offered, and they both burst out laughing. 'Where are we going anyway?'

They were driving out of town in a direction Claire didn't often go in.

'Surprise,' he said mysteriously.

'I feel as if I'm being kidnapped.'

'Actually, I have the ransom note written already.'

'Just tell me where we're going or I'll throw myself from the car at the next junction.'

Stefan glanced at her. 'I know you can't run. You've told me that. I'll just catch you and put you back in the car.'

She laughed. 'I knew I should never have told you about sports day.'

The little car went surprisingly fast down the high-hedged lanes. Wild roses and cow parsley brushed against its cream paintwork and shiny chrome.

After a few minutes silence, he relented. 'OK. You've worn me down with your sophisticated interrogation techniques. We're going to a little place I photographed for a magazine feature a few months ago. It's a Jacobean mansion converted into a five-star hotel. They lay on the most fantastic afternoon tea.'

'Sounds lovely.'

The car stopped at a junction. Stefan looked at her and smiled. He arched an eyebrow. 'They have the most delicious cakes.'

They drove for another half an hour. The smell of freshly cut hay came in through the open windows and Claire started to relax. Stefan told her about a house he'd been photographing in Scotland the day before.

'It was a fortified house. A castle, really. Parts of it medieval. The old couple who live there are quite mad. They have fourteen Great Danes and a huge black goat with a big red collar that sleeps in a basket in front of the Aga.'

'Makes a change from a cat, I suppose.'

'Maybe William would agree to a goat instead of a dog?' Stefan threw her a fleeting look.

'It would keep the grass short too,' Claire said, laughing, but she wished he hadn't mentioned William.

At last the car swung through stone gateposts and down a long drive. The hotel stood on the side of a steep hillside looking over a wooded valley below. Ancient weatherworn carvings adorned its walls. Stefan parked outside and they walked up wide stone steps into a cool, marble-floored foyer. Claire gazed around at the sofas and armchairs arranged in sociable groups around huge fireplaces. Elaborate floral arrangements filled vast urns.

'Stefan, how lovely to see you again.'

A man in a pin-striped suit appeared and shook Stefan's hand enthusiastically.

'I've wanted to come back ever since we did the shoot here.'

'Your pictures looked superb in the magazine. It did business no end of good.' His accent was faintly European – French or Italian, maybe.

'This is my friend Claire,' said Stefan. 'I've told her about your fabulous cakes.'

'Tea for two then? No problem,' said the manager. 'Would you like to sit on the terrace? It's a beautiful day.'

He led them through a blood-red dining room. Crystal glasses glinted on crisp white tablecloths and Venetian mirrors reflected back at each other into infinity. They came out through French windows onto a long terrace. The sunlight was bright after the cool darkness of the interior.

The manager seated them at a table looking out across the view. In the bottom of the valley Claire could see a river twisting between the trees.

'This is very nice,' she said when the manager had left them alone.

'I knew you'd like it. Would you just excuse me? I'll be back in a minute.' Stefan got up and disappeared the way they'd come.

Claire looked at the other guests sitting around the terrace. They all looked extremely glamorous. She was sure she recognised a woman in a wide-brimmed hat and elegant cream trouser suit. Wasn't she someone on the television? The older man sitting with her looked vaguely familiar too. Claire couldn't help but stare at them.

When she looked away from them she realised that Stefan was back and had been watching her.

'I can't work out where I've seen them before either,' he said sitting down and nodding towards the couple.

A pretty waitress dressed in black and white appeared and laid out plates and silver cutlery between them. Claire saw Stefan smile at the waitress and then give her the smallest suggestion of a wink. The waitress winked, more obviously, back at him and with a little giggle walked away. *How dare he?* Claire thought. How dare he flirt so brazenly in front of her? She contemplated getting up and leaving but the waitress was back with a tray of steaming tea-pots, jugs, cups and saucers. She placed a cup and saucer in front of Stefan and Claire saw a smile pass between them again; she decided she was definitely leaving. It had been a mistake to ever see Stefan again. A clink of crockery made her glance down at the cup and saucer the waitress placed in front of her.

Claire's eyes widened in astonishment as she picked up the porcelain cup. For a moment she let her fingers trace the delicate brush strokes that made up the pink camellias swirling around the

124

fine white glaze; on the rim a band of gold lustre glinted in the sunlight.

'It's beautiful,' whispered Claire still staring at the exact replica of her grandmother's tea cup. 'Where did you get it?' she asked, looking up at Stefan's smiling face.

'I have a friend who decorates china. I took her a piece of your broken cup and asked her to copy it for me.'

Claire shook her head in amazement. 'I can't believe it. What a lovely thing of you to do.'

The waitress was still standing beside them grinning. 'Your friend wanted it to be a surprise. It's beautiful, isn't it?'

'I just wanted to say thank you,' he said, when they were alone again. 'For my sister's present. Shall we christen it?' He leant across to pour tea into the cup.

'You don't need to thank me like this,' said Claire. 'A cheque in the post or a credit card number is usually enough.'

'I've got your money here,' he handed her an envelope. 'But I wanted to thank you for the lovely time I had photographing your house as well. I don't normally enjoy my job so much.'

'Well, thank you for the thank you,' she said, suddenly feeling shy. With one hand she played with the corner of her napkin, rolling the stiff white hem between her finger and thumb.

The waitress reappeared with a three-tiered stand of cakes. Chocolate gateaux, creamy éclairs, custard tarts, and fruit pastries. Butterfly buns, fruit cake, scones, and little cream-filled pink meringues. Claire had never seen so many cakes.

'Wow,' she said, wide-eyed.

'You choose first. You look like you need feeding up. What can I tempt you with?' he asked, turning the cake stand around so that she could view the selection.

Claire took a slice of Victoria sponge oozing with jam and cream. It tasted light and fluffy. She was suddenly starving after weeks of having no appetite at all.

'I wish I could make a sponge that tasted like this,' she said, wiping crumbs from the corner of her mouth.

'Do you want to try a bit of this one? It's delicious.' Stefan didn't wait for Claire's answer but held out a forkful across the table. The pile of chocolate sponge and mousse slipped sideways on the fork. 'Quick!' he said, laughing. 'It's going to fall off.' Claire leant forward and took it in her mouth. It felt delectably soft and silky, melting on her tongue.

'Do you want some of this?' She offered a forkful of her own sponge.

'That's really good.'

'What shall we try next?' he said when their plates were empty.

'You've got jam on your chin,' Claire told him, handing him his napkin.

The afternoon passed quickly in a blur of cake-tasting and cups of tea in her beautiful cup on the sun-drenched terrace. Stefan was so funny it almost made Claire forget how gorgeous he was. He made her laugh, gently teasing her and telling her stories about his friends and the houses he had photographed. They talked about their favourite food, favourite music and artists; about novels they'd both enjoyed and films he'd seen that she would have liked to have seen, if going to the cinema to see grown-up films were still possible. Claire couldn't remember the last time she'd talked to anyone about these things – things that used to be so important to her before the children, before William, before the house.

Stefan told her about his ten years spent wandering the globe: India, Russia, China, America – north and south. For the first time Claire wished she'd listened to her mother's advice and seen the world before she settled down.

Stefan's ambition had once been to be a travel photographer.

'But somehow I got sucked into interiors. Wherever I went it seemed that I always ended up photographing houses until that's what I became known for and no one cared about my shots of Kilimanjaro at dawn or street vendors in Beijing.'

'It's not too late,' she said. 'Can't you have another go?'

He stared into the distance. 'I don't know. Now I'm back in Britain I feel like I'm stuck in this rut for good.' He seemed lost in his own thoughts. Claire reached out and touched his hand; effortlessly their fingers entwined. For an exquisite moment they remained like that. Somewhere inside the hotel a clock struck six.

'I've got to go,' she said. Stefan let her hand go. 'I promised I'd be picking up the children now.' She couldn't believe it could have got so late.

'I wish we could stay.'

*Stay for what?* Claire wondered. *More tea and cakes? Dinner? The night?*

'I've got to go,' she said again and stood up, taking her jacket from the back of the chair.

They walked back to the foyer. Stefan went to the large oak desk to pay.

'It's on the house,' she heard the manager say. 'Please come back soon.'

'I will,' said Stefan.

'Bring your lovely lady-friend again,' the manager called as they went through the large double doors.

'I'll see if I can persuade her.'

As they drove back Claire felt happy, full of cake, and sleepy. She could still feel the touch of his fingers laced in hers. Stefan turned on the CD player.

She smiled. 'Leonard Cohen; I haven't listened to him for years. I used to play his albums all the time when I was at college.'

'I would have thought you'd have been more of a George Michael sort of girl.'

'I have hidden depths beneath my façade of pretty ribbons and lace and lavender cushions,' Claire said, turning the music up a fraction. Stefan looked at her with half a smile and raised his eyebrows.

'I saw an exhibition at the Royal Academy last week,' he said. '"Matisse's Women"– paintings mostly, a few drawings and a little bit of his ceramics. You would really like it.'

'I can't remember the last time I went to an exhibition.'

'Lots of lovely use of pattern, beautiful colours, very vibrant. I

127

think it's on for a while.' He looked across at her and his deep brown eyes met hers. 'I could take you to see it.'

Claire didn't answer. She had deliberately put all thoughts of any future out of her mind, trying to enjoy each minute as it came.

'Do you think you could escape to London at all?' he asked.

'I don't know. Maybe.'

Her mind raced. The school summer holidays were long. William would be working right through them. Could she possibly ask Sally to have the children again? It was hard enough to find time for Emily Love at this time of year.

'When?' she asked, looking straight ahead. On the horizon she could see an empty shell of a derelict house, ivy outlining its roofless walls.

'Next week? Is Tuesday a good day?'

'I'd need to work it out,' she replied. 'I could ask Sally to have the children again, but I don't want her to get suspicious.'

'Suspicious of what?'

'I don't know. Nothing. I don't know.' She felt flustered.

'There's nothing to be suspicious about, is there?' He looked at her.

'No, of course not. I just don't know what she'd think.'

'Where does she think you are this afternoon?' His eyes were back on the road.

'With a customer.'

'Well, I am a customer, aren't I?' Stefan asked innocently.

'Yes, I suppose you are,' she said slowly.

'You could be with a customer again,' he said.

'Yes, I suppose I could.'

'Anyway, you'd find this exhibition inspirational, I'm sure, and so it would really be research for your work.'

'I'll see,' said Claire. 'I'll ask my mother to come over and look after the children. I'll email you.'

'Text me,' he said, parking the car back in the car park. 'My number's at the bottom of my emails.'

Claire opened the car door and turned to Stefan.

'Thank you for a really lovely afternoon.'

'Thank you. I've enjoyed it very much.'

'And thank you for this,' she said, holding up her cup. The waitress had washed it and wrapped it in a napkin to keep it safe for the journey home. Claire got out of the car.

'Send me a text about next Tuesday,' he said, and she closed the door and walked away. No goodbye kiss or hug. She didn't look back. As she started reversing her car from the parking space she saw the little sports car drive away behind her. She could still hear Leonard Cohen's languorous voice in her head.

Her mind was a blur as she drove back to Sally's to collect the children. Of course she wanted to see him in London. How could she not? She'd only left him minutes earlier, but she was desperate to see him again, just one more time, just to be with him for a few more hours.

Stopping the car on the pavement outside Sally's terraced cottage Claire carefully unwrapped the cup from its linen napkin. She turned it over in her hands and for the first time noticed the inscription painted underneath.

'*With very special memories, Stefan.*'

'Would you be able to come over and look after the children for me next Tuesday?' Claire bit her lip hoping that her mother wouldn't ask her where she was going; when Claire was a child Elizabeth could always see straight through any lie she told her.

'I can't next Tuesday.' Elizabeth's voice sounded faint and crackling; Claire had had to call her on her mobile having failed to get her at home for two days. 'I'm going to Brighton.'

'Brighton!'

'There's no need to sound so surprised.'

'What are you doing in Brighton?'

'Eating ice cream on the pier, I expect.' Claire wasn't sure if she was being sarcastic. The line went dead.

'Hello,' Claire called into the receiver. 'Hello.'

'Sorry.' Elizabeth was back. 'Went through a tunnel.'

'Are you on a train?'

'No.' There was a noise in the background that sounded like an engine.

'You're not driving are you? Do you know that it's illegal to talk on your mobile at the same time?'

'Of course I'm not driving!'

The noise sounded a bit like a motorbike.

'Where are you, Mum?'

'Here comes another tunnel, better go. Bye, dear, remember to let me know about –' She was gone.

Claire guessed she had been going to ask if she'd made up her mind about Cornwall but at that moment all Claire could think about was how she was going to get to London without three children in tow.

'I have a huge favour to ask you,' she said to Sally as they sat on the riverbank after a picnic with the children. 'Is there any way you'd have the three of them again next Tuesday?'

'OK,' said Sally, finishing off a packet of Pringles. 'They're no trouble at all. I think they actually manage to instil a bit of calm into my boys. Where are you going?' She handed Claire the last crisp and started pushing the empty sandwich wrappers and apple cores into the tube.

'I have to go to London.' She could feel herself blushing with guilt.

'Oh,' said her friend inquisitively. 'To see another customer?'

'To see an exhibition,' said Claire, breaking off little bits of Pringle nervously. 'Matisse at the Royal Academy. I really want to go. Inspiration for work. A business trip, really.'

'I saw a bit of a programme about that on BBC4, before Gareth changed the channel to watch rugby. I'd love to see it myself. Why don't we go together one weekend? It would be more fun together, a girly day out in the city. A bit of shopping, lunch – maybe an afternoon gin and tonic at The Ritz. What do you think? We could ask the men if they'd look after the kids.'

'Actually,' said Claire, panicking, 'I think it would be better on my own so I can concentrate properly. I might go and look in that lovely department store that I dream of stocking one day, see what the competition is like there.'

Sally looked quizzically at her face.

'Are you all right, Claire? You really don't seem quite yourself lately. If I didn't know you better I'd think you were hiding something from me.'

*Was it that obvious?* thought Claire.

'It's not Gareth, is it?' Sally's hands flew to her face. 'Oh my God! I should have realised before. The two of you are having some sort of torrid affair behind my back, aren't you? Is that why he's smartened up his act and you've got skinny; you're meeting up for passionate trysts?'

'Oh, Sally, now you're being paranoid.'

Sally laughed. 'I'm only joking; of course I wouldn't expect you to want to have anything to do with Gareth.' She looked thoughtful for a moment. 'Though I'd happily do a swap for William if you didn't want him.'

Claire started choking on a Pringle crumb. Sally peered at her face again. 'You look like you're having some sort of hot flush. Maybe you're going through an early menopause?'

When the children were in bed, and while William fiddled with wiring in the summer house, Claire took her mobile phone into the study.

*I'll meet you outside the exhibition on Tuesday. 2 p.m.? C*

131

# Chapter Sixteen

*'A palette of chalky white shades compliments the antique
furniture and richly coloured oriental rugs, creating
a stylish effect throughout the house.'*

*Just once more*, she repeated over and over in her head in time to the
rattling of the train. The journey to London took an hour, but it
seemed much longer. She'd bought a magazine at the station; it lay
unread on her lap. She couldn't concentrate. Her eyes were constantly drawn to the countryside speeding by outside, willing it to
go by faster.

She'd had another trip to the lovely clothes shop, bribing the
three children with comics to sit in the corner while she hastily
tried on a mountain of outfits. She had bought a swirling raspberry-
red skirt which she wore with a vintage lace blouse she'd had since
her college days. It fitted for the first time since the children had
been born. She'd made a brooch, looping a length of dark pink
ribbon into loose petals secured in the middle by a pearly button
to make a flower. She pinned it to her blouse and slipped into her
new sandals.

'Looking gorgeous again,' said Sally as Claire dropped the children off. 'Have fun in the big city – don't get up to mischief.'

From the station Claire took a taxi. She couldn't face the busy
hustle of the Tube, the hot walks down long, tiled corridors, the
jostling on crowded platforms. After a frustratingly slow crawl
through London traffic the taxi drew up outside the imposing

building of the Royal Academy of Arts. Long banners advertising the exhibition hung down the length of the stone façade. The street was crowded with fast-moving Londoners and loitering Japanese tourists. Fumbling in her purse for the fare, Claire was aware of buses beeping at her double-parked taxi. In her hurry, her change spilled onto the rutted rubber floor of the cab.

'Come on, darling,' said the taxi driver as she scrabbled to pick up the coins. 'I can't sit here all day waiting for you.'

Flustered, Claire handed the driver a twenty-pound note.

'Haven't you got anything smaller?' More beeping came through the open window.

'Keep the change and what's on the floor,' she said, opening the door to hot traffic fumes and the noisy street. She took a deep breath and wove her way across the dense crowd of people in front of her.

Walking into the sudden quiet of the large entrance courtyard, she could see Stefan sitting on the steps. As she walked towards him she straightened her skirt and checked the buttons on her blouse weren't coming undone; they had a habit of popping open and revealing more than she intended. He hadn't seen her. As she got closer Claire realised he was on his phone. He was talking, looking down, running his hand through his hair, laughing. Only a few feet separated them now. Claire slowed down her steps, waiting for him to notice her.

'Let's meet up for a drink some time,' Claire heard him say and then he laughed again, throwing back his head. Suddenly he saw her. 'I've got to go.'

He stood up smiling and slipped his phone into his pocket.

'An old friend I haven't seen for ages,' he said. Claire wondered if it was an old girl friend. 'He's called Mark,' Stefan said with a smile as though he'd read her mind and wanted to reassure her.

'It's none of my business.' Claire felt slightly flustered.

'It's great to see you.' He took both her hands in his and kissed her cheek. 'Was the journey all right?'

'Fine,' she said. 'I haven't been on a train for ages.'

'Do you need a cup of tea to recover?'

'No, let's see the exhibition first.'

'Come on then, I've bought the tickets already.' Stefan touched her back lightly as he led her up the steps. 'You look lovely,' he said. 'Nice brooch.'

Claire touched it and she could feel her heart beating rapidly under the white lace of her shirt.

Inside the gallery they moved slowly around the hushed white rooms looking at the brightly coloured paintings on the walls. Matisse's women stared out at them, serenely beautiful; their flat calm faces looked at Claire amidst a riot of bold pattern and colour. Sensual feline bodies silently reclined on sofas upholstered with chaotic patterns, or sat upright, waiting, on bright wooden chairs. In front of the figures, fruit or flowers in decorated vases sat on sumptuously patterned tablecloths. In the last gallery the female figure was stripped down to cut-out shapes of paper – so simple, yet strangely erotic. To Claire these women looked strong and confident, at ease with their bodies, happy in their eternal settings. It made her feel aware of her own body; conscious of herself, her limbs, the way she walked. She and Stefan didn't speak as they moved around the quiet rooms side by side but Claire felt powerfully aware of him beside her, the inches between them charged with a magnetic energy drawing them together, pushing them apart. Her skin prickled with his proximity to her. They didn't speak until they were outside again, blinking in the bright August sun.

'Now what?' asked Stefan. 'Tea? Coffee? Something stronger?'

'Tea would be good.'

'Do you like champagne?'

'It's been a long time since I've had any real champagne,' she admitted. 'Cava and a bit of fizzy Australian is the closest I get to it these days.'

'I'll take you to my favourite bar,' he said. 'They do great champagne cocktails. It's not far.'

They walked out into the busy pavements of Piccadilly and up Regent Street. Claire caught tantalising views of clothes in shop windows as Stefan led her quickly on down the side of Liberty's and into the narrow streets of Soho. Her feet began to sting in her high strappy sandals as they negotiated the fruit barrows of Berwick Street. Stefan obviously hadn't heard of 'taxi shoes'. He took her hand as she slowed down and lost pace with him.

'Nearly there,' he smiled at her.

He kept hold of her hand. Claire forgot about her painful feet.

At last Stefan stopped outside a narrow doorway. A tall man in a black suit stood just inside the door, and Stefan said something she couldn't quite hear and signed a large, lined book then together they passed into a darkly lit corridor. As she followed Stefan up a steep staircase, Claire felt nervous. She remembered that she didn't really know him at all. At the top of the stairs a door was open and light flooded out. Claire stepped into a huge, high-ceilinged room. Along its longest wall a bar stretched the entire length. It sparkled with every bottle of spirit imaginable, suspended, like glistening jewels, on a mirrored wall behind it. Long windows looked out over a leafy square on one side and into a busy Soho street on another. Each wall was hung with large black and white abstract paintings. Pale suede sofas and low glass tables were arranged around the room. It was empty apart from a group of businessmen seated beside one window and an eccentrically dressed man with a beautiful woman, both reading magazines. She was surrounded by shopping bags. Moschino, Chanel, Donna Karan, Burberry. Serious shopping bags.

'What sort of bar is this?' she whispered to Stefan.

'It's a members' bar,' he said, leading her to a cream-coloured sofa looking out over the square.

'Like a private club?' He sat down beside her so that they were both facing the window.

'Sort of. For creative media types. Do you like it?'

'I don't know,' she admitted. 'It's a far cry from our local pub in the village.'

He laughed. A waiter, young, blond, and chiselled, silently put down a bowl of olives on the table in front of them.

'Hello, Barney,' Stefan said to the waiter. 'Any luck with the auditions?'

'No, I never seem to get a break. Thanks for asking though, Stefan. What can I get you?'

'Could we see the cocktail menu, please?'

In seconds the waiter re-emerged and handed them both a long, cream-coloured menu of champagne combinations that Claire had never even imagined.

'You choose,' Stefan said to her. 'For us both.'

'I think the responsibility is too much.' The list seemed to blur in front of her. She pointed her finger randomly. 'Elderflower liqueur and champagne sounds lovely.'

'Two elderflowers,' Stefan said to the waiter.

As they waited for their drinks they were silent. Stefan's phone rang and he apologised as he took the call. Claire stared out of the window at the chestnut trees in the square below; their leaves moved gently in a breeze. Couples lay splayed out on the grass relaxing in the summer weather. Office workers sat on benches drinking out of cardboard coffee cups or hurried down the narrow paths criss-crossing the square, eager to get to wherever they were going. After a few minutes a dishevelled man staggered into the square, shouting and waving a bottle shrouded in a crumpled shopping bag. A tangled mat of grey hair half hid his face. As Claire watched him he looked up. She felt as though he was looking at her, shouting at her.

Inside the long closed windows she couldn't hear the world outside, only the crisp clink of glass meeting glass and the hushed, low murmur of conversation. Below her the man was mouthing silent, angry words up towards her. Suddenly he sank down onto his knees, his face twisted as though in tears. The people in the square ignored him. Claire looked away as well. On the other side of the room the barman was mixing their drinks in tall champagne flutes. When she looked back down again the man was shuffling away, hunched up beneath his thick layers of coats. He threw his empty bottle towards a bin. It missed and smashed silently on the path.

Claire suddenly wished she was at home in her beautiful house, in her comfortable kitchen, cooking, cleaning, and weeding the garden, playing games with the children. She was a married woman, a mother of three. She didn't belong here in this life, in Stefan's life. She had been wrong to come to London. Wrong to see Stefan again.

'Are you all right?' he asked, putting his phone away. 'I'm so sorry about that. It was about a job I'm doing next week. I've turned my phone off. I'm all yours now.' He turned to face her, studying her with concern. 'You look sad.'

'This just doesn't feel right,' said Claire.

'Here?' Stefan asked, looking around the room. 'We could go somewhere else. Just a cup of tea in a café if you like?'

'No. I mean I don't think I should have come to London at all.'

'You didn't like the exhibition?' His expression looked hurt. Claire reached out and didn't quite touch his arm.

'No,' she said. 'I liked the exhibition very much, just like you thought I would. I mean, I don't know what I'm doing here, with you. I'm not sure it's a very good idea.'

'Being with me isn't a good idea?' he asked her slowly.

'Yes,' she said, nodding, then shaking her head. 'I mean, no, it's not a good idea.'

The waiter appeared and placed two tall champagne glasses in front of them. Claire picked up her glass and took a sip; it was delicious, like a fizzy elderflower cordial. Stefan put down his glass and leant forward. His hair fell forward across one eye and he pushed it back to look at Claire, his face serious.

'Do you want to go right now?' he asked.

'Yes. I think I ought to.' She finished her drink much too quickly and reaching for her bag stood up. Stefan watched her but he didn't move. Claire felt light-headed as she fumbled for her purse. 'I'll just pay for the drinks.'

'It's all right; they just go on my bill. I settle up at the end of every month.'

'Oh.' Claire felt suddenly awkward. 'I'll just leave now then. Thank you for taking me to the exhibition.'

She took a small step away from the sofa towards the door. Stefan didn't make any attempt to follow her or to ask her to stay. She stopped and looked down at his face for one last time.

'If you ever need any more aprons or perhaps a cushion or some bunting or a Christmas stocking . . . You know my email address, or text me, or, you know, just order on my website.'

Stefan stared up at her, a flicker of a smile playing on his lips.

'I can make anything you like,' she continued, unable to stop talking, unable to drag her gaze from his. 'I'm sure I could do something more macho for your flat if you want . . .' *Just walk away and stop making a fool of yourself*, she pleaded with herself.

'Claire,' Stefan said and reached for her hand. 'I don't want any black leather cushions or whatever you have in mind for macho soft furnishings.' He was laughing. 'I just want you to sit down.'

In an instant Claire found herself sitting beside him again as though pulled by some irresistible force. He moved slightly nearer to her, his thigh nearly touching her own, his hand still holding hers. Claire looked into his soft, dark eyes as his thumb began to make slow, tiny circles around her palm; it felt exquisite.

'What are you doing?' she asked.

'What are we doing?' he replied.

'I don't know.'

'Can I kiss you?' his face was already dangerously close, his breath warm on her cheek.

'OK,' she whispered.

He softly touched her lips with his. The feeling was so intense it almost hurt. He moved away, looked at her, and then kissed her again. Claire closed her eyes, but bright colours swirled in front of her. Her lips parted; he tasted of champagne. She felt dizzy. The kiss seemed to last forever.

When Claire finally pulled away, she was amazed to find the room still there, the bottles still sparkling on the shelves, the other customers still talking and drinking at the tables, as if nothing had happened at all.

'Are we allowed to do this here?' she asked.

'I don't know. I've never tried before,' he said and kissed her again.

After what seemed like a long time they sat side by side again, only their hands still entwined.

Stefan ordered more drinks. 'Are you glad you didn't go?' he asked turning to Claire; he put his arm along the top of the sofa and his fingers gently stroked the back of her neck.

Claire felt too dazed and happy to reply. 'I've wanted to kiss you since the moment I first saw you,' Stefan continued. 'When I walked into your garden and found you, covered in flour, making mince pies on that boiling day, I thought you were the most gorgeous thing I'd ever seen.'

Claire looked at him; she hardly dared to breath. It was impossible to think of anything to say, so she took a sip of the new champagne cocktail that Barney had placed in front of her.

'I can't explain it,' he went on. 'It was like an instant connection. I knew you at once. I recognised you as if we'd known each other before. I knew how you would be – intelligent, kind, funny, easy to talk to, beautiful. And you were all those things; you are all those things and more.'

Claire laughed. She wondered if she were asleep and dreaming.

'This isn't sounding right,' he said. 'I sound ridiculous, I know, but that's how I felt. How I feel. I thought maybe we could just be friends, but I can't. I can't pretend not to feel the way I do about you.' She felt Stefan looking at her, searching her face for a response, waiting for her reaction. She looked back out over the square below and took another sip of champagne.

'When I first saw you standing in my garden that day,' she said, without looking at him. 'I expected you to be arrogant, conceited; full of yourself, maybe. But within minutes I felt as if I knew you too, as though you understood me. It was so easy. Just being with you felt so easy. You're right; it was like an instant connection between us. When you left after the photo shoot I couldn't believe that you would go; I thought you would come back . . . And then your sister's apron and you said you'd come and collect it, but then you didn't and your email sounded cold and so detached.'

'I couldn't come,' interrupted Stefan. 'I decided I couldn't see you again. It would be too difficult to hide the way I feel. I thought you'd send the apron and I hoped I'd be able to forget you.'

'And I thought I'd send the apron and try to forget you.'

'But I couldn't forget you. I needed to see you again.'

'After you came to the house to take the pictures I couldn't breathe properly for days,' Claire told him. 'I had to remind myself to breathe. I couldn't eat. I couldn't sleep. I was hardly safe to drive the car. You were in my head the whole time.' She looked at him. It was a huge relief to tell someone, to confess it all, to confess to him.

He raised her hand to his lips and gently kissed the tip of each finger. 'Are you very happily married?'

Claire laughed. 'What do you think? Would I be doing this if I was?'

'I don't know,' he said. 'You tell me.'

'No, I'm not happily married,' she said. 'I'm miserable. I don't think I realised how unhappy I was until I met you. I hardly recognise William any more. He's obsessed with the house, with making a perfect home.'

'It is a perfect home.'

'But what's the point of it if everything else is sacrificed? You said you thought I might be jealous of the house. I was cross with you for saying that at the time but the more I think about it the more I think you were right. I have been jealous. The house has come between us, he changed when we moved there, when we had the children; he seemed to fall in love with the house and out of love with me. But since I met you I'm not jealous any more. Now I just don't care.'

'How could he not love you?' Stefan asked, pulling her close to him again. After a little while he said, 'You don't have to stay with him.'

'It's all so complicated. I have three children to think of.'

Stefan ordered another two champagne cocktails. Claire drank hers quickly. He ordered more.

'I feel like I've waited years for you,' Stefan said quietly.

She gently touched his face. He took her in his arms again and kissed her cheek, her neck, her lips.

She pulled away from him. 'I should go.'

'I don't want to let you go,' he said. 'I need to be with you.'

'And I need time to think.' She looked out of the window into the square again. The shadows were long. She looked at her watch. 'I really have got to go. I'll miss my train. It's at five thirty.'

'We'll never get there,' he said, looking at his own watch. 'You'll have to get the next one.'

'I'll be late for the children. Late for Sally again.'

'Phone her,' he said. 'If we leave now, you'll definitely get the six thirty.'

As they stepped out into the street, Claire felt her head spin. She wasn't used to champagne in the afternoon, and she remembered that she hadn't eaten lunch. Stefan took her hand.

'Shall we get a cab?' he asked.

'You don't have to come too.'

'I want to. I want to be with you for as long as possible.'

The bright light and sounds of the London evening brought reality back to Claire like a blow.

'Do you smoke?' she asked suddenly as Stefan searched the street for a taxi.

'I gave up recently. Why, do you?'

'I gave up years ago, but I need a cigarette right now. I think it might help me think more clearly.'

He laughed 'You are full of surprises. Do you really want a cigarette?'

'Yes,' she said. 'I do.'

'OK, let's buy some then.'

They walked to the square that they had been looking down on from the bar, and sat on a bench. Claire took a cigarette from the packet. Stefan held out a lighter to her.

'I'll light it,' she said, taking the lighter from his hand. As she breathed in she felt dizzy, but she also felt calmer.

'Nice?' he asked, putting one hand around her shoulder and lighting his own cigarette with the other.

'I'm sorry,' she said. 'I don't know what has come over me and now I've made you smoke again after giving up.'

'One won't hurt,' he said, smiling at her.

'I don't know how we got from fairy cakes and cups of tea to champagne and cigarettes so fast.'

'I really am leading you astray,' he said and blew out a long stream of smoke.

She grinned at him. He kissed her. She didn't want the kiss to ever end. At last she pulled away.

Her blouse had come undone of its own accord. She hastily did it up before she exposed her bra to half of Soho.

Stefan laughed. 'I had no idea it would be so easy to undress you.'

'Look at me.' Claire was laughing too. 'Snogging on park benches, clothes falling off, illicit cigarettes. I feel about fifteen years old.'

Stefan tenderly took her face between his hands and kissed her again.

'When can I see you next?' he asked.

'I'm frightened,' she said.

'Of what?'

'That you'll hurt me.'

'I'd never do that.'

'Promise?'

Their eyes met.

'I promise,' he said, gently kissing the palm of her hand.

They were silent in the taxi to the station. Stefan held her close against him, his arm around her. He stroked her hair.

'Don't come with me,' she said, as the taxi stopped outside the entrance. 'I don't think I can manage an emotional goodbye on the station platform.'

'No *Brief Encounter* moment?'

'No,' she said softly, gently cupping his face with her hands, pulling it to hers, and kissing his lips.

'When can I see you?' he asked her again.

'Next week?'

'I'm going to New York next week,' he said. 'I'm doing a job there.'

Claire raised her eyebrows. 'Are you sure you want to be with me? I don't think I fit in with your sophisticated jet-set, bachelor life.' She was only half joking.

'You are a beautiful, stylish, and talented woman,' he said, kissing her briefly between each word. Then he sat back from her and looked at her seriously. 'I don't know if you really want to get involved with me. A lonely, middle-aged photographer who photographs other people's happy lives instead of making one for himself.'

The taxi driver looked over his shoulder from the driver's seat. 'Are you getting out or what?'

'Will you be back by Friday?' She'd have to ask Sally again to mind the children. Or maybe she could ask her mother.

'Yes.'

'Meet me in the car park again,' said Claire, opening the taxi door. 'Two o'clock.'

'Where shall we go?'

'Surprise me!'

She shut the door quickly and the rush-hour commuters absorbed her in seconds. Now she was late for the six-thirty train. She only just made it, running down the platform, getting on just as the whistle blew for the train's departure.

Trying to catch her breath, Claire flopped into a seat. She felt stunned. Wasn't this what she had longed for: a declaration of his feelings, an opportunity to express hers? Why did she feel so shocked? So terrified? As the train slowly pulled through London's suburbs she felt calmer. She started to think back over the afternoon, remembering his kisses, his hands, the strong hard muscles of his back she had felt through his shirt. She remembered what he had said, how he had made her feel. Putting her hands to her cheeks she felt her face flush with the memories.

She tried to think about something else. *Supper.* What to cook for supper? Pasta? Sally would have fed the children, so it would be just her and William. *William.* She felt a huge wave of guilt wash over her. How could she face him tonight? Her head began to ache. She felt sick. Too much champagne. That cigarette had been a mad idea. The whole afternoon had been mad. Spaghetti Bolognese? She thought again. Pork chops and baked potatoes with peas? Stir-fry chicken and noodles? *Stefan lying on a bed.* How lovely it would be to be lying beside him. She closed her eyes, and tried to get rid of the image. *Trifle*, there was still trifle left from Sunday lunch – that would do for pudding.

Her phone buzzed with the sound of an incoming text.

*I can't stop thinking about you.*

She didn't reply, couldn't think how to reply.

She thought of the nice mothers at Ben's nursery, Mrs Wenham the headmistress, her own mother – what would they think?

'Are you all right?' said Sally, opening the door to her. 'You look really pale.'

'I've got a migraine,' Claire replied. 'I'm so sorry I'm late.'

'It's fine. Everyone has been fine. We've had tea and Ben has had a bath after an accident with some spaghetti hoops.'

'Thank you so much,' said Claire. 'I owe you such a big favour.'

'It's OK,' said Sally again. 'Are you sure you're all right? You really don't look well.'

'I just need to get home.'

'Tell William to put the children to bed.'

'I don't know when he'll be home. I think he said it would be late tonight.'

'Well, you go to bed yourself as soon as you can,' said Sally, looking concerned. 'This is what happens when you go gallivanting in the city on your own. Next time take me!'

144

'I know,' said Claire. 'I think I could have done with a chaperone.'

Bedtime seemed to take ages. Ben went to sleep in the car on the way home. She desperately hoped that he would stay asleep and she could just carry him to bed. No such luck. He started screaming as soon as she lifted him from the car seat and then wanted *The Gruffalo* read four times in a row to get him to stay in bed. Emily had left her DS in Sally's house and demanded to be taken back to fetch it. When Claire said no she refused to get into her bed and locked herself in the bathroom.

'Why are you such a horrible mummy?' she shouted from behind the door.

Oliver was hungry and decided to pour himself a bowl of Rice Krispies, spilling half the packet all over the kitchen floor, followed by a large splash of milk.

Claire was exhausted. At last they were all asleep. With great relief she was able to lie down in her own room. From her horizontal position on the bed she slipped off her skirt and blouse and slid between the cool sheets, still in her underwear. William wasn't home, and the house was blissfully dark and quiet. She lay with her head buried in her pillow, trying to smother the throbbing pain, trying to go to sleep.

Somewhere downstairs she could hear a phone, her mobile. It was the sound of a new text message. Could she wait until morning? She lay there feeling ill, but the thought of a text from Stefan gave her the strength to get up and go downstairs.

Moonlight through the windows cast deep shadows in the hallway. Claire found her bag on the new console table and searched through it in the semi-darkness for her phone.

*Goodnight. I'll be dreaming of you.*

Suddenly Claire heard the key turn in the lock of the front door. She was standing beside it. Quickly she turned her phone off and threw it into her bag; she dropped the bag onto the floor and kicked it under the table.

The door opened. William walked in and switched on the light.

'What are you doing?' he asked, looking at Claire standing in her bra and pants in the middle of the hall.

She started to laugh, despite her headache, suddenly aware that this could look like some misjudged attempt at seduction.

'Why are you laughing?' he said crossly. 'What's going on?'

'I thought I heard a noise,' she said. 'I've been in bed. I've got a really bad headache, but I heard something, so I came down to check.'

'I've got a bit of a headache too,' he said, rubbing his temples. 'Though after the day I've had, I'm not surprised!'

'Oh dear,' said Claire, trying to sound sympathetic, but starting to climb the stairs at the same time.

'Why were you in bed in your underwear?' he asked.

'Because I couldn't be bothered to take it off,' she sighed, slowly climbing a few steps more.

'What's for supper?' William called up after her as she made it through the bedroom door.

'Trifle,' she replied and collapsed back into bed.

# Chapter Seventeen

*'The overall effect is stunning.'*

Claire had waited until William had left for work before turning on her phone.

*Good morning. S.*

*Good morning. C.*

*What are you doing?*

*Making breakfast. What are you doing?*

*Lying in bed remembering yesterday.*

*Nice memories?*

*Very.*

*I wish I was with you.*

Claire was making pancakes. It was a breakfast treat usually reserved for Sundays, but she wanted to do something special for the children to make up for her day away from them. They were still asleep. In a minute she would wake them up.

Her phone buzzed again. She looked at the message, expecting it to be another from Stefan. It was from her mother.

*Hello darling. Are you coming to Cornwall? Love Mum x*

Claire couldn't think about Cornwall. She couldn't think about the future at all. The next time she could see Stefan again was as far as she could go.

All day Claire felt as though her mind was whirling, her stomach tight with fear and happiness. She went over and over the previous afternoon in her head, remembering every detail, every moment, every word.

*I miss you*, he sent as she walked down the aisles in Waitrose, trying to concentrate on what to buy and stop Oliver and Emily filling the trolley with sweets.

*Thinking of your beautiful eyes*, as she sat with a group of other mothers at a Play Barn birthday party, drinking a tasteless cappuccino and trying to keep Ben in sight as he careered down terrifying slides into a ball-filled enclosure.

*This time yesterday you were in my arms*, as she scraped ground-in Play-Doh from the coir matting on the stairs.

As she was making macaroni cheese for tea, her mother phoned.

'Did you get my text?'

'Yes, Mum,' said Claire, trying to stop Ben from climbing onto a chair beside the stove.

'And I sent an email you haven't answered. I was ringing all day yesterday and you weren't there. Are you all right?'

'I'm fine, Mum. Just a bit busy.'

'You sound odd.'

'Thanks! Are you all right?'

'I'll tell you how I am when I see you,' her mother replied mysteriously. 'Can you get away for a few days to come to Cornwall?'

'I'm still not sure,' said Claire, stirring pasta into the cheese sauce. 'No. It's too hot!'

'Pardon?'

'Sorry, Mum. Ben is trying to steal bits of pasta from the saucepan.'

'Just for three or four days. I'd love to see the children playing on the beach by the cottage. It looks beautiful on the internet. The children will love it.'

'Yes, I know,' said Claire. 'I'll try my best. Ben, get down and go and play with Emily.'

'Do you have a webcam on your computer? I've just bought one. If you have one we could talk and I could see you at the same time.'

'No, we don't have a webcam,' Claire said, wondering what other pieces of technology her mother was about to embrace.

'Well, you'll have to get one. You've got to keep up, Claire.'

'But what if I can't come to Cornwall? Can you cancel the cottage?'

'Oh, that doesn't matter; I'll be going there anyway.'

'Are you sure you're all right?' asked Claire. She was worried about her mother, she realised she hardly ever phoned in the evening and it was two weeks since she'd been to visit.

'Better than ever. Let me know if you can come. I'd love you to be there.'

'Would you be able to come and look after the children for me next Friday?' *Please say yes*, thought Claire.

'Sorry, I'll be busy next Friday. Is it something important? If it's work you should make William take some time off to look after the children. He really should take what you do more seriously.'

'It's all right, Mum, I'll sort something out with him.'

'Look, I must go. I'm running late.'

Claire suddenly had a huge urge to confide in her mother. She took a deep breath.

'Mum, I want to tell you something . . .'

But her mother had already gone. Claire stood staring at the phone in her hand.

'It's probably for the best; I don't need to tell anyone. Just my little secret.'

'Secret, secret,' echoed Ben.


William was home early with flowers.

'What have I done to deserve these?' asked Claire, looking at the bunch of white lilies in his hand. She hesitated before taking

149

them from him. Her grandmother always told her white lilies were for innocence and she felt drenched in guilt.

'I just thought I'd been neglecting you lately,' he said. 'When I saw you last night with your bad headache, looking so thin, I was worried about you. I wanted to let you know that even though I might work late or be busy building the summer house, I do think of you.'

He took her in her arms and hugged her. Claire hadn't expected this at all.

'I think you need a little treat,' William said, still holding her.

'Do I?'

'I've booked a table for two, just you and me, at the Italian Bistro in town for this Saturday night. I've asked my parents to come down to babysit.'

'Oh, how lovely,' she said, trying her best to sound enthusiastic.

'You deserve it, darling,' he said. 'I know how hard you work with the children and your little business.'

He lifted her chin and kissed her mouth; his lips felt dry and rough.

'Yuk,' said Oliver, walking in the room. 'That's disgusting. Stop it.'

William let go of Claire and scooped Oliver up into a fireman's lift and ran with him around the room.

'Mum,' Oliver called through breathless laughter. 'Your phone was ringing.' He held it out in his hand from his position over William's shoulder.

Claire grabbed it from him as they passed her.

*I can still feel your lips on mine, more delicious than any cake or champagne.*

She quickly turned her phone off and pushed it to the back of the tea-towel drawer. Then, lifting down the Moorcroft vase from the dresser, she started to arrange the lilies.

'I do love you, Claire,' said William, coming up behind her and encircling her in a tight embrace. She felt sure that he would feel her heart thumping through her shirt and wonder what was wrong but he quickly released her and headed for the door.

'I'll just go down to the summer house and do a few things before supper. Call me when it's ready.'

# Chapter Eighteen

*' "I know how lucky I am . . ." says Claire.'*

The lilies lasted a week. The air of the house hung thick with their sweet, heavy scent, making Claire feel slightly sick. In that time she had taken the children swimming three times, been to town to buy them new shoes, had two picnics with Sally and the children, four trips to Waitrose, two to the organic farm shop, had the car serviced, taken Macavity to the vet with a cut nose, sent out numerous orders she'd received from her website, sent some cushions to a shop in Tunbridge Wells, cut out and appliquéd twenty peg bags for the gallery in town, entertained and fed her parents-in-law, and had been out for a meal with William.

In that time she had also had forty-two texts from Stefan and she knew that he had photographed a converted windmill near Cambridge and a gothic mansion in Yorkshire, got a plane from Heathrow to New York, photographed a Manhattan loft apartment, bought a new jacket, been to an opening at the Museum of Modern Art, had dinner with an actor friend, seen a play on Broadway, and at the time she was throwing the wilting lilies on the compost heap he was somewhere above the Atlantic on his way home.

Two days left until she saw him again.

She had been nervous about the meal with William. She couldn't envisage them sitting across a table from each other with anything to say.

His parents had arrived later than arranged on Friday night, his mother showering the children with presents, cuddles, and games and then expecting Claire to get them into bed and asleep in time for the adults to eat at a reasonable hour.

'You should be much firmer with them,' she said, as Claire stopped stirring the risotto yet again to put Ben back to bed and to ask Emily and Oliver to get back into theirs.

'They're just very excited about your visit,' said Claire through gritted teeth. 'That's why they can't sleep.'

'Lights out, door closed, no nonsense,' said her mother-in-law. 'That's how it was for William. He knew I meant it.'

'Maybe you could go up and have a go then, dear,' suggested her father-in-law from behind his glass of whisky.

'What a good idea,' said Claire. 'I'll get on with this risotto, or we'll never get to eat.'

'You look much too thin,' said her mother-in-law, as Claire came downstairs dressed in a simple black silk dress the following evening. 'You girls and your ridiculous diets. I don't know why you can't accept that you should be filling out by the time you get to your age. You can't hold back time.'

'I haven't been on a diet,' protested Claire.

'It's probably running around after three children that keeps her so lovely and slim,' said her father-in-law, smiling at her.

'I knew three would be too many for you to cope with,' put in her mother-in-law. 'I told that to William before Ben was born. He agreed with me. He said he'd never wanted another child, but it was too late by then. You'd got your way.'

'I cope as well with three as I did with two,' Claire insisted, slipping into a pair of black stilettos and trying to stop herself from stabbing her mother-in-law with a very spiky heel.

'And they're a credit to you,' said her father-in-law kindly.

'Thank you,' said Claire, wondering how he had managed to live with his wife for so long.

'I'm only saying it's a strain on you both. Poor William, working all hours to keep you all.'

'I do contribute financially as well,' said Claire, trying to keep her voice steady. 'Emily Love is already making a profit.'

'Well, maybe when Ben's in full-time school, you'll be able to get a job again,' her mother-in-law continued.

'Are you ready to go?' asked William, coming downstairs.

'Definitely,' said Claire, stepping out of the door as quickly as she could.

Claire needn't have worried that they would have nothing to say to each other over dinner. From the moment they opened the car doors William was talking about 'Project House'. As they drove into town he was distracted by a site on which three new houses were being built.

'I can't understand it. How did they ever get permission to build those hideous eyesores here?'

'I like them,' she said. 'They look like nice family homes with fair-sized gardens too. It would be lovely to have a view of the river and be so close to town.'

'Modern monstrosities,' said William with a shudder, and then he started talking about their house again.

On and on he talked over the meal: worries about the roof; windows that he wanted to replace; a plan to move the outside tap. By the time their puddings were served, Claire realised she had hardly said a word all night. She took a chance to change the conversation when William stopped talking to take a large mouthful of chocolate cheesecake.

'I wonder if your mother's got the children into bed yet?'

'My parents are so good to come and look after them,' he said. 'It's a shame they don't live nearer.'

'The children always seem to enjoy seeing them,' said Claire, delicately cracking the sugar crust of her crème brûlée with her spoon. She was imagining what it would be like to be sharing a meal in this intimately lit restaurant with Stefan.

'I've been having more thoughts about an ensuite in the

154

guest room.' William paused to shovel in another mouthful of cheesecake.

'Good idea,' she said, not really listening.

'It would be easier when my parents come to stay – we might be able to tempt them to come more often.'

'Actually, I think the guest room is fine as it is,' she said, suddenly taking notice. 'An ensuite would never fit into that room.'

'Emily's bedroom next door to it is a very good shape and size for a small bathroom.' He took a pen from his shirt pocket and started drawing a sketch on a paper napkin. 'Toilet here, sink unit, maybe a double one here, shower where the cupboard is. Knock a door into the guest room. Move the bed against this wall here.'

Claire stopped him. 'That's all very nice, but just where is Emily supposed to sleep?'

'Above the kitchen.'

'There's nothing but air above the kitchen. It's only a single storey.'

'Yes,' he said. 'At the moment. But what if we build on top of it?'

'How?'

'I've planned it all out,' he went on, drawing sketches on a separate napkin. 'Lower the kitchen ceiling. Raise the roof so that it's more like a large attic space. There would be plenty of room to stand up in the middle. Cupboards down the sides, like this; a dormer window at the back. Redesign the whole kitchen below, new units, new floor, get rid of that old Welsh dresser.'

'But I love the kitchen, it's my favourite room.'

'It's got very shabby since Ben's been born, it needs a complete overhaul. We'd need planning permission, of course. It could take time to win them round. They're all bloody control freaks in the local planning department. They let those horrible new houses go up, but I bet we'll have to fight for this.'

'And it would all be so that your parents could have an ensuite bathroom when they come to stay?' asked Claire, trying not to sound annoyed.

'Remember how good they have been to us, darling.' Claire thought she could detect a slight edge in his voice that stopped her from going any further.

'It will be nice to see the summer house finished,' she said and then William, distracted by his new favourite project, started talking about the tongue and groove he was going to panel the inside walls with and the insulation he was going to put in the ceiling. 'Have I told you my mother wants to buy us a hot tub as our Christmas present?'

'That was nice, wasn't it?' he said as they drove home, giving Claire's knee a squeeze with his hand.

'Yes, lovely. Thank you.' Claire let herself daydream about Stefan as she stared out into the night.

'Couldn't believe the bill though. We can't afford to be doing that sort of thing too much.'

'No,' she sighed.

'Not if we're doing this attic conversion and ensuite and remodelling the kitchen.'

She changed the conversation. 'My mother wants us to go to Cornwall with her for a few days to a cottage.'

'It's a bloody long way for a few days,' he said. 'I can't go. God knows, I've little enough time to get everything done as it is. I have to finish the summer house and I need to sand down the living-room floor over the next few weeks. It's covered in scratches from Ben and his ride-on toys.'

'I haven't noticed the scratches,' she said, looking out into the darkness beyond the window.

'And there's still that stain you made with the raspberries. I'll have to re-wax the whole floor. We won't be able to use it for a few days.'

'Then maybe the best time to do it is when I'm in Cornwall with the children.'

'What about me?' he asked. 'Are you going to leave me on my own?'

'It's only for a few days. It will be nice for the children to have a bit of a holiday and I'd like to see my mother. I'm worried about her. Lately she hasn't seemed herself at all.'

'Thank God for that,' he said.

'William!'

'It was a joke, darling!' He squeezed her knee again.

'I was thinking about encouraging her to join something – an evening class or maybe a walking group.'

'A walking group? They'd never put up with her. They'd probably all walk much faster trying to get away from her. They'd probably run!'

'I suppose that's another joke?' she said, looking at his silhouetted profile and deciding that sometimes she really didn't like her husband at all. 'It's not funny. It's mean.'

'You're being overly sensitive about her, as usual.'

He swung the car into the drive and stopped with a jolt. The front door opened and the bright light of the hallway flooded out. William's mother stood in the porch in her peach silk dressing gown. She put her hand up to wave. William got out of the car and went to greet her.

# Chapter Nineteen

*'Set amongst idyllic country scenery . . .'*

'I'm afraid I can't do Friday,' Sally said as they sat on a bench at the adventure playground watching the children careering up and down climbing frames and rope swings. 'Anna needs me to do an extra day at the gallery. God knows what I'll do with the boys. Can you change your dental appointment and have my boys on Friday and I'll have your children next week?'

Claire's heart sank; she couldn't possibly wait until the following week to see Stefan. Sally sensed her disappointment.

'It's just that the gallery is really busy with holidaymakers.' She smiled. 'It's your own fault, Claire, people are coming from all over to buy your stuff, especially those new flower brooches you've just started to make, they're flying out of the door.' She pushed one large breast towards Claire. 'Look, I've even bought one.' The bright pink ribbon petal brooch looked jaunty against Sally's blue and white striped T-shirt.

'You didn't have to buy one,' said Claire. 'I could have made you one.'

'You can make me one to go in my hair.' Sally pushed a tousled strand of blonde hair up above her ear. I want it to go here; a really big red one on a clip. I think they'd sell well too, I'm sure Anna would try them out in the gallery for you.'

'Mmm,' said Claire, as she desperately tried to work out what

158

she could possibly do with the children on Friday afternoon. The thought came to her – did she dare?

Sally waved her hand in front of Claire's face. 'Are you listening? Did you hear my wonderful new idea?'

Claire looked up at her with a sigh.

'I think I'm just going to have to resign myself to asking William's mother to look after them on Friday.'

'Great,' said Sally, grinning. 'You can ask her to have my boys as well.' As she looked at Claire's horrified face she let out a guffaw of laughter. 'Even William's mother doesn't deserve having to look after my two hooligans.'

'Where did you say you were going again?' William's mother was unpacking pieces of a large carved oak plant stand from the boot of her car. 'This will look wonderful in the conservatory when it's put together. It just needs something to cascade down the pillar – some sort of fern or trailing geranium.'

'I'm going to see an extremely chic gift shop that's very interested in stocking my work,' said Claire, answering her question and finding she quite enjoyed making up the lie. 'They saw my cushions on my website and they say they'd like to see some more of my designs. They're really enthusiastic, the lady on the phone said my work is just the sort of thing her upmarket customers will love – it all seems very posh.'

William's mother sniffed. 'I'm surprised that people want things made out of second-hand fabric. Why don't you just get some lovely lawn from Liberty – so much nicer than dirty old material that could have come from anywhere?'

Claire smiled benignly at the older woman. She didn't care what she said to her, she was going to see Stefan and that was all that mattered. She had received a text the day before:

*Plane just touched down. Not long now. X*

And one more as she was making the beds that morning:

159

*Counting the hours.* X

*I'm counting the minutes.* X, she replied.

Claire drove down the small back lane beside the river – using the high street was too risky with Sally working at the gallery today. She wore a simple white dress, 1940s in style with a fitted bodice that did up with tiny covered buttons down the front; a full skirt fell below her knee, and she had chosen a pair of simple pale blue ballet pumps instead of her high heels.

Stefan was waiting for her in the car park, leaning against his car in a checked blue shirt and khaki chinos. Claire's heart lurched when she saw him. He was smiling, she was smiling, she could hardly concentrate on manoeuvring her car into a parking space and turning off the engine. In seconds she was beside him. He opened the passenger door without a word and she slipped in. As he sat down beside her he leant across and kissed her on her lips; the kiss felt warm and familiar and right.

'I missed you,' he said and started to drive out of the car park.

'Where to this time?' asked Claire.

'A little field I know.'

'A field!'

Stefan pointed to the back seat, Claire turned and saw a wicker hamper and folded tartan rug beside it.

'I thought you might like to have a picnic. There is a very secluded spot near here where we could be alone.'

Claire raised her eyebrows.

'How do you know secluded spots round here?'

'I once came on a Scout camp to a place just up the road and I distinctly remember a rather lovely place beside a little river.'

'I never had you down for being a Boy Scout,' laughed Claire.

'I had a stepfather who was a Scoutmaster. He threw me out of his troop when he found me siphoning off his homebrew and selling it disguised as bottles of cola at the annual jamboree.'

'I bet you were really naughty when you were younger.'

Stefan grinned at Claire.

'I still am.'

He stopped the car beside a stile leading into woodland.

'The river is just beyond the trees,' he said, taking the picnic hamper out and handing Claire the blankets to carry. 'I did check on Google Maps to make sure it hasn't been turned into an out-of-town shopping centre or industrial park.'

Dappled sunlight made patterns on the woodland floor; the dry earth beneath Claire's feet smelled musty. Somewhere in the distance she could hear a woodpecker tapping on a tree.

*Thank goodness I wore flat shoes*, thought Claire.

Before long they reached a strip of buttercup-strewn grass and the river sparkled like a string of diamonds in front of them.

'It's idyllic,' said Claire, looking at the clear water that rippled over smooth grey rocks and pebbles.

'I thought it might be more private here than some fancy bar or restaurant.' Stefan put the picnic basket down and bent and kissed her.

'Are you sure there are no Boy Scouts hiding in the bushes?'

'I don't think you get a badge for voyeurism.' He kissed her again and then drew away to take the blanket from her. Together they laid it on the ground and Stefan started to unpack the basket.

'I'm impressed,' said Claire as she looked at the selection of cheese, salami, tomatoes, olives, rolls, and hand-cooked crisps. 'But where are the Marmite sandwiches?'

'Oh no!' Stefan put his hand to his head. 'I knew I forgot something. But I have got this.' He produced a bottle of Chardonnay from a cool-bag. 'Will a glass of wine do instead?'

They lay side by side, each propped up on one elbow facing each other as they ate and drank and talked and gazed without touching as if saving that as a treat for later. Claire loved talking to him; she wanted to just talk to him almost as much as she wanted to kiss him.

They talked about the children and she wondered about telling him about Jack. Her grief for her lost baby was like a scar she felt he ought to know about. Just as she was about to start to tell him her phone rang in her handbag. She ignored it but in the brief pause it created Stefan suddenly sat up.

'I've got something else for you.' He said, delving into the bottom of the hamper.

'Pudding?' asked Claire. 'Cigarettes?' Stefan shook his head and produced a small gold and turquoise box . He held it out to Claire. She took it from his hand. Slowly she lifted the lid. Inside, coiled on a bed of pink tissue, was a delicate necklace, its silver links interspersed with opaque beads and tiny mother-of-pearl buttons. 'When I saw it I immediately thought of you. The buttons. I had to get it for you.'

Claire slowly lifted the necklace out of the box. It was very pretty.

'I can't accept this.'

'I can't take it back,' he said. 'I bought it in New York and I'm not going back there for a while. Don't you like it?'

'Oh, yes,' Claire said, examining the necklace in her hand. 'It's beautiful. Just perfect. Thank you.' She looked up at Stefan and smiled. 'I'll try it on.' Putting it up to her neck, she fumbled with the clasp. One end dropped; it slid into her cleavage. She fished it out and tried to do it up again feeling self-conscious and clumsy.

'Let me help you.'

Stefan got up and walked around behind her. She held up each end of the necklace to him. He lifted her hair, gently laying it across her shoulder before taking the necklace in his hands. For a second Claire could feel his fingers lightly on the back of her neck as he carefully fastened the clasp. He sat back down and looked across at her, smiling.

'I thought it would suit you,' he said. 'It looks just right.'

Claire touched it; it felt cool against her sun-warmed skin.

Suddenly she had an urge to stand in the river, to feel the water swirling around her feet; as she got up and kicked off her shoes her

162

phone rang again, but she was already picking her way across the grass towards the water.

'What are you doing?' called Stefan.

'Paddling,' she said, stepping boldly onto a large flat rock. The water was ice cold as it flowed over her toes and around her ankles. She bent down to let it run between her fingers.

'You're getting the hem of your dress wet,' said Stefan, standing on the bank.

'It doesn't matter,' she said. 'It will dry.'

Suddenly she flicked her hand in the water sending an arc of droplets through the air across to Stefan. For a brief second she saw a rainbow form and then disperse.

'Hey!' Stefan cried, stepping back. 'You've got me wet now.'

'Don't be such a townie,' she laughed. 'It's only water.'

'Right!' He bent down to take off his shoes and rolled up his trousers. 'You'll be very sorry about that.' Claire stood on her rock, hands on her hips, defying him to take revenge. Tentatively he stepped into the river, finding his balance on the slippery stones, then with a sudden kick of his foot Claire was drenched, water all over the front of her dress.

'I'm soaking,' she said, holding out a dripping skirt.

'It's only water!'

She kicked back and his linen shirt stuck to his chest with water.

'Now you're asking for it,' he laughed and leant forward to throw a wave of water at her just as she was leaning forward to do the same to him. Water cascaded over her head. She stood up in surprise; her hair dripped in streams down her face. She wiped her eyes and stepped onto a rock beside Stefan. She pushed him, aiming to make him fall into the shallow water but it was her who felt herself slip and lose her balance; just as she thought she was about to fall, Stefan caught her in his arms and pulled her towards him, his face next to hers. He drew her into an embrace and kissed her. She could feel his damp chest against her own, feel his heart beating hard against hers. His hands moved slowly down her back, pulling her close to him,

163

then in an instant he had picked her up and, stepping out of the river, laid her down on the blanket. He lay beside her, kissing her, his hand moving over the wet bodice of her dress.

'You're so beautiful,' he whispered into her neck.

His fingers deftly undid the buttons of her dress and lightly touched the damp skin underneath. She heard herself breathe in sharply at the pleasure of it. Her phone rang again. She let it ring until it stopped but when it immediately rang again, she couldn't ignore it. Claire struggled to sit up.

Stefan tried to pull her back down towards him.

'Can't you leave it?' he asked.

'It's the fourth time it's rung, it might be important. It might be one of the children.' She answered it and was startled by William's loud voice.

'Where the hell are you?' She glanced at Stefan and put her finger to her lips to silence him.

'I'm at a shop, talking about them stocking my work.'

'My mother has been trying to get hold of you all afternoon. She phoned Sally to see if she knew the number of the shop you'd gone to and she said you were at the dentist's, she said she could see your car in the car park in town.'

Panic flew through her; she knew she was too bad at lying to do this.

'What's wrong? Has something happened?' she asked.

'It's Ben, he's had an accident.'

Claire scrambled to her feet.

'How? When? Where is he?'

'I don't know exactly, a head injury apparently. I'm still at the office, he's in the hospital; my mother is in a terrible state.'

Claire felt tears pricking in her eyes, she never should have left the children with William's mother – of all people, what had she been thinking?

'I'll meet you there,' she said to William and turned off the phone. Snatching up her shoes and handbag she turned to Stefan. 'I need to go,' she said. 'I need to get to the hospital, it's Ben.'

Stefan quickly gathered up the remains of the picnic and followed Claire who had already set off at great speed towards the stile.

As he started the car he looked at her. 'You're shivering; here, have the blanket, let me put it over you.' He had already turned to pick it up from where he'd thrown it onto the back seat.

'No! Just drive.' Her voice was loud and he looked taken aback.

'Try to calm down, Claire; are you all right? You look as white as a sheet.'

'Of course I'm not all right, my child is in hospital. All I want is for you to drive the bloody car!'

It took three-quarters of an hour to get to the hospital, it seemed like an eternity to Claire. Images of Oliver and Jack kept flashing into her head, their tiny bodies covered with tubes and wires and monitors, was this how Ben would look when she got to him?

She tried William's mobile, then Sally's – she needed more information to stop herself imagining the worst. No one picked up. She started to cry and Stefan reached across and tried to touch her reassuringly, she pushed his hand away; she couldn't look at him, she couldn't speak to him. Was this the price she had to pay for a few moments of guilty pleasure? She couldn't bear that anything should happen to Ben.

'Stop here!' she said a few hundred yards from the hospital gates.

'I'll drive you to the entrance.'

'No, I don't want William to see me arrive with you.'

Stefan stopped the car, she was out of the door before the wheels stopped turning.

'Let me know how he is,' Stefan called from the window but Claire hardly heard him. She was running fast along the grassy verge and through the big stone gates and across the tarmac car park to reception where she was told to go to A& E.

'Where is that?'

'The other side of the building,' replied a dumpy woman with *here to help* written on her name badge. 'Follow the yellow arrows.'

She ran faster, her footsteps echoing down the linoleum corridors, her hands pushing through double doors, each breath escaping from her lips in little gasps.

Suddenly she was there, emerging into the bright new A&E extension. She looked wildly around her – massive televisions glared brightly on every wall, people were lined up on multicoloured plastic chairs and a crowd was gathered around the drinks machine, banging it to make it work. Finally she saw Sally sitting on the window ledge with Oliver and Emily and sitting on her knee, swinging his legs and eating a packet of Smarties, was Ben.

'At last!' said Sally.

Ben beamed up at Claire with a chocolaty smile. Claire crouched down in front of him, reluctant to take him in her arms in case she exacerbated whatever injury he had. She stroked his face.

'What happened?' she asked Sally.

'Apparently some sort of plant pot fell on top of him.'

'No,' interrupted Emily in an exasperated tone. '*Not* a plant pot, a plant stand. The one that Grandma was trying to put together. Ben climbed up it and she hadn't put it together right and that column thing fell off the bottom bit and Ben fell down and that funny platform on the top hit him on the head.'

'There was blood gushing everywhere.' Oliver sounded impressed.

Sally gently turned Ben's head to one side and Claire saw a square shaved patch amongst his blond curls and a row of stitches along a short cut on his scalp.

'For a little while they thought he might have mild concussion,' said Sally. 'But now they think he's absolutely fine.'

'Where is William's mother?'

'William's dad came and took her away, she got rather hysterical, she said she needed to get home to have one of her pills,' said Sally.

'She meant gin,' said Emily in a conspiratorial whisper. 'I heard her telling Grandpa a stiff G&T was all she could think about.'

'Anna very kindly let me come here to stay with the children till William or you arrived.'

With an overwhelming feeling of relief Claire took Ben from Sally and held him closely to her.

'Thank goodness you're all right, my love. I've been so worried.'

Ben pulled back from her tight grasp.

'Wet hair, Mummy!'

'You do look rather damp,' said Sally, looking Claire up and down. 'And a little more dishevelled than usual. Is that a new necklace?'

'Sorry it's taken me so long.' William appeared beside them. 'Looks like things aren't quite as serious as they seemed at first anyway.' He turned to Sally. 'Thanks, you've been a star. I don't know how we would have managed without you.'

'Any time,' smiled Sally. 'Family crisis? I'm your girl!'

'Let's get everyone home.' William had on his most authoritative voice, the one he usually reserved for public fatherly duties. 'Who's going to go in whose car? Emily and Oliver, would you like to go with Mummy and Ben?'

Claire stiffened. The car; it was still in the car park miles away, how was she going to explain that?

'The car has broken down,' she said.

'How did you get here?' William and Sally said at the same time.

Claire paused, desperately trying to think of an explanation; were there any buses round here any more?

'I hitched a lift.'

William looked incredulous.

'What a dangerous thing to do. You don't know who might have picked you up.' He marched towards the huge revolving doors, shepherding Oliver and Emily in front of him. Claire hung back, still holding Ben in her arms.

'Come on,' said Sally, putting her arm around Claire's shoulder. 'I'm sure he doesn't mean to sound so pompous – you've got to

167

remember the sort of mother he had to grow up with – he's turned out well considering that!'

Claire laughed but inside she felt leaden with self-loathing and incompetence. If only she hadn't been with Stefan, this would never have happened. She vowed to forget him, never to see him again.

Sally steered Claire towards the doors.

'I think we all could do with a stiff G&T right now, but I also think you ought to know you have a squashed cherry tomato on the back of your dress.'

# Chapter Twenty

*'The taupe and cream décor of the landing is cool and refined.'*

Days passed and Claire's sense of guilt began to fade. Stefan sent a text asking about Ben, she answered politely and tried not to encourage him in any way. Stefan sent another text but when she didn't reply he didn't try again.

After a week she slowly started to let herself remember the picnic and the river and Stefan's hands on her skin.

On a hot and humid evening, while William put cladding on the summer-house roof, Claire sat at her dressing table and took the button necklace out from the back of the drawer where she had hidden it. She held it at her bare throat and looked at her reflection. The buttons felt smooth and cool, their pearly sheen complimented her summer tan. She thought of Stefan's fingers as he had undone the buttons on her dress and felt her heart twist with desire. She wished she'd been calmer when she heard about Ben's accident; she thought that Stefan must have thought she was some sort of lunatic woman. If only she'd managed to tell him about Jack then he might have understood.

*I'm sorry I was so rude to you. I miss you. X.* She sent the text as soon as she'd written it so there'd be no time to change her mind.

*I miss you too. X,* came back immediately, followed a few minutes later by: *Can I see you again?*

*Meet me at the hotel with the lovely cakes.*

*Next Thursday?*

*Yes. 2 p.m. X*

At last Thursday arrived.

Everything had been arranged. Sally had agreed to have the children, yet again. Claire hoped her friend had been joking when she made her promise to have the twins to stay for a week to pay her back.

Claire woke up early, not sure if she'd managed to sleep at all. At last every bit of her seemed to ache with longing to see Stefan. Was she ready to be that sort of woman? *Yes, yes, yes*, said Bad Claire in her head. *Maybe*, said the respectable housewife and mother she tried so hard to be.

The early morning dragged. She unloaded the dishwasher and swept the floor. William got up and Claire made him coffee and set the table for his breakfast. The children woke up and she sorted out the usual arguments about cereal. Her husband left for work and she checked her phone.

*I can't wait to see you. X.*

She watered the red geraniums on the kitchen windowsill, looking out at the bright blue sky which heralded a perfect day. She heard a new text arriving and picked up her phone.

Claire hadn't started reading when suddenly the back door was flung open and Sally's boys tore through the kitchen, shouting for Oliver and demanding games on the computer. She barely had time to feel confused before Sally walked in and threw herself down on a chair.

'I've chucked him out,' she said.

'Who?' asked Claire. She still had the phone in her hand, message half unread. She turned it off and slipped it into her pocket.

'Who do you think?' Sally threw her arms up in exasperation. 'That bastard husband of mine.'

'Gareth?'

'I hope that he's the only bastard husband I have, otherwise I'm more unlucky than I thought. Yes, of course I mean Gareth – the sneaky, no-good lump of pigs' crap.'

'Oh, Sally,' said Claire. 'So, he has been having an affair after all?'

'In his dreams he has.' She got up and opened Claire's biscuit tin. 'He's having a virtual affair. I might have known he'd be too lazy to actually get off his backside and exert himself in some other woman's bed.'

'What do you mean?'

'Even you must have heard of cyber-sex, Claire.' Sally finished chewing a mouthful of flapjack and took a deep breath. 'The lying piece of shit got himself onto a dodgy internet dating site calling himself Big Bad Bear and has been sending dirty messages to some woman who goes by the name of Sweet Betty.'

'He told you this?' Claire had to resist the urge to laugh at Gareth's cyber-name.

'Oh no.' She took another flapjack. 'I found out for myself last night. He forgot to turn off the website before he went to the pub. I sat down to do my Tesco shop online and found this message from Ms Betty, or whoever she is, telling me that all she's wearing is a pair of crotchless knickers and an eight-foot boa constrictor – did I want to turn on the webcam to see her?'

Claire did laugh then; she couldn't help it. It seemed too ludicrous to believe. Sally shot her an angry look.

'I can tell you, Claire, there was nothing funny about reading the whole backlog of messages they've been sending back and forth for weeks. It was disgusting, tasteless, tacky stuff. No wonder Gareth started smartening himself up a bit – not to go and meet this woman but rather to sit in our back room while she ogled him on her computer. Probably while I'm upstairs checking the boys' heads for nits or in the living room with a pile of ironing.'

'What did you do?'

'I turned on the webcam and told her where she could shove her bloody boa constrictor and what she could do with her crotchless knickers – and believe me, by the look on her scraggy face, I don't think it was what Gareth would have told her to do with them.'

'Oh, Sally, this is awful.' Claire gave her a hug. Sally's well-upholstered body felt tense, as if she were trying to keep herself from breaking down. 'What did you say to Gareth when he came home?'

'There wasn't much to say.' Sally moved back to the chair, sat down and put her head in her hands, burying her fingers into her unbrushed mane of hair. 'By the time Gareth came home I'd put all his stuff in bin liners and dumped it in the front garden, apart from his Iron Maiden T-shirt which I cut into little pieces and sprinkled up the path.'

'What did he do?'

'He was upset about the T-shirt, but when I told him I'd found out about Sweet Betty he just turned around and started loading the black bags into his car. Obviously it didn't all fit in – there's only so much of a man's life that can fit into a Ford Fiesta – so I expect he'll be back this morning to collect the rest. I didn't want to stay around to see him.'

'Where do you think he's gone?'

'Absolutely no idea. And do you know what? I just don't care. I'm so angry.'

'Is it that bad?' Claire asked. 'It's not as if he actually met up with her. Couldn't you try and work things out together?'

'No way,' said Sally. 'It doesn't matter if he met her or not. It's what was going on in his head that counts.' She sat up straight in the chair and tucked her shirt into her jeans in a businesslike manner. 'He's not getting any second chances. That's why I've made an appointment to see a solicitor at two o'clock this afternoon. I want to know where I stand when I divorce the cheating ratbag.'

'Two o'clock?' Claire said quietly. 'What about . . .' Her voice trailed off. Suddenly she realised what Big Bad Bear's cyber-infidelity meant for her: she wouldn't be able to see Stefan today.

Sally seemed oblivious. 'Obviously I'd be entitled to the house. It's the twins' home and I reckon he'll have to pay quite a lot

172

towards their upkeep. But what I'd really like to know is how often he legally has to have the boys to stay with him. I'm hoping it's every weekend at least. That reminds me, would you have the boys this afternoon while I see this solicitor? I know I said I'd have yours but the last thing I expected was this marital bomb going off. I'm sure the gallery you were going to see will understand.'

'Don't worry,' Claire said, sitting down beside Sally and taking her hand. 'You do whatever you have to do and I'll help in any way I can.' Inside she wanted to weep with disappointment and frustration.

Sally stayed all morning drinking tea, eating flapjacks, and pouring out her fury and pain in a tirade of insults about Gareth and bravado about her future as a single woman.

After a couple of hours, Claire managed to extricate herself with the excuse of needing the toilet. Once in the bathroom she took her phone out of her pocket and sent a text.

*So sorry. Something's come up. I can't make it today x*

After lunch Sally set off for the solicitor's office, leaving Claire to deal with her boys; one of them had somehow got up on to the roof of the summer house. Once she'd lured him inside with a bowl of microwave popcorn, put on a DVD, settled all the children in front of it, and locked the back door, she turned on her phone again. One new message.

*Don't worry, it's fine. I understand.*

Claire read it three times. She could have done with more regret, more disappointment.

*What about tomorrow?* she replied.

*I've made plans. I'm free on Sunday afternoon?*

*Can we rearrange for Sunday then? x*

173

*Fine. 2 p.m.?*

*Great, I'll look forward to seeing you. Xx*

And that was it; no more. Claire spent the rest of the day trying to shake off a sense of unease, though it was hard to pinpoint exactly where it came from.

Sally came back from the solicitors full of determination to file for a divorce.

'Don't you think you should wait?' said Claire. 'Let things settle. Talk to Gareth. What about counselling?'

'I'm not having some soft-spoken counsellor tell me I should try and understand Gareth because he's still coming to terms with being weaned from his mother, or once found his father dressed in a twinset and pearls, or some other rubbish I no longer care about. I've decided. As far as I'm concerned, Sweet Betty and her overgrown grass snake are welcome to him.'

# Chapter Twenty-one

*'Mixing textures in similar tones ensures
a versatile and interesting finish.'*

'I need to go out on Sunday afternoon,' said Claire as she sat opposite William at the kitchen table. She topped up his wine glass and passed him another slice of ciabatta.

'Why?'

'I've had an enquiry from another shop a few miles away, a really good one, and I've said I'll go over and show them samples. They're too busy in the week, but the shop is closed on a Sunday, so they said that's the best time.' She'd been practising the line all day.

'I thought I might make a start on sanding the living-room floor,' he said.

'I thought you were going to do that when we're away?'

'I've got loads of other things to do as well. I want to repaint the wall on the landing where Ben has scribbled in Biro and I'll have to mow the grass.'

'OK,' said Claire, playing what she hoped would be her trump card. 'I'll ask my mother to come over and look after the children.'

'All right,' he said. 'I'll do it. But you won't be too long, will you?'

Leaving the children was like a military operation. Claire had given them all an early lunch and loaded and turned on the dishwasher. Oliver and Emily both had birthday parties to go to in opposite directions. She had presents wrapped, cards written, step-by-step instructions printed out on how to find each venue, with arrival and pick-up times highlighted. The children were dressed – Oliver in a pirate costume and Emily in a pink T-shirt and tutu skirt with her brand-new school shoes, which she insisted on wearing. Claire left Play-Doh and a 'magic water' painting book on the kitchen table to keep Ben occupied while he was on his own with William. The biscuit tin had been refilled with home-made jam tarts and a big pan of tomato soup sat beside the Aga for the children's tea. The house was clean and tidy, Macavity fed, plants watered. Claire had hardly had a chance to think about where she was actually going.

It wasn't until she was in the car driving out of the village that she let herself remember what she was doing. In the last few days, her emotions had swung wildly from ecstatic joy to guilt, despair, terror, and back to joy again. For days she had been numb with indecision, completely unable to think of what to do or what she wanted, but in the last forty-eight hours she had emerged from a fog of confusion and the future seemed clearer. Again. She dared to imagine a life without William, a life without the house. A life with Stefan.

It was not impossible. *People do it all the time*, she told herself, thinking of Sally, who was behaving as if separating from Gareth was the best thing that ever happened to her. She had spent the whole of Saturday in Claire's kitchen extolling the joys of being a single woman.

'Good for her,' William said to Claire after she left. 'She deserves someone better than that layabout.'

'I always liked Gareth,' Claire said, ironing a dress she planned to wear the next day. 'Remember all the help he gave me with the Emily Love website?'

William shrugged and flicked on the evening news.

Claire drove down the long, high-hedged roads too fast. She needed to be with Stefan as soon as possible. The weather had been dry all week; the bushes and trees looked parched and dusty. Most of the hedgerow flowers were over and the hay was piled in neat blond blocks across the close-cropped fields. She hardly noticed the scenery. Her mind was focused on the destination and the excitement of seeing Stefan again.

Claire needed to ask him questions, to find out more about who he really was. He had spent two days with her, observed her daily life, seen her home in detail. He knew where she spent her working day: where she woke up, where she ate her meals, where she brushed her teeth. She had no idea what his flat was like, where or how he spent his time. She wanted to know about his friends, his sister, what he watched on television, his favourite beach, mountain, castle. All this information seemed somehow vitally important. But most of all she just wanted to be with him again, existing in his space, even if they didn't talk at all.

She had only had one text from him since Thursday.

*Might be held up. Could we make it 2.30?*

As her car crunched onto the gravel parking area, Claire could see immediately that his car wasn't there. She looked at her watch. She was five minutes early. She got out and waited, leaning against the warm body of her car. She looked at her reflection in the tinted window of the Mercedes parked beside her.

Her hair was loosely caught up in a clasp at her neck; wisps fell down in curls onto her shoulders and blew gently on the light breeze. She had on a broderie anglaise shift dress that she hadn't worn for years, the short, capped sleeves showed off her smooth, sun-browned arms. The fit was perfect – lightly skimming her hips and ending just above the knees. She had bought it from Portobello Market before any of the children were born. Teamed with her new sandals, a pair of large sunglasses, and the necklace Stefan had given her, she felt particularly pleased with how she looked.

She willed herself not to look at her watch. The time came,

then passed. He was late. He hadn't been late for her before. She touched the necklace, the smooth, round buttons reassured her. He would surely come soon. After twenty minutes she decided to go into the hotel. The manager recognised her at once.

'You are Stefan's friend,' he said, coming round from behind his desk to take her hand and shake it enthusiastically.

'I'm supposed to meet him here,' she said.

'Yes, yes, he made a booking. A table for two on the terrace,' said the manager, consulting a big red book on his desk. 'He should be here now. Come with me.'

He took Claire by the arm and gently directed her through the dining room, onto the terrace, and to a table beside the balustrade around the edge. White teacups and silver spoons were already set out neatly.

'Do you like it here, in the shade?' the manager asked her, pulling out a chair. 'The shade is nice on a hot day like today.'

'Yes, thank you. It's lovely,' she said. *Where was he?*

'Don't worry. He will be here soon,' said the manager, as if reading her mind. 'I expect the traffic was bad getting out of London.' He shrugged his shoulders. 'Would you like a drink? Wine? Coffee?'

'Could I have a glass of water?' Her mouth felt dry, her stomach tight.

'Of course.'

He left her on her own.

She tried not to watch the wide double doors leading out from the hotel's interior. Instead she looked at the other people seated on the terrace: families finishing their Sunday lunches, couples lingering over coffee, and the odd lone customer reading a paper or talking on the phone. They all looked so self-contained and happy.

Claire felt anxious. Supposing he'd had an accident or suddenly been taken ill? She noticed the single dark crimson rose in a small vase on the table – in flower language dark red roses were for mourning. Now she really was counting the minutes. Each one seemed like an hour.

A waitress brought her a clinking glass of iced water. A different waitress from the one who had colluded with Stefan to present her with the painted cup.

'Thank you,' she said and took a sip. Then, at last, Stefan was walking towards her.

He looked beautiful in a pale cream linen jacket and white shirt – more tanned than when she had last seen him. She saw a woman look away from her lunch companion to watch him as he passed her table. Claire's heart soared as he approached, suddenly excited. She had to resist the urge to get up and run to him.

'I'm so sorry,' he said, leaning over and kissing her cheek. 'My car wouldn't start. I ended up having to borrow a friend's.'

'Oh dear. The beautiful Claudia. Will she be all right?'

'Yes.' He took off his jacket and draped it over the back of his chair. 'I know a very clever mechanic who does wonders with old cars.'

He sat down, and they were silent for a moment. There was something about him that made Claire nervous. He seemed detached from her; distant. The softness was missing from his eyes. He wasn't smiling.

'I've missed you so much,' she said, putting out her hand, touching his. He didn't take it. She withdrew and took another sip of her water.

'I'm so sorry about my behaviour when I last saw you. When I heard that Ben had had an accident I was just so frantic with worry. I know I must have seemed very rude.'

He shook his head as though it didn't matter and looked at her with a serious expression.

'Claire.' From his tone she knew he was beginning something she didn't want to hear. 'This isn't going to work, is it?'

She was silent; she couldn't reply. She felt as if he had physically hit her. Part of her wanted to get up and walk away immediately. Go home. But she sat very still and stared at him.

'You know it as well as I do, don't you?' he said, looking at her

179

across the table. He shrugged his shoulders slightly, as if waiting for a response.

'Why?' she asked quietly.

He sighed. 'Because it's an impossible situation, you and me. You're married with children. You have a life with someone else. You don't want to hurt your children, to destroy your home. So what are we doing?'

With her eyes she studied the lichen on the stone balustrade behind him, yellow and white and grey. It looked like a landscape – trees, bushes, hills – as if someone had painted it on to the stone for decoration.

'But I thought . . .' she said, but couldn't find the words to continue.

'What?'

'I don't know what I thought. I thought it could work, that I couldn't feel the way I feel about you and it not work. I thought you felt the same. What you said when I met you in London? All your texts?'

'I know, I know,' said Stefan, running his hand through the dark waves of his hair. 'I meant what I said. About the way I felt about you.'

'And now, suddenly, you don't feel like that?' she interrupted. 'How can you have changed your mind so quickly? Did you see me again as you walked through the door and decide that actually I wasn't quite as attractive as you remembered, not quite so desirable?'

'No,' said Stefan, taking her hand in his. 'No. I walked through those doors and saw you and you looked more beautiful than ever, so lovely in that dress. I knew it was going to make it even harder to say this – to do this – but I have to. I've spent the last two days trying to decide what would be best.'

'I don't understand,' she said, looking at the cubes of ice melting in her glass.

'I can't destroy your life. I've seen it, photographed it. Your home. Your children. William. It's perfect. I can't destroy that.

180

When I think of you so distraught about Ben I realise I could never destroy your family. You'd never forgive me; I'd never forgive myself.' He let go of her hand.

'But the things you said? The way you said you felt about me?' said Claire, still looking at her glass. 'Why did you bother saying anything at all if this is how you feel?'

'I wasn't thinking properly. I was being selfish. I was only thinking about myself and how I felt about you; what *I* wanted. Now I realise how impossible this is. You don't really know me. You don't know what I can offer you. I don't know what I can offer you. You've got three children. I don't know anything about children. I can't even fit them in my car. What would it do to them if your marriage broke up? I know what my parents' divorce did to me and my sister. You told me how you felt when your father divorced your mother. You don't want to have an affair. I don't want you to have an affair – all the deceit, the lies, the guilt – so what would we do?' He sat back in his chair and looked at her.

Claire wondered if this was some kind of test.

'Would you like to order now?' A waitress appeared beside them.

'What would you like?' Stefan asked Claire. 'A cup of tea? A glass of champagne?'

'No,' she said. 'I definitely don't feel like champagne.' She looked at the waitress. 'Could I have a gin and tonic, please?'

'A glass of white wine,' he said. The waitress moved away.

'I still don't understand what made you change your mind so suddenly,' said Claire, looking up at him.

'I sensed your hesitancy. When you didn't answer my text, I knew that you felt uncomfortable. I'd pushed you too fast into something you obviously weren't happy about and . . .'

'Stop, stop!' She was staring at him. 'What text didn't I answer? What wasn't I comfortable with?'

'My text on Friday,' said Stefan. He looked slightly embarrassed and lowered his voice. 'When I suggested that I book a room for us here.'

'I never got a text about that.' She thought back to the texts that they'd sent each other on Friday morning before Sally had come crashing in with her news. There had been the text she was about to read when Sally arrived. Had she ever finished reading it?

'And then a few hours later you cancelled the whole thing. I thought you'd decided it would be wrong to see me at all.'

Claire took her phone out of her bag and checked back through all the texts. She hadn't been able to bear to delete any of them. There it was. If Sally had entered a few seconds later she would have had time to read:

*. . . I'm so tempted to book a room for us. What do you think?*

Claire let out a little groan of dismay.

'I never read this. I didn't cancel because I thought what you had suggested was inappropriate or too fast or whatever other reason you've been concocting in your head. I cancelled because my best friend and nominated childminder for that day threw her husband out of their house for cheating with a woman with a boa constrictor.'

'Hey, now it's your turn to stop.' Stefan laughed for the first time that afternoon. 'You're losing me. I'm not even going to ask about the boa constrictor but you're saying that you never even saw that text?'

'I never saw the text. It had nothing to do with why I had to cancel. I had no one to look after the children and I just didn't think it was going to work if I brought them all with me – no matter how many packets of crayons I had in my bag.' Claire smiled at him. She wanted to reach out and touch his beautiful face, trace the laughter lines around his eyes with her fingertips. It had all been a misunderstanding. Now everything would be all right.

She put her arms out towards him on the table, willing him to lean forward. Instead he leant back in his chair and stared out across the valley.

'I was so looking forward to seeing you. I was desperate to see

182

you, longing for you all the time I was in New York,' he said at last.

'And now?'

'On Friday, when you cancelled, it was as if reality suddenly hit me. The bubble burst and I realised it would be wrong. I've spent two days thinking about this. Even now that I know you didn't see the text, I still know that it wouldn't work. The guilt would eat away at us, destroy us in the end.'

'How can you be so sure?' she asked.

'I know how I would feel. I can't do it, Claire. I've met William. I can't do it to him. I'd feel awful.'

'What about me?' she said, suddenly angry. 'Are you thinking about me at all?'

'I'm sorry but I've made up my mind.'

He took a packet of Marlboro from his pocket and lit one. He didn't offer one to Claire but left the packet and the lighter beside the vase in the middle of the table. After a few seconds Claire slid a cigarette from the box and lifted it to her lips. Stefan picked up the lighter and lit it for her. She inhaled deeply and then blew out a long stream of smoke. She felt a little better.

Stefan said nothing. His expression seemed impenetrable.

'To protect yourself,' she said, 'you're hurting me first.'

'No, Claire,' he said, suddenly looking at her again. 'I would never hurt you.'

'That's what you said in London,' said Claire. 'That's what you promised. But you are hurting me. This hurts.'

'I'm not doing this to hurt you,' he said, looking upset. 'I just think of everyone else that would be hurt. It's not what I want. I'm only being realistic.'

'I can't decide if you're being realistic, honourable, or just a coward,' she said angrily.

The waitress put their drinks on the table and quickly walked away.

'It's not as if I have some sort of idyllic marriage,' Claire said, her fingertips touching the ice cold glass in front of her.

'I know,' he said. 'I know you're not happy, but it's up to you to sort things out. You have to decide what happens between you and William.'

'Would you wait for me to make a decision?' Claire asked.

Stefan flipped his lighter over and over in his fingers, concentrating on it silently.

'I see,' she said. 'Fine. I understand.'

She stubbed her cigarette out in the ashtray, stood up, and picked up her bag.

'I'd better go.'

'Don't,' he said, suddenly flinging down the lighter so that it skimmed across the table. 'Don't go yet. You haven't even started your drink.'

Claire stood still. She knew she should just turn and walk away across the terrace, get in her car and leave. She sat down again and took a sip of her gin.

'This doesn't make me at all happy,' he said, looking across at her.

'It doesn't make me happy either,' she sighed, 'but maybe you're right. I just don't know how you can suddenly be so detached from your emotions.'

He shrugged. 'You are so lovely, Claire,' he said, taking her hand in his. 'I want you to know this isn't easy for me. I feel awful about it.'

'But you've made up your mind?' She looked at him; he had a look of resigned decision on his face that reminded her of a parent determined to not let a child have another biscuit before dinnertime.

'Yes, I've made up my mind. I can't see you again.'

Claire felt as if everything was crumbling in front of her. She didn't know how she could cope with this loss, this rejection. Despite the warmth of the afternoon she suddenly felt cold. She picked up her drink and took another sip.

'There's something I haven't told you,' said Stefan, lighting another cigarette. 'Something that might help you to understand me a bit better. Understand me or maybe even hate me.' He shrugged.

Claire took another cigarette as well. 'Tell me.'

'I've been in this situation before.'

'What do you mean?'

'I mean I've been involved with a married woman before.'

She looked at him and then past him, down the valley, through a thick copse of trees. She wasn't sure she wanted to hear Stefan's story after all. She imagined kicking off her high heels and running across the hotel lawn, into the woods, and losing herself in the dense summer foliage.

'It was when I was in Australia.' He took a drag on his cigarette.

'Go on,' she said cautiously.

'She was the wife of a wealthy business man – he'd made a fortune buying up land around Sydney. He had a luxury yacht that they lived on. I was asked to photograph it for a magazine. That's how I met her.'

'Oh,' Claire said. 'You really have done this before.'

'No, it was different. I don't want you to think I make a habit of picking up married women when I photograph their homes.'

'Only twice then?' She gave him a quick, ironic smile.

'Yes, only twice.'

Their drinks were finished. The waitress cleared the glasses on to a tray.

'Two coffees,' Stefan said to her. He glanced at Claire; she nodded. The waitress seemed to melt away.

'So what happened?' Claire asked.

'She'd only been married a few months. Things weren't working out the way she'd hoped. He'd made her leave her job, he was out all day. I suppose she was lonely when I met her. We had an affair.'

'For how long?'

'Three years.'

'Three years!' she repeated.

'She kept promising to leave her husband. We'd make a plan for the future and then she'd always back out at the last minute. My coming home to England was part of the last plan. I told her I'd

185

had enough. I was going home and if she was serious about me we could meet at the airport and she could come with me. I remember sitting in the departure lounge and slowly realising she wasn't going to show up. I so nearly walked out of the airport and went to find her.'

'But instead you got on the plane?'

'Yes, I got on the plane, came home, found a flat, a job. I had a few short-lived relationships . . .'

'And here you are,' said Claire. Jealousy, anger, hurt, betrayal: it all seemed to be filling her up, oozing out of every pore. What a fool she'd been.

'I don't want you to think that I still have any feelings for her,' Stefan continued. 'I realise now how shallow my relationship with her had been. How little we had had in common. I never felt the way I feel about you. It never felt so overpowering, so intense.'

Claire said nothing.

'Do you despise me?'

Claire shook her head.

The waitress appeared with their coffees. Claire slowly poured milk into hers and took a sip.

She knew that now it was time to leave, but she felt unable to move, weighted to her chair by sadness.

'Do you understand why I don't want to get into that situation again?' asked Stefan, looking into her eyes.

He leant forward and kissed her lips. His mouth felt velvet soft. She wanted more, and kissed him back, unable to stop herself, then pulled away.

'I'm going home now.' She stood up and started to walk away. Stefan followed her.

With every step they took together across the terrace, through the hotel restaurant and lobby, Stefan became more distant. A barrier had come down between them.

By the time they reached the car park Claire knew she had lost him completely.

'I'll be in touch,' he said.

'No,' she said. 'Don't. I don't want any room for hope.'

'Are you all right?'

'I'm fine.'

'Good.' He took his car keys from his pocket. 'You'd better go now or you'll be late.'

Claire turned and opened the door of her car. She looked back at him.

'You never told me why your car is called Claudia,' she called.

He was already walking across the gravel to the small blue hatchback parked on the other side of the car park. He stopped and walked back to her.

'Was that the name of the woman in Australia?' Claire couldn't stop herself from asking.

'No.' He touched her cheek. 'Claudia was one of my primary school teachers. Mrs Casanovas. My very first love. When my parents split up and we had to move, leaving Mrs Casanovas upset me most of all.'

'So you were into married women even then,' she said with a tight smile.

'This isn't about some married-women fetish.' Stefan's face was serious. 'I wish with all my heart that you were single.' He turned and walked away.

Blinking back tears, Claire got into her car and quickly started the engine. She tried to make her mind blank, tried not to think about the ache that throbbed in her heart as if she had been physically beaten.

'Just drive,' she told herself, and slowly pulled away across the car park. She didn't look at Stefan's car as she passed it, and she didn't look behind her as she drove down the long drive back into the maze of country lanes that would take her home.

'Ben turned the hose on and made a huge mud puddle in the flower bed,' said Emily, running to the car as Claire opened the door.

Oliver ran after her. 'Then he sat in it and rubbed himself all over with mud,' he told her eagerly.

'Daddy was really cross,' said Emily.

'Where is Ben now?' asked Claire.

'Over there,' they chorused together, pointing to a completely mud-encrusted Ben happily jumping up and down on a mini trampoline. Bits of dried mud flew off him with every bounce.

'Where have you been?' William came through the front door wiping a large paintbrush with a spirit-soaked rag.

'I've only been as long as I said I'd be,' said Claire defensively. 'Why haven't you given Ben a bath? He's filthy.'

'I've been trying to paint the wall on the landing. The last thing I need is him coming in and getting mud all over the wet paint.'

Claire sighed. She wasn't capable of getting cross. She looked at Oliver and Emily and held out her arms to them. They cuddled into her, and she hugged them tightly.

'Was it worth it?' asked William.

Claire looked up from the children. 'Was what worth it?'

'The shop. Did they order anything?'

'Oh,' she said. 'I don't think I'll hear from them again.'

'A waste of time then,' he said and disappeared back inside.

'Yes,' said Claire quietly. 'A complete waste of everything.'

# Chapter Twenty-two

*'The master bedroom reflects Claire's love of simple
country style. "I wanted this room to feel as peaceful
and tranquil as possible," she says.'*

Dear Stefan.

It was four thirty in the morning. Claire had lain awake
all night, her body physically aching with sadness and loss.
At about three o'clock, as William sweated and snored beside
her, she began to compose an email to Stefan in her head.
When a thin line of grey appeared between the shutters she
got up. Silently, she went downstairs into the study. The
computer whirred into life at her touch. Claire sat down and
started to type.

*Dear Stefan,*

*I feel so sad. I don't want to lose you from my life. I feel so sure we
could work things out. I don't think I can go on living with William, especially not feeling the way I feel about you. I know it will
be painful and very difficult, but that will pass in time. If you could
wait for me to sort things out here, then we could see how things
work out between us – just take it slowly, no commitments, no guilt
(leave that to me). Surely the way we feel about each other is too
precious to throw away so easily? Please don't let this chance of*

*happiness for us both disappear. Maybe we could meet in the week
to talk?*

*I miss you.*
*Claire x*

She pressed 'send' before she could change her mind and went
into the kitchen to make a cup of tea.

Claire stood outside, her feet bare on the damp grass. In her
hands she nursed her mug of steaming tea; in her heart the sadness
started to lift a little, to be replaced by hope. What time would
Stefan wake up? What time would he look at his emails? How
long would he take to answer? What would he say?

She wondered if she'd sounded too desperate. Could she really
leave William? In the darkness of the bedroom she had suddenly
felt so sure she could, so sure she would, but now as the sun started
to rise behind her she thought of her children and felt a stab of
pain. To put them through this tangle of adult emotions, adult
complications and confusion, seemed cruel and selfish. To make
them divide their time and love between her and William, to
introduce a complete stranger into their lives – how could she do
that to them? But then she thought of Stefan.

'Mummy, what are you doing?'

Emily was crossing the lawn towards her, sleepily rubbing her
eyes, her cotton nightdress creased and crumpled.

'Mummy!' A cry from the kitchen door as Ben appeared, hair
on end, his arms held up towards her. 'Cuddle me,' he pleaded.

Claire walked towards them. She hugged Emily and picked up
Ben and squeezed him tightly.

'Would you like to go for a walk before breakfast?' Claire
asked. 'We could take some jam sandwiches and juice and have a
picnic in the woods.'

'Yes, please,' said Emily excitedly. 'Shall I wake up Oliver?'

Wild fuchsia and honeysuckle jostled for space in the shaggy
hedgerows that lined the lane from their house. Bees and hoverflies

buzzed above them. Claire walked holding Ben's hand as Emily and Oliver ran on ahead picking and blowing at dandelion clocks in the early-morning sun. She had left William sleeping. The alarm clock hadn't yet gone off. In the kitchen she had laid his bowl and spoon on the table and beside them his breakfast cereal and a small glass of orange juice. In her mind, Claire formulated a plan of action. She would talk to William tonight; tell him she wasn't happy with their marriage. She would make an appointment to see the solicitor Sally had seen to find out exactly what would happen if they got divorced. She thought about the house; she couldn't deprive William of his beloved house. It was beautiful, but in so many ways it had never felt like hers. Could she move? She thought of the pretty Georgian houses in the town. Some had lovely gardens.

She tried to think of herself and the children in a different environment. Meals in a different kitchen, the children getting used to different bedrooms. Not so much space. It would be a challenge. It could be fun, liberating; her own home – maybe Stefan's home too? She felt sure they could make a home together despite what Stefan had said. They could buy something together, a tumbledown cottage, a house with lots of character that they could make their own.

*Her and Stefan decorating another house, furnishing it together, living in it together. Waking up with him every morning.* Her heart leapt at the thought. William would see the children at weekends and holidays. She didn't think he'd want much more than that, though the thought of spending time without them made her sad. The children would be upset, of course, but they'd soon get used to it. Lots of children did. Maybe they could explain it all to them at the weekend.

Her mind raced on and on with plans and dreams, but at the back of it there remained a nagging anxiety. *How would Stefan answer her email?*

When they got home, William had left for work, his breakfast bowl and glass and mug empty on the kitchen table. While the

191

children went out to play in the garden, Claire checked her emails. Nothing. She went into the kitchen to tidy up. She decided to make chocolate fairy cakes for a lunchtime treat. In between greasing the tray, sifting flour, cracking eggs, and melting chocolate, she went in and out of the study constantly to check on the computer. She was just sliding the cakes into the Aga when her mobile phone buzzed. A text. Her heart jumped as she picked up her mobile.

*Cornwall? Confirm? Mum x*

She texted back.

*Yes! Love Claire.*

She wondered what her situation would be by then. It was two weeks away, yet her whole life could have changed. She looked at the clock on the kitchen wall. It was only ten to eleven, but she felt as if a full day had passed already. She went into the study again. 'One new message,' she read on the screen.

*Dear Claire,*

*Thank you for your email. As I said yesterday, I don't want to be responsible for breaking up your marriage. You must make your own decisions, I cannot be involved. I think it's best to end things between us at this early stage. Thinking of you. Take care of yourself.*

*Stefan x*

Claire read it again and then another time. She felt numb. His words sounded so detached, so unemotional, so definite. She stared ahead out of the window at the children playing on the grass; she was unable to get up. Remembering all the plans she'd made earlier that morning, she felt stupid and naïve. She sat motionless in front of the computer for a long time. Stefan's message blurred and distorted on the screen. Emily tapped on the window and asked for a drink.

In the kitchen she handed out three cups of orange juice, then sat down at the table and was still again for another long time. She stared blankly at the shelves of the dresser, cluttered with an assortment of plates, mugs, photographs, bits of Lego and children's paintings.

Emily came in.

'When are we having lunch?'

She looked at the dirty bowls waiting to be washed by the sink.

'Have you made chocolate cakes?' she asked, dipping her finger into the remnants of the thick dark goo of sponge mixture and licking it.

*Cakes.* Claire had forgotten the cakes. She got up and opened the Aga door. The hot smell of burning hit her. She pulled out the cake tray and looked at the three rows of beautifully domed but blackened tops, cracked and gently smouldering.

'Oh, Mum. Why didn't you take them out before?'

Claire felt tears sliding down her cheeks. All she could do was stare down at the tray in her oven-gloved hands.

'Oh, Mummy.' Emily wrapped her arms around Claire's waist. 'Don't cry about the cakes. We can go to the shops and buy some more. It doesn't matter.'

Oliver ran in. 'Sally's here, Mum. She's just parking the car.' He looked at his mother, surprised. 'What's wrong?'

'She's burnt the cakes,' explained Emily, still with her arms around Claire.

'Oh,' said Oliver, uncomfortably shifting from one leg to another and then quickly returning outside to play with Sally's boys who had just appeared in the garden.

Sally's voice came from outside the back door.

'I've only popped round for a minute,' she called. 'I just had to tell you what I've done this morning.' She came through the door and stopped. 'Claire, whatever is the matter?'

Claire stood shaking with sobs, tears dripping onto the burnt cake crusts.

'It's the cakes,' said Emily. 'They're burnt. Can I go out and play now, Mummy?'

Claire seemed unable to reply.

'Of course you can,' said Sally. 'I'll sort out Mummy's cakes. You go outside.'

Sally gently took the cake tray from between Claire's hands, slid off the oven gloves, and steered her towards a chair.

'Never any good crying over burnt cakes,' she said. 'Over burnt anything, for that matter. Otherwise I'd be in tears most days in my kitchen.' She wiped Claire's cheeks with the oven gloves, dabbing softly as though she were a child.

Claire didn't say anything, couldn't say anything. She put her head in her hands and continued to cry.

'Come on, love,' said Sally kindly. 'It can't be that bad.' She rubbed Claire's back as she sat down beside her. 'What is it?' she tried again. 'The children all look well and happy. Is it your mum? Is your mum ill?'

Claire shook her head.

'Is it William?' asked Sally. 'Is William all right?'

'He's fine,' she said in a muffled voice.

'Has he done something to upset you?'

Claire cried harder. The oven gloves could no longer contain the flow of tears and Sally passed Claire a nearby tea towel. She buried her wet face in it and was unable to answer any questions.

Sally picked up a fairy cake from the tray and peeled off the thin paper cup around it.

'Look, they're fine on the bottom,' she said, picking off a bit of soft sponge and putting it into her mouth. 'Delicious! You see, sometimes things look disastrous, but it's only on the surface and everything is all right underneath.' She put out her hand and stroked Claire's arm.

'Is it something William's done?' she asked. 'Has he suggested one home improvement job too many? He's not having an affair is he? William wouldn't do something like that. He's not like the devious skunk that I've been married to for far too long.'

'He's not having an affair,' sobbed Claire through her tea towel. 'It's me. No, it's not. I'm not having an affair. I haven't had an affair. Well, I don't think I have. I don't know.' She burst into an-other fit of sobbing.

'You don't know if you've had an affair? You're not making any sense.'

Claire sighed and sat up, wiping her eyes. She didn't look at Sally but stared at the spots on the tablecloth.

'I fell in love with another man,' she said quietly.

Sally gasped.

'I fell in love with another man and I think I would have left William, but now he doesn't want to see me any more,' Claire went on.

'Who doesn't want to see you any more?'

'The other man. He says too many people would get hurt.'

'He's got some sense then,' said Sally. 'Who is he?'

'The photographer who photographed our house.'

'You've been having an affair with the bloke who came to photograph your house and family?' Sally sounded incredulous. 'Do you think the magazine knows he goes around destroying the lovely homes and lives he photographs?'

'I don't think he does go around destroying other people's lives.'

'Only yours then,' said Sally.

Claire decided not to tell her about the woman in Australia.

'I can't believe you've been having an affair.'

'I don't think I've had an affair with him, really,' said Claire, wiping her eyes again. 'I just liked him a lot and saw him a few times over the past few weeks and kissed him a bit.'

'And?' asked Sally. 'Anything else?'

'No, not really.'

'Mmm,' said Sally suspiciously. 'Big Bad Bear and Sweet Betty didn't even meet but my solicitor says it could still be classed as adultery.'

'Mum, we're starving.'

Oliver stood at the door to the garden.

'You can have some chocolate cakes,' said Sally.

'Yuck, they're all burnt.'

'I've brought different ones,' said Sally. 'You go on back and play, and we'll bring them out in a minute.'

Reluctantly, Oliver disappeared.

'Right, here's a knife,' said Sally, handing it to Claire and taking out a brightly coloured melamine plate from a cupboard. 'If we just take them out of the paper cases and cut the burnt tops off, they'll never recognise them.' Sally smiled. 'You see, you're not the only one who can be deceitful here.'

'I haven't been deceitful,' Claire protested. She had stopped crying.

'You never told me what was going on.'

Claire wanted to wince at her reproachful tone.

'And I'm your best friend. I'm presuming that you only pretended to be visiting galleries and seeing customers and going to the dentist while I looked after your children. That's what I would call deceitful. Though when Ben had his accident and you were nowhere to be found, I did suspect something funny was going on – and that tomato on your dress; I still can't quite understand how that got there.'

'I couldn't tell you,' Claire tried to explain. 'I couldn't even admit how I was feeling to myself for a long time.'

The round remnants of the fairy cakes looked quite appetising, especially when Sally topped each one with a Smartie stuck on with a tiny spot of butter. The children fell on them as she took them into the garden.

'That should keep them happy for a while,' she said, coming back in. 'Are you feeling any better now?'

'A bit.'

'I just can't believe it,' said Sally, popping a charred cake top into her mouth. 'I thought I was the one with the unhappy marriage. I thought you loved William. I thought you had the perfect marriage.'

'All this is perfect,' said Claire, waving her arm around the room. 'The house, the garden, the stuff. But it doesn't feel real. It doesn't feel like part of me. Just because the home is perfect doesn't mean the marriage is.'

'I know William loves you.'

Claire shrugged. 'I think he loves the house more.'

'What are you going to do?'

'This morning I really thought I could leave William, get a new house with the children, start again. I thought, naïvely, that I could start again with Stefan. I had stupid fantasies about choosing furniture, having breakfast together.'

'Your fantasies are a bit on the tame side,' said Sally, laughing.

Claire ignored her. 'Then I got his email. I burnt the cakes and you came in.' She started sobbing all over again.

One cup of tea later, Claire took Sally into the study and showed her Stefan's email.

'Sounds like he's made up his mind.' Sally peered at the screen. 'I think he's being very sensible. Think of those poor children out there in the garden. I think he's doing the right thing, putting a stop to it before innocent people get hurt.'

'What about you?' asked Claire. 'You've left your husband. What about *your* children?'

'For one thing, I didn't have much choice. The man was doing goodness knows what in front of a computer screen. Please don't tell me I should have just ignored it and carried on as before. I will never get the image of that barely dressed snake woman out of my head – I'm seriously traumatised. And secondly, I didn't have a home like this to deprive the twins of.'

Sally took Claire's face in her hands.

'I'm sure you can make things work with William. He's the father of your children, you've lived with him for years, and you've made a lovely home together. It's not worth walking away from. You hardly know this Stefan man.'

'It's all right,' said Claire with a sigh. 'I can feel all my determination seeping away. I'm not going anywhere.'

'Good!' said Sally. 'Now I want you to promise me one thing.' She smiled at Claire. 'Next time you don't really, sort of, have an affair and fall in love with another man, could you let me know sooner so it's not such a shock? Between you and Gareth I feel as if I've started living in a bloody soap opera.'

'I can promise you now,' said Claire, 'there won't be a next time. I can't ever go through this again.'

'Look at me being all domestic!' Sally took away the barely touched sandwich she had made Claire after she'd fed five children beans on toast.

'Thank you,' said Claire gratefully.

Sally sat down beside her at the table and feigned exhaustion.

'All that cooking's worn me out for the day!'

'Can I ask you something, Sally?'

'If it's my recipe for beans on toast, I can't tell you, or if I did I'd have to kill you – it's top secret.'

'Are you really as happy as you seem, now that you've separated from Gareth?'

'No,' replied Sally. 'It's been the worst weekend of my life. If I'm being honest, I'm heartbroken. I miss his lazy body lounging on the sofa. I miss his smelly clothes left lying all over the floor. I miss the way he always held me close to him in the night. I miss the greasy frying pan he always left on top of the hob. I suppose I just miss *him*. I keep finding bits of his Iron Maiden T-shirt all over the garden and holding them up to my face to see if I can catch his smell. I've been crying myself to sleep, the boys are playing up even more than usual, and Gareth keeps phoning me in tears. I love him. I don't want to live my life without him, but I'll never forgive him for what he put me through, for what he destroyed, so this is how it has to be.'

Claire took Sally's hand in hers. She looked so sad.

Suddenly Sally pulled herself up and smiled. 'I'm hoping this could be the start of a whole new me though. Fitter, slimmer, more dynamic. I'm giving up sugar, including Jelly Babies, and crisps, and eating more than one family-sized pizza at a time, and I bought some running shoes this morning and I'm going to sign up for a retail management course in September. I'll show Gareth that I don't need him any more. Then he'll be so sorry.'

'Good for you, Sally.'

Sally stood up. 'Now, I think, Madame Bovary, that it's time to cheer ourselves up. I've already put a bottle of William's best Chardonnay in the freezer to chill and I'm going to open that box of Thornton's chocolates I found in the back of your jam cupboard. The new me doesn't start until tomorrow.'

# Chapter Twenty-three

*'Dark rooms were easily opened up into light-filled living spaces.'*

The week passed slowly, painfully. Claire cooked meals, took the children to play at friends' houses, drove them to an endless stream of birthday parties, Ben had his stitches out, and she pushed a trolley up and down the aisles at Waitrose almost every day.

'You look peaky, dear,' the woman on the checkout said. 'Summer cold?'

'Yes,' said Claire, not meeting her eye.

She couldn't sleep. At night she sat for hours in the silence of the house drinking tea out of her camellia cup, ironing, answering Emily Love emails, sweeping the floor, and trying not to hope for word from Stefan.

She wondered where he was, what he was doing. She had nowhere to picture him. He knew exactly where she was. If he thought of her she would be in the house, the village, the town that he had seen her in before. Trapped in her domesticity; forever walking through rooms, down lanes, down pavements, down aisles, while he could be anywhere in the whole world.

Two days after she had last seen Stefan, Claire had gone to a run-down petrol station on the other side of town. Guiltily, she asked the bored teenager behind the counter for a packet of cigarettes. As he fetched them down she looked out of the smeared glass window at her children waiting in the car on the forecourt and felt ashamed. She added three packets of chocolate buttons and hid the cigarettes in a zipped compartment in her bag.

At home she put on a video and while the children sat engrossed in front of it she went outside, stood behind the summer house, and smoked two in quick succession. Briefly, the nicotine took away the pain.

As each day passed, she felt as though she was losing Stefan – losing him in her mind, in her memory. Bit by bit his face seemed to slip away until after a week it was a blur beneath the dark waves of his hair. She tried to recall their conversations. At one time she could remember so many things he'd said – little things, insignificant things, huge things – but soon she doubted her ability to recollect and wasn't sure what things were real or simply hoped for. Sometimes a brief image would flash into her consciousness: his hand on a glass, the curve of his fingernail, a tiny brown mole on the side of his neck. Then the image would be gone and though she'd try she could not bring it back. As her memories drifted away, her heart seemed to ache more with the loss, until she wondered if one day she would be left with no memories, no recollections at all, only pain.

Cigarettes became a kind of refuge. Something to look forward to. Something that eased the pain, if only for a few minutes.

She smoked guiltily, secretly – round corners, crouched beneath windowsills, leaning against the back of the summer house. Instead of having an illicit affair with Stefan she was having one with nicotine.

One rain-dreary August afternoon, Claire slipped the button necklace into a padded envelope and wrote Stefan's address on the front. Before she could change her mind she bundled the children into raincoats and walked them down to the village postbox. They squabbled over who would post the envelope through the slit in the red Victorian box on the corner of the green. Finally it was Claire who put an end to the argument by posting it herself. Immediately she regretted it and wished there was some way of fishing it out; but it was done, the necklace was returned, line drawn, a definite end. As Claire trudged the damp children back up the hill she knew that sending back the necklace made no difference, it couldn't end so easily, there was no simple cure for the aching in her heart.

Sally was kind, but there were only so many times that Claire could tell her that she missed Stefan, that she thought her heart was breaking with sadness. William seemed to notice nothing; he was too tied up with his own distractions, too tired to wake up to the sound of Claire's nocturnal wanderings, too engrossed with building the summer house to notice how silent she had become.

Cornwall was the last place Claire wanted to be. Every day she hoped that Stefan might just appear or text or email or write or come in his lovely car and take her away. She didn't want to go too far from home, just in case. Cornwall seemed too many miles away for Stefan to find her if he changed his mind.

# Chapter Twenty-four

*'Organised disorder has its own intrinsic charm . . .'*

With a sinking heart, Claire drove south; the children squabbling and then finally sleeping in the back of the car. Endless miles of motorway gave way to dual carriageway, then smaller roads, threaded with villages and farms, then lanes, narrow and green with ferns and long grasses.

Claire stopped and consulted her mother's directions. She drove on down tightly bending lanes. Occasional flashes of silver on the horizon reminded her that she was headed for the sea. She reached a holiday resort – little white apartments piled up the steep valley slopes and static caravans lined up along the cliffs in the distance. Her mother's directions took her out of this village through even smaller lanes until, just as she was sure she'd gone too far, she saw a sign for the cottage. She pulled onto a gravel drive lined with pots of scarlet geraniums. Claire looked around for her mother's small brown Mini. All she could see was a bright red motorbike with a silver sidecar.

She hardly had time to wonder about the motorbike before her mother appeared in the doorway and ran towards Claire's car. As Claire got out, stiff after the long drive, her mother embraced her so enthusiastically that they almost toppled over together.

'Look at you,' Elizabeth said, holding her daughter at arm's length. 'You look terrible. Are you ill?'

'Just tired, Mum.'

'Well, let me look after you now.'

The children woke up and were immediately excited to see their grandmother – then, after a few seconds, desperate to get to the beach.

'Where's your car? Whose motorbike is that?' Claire asked as Elizabeth herded them all towards the cottage.

'I'll tell you later,' she replied. 'Let's get these poor children on to the beach first.'

Elizabeth led them into the small, neat cottage (faded dried flowers seemed to adorn every available surface) and then out through French windows at the back. They opened almost directly onto a tiny cove. Seaweed-covered rocks and pebbles lined the higher shore, but they gave way to the soft yellow sand of a completely empty beach. The children immediately took off their socks, shoes, and shorts and ran into the sea in their pants and T-shirts, screaming with delight. Claire thought how cross William would be with her for not telling them to put on their swimming things first. She didn't care. He wasn't there.

'I'll bring you down a mug of tea,' Elizabeth said, disappearing inside.

Claire stood on a large rock, watching the children. They were playing chase with the tide as it moved lazily up and down the flat wet sand. She looked up to the cliffs above the cove and could see the outline of a man and a dog walking on the path. The man walked slowly, limping along with the help of a stick. The dog seemed to be patiently keeping the same slow pace, though every now and then he ran in front a few yards before returning to his master's side again.

Elizabeth walked towards her with two large mugs of tea. Claire noticed that she'd had her hair cut shorter. Her usually severe grey bob had been layered softly around her face; Claire thought she could detect some golden highlights running through it. The new style made her look younger, prettier. She had put on a little weight; it suited her. Her fuller figure was flattered by a long linen tunic worn over ankle-skimming jeans. Turquoise beads around her neck complemented her bright blue eyes.

'You're looking well,' said Claire as her mother handed over her tea.

'I am well,' said Elizabeth. 'Very well.'

'This is a lovely place you've found.'

'It's even lovelier than it looked on the website,' agreed Elizabeth. 'Just as nice as an old Italian shed. William's mother can stuff Tuscany in her hot tub and boil it and she can throw in that pedestal thing she clobbered poor Ben on the head with while she's at it.'

Claire laughed. 'She didn't clobber him; it fell on top of him.'

'Same difference,' Elizabeth sniffed and folded her arms across her chest. 'If she hadn't been forcing things on you that you never wanted in your house in the first place it wouldn't have happened, would it?'

'You know, we can only stay here for four nights,' said Claire, changing that particularly painful subject. 'The children start school again on Monday.'

'I know, but we'll stay on and finish the week anyway.'

'We?' said Claire, surprised.

'That's what I wanted to tell you,' said Elizabeth, her cheeks flushing pink.

Claire sat down on the rock she had been standing on.

'Yes, you might need to sit down, dear. Shove up and I'll join you.' Her mother sat down beside her.

'Well, go on, tell me then.'

Elizabeth took a deep breath.

'I've met a man,' she said. 'A really nice man. Wonderful, actually. Well, I think he's wonderful.'

Claire was amazed. After a few seconds staring at her mother, unable to think of what to say, she managed: 'Who is he? How did you meet him? Where is he?'

'He's called Brian,' Elizabeth explained. 'I met him two months ago. I've been longing to tell you but I wanted you to be able to meet him at the same time.'

'How did you meet?'

'I ran him over.' Elizabeth took a sip of tea.

'What?'

'I ran him over with my car.' Elizabeth gave a short laugh. 'I didn't mean to. It was an accident.'

'You ran him over?'

'He was rather in the way,' said her mother. 'He should have been more careful where he put his easel. He admitted that right from the start.'

'His easel?'

'Brian is an artist,' Elizabeth explained. 'He and his wife used to run painting courses from their house in France.'

'He's got a wife!' Claire exclaimed.

'No. She died three years ago,' said Elizabeth. 'Breast cancer. Very sad. Poor Brian hadn't painted at all since she died and then the first time he decides to get his brushes out again I come along and plough into him.' She laughed again.

'It doesn't sound funny, Mum.'

'Obviously it was a terrible thing to happen but there was a funny side to it too. When you meet him you'll realise it's very hard not to laugh around Brian.'

'Did you hurt him?' asked Claire.

'He broke his ankle. I think he was quite lucky. It could have been so much worse. He'd just stood up to gauge the angle of the church tower he was painting when I reversed straight into him. I don't like to think what would have happened if he'd still been sitting down. I was trying to get out of a very tight parking space in the car park. I was late for an optician's appointment. I didn't realise he was painting just behind me.'

'Did you not see him in your mirrors?'

'Oh, no,' Elizabeth assured her. 'You see, he was in my blind spot. As I've said, it was a silly place to set up an easel.'

'So you ran this man over, broke his ankle, and now you're on holiday with him in Cornwall?'

'I know it sounds like an unlikely way to start a relationship.' Her mother smiled. 'He forgave me almost immediately. I drove him to the hospital but I didn't feel I could leave him waiting there on his own. We were in the X-ray department for three hours until he was seen and then we had to wait another two hours before he had his ankle put in a plaster cast. We never stopped talking. He made me laugh. We found we had so much in common. It felt as though we'd known each other for years. An immediate connection. Do you know what I mean?'

'Yes,' Claire replied. 'I know exactly what you mean.'

'I think I fell in love with Brian in that hospital waiting room. Hard seats and weak coffee from a machine never seemed more romantic.' She grinned and Claire could suddenly imagine what she must have been like as a girl. 'He lives with three cats, two pigs, twelve ducks, and a dog called Buster. He's good and kind and he makes me laugh. I'm so happy. I can't believe it.'

Claire put down her mug and gave her mother a hug. 'That's fantastic,' she said. 'It's wonderful.'

'Do you really think so? I've been so nervous about telling you.'

'Why?' asked Claire. 'I've always said you should find someone else.'

'Have you?'

'I'm sure I have, loads of times. I know I'm always wishing you would find someone.'

'Someone to take care of me in my old age?' Elizabeth raised her eyebrows. 'So you don't need to worry about me so much?'

'Someone to have fun with while you're still young enough to enjoy it,' said Claire. 'You only live once so you might as well make the best of it. Is that his motorbike?'

'Yes,' replied Elizabeth. 'Isn't it fabulous? Buster goes in the sidecar.'

'Where do you go?' asked Claire.

'On the back, of course. I've bought some leathers and a helmet. You should see me. It'll make you laugh. Of course poor Brian hasn't been able to ride the bike for weeks because of his ankle. So coming here was his first long ride. It was my first time on the back of a bike since before you were born. It was wonderful. The wind on my face. It's like the good times with your father all over again.'

'I didn't know there were any.'

'Oh yes.' Her mother looked out across the sea. 'There were good times. That's why I couldn't understand why he always wanted other women. Why he wanted to leave.' She was silent for a while and then turned to Claire and shrugged. 'But that was all years ago. I think it's time I let him go now.'

'Yes,' said Claire and took Elizabeth's hand in hers, squeezing it gently.

A dog barked and looking up Claire saw the man from the cliff walking stiffly down steep wooden steps towards them.

'Oh, here he is.'

Elizabeth got up and walked towards him. She kissed his cheek and Claire could see she was telling him something. They smiled at each other, an exchange so intimate that she had to look away. The children were digging a hole for the tide to fill. They were surprised by the golden retriever running towards them. Ben screamed.

'Gently, Buster,' the man called to the dog. 'He won't hurt you,' he assured the children as the dog jumped into their hole and started barking and turning in circles, brushing their faces with his wagging tail. 'He only wants to say hello.'

Claire stood up and walked across the sand to meet her mother and Brian. Her first impression was of someone solid – wide-shouldered, medium height, his stomach gently rounded over corduroy trousers pulled in with an ancient-looking leather belt. His weather-beaten face was bearded, his grey hair thick though somewhat wild. Deep lines fanned out on each side of lively eyes. You could see that he had been a very handsome young man – he was still a handsome man.

He held out his hand to Claire.

'It's lovely to meet you,' he said, smiling warmly.

His hand felt smooth, his handshake firm.

'Mum has been telling me all about you,' said Claire.

'Good things, I hope.'

'Oh, yes.'

'She has certainly made me a very happy man.' Brian took her mother's hand in his.

'I think it's time for a celebratory drink,' said Elizabeth. 'It's well past five o'clock. Gin and tonics all round.'

'Yes, please,' Claire and Brian chorused together and they all laughed.

'That's a shock too, Mum,' said Claire. 'You never drink.'

'Well, you only live once, as you said yourself, dear.'

Claire called to Ben, scooped him up, and walked with Brian up to the cottage garden as her mother went inside to fetch the drinks. From a wooden table they could still watch Oliver and Emily running in and out of the waves with a very excited Buster bounding beside them.

Brian carefully stretched out his leg in front of him. He winced with pain.

'How is your ankle?' asked Claire, cuddling Ben close to her to keep him warm.

'Getting better, but I think getting back on the old bike and driving a hundred and fifty miles wasn't that great for it. It certainly feels stiffer today.'

'It was an awful thing to happen,' said Claire. 'To get knocked down like that.'

'No, not awful at all.' Brian smiled. 'Actually it was one of the best things that's ever happened to me.'

'I'm sure there are easier ways to meet someone.'

'Well, your mother certainly has an unusual way of getting a man's attention.'

'She seems so happy,' said Claire. 'Quite changed. Would I be right to think you are responsible for dragging Mum into the twenty-first century?'

'If you mean introducing her to the wonders of the internet, then yes, that was me. She's a fast learner. She's never off her laptop now.'

Elizabeth returned with a tray of glasses, a bowl of cashew nuts, and a towel to wrap around Ben.

'Cheers,' said Brian, raising his glass. 'To a very happy future.'

'To a happy future,' mother and daughter echoed.

'So, you used to live in France?' Claire asked Brian. He was throwing nuts into the air to catch them with his mouth. Ben squealed with laughter at his display.

'I still live in France,' he replied, handing Ben a square of chocolate that he had produced from the pocket of his denim shirt. 'I have an old farmhouse that I renovated years ago. It's in the Dordogne. I had only come over here for a day or two to meet my son's new baby. My first grandchild. She's called Alice, she's gorgeous. I was painting them a picture of the church where Alice will be christened when I met your mother.'

He squeezed Elizabeth's hand across the table.

'Now I've got my ankle out of plaster and I'm back on my wheels again I need to get back home. The animals are being looked after by my neighbour but they'll be missing me. I also want to get the painting classes back up and running and,' he hesitated and exchanged a glance with Elizabeth, 'I want to take your mother with me.'

'For a holiday?' asked Claire.

'No,' Elizabeth replied. 'I'm going to move to France to be with Brian. To live there. My flat is on the market already.'

'Wow!' said Claire. 'That's a big life change.'

Her mother looked at her, and smiled nervously. 'Do you think it's too big?'

'No, it's not too big. Do it if you want to, Mum,' said Claire. 'You were a French teacher for thirty-five years – you speak fluent French. I remember how much you wanted to live in France when I was little, but Dad wouldn't even go there on holiday. It could be fantastic. Why not grab all the opportunities you can?'

'That's what I say,' said Brian. 'At our age you never know how long you've got left. You could get ill or have a heart attack or some mad woman in a brown Mini could run you over.'

Claire's mother swiped at him crossly. He caught her hand in his and kissed it. They both laughed and Claire couldn't help smiling.

'I thought you might not approve.' Elizabeth's face was serious again. 'It's not as if we've known each other very long.'

'Two months is a long time if you love someone,' Claire said.

'I thought you'd be upset about my leaving you and the children.'

'We'll be over all the time,' said Claire. 'It will be a great excuse to have French holidays. The children will love it.'

'What do you think William will think?' asked her mother.

*Who cares?* thought Claire.

'Well, I expect he'll foresee all sorts of potential problems and pitfalls – you know how he worries. But I hope he'll be very pleased for you.' She touched her mother's hand across the table. 'I'm really happy for you anyway.' She looked at Brian. 'For both of you.'

'Can we put our swimsuits on now?' Emily shouted as she ran towards them, T-shirt dripping. Oliver followed, equally soaked.

'I think it's a bit late for that!' Brian laughed. 'You're already drenched.'

'Who are you?' asked Emily, looking at the stranger suspiciously.

'I'm Brian,' he said. 'Your grandmother is a very special friend of mine.'

Just then Buster ran up to the table and shook himself violently. Sea water sprayed out all over everyone.

'And this is my other special friend,' said Brian, patting Buster's soggy coat. 'Now, I should go in and make a start on supper. Any volunteers for giving a hungry dog his dinner?'

They ate looking over the little cove and beyond to a far-off headland. The setting sun was still warm and Claire began to feel herself relaxing for the first time in weeks. Brian made them large crêpes which he served with melted cheese, ham, and fried eggs.

He told Claire and the children that it was a traditional Dordogne speciality. Claire was suddenly ravenous in the fresh sea air; it had been a long time since she had enjoyed a meal so much.

Brian told the children about all the mischief Buster got into on their walks and let them feed the dog small treats from their plates. They laughed, delighted, at the big yellow dog pushing his nose around their toes looking for dropped food, his shaggy tail slapping against their bare thighs.

After the meal, Brian suggested he take the children back to the beach where he directed them in a scramble over the rocks and pebbles to search for driftwood for the cottage fire. He stood on the highest rock holding Ben's hand and pointing out with his stick branches for Oliver and Emily to collect.

'He's lovely, Mum,' said Claire, watching them as she collected up their plates from the table.

'I think so.'

'He's a big hit with the children,' Claire added. 'I think they're going to have a lot of fun with Buster too.'

She could see Oliver and Emily climbing over the large flat rocks, Buster close beside them, sniffing in between the crevices. Ben was picking up pebbles from the foot of the rock he shared with Brian. He handed them with great importance one by one to Brian and watched in wonder as Brian skimmed each pebble across the incoming water, making them hop across the waves.

'Are you all right?' Elizabeth asked her. 'I'm worried about you. You've lost so much weight.' She came and put her arm around her daughter's shoulder. 'You seem sad.'

'I think I just need a bit of a rest,' said Claire. 'Don't worry about me. I'll be fine.'

After Claire had put the three exhausted children to bed, Brian and Elizabeth showed her pictures of the house in France on Brian's laptop. It was a beautiful rectangular farmhouse with shuttered windows, ochre-coloured walls, and an undulating terracotta roof. The garden was a wilderness of trees and flowers bordered by a wide, shallow river. A duck pond was fringed with irises and a painted wooden duck house sat on an island in the middle. They showed her pictures of the little medieval town nearby. Pretty golden buildings clustered on a steep hillside leading down to a medieval bridge.

'Proper shops there,' Brian said. 'Patisseries, boulangeries, hardware shops selling everything you'd ever need. The people are so friendly. I've know them all for years. They were all so good to me when my wife died.'

Brian made a fire as the late-summer chill set in and they sat around it drinking wine, telling Claire more of their plans for the future. Buster gently snored at Brian's feet.

'The children will love it over there,' he said. 'We'll soon have them fishing in our river and there are loads of fossils in the rocks around the house, and a lake nearby to swim in.'

'We'll come as often as we can,' said Claire, genuinely looking forward to it, though she couldn't help thinking how much Stefan would like it.

She found herself imagining being there with him: sitting drinking wine in the shady garden, watching the children playing in the river, walking down the narrow lanes of the town hand in hand, leaning over the bridge as the water flowed beneath it. She felt sure he'd get on well with Brian.

'You look miles away,' her mother said, bringing her back to reality. 'You must be tired after your long drive. Don't let us keep you up with all our talking.'

'It must all be a bit much to take in,' said Brian kindly. 'You didn't even know I existed until today and now I'm whisking your mother away to foreign parts.'

'I know I should have told you before but I haven't seen you for so long,' said her mother. 'And I wanted to talk to you face to face, for you to meet Brian yourself.'

'I wish you both lots of happiness.'

'You're very generous,' said Brian.

'No, not generous,' said Claire. 'I just think if you can find someone you want to be with and you can be with them, then you're very lucky.'

She got up.

'I'd better go to bed; I suddenly feel exhausted. Must be the sea air.'

She kissed her mother's cheek. 'Night, Mum,' she said and kissed Brian too. 'It's so lovely to meet you.' She smiled at them both and left the room.

In bed she could hear them quietly talking as they washed up, laughing together, whispering, so obviously happy in each other's company. She realised that there was only one other bedroom in the cottage. She remembered a patchwork-covered double bed she had glimpsed earlier and tried not to feel shocked.

Claire woke up early. Ben had got into her bed sometime in the night. She held his warm, soft body close to hers, feeling his gentle breathing on her cheek. After a little while she extricated herself from his embrace and got up and pulled on jeans and a jumper.

She left the children sleeping in their room and made herself a cup of tea in the silent kitchen. Taking it outside, she stood looking at the sea. The tide was high and the air crisp and cold. Gulls soared against another bright blue sky. The rhythmic sound of the waves rolling onto the shingle edge of the beach mixed with birds' calls high above her.

She walked up the steep cliff steps until she reached the top, looking down on the clear green water glistening in the morning sun. Sitting down on the short grass beside the coastal path, she took a cigarette from a box of ten in her pocket. As she lit it and inhaled she thought of Stefan and wondered where he was. Waking up to the noise of London traffic, or somewhere hundreds of miles away in another country? Maybe he was on the other side of the large expanse of water in front of her. She gazed out across the sea and her heart ached with the longing that had become so familiar.

'Those things will kill you,' said a voice.

Brian and Buster appeared from the opposite direction. Claire jumped at being found out.

'Don't tell my mum,' she said as he sat down beside her.

'You're a grown woman,' he laughed. 'Not a twelve-year-old behind a bike shed.'

'I know,' she said. 'But I still think she'd be cross with me.'

'Only worried about your health.' Brian smiled at her. 'But I'll keep your secret, don't worry. I'm sure you have your reasons. We all need the odd vice to make life worthwhile sometimes.'

'Yes,' said Claire, looking down onto the rough grey rocks of the cliff.

'I know I drank too much when my wife was ill,' Brian went on. 'The odd nightcap gradually turned into half a bottle before bed and then a couple of glasses of whisky in the morning as soon as I'd made her breakfast. Whisky with lunch, whisky with tea and supper. I felt very guilty at the time but, looking back, I think it helped me through it. I needed something otherwise I'd have gone mad.'

'That must have been a terrible time for you,' said Claire.

'I thought my life was ending too,' he said. 'Wished I could go with her when she died. Seriously thought about making that happen. It was a very bleak year, the year after her death.'

'You must have loved her very much to feel so sad.'

Claire thought of the agonising months after Jack had died. She wondered if her mother had told Brian about him.

'I adored my wife,' Brian went on. 'We'd been together since we were fifteen. I never imagined I could love another woman. But then I met your mother.'

He looked at Claire and smiled.

'She's a very special person. She's been like a gift for me, an unexpected gift. An explosion of light out of all the darkness of my grief. It just shows you – even if you think everything is lost and that only loneliness and despair remain, the most amazing things can happen. Never give up hope. If life has taught me anything it's that things always get better.'

'I hope you're right,' she said, finishing her cigarette and stubbing it out in the short grass.

'Did your mother tell you that I've asked her to marry me?'

'No,' said Claire, looking up at him surprised. 'What did she say?'

'She refused,' said Brian. 'She says she'll never get married again.'

'Give her time. It was dreadful for her when my dad left. She was so upset, felt so betrayed and hurt. Does it matter to you if you're married or not?'

'I'd just like to show her how much she means to me,' he said. 'Show the world how I feel about her.'

'Give her time,' Claire said again. 'It's not been long since she met you. She'll need to learn to trust again after all these years.'

From where they sat she saw her mother and the children on the beach below. Buster barked and got up to go and join them.

'Your mother is worried about you,' said Brian. 'She thinks you might be going through a rough patch.'

'If what you said just now is right, then things will get better.'

Claire stood up and waved at the little group below.

'I can understand if you don't want to talk about it,' said Brian. He stood up and put a hand on her arm. 'But don't give up hope.'

Together they slowly walked down the steps onto the sand. Ben ran over to Brian and threw his arms around his leg.

'I found a shell,' he said proudly, holding out his hand.

'We saw a seal,' shouted Oliver excitedly behind him.

'I saw two,' called Emily.

Elizabeth gave Claire a hug. 'It's so lovely having you all here.'

'It's lovely to be here,' said Claire, hugging her back.

The four days passed quickly – playing with the children on the beach; walking on the headland; drinking endless cups of tea, gin and tonics and glasses of wine with Elizabeth and Brian on the terrace; laughing at Brian's funny stories. The children loved him. He gave them rides on his motorbike – Emily and Ben in the sidecar, Oliver proudly on the back. Brian drove them slowly up and down the lane while they called and waved to Claire and Elizabeth as though they were on a fun-fair ride. Ben was constantly demanding his attention and Brian was happy to give it to him. He took Oliver and Emily bird-watching on the cliff tops and they all went out on a boat trip, joined by a school of dolphins swimming along beside them in the waves.

Buster was an endless source of fun, never tiring of chasing a stick or jumping in and out of the tide, chasing the three children. Brian and Elizabeth cooked together in the evenings, slicing vegetables and stirring pots side by side, creating lovely meals 'to fill you out a bit', as Elizabeth said to Claire.

Claire had never seen her mother so happy, so good-natured. Gone was the constant underlying note of bitterness in her voice; gone her unrelenting cynicism and suspicion of life. She was cheerful, lighter in her tone and attitude, relaxed and full of fun. She played cricket on the beach with the children and had bedtime games of Monopoly with Oliver and Emily, cheating disgracefully, then denying it outrageously when found out.

To Claire it was like the family holidays she'd dreamed of as a child. Happy days together on a beach in the sun, rather than the quietly tense times the three of them had spent looking at prehistoric burial mounds or stone circles – her father's great passion.

He would take endless photographs and measurements for a book he never even started to write. They rented musty caravans and spent nights in dark guesthouses eating tinned grapefruit for breakfast and sleeping on scratchy nylon sheets.

As an adult, Claire could still feel mild depression sweep over her as they sped past Stonehenge on the A344. It always seemed strange that her father had settled in California, so far away from his beloved ancient British sites. After he left they never had any holidays. Had it been because of lack of money? Maybe Elizabeth had simply lacked the inclination.

Claire felt sad as she and the children hugged Brian and Elizabeth goodbye at the end of their visit. The children begged her to let them stay until the end of the week and cried as she bundled them into the car. Claire felt like crying too and longed to stay, but the thought of explaining to a pursed-lipped Mrs Wenham why Oliver and Emily were starting the new school term late kept her firm in her resolve to head for home.

Claire got in the car and drove away, beeping the horn and waving until the little cottage was out of sight.

'She's doing what?' William exclaimed when Claire got home and told him her mother was moving to France with Brian. 'Does she really know this man? He could be anyone!'

'He's lovely,' said Claire, the happiness she'd found in Cornwall slowly ebbing away as she faced her husband across the kitchen.

'You hear about men like him, seducing old women, making them sell their houses, and then going off with all their money.'

'I don't think he's like that,' she said, sighing. 'He's just a nice man. I could tell how happy they were together.'

'Well, I wouldn't trust him,' said William. 'Just you wait and see. She'll be left heartbroken and penniless. And what about the children?'

'What about them?' asked Claire, trying not to get cross.

'What about their inheritance if it all disappears in your mother's mad adventures?'

'Why do you have to be so cynical?'

'I'm not cynical,' he replied. 'It's you and your mother who seem to be naïvely taken in by this complete stranger.'

'You'll have to meet him and then you'll see how nice he is.'

'I hope your mother doesn't think we'll have the time or money to be constantly going back and forth to France.'

He noisily opened cupboards looking for a jar of coffee.

'We must have run out,' said Claire, suddenly feeling tired after the long drive home.

'We're low on a lot of things,' said William, making himself a cup of tea.

'Are we?' she said, inwardly fuming at William's inability to find time to shop for himself while she was away.

'The children liked him a lot.'

'Who?'

'Brian.'

'I hope you didn't leave them alone with him, Claire. As I said, you've no idea who he is.'

Claire got up and decided to check her emails.

Already there were Christmas orders from shops wanting new Emily Love stock, a lot of website mail orders, the usual junk, but nothing else. Claire stared blankly at the screen until William shouted from the kitchen that they were out of milk now too.

# Chapter Twenty-five

*'A comfortable home that's always welcoming. Claire has created the perfect environment for her family and friends to enjoy.'*

Oliver and Emily returned to the competent care of Mrs Wenham and Ben went back to nursery to give Claire more time to work. She was frantically busy but even the hectic after-school schedules and the demands of Emily Love didn't stop her thinking about Stefan.

The summer turned to autumn. The days were shorter and the hedgerows started to turn brown, shed their leaves, and slowly rot. The new season made Claire even more depressed. The damp October cold made her summer memories seem remote. She put away her thin cotton skirts and dresses and got out jumpers, trousers and long boots that Stefan had never seen her wear.

She bought new clothes to make herself feel better. A red velvet coat, a tight tweed pencil skirt, a knitted dress. A new underwear shop opened in town and Claire let herself be measured and cosseted by the shop assistant who brought her an endless succession of bras to try. The cheery woman talked on and on about the supportive benefits of each one, tightening, lifting and adjusting.

'This one gives you the most fantastic cleavage. Your husband will love it!'

Claire looked in the mirror and wondered which one Stefan would most like to find as he slowly unbuttoned her shirt.

As she waited to pay for the bra she'd finally chosen, her fingers stroked the pale peach silk and delicate embroidery, a tiny tear of pearl nestled in between the two softly padded cups. At the last minute she bought the matching knickers as well.

'Hubby will be pleased when he sees you in these,' said the shop assistant as she wrapped them in crisp white tissue and slid them into a bag adorned with golden cherubs. The bra and knickers stayed unworn, still wrapped, at the back of Claire's underwear drawer for a long time.

'What are we doing about your birthday?' asked Sally, as they sat enjoying *après*-school-run cappuccinos in the hotel lounge in town. Sitting in front of a warm log fire, on soft suede sofas, they were flicking through the hotel's glossy magazines. Now Sally had started her retail management course at the local college, Claire hardly ever saw her.

Although it was good to catch up, Claire was only half-engaged in conversation. She was looking through the latest copy of *Idyllic Homes*, looking at the names of the photographers in the articles, searching for Stefan's name.

'Earth to Planet Claire?'

Sally waved a magazine in front of Claire's face.

'Sorry. What did you say?'

'I said, what are we going to do for your birthday?' Sally repeated her words slowly.

'I don't feel like doing anything much.' Claire knew she sounded flat but these days she found it hard to sound enthusiastic.

'Well, what about me? Don't I deserve a night out? I've worked really hard these first few months on my course and I've already lost two stone.'

It was true that in the last two months Sally had transformed herself from dishevelled housewife and mother into a svelte and sexy mature student. Running and a strict diet regime had done wonders for her figure. Her toned thighs were now clad in skin-tight denim, tucked into a pair of knee-high black leather boots. A cashmere jumper showed off her newly discovered waist. Lately she'd started dating a blond and brooding twenty-two-year-old called Josh.

'I thought you were having enough nights out with your toy boy.' Claire raised her eyebrows.

'I know,' Sally said. 'But I miss having a good old chat. There's only so much conversation you can have with someone fifteen years younger than you.'

'I didn't think it was the conversation you were interested in.'

'Well, I wouldn't like to waste too much time talking when there are so many other things to do with Josh.' She winked at Claire and laughed. 'If you know what I mean.'

'You certainly didn't waste any time finding ways to fill those lonely nights when Gareth has the boys,' Claire said. She couldn't help but feel slightly envious.

'I never realised there was so much fun to be had as a single woman. Maybe Sweet Betty did me a favour in the end.' Sally hesitated and glanced at Claire. 'But being married is good too – if it's not Gareth that you're married to, obviously. Things are all right now between you and William, aren't they?'

'Fine,' Claire replied, looking back down at the magazine on her lap.

'Good,' Sally said. 'Now, what about your birthday? It's only three weeks away. Let's do something fun to celebrate instead of the usual fireworks with the kids on the village green. You're only thirty-six once, after all. We could book a table in a restaurant – get some of the other mums together as well.'

'OK.' Claire flicked absentmindedly through the pages of *Idyllic Homes*. Suddenly there was Stefan's name blazing out at her from the glossy pages. She stopped breathing. A full-page photograph of a neatly proportioned red brick Victorian house. *An exquisitely renovated former rectory, elegantly furnished with period pieces with a modern twist*. She turned to the first page of the feature: a picture of a sumptuously decorated living room, all cream, beige and chocolate. A long-limbed redhead sat on a chaise longue, one arm draped along its velvet back, her slim legs crossed, a cream silk

222

shirt casually unbuttoned to reveal a hint of cleavage. She was smiling confidently at the camera. She was smiling at Stefan. Claire skimmed through the text.

*"This house is very special,"* says Jilly, *who combines running a four-star restaurant, a successful interior design business, and life as a busy mother. "We feel really at home living here."*

Claire immediately hated Jilly. She wondered if Stefan had invited her to share cakes and champagne cocktails with him. She wondered if her unnaturally full lips had kissed Stefan's, if her slender arms had wrapped themselves around him, and if his hands had wandered underneath that luxurious shirt.

'Are you listening to me at all?'

Claire looked up to see Sally staring at her.

'If you would rather read magazines than organise your birthday party, that's fine. I'll just have to organise it for you.'

Sally booked a table for thirteen at the hotel's restaurant for the night of Claire's birthday. Excitement fizzed amongst the mothers at the school gate. Outfits were planned, hairdresser's appointments booked. Claire bought a new olive-green silk dress and high-heeled gold shoes in an effort to get as excited as everyone else. The outfit would do for Christmas Day as well. Elizabeth and Brian had invited them for Christmas in France, but William had already arranged the usual visit from his parents.

Claire had to work most evenings after the children had gone to bed. She cut out cushions, aprons, lavender hearts and bunting till the early hours of the morning. She packed up orders and wrote out invoices. The children needed to be taken to Cubs, swimming, ballet, judo and violin classes after school. She endlessly tidied the house, cooked meals and ironed clothes. She had so much to do that she felt as if she was wading through thick mud, struggling to get somewhere, but sinking deeper with every step.

'You'll wear yourself out if you don't stop working so hard,' her mother warned, when she called from France. 'I hope William is helping out with the children and doing his bit around the house.'

'He's working a lot as well,' said Claire. 'He's home late every night and he's finishing off the inside of his summer house at weekends.'

'Just try to make sure William realises how hard you're working too. He's not the only one with a demanding job.'

'I'll be fine,' said Claire. 'It's only this mad rush up to Christmas.'

Claire felt as though each day was hurtling her faster and faster towards her birthday. It wasn't being older that she dreaded, but the thought of so many more years to come. Years of school runs, cleaning, cooking, shopping, William. She tried to remember if it had been enough for her before – before Stefan came and ripped open the box where she had kept her needs and wants and emotions so neatly packed away. Now they were out and running wild, refusing to be put back in the box again.

It was the Monday before Claire's birthday and they had woken to the first frost of the winter. The grass had been so white that Ben thought it must be snow and ran out to try to gather it up into snowballs and Oliver and Emily slipped and slid across the patio pretending to ice skate.

Claire watched them from the kitchen window; it was such a magical scene. She realised she felt happier than she had for a long time. Cradling a cup of tea in her hands she leant back against the warmth of the Aga, and thought about her birthday. She was beginning to look forward to going out with the girls and having a bit of fun.

The sound of wheels on gravel and a thump from the direction of the doormat heralded the morning's post.

As soon as she walked into the hallway Claire could see the copy of *Idyllic Homes* lying on the dark slate tiles. She picked it up, tore off the cellophane wrapping, and held the pristine magazine in her hands. On the cover 'Special Christmas Issue' was picked out in dark red letters against a picture of their fireplace dressed with holly and candles, Emily Love stockings hanging down towards a blazing fire; tempting ribbon-wrapped boxes peeped out of each one – it was their fireplace! A picture from their shoot had made the cover. Claire stared at it and wondered if Stefan was pleased to have his photograph on the front; had he thought about her when he'd seen it? A list of smaller captions were printed beneath the title: 'The Perfect Gift Guide', 'Fresh Ways with Seasonal Foliage', 'A Textile Artist's Inspirational Country House'. Claire flicked through until she found the article. The children had come in from the cold garden and jumped excitedly beside her. The pictures looked beautiful on the glossy A4 pages.

She took the magazine with her to show Sally as she dropped the children off at school.

'Did you really say this?' asked Sally, as she started reading the text beside the pictures.

Claire hadn't had time to read it in her mad dash to get everyone out of the house.

Sally started to read out loud: '*Christmas is Claire's favourite time of the year; a time to gather her friends and family around her in her beautifully restored thatched farmhouse. She likes nothing better than to spend the weeks leading up to Christmas Day making heavenly handmade gifts for family and friends, each one uniquely crafted out of carefully sourced vintage fabrics and antique lace and buttons. When all her gifts are exquisitely wrapped beneath her tree, Claire can sit back and relax beside her open fire and reflect on the years of hard work that have made her house such a special place to be at Christmas.*'

'Where have my heavenly handmade gifts been then?' asked Sally. 'And if you've got enough time to sit beside your fire and reflect at Christmas, you can come round and give me a hand instead.'

'I never told the journalist any of that,' said Claire, trying to get the magazine from her.

Sally turned away from her and read on in an exaggerated voice: '*On Christmas morning, Claire enjoys preparing her festive feast in her pretty pastel-coloured kitchen. Cooking her turkey slowly in her pale blue Aga the night before gives her and the children lots of time to welcome their many guests to their home and sit beside the tree exchanging presents and drinking mulled wine.'*

'What?' exclaimed Claire. 'What really happens is that I race round trying to tidy up all the early-morning present-opening carnage before William's parents arrive at nine, and then I re-member I've completely forgotten to take the turkey out of the fridge. My mother arrives, William's mother upsets her and makes sarcastic comments about everything, William starts making shelves just as I ask him to help me prepare the vegetables, and I end up drinking a bottle of cheap rioja (that I haven't had time to make into mulled wine) alone in the kitchen, trying not to throw bread sauce at the walls.'

'So you didn't tell any of this stuff to the journalist?'

'What do you think?' said Claire. 'I told her about the house and what it had been like and all the work William did on it and about how I started my business.'

'I hate to tell you this,' said Sally, who had been finishing the article. 'It doesn't actually mention William's hard work anywhere in this. In fact, it doesn't mention William at all.'

William phoned at lunchtime.

'Did you know the magazine is out?' he asked as soon as Claire answered.

Claire felt herself inwardly bracing. 'We got a copy sent to us in the post this morning after you'd left.'

'Someone brought it in to work,' William said. His voice was quiet.

'The house looks lovely, doesn't it?' she said hesitantly. There was silence on the other end of the phone. 'The children were so excited. They've taken it in to show at school.'

'Did you read it?' asked William. She could tell he was trying to control his voice.

'Yes, I did, but it's not . . .'

'Not what, Claire?' he asked. 'Not my house too?'

'I know but . . .'

226

'When you did the interview did you just forget to mention that I live there as well? Did you just forget to mention your husband, who has worked so bloody hard turning it from a wreck to the sort of house they want to feature in their magazine?'

'I didn't forget, I . . .'

'I thought they hadn't even used the photograph that photographer bloke took of us together, but then I realised that there is the picture of you on our kitchen sofa and that I'd been airbrushed out.'

'I hadn't noticed that. Oh, William, I'm so sorry.'

'Don't you think people will wonder how you managed to do all that work on the house and produce three children? A team of friendly builders and immaculate bloody conception?'

'I'm so sorry, William. I didn't know they were going to make it sound that way. Of course I told the journalist all about you and your amazing hard work. I don't know why she didn't mention you. I'm really upset as well.'

He was silent again.

'William?' Claire wondered if he was still there. 'I am sorry, but it's not my fault.'

'They just used you and our children to fill their pages. Your naïvety in agreeing to do it in the first place amazes me, Claire.'

'You seemed happy to let them do it too, if I remember rightly.'

'I didn't realise that it would be such a waste of time. What did we get out of it – absolutely nothing!'

'No, it's not like that,' she said. 'I've had over twenty orders on my mail-order website this morning and the phone hasn't stopped ringing with enquiries. It's been great free advertising for Emily Love.'

William made a huffing noise and put the phone down.

Claire stood with the receiver still in her hand for a long time. She felt awful. She could understand how hurt he must be.

As she made herself a cup of tea, the phone rang again. She let it ring. She'd spent all morning answering it and couldn't face talking to anyone else. After she'd had an illicit cigarette to recover from her conversation with William she checked her phone messages. It had been William's mother.

Her voice barked out from the answering machine: 'I saw the magazine today. My cleaner brought it with her. I was surprised, I hadn't realised that it was such a poor publication. What a dreadfully written article. Why didn't they mention William or the help we gave you to buy the house in the first place? And you say that you found all your furniture yourselves, but what about the oak dining table and the console table and your lovely bed? Not to mention the grandfather clock – that clock belonged to William's Great Aunt Rosalind, it wasn't from a reclamation yard, and that watercolour painting in the hall was done by William's father's grandfather, not found in a junk shop! And they didn't show any pictures of the dining room, why are there so many of the kitchen? I've never liked what you did to that room. I hope you –' She was cut off by the bleep. Claire decided to have another cigarette.

By the time Claire realised she was late to collect the children from school, she was taking orders for delivery well after the New Year. The phone had rung and rung. Several shops had placed orders. There had been endless enquiries about one-off commissions. Her mother had sent an email to say how lovely the pictures looked, but wasn't it a shame the article hadn't mentioned that all Claire's Cornishware had been inherited from her great aunt, not bought in car boot sales, as it seemed to imply.

Claire felt exhausted. It was wonderful to have so much interest in Emily Love, but she wished she had asked to see what had been written before publication.

The children came out of school – the only children left as Claire was so late. Mrs Wenham their headmistress bustled behind them, holding a copy of the magazine.

'What lovely pictures,' she called to Claire as she approached. 'Oliver and Emily have been like celebrities for the day, haven't you?' She smiled at the two children who looked as tired as Claire felt.

'It's just a pity,' added Mrs Wenham, as Claire began to walk away with Oliver and Emily, 'that they couldn't have been wearing their school uniforms in any of the pictures. You know, to give us a bit of a plug.'

Claire thought she was going to scream. Instead she smiled brightly at Mrs Wenham and led the children to the car.

She sat in the driver's seat resting her head on the steering wheel. How many other people could the article possibly upset or disappoint? Perhaps William was right; she had been naïve to agree to it in the first place. More naïve than he could possibly imagine.

'Why didn't they show any pictures of my doll's house, Mummy?' asked Emily, flicking through the magazine again. 'I tidied it up specially.'

Oliver sunk down in the passenger seat beside Claire.

'What's wrong with you?' she asked her scowling son.

'Charlie Bennett laughed at me all day for wearing those stupid striped pyjamas. I'm *so* embarrassed, why did you force me to be in the pictures in the first place?'

'Want it!' Claire heard Ben's shout as she moved the car away from the curb.

'No, I'm reading it,' said Emily.

'Mine!'

'Mum!' Emily shrieked. 'He's ripped it.' There was a muffled thump and Ben started to cry.

'Let him rip it up,' muttered Oliver. 'I don't want to ever see it again.'

'It's ruined,' Emily cried.

Claire took a deep breath and started to count slowly in her head.

'We have to go and buy another one *now*, Mum!' Emily's angry voice was piercing.

'No way!' Oliver turned round to try to grab the magazine from his sister's hands. Emily walloped him over the head with it. 'Mum! Did you see what she did?'

Claire put on the radio and turning it up very loud tried to pretend she was on her own.

# Chapter Twenty-six

*'Informal floor-length curtains introduce*
*a country feel to the upstairs rooms.'*

William was still only speaking to her in reluctant monosyllables by the morning of her birthday. He grudgingly gave her a cup of tea in bed and handed her a small black box. Inside there was a pair of tiny pearl earrings, just like the ones his mother wore. Claire hadn't worn earrings for years.

'They're beautiful,' she said, trying to sound grateful. She leant over and gave him a kiss. William grunted.

Oliver and Emily came in with pictures they'd got up early to draw for her. Oliver's was of Macavity engaged in some sort of battle with a fire-breathing robot dragon; fighter planes blasted them from overhead.

'Lovely,' said Claire.

'This is you,' said Emily, getting into bed beside Claire to explain her own brightly coloured picture. 'This is lots of Emily Love bunting and these are some Emily Love cushions, and this is your cake with loads and loads of candles, and here are your presents and some flowers and butterflies.'

'They're fantastic pictures,' said Claire, hugging the two children. 'I'll put them on the wall when I get up.'

'Be careful what you use to put them up with,' said William, who was getting dressed. 'That sticky stuff you used before left marks and took out a chunk of the paint.' At least he was speaking normally to her again.

Ben tottered in with a large armful of his toys.

'For you,' he said, dropping them on the bed on top of Claire before climbing in and snuggling down beside her.

'They're not proper presents,' said Emily. 'That's just your stuff, Ben. Mummy doesn't want toys and I bet you'll want it all back in a minute.'

'It's very thoughtful,' said Claire and kissed the top of Ben's blond head.

Her mother and Brian had sent her a lovely 1950s silk scarf with a Paris street scene printed on it and a book about antique French fabric. William's mother sent a very expensive-looking jar of revitalising eye cream (*A unique mineral complex firms, lifts and reduces the signs of aging*) and a step-by-step cookery book (*Simple recipes and instructions for those just starting out in the kitchen*).

The phone started to ring with more enquiries and orders for Emily Love before Claire had even got the children off to school. Somehow she managed to get them all dressed and out of the house before nine o'clock.

After a quick cup of coffee in the hotel with Sally, Claire went home to try to tackle all the orders that were still pouring in as a result of the *Idyllic Homes* article.

As she drove through the village she passed the huge bonfire that had been built on the green for that night's fireworks party. This would be the first time William would have taken the children to it on his own. *In fact*, Claire thought, maybe it was the first time he had ever been to the village fireworks night at all; usually she was on her own performing a terrifying juggling act with sparklers, hot potatoes, scalding soup, and children in the dark. She shivered with anxiety at the thought of it. She hoped William would have the sense to keep everyone away from the bonfire; she'd advise him to avoid the soup and sparklers and keep Ben strapped into his pushchair at all times.

A pile of colourful envelopes welcomed her as she pushed open the front door. Claire made herself a cup of tea and sat down at the kitchen table and started opening her cards. The postcard had been hidden between two envelopes of vibrant pink; it slipped onto the table just as she opened a card from Zoë.

She hadn't heard from Zoë since the year they finished college and Zoë had told her she was making a big mistake marrying William. *Haven't you noticed his CD collection is in alphabetical order?* Claire felt a stab of guilt as she remembered that after sharing a flat with her for over two years, Zoë hadn't even been invited to their wedding. She read Zoë's brief note underneath her birthday greeting:

*Never can see fireworks without thinking of you, Girl!*
  *Saw the feature about your house in the magazine – what a lovely life you've made. What happened to William? No mention of him in the article so I presume you saw the light! I'm still in London. Let's meet up soon and we can catch up on all those long years since college. I've missed you,*

*Zoë xx*

Her delight at finding Zoë's card was almost immediately forgotten when she noticed the picture on the postcard in front of her; a regal woman in a gown of Virgin Mary blue was seated on a red and yellow sofa, the bowl of flowers behind the woman's head looking almost like a golden crown. Claire recognised it at once, *The Lady in Blue*; it had been her favourite painting in the Matisse exhibition. In her mind she had a vision of standing slightly apart from Stefan as she gazed at the large canvas; had he guessed how much she liked it?

With a quickening heart she turned the card over. Her vision seemed to blur for a moment then cleared and slowly she let her fingers trace the black ink writing, hardly daring to breathe as she read the short inscription:

*Dear Claire,*

*Happy Birthday,*

*Stefan x*

How did he know it was her birthday? She recalled a brief conversation in the garden, where she'd mentioned it was on fireworks night, could he really have remembered?

Claire sat looking at the postcard for a long time until Macavity's long, sleek body wound itself against her and brought her out of her reverie. She took her phone from her handbag, typed out a message, re-read it several times and finally pressed send.

*Thank you for my card. How are you? C*

He didn't reply.

She loaded the washing machine, unloaded the dishwasher, loaded the dryer, hoovered the floor. He still didn't reply. She couldn't concentrate on work. Sitting down at the table she picked up the postcard for the hundredth time that day. She picked up the phone and checked it one more time.

The kitchen door opened. Claire jumped.

'Did I frighten you?' said Sally, standing in the doorway with a purple-sequined beret pulled down hard on her head. 'I know I look scary.'

'Yes,' said Claire, flustered, putting the phone down on the table behind her. She laughed. 'I mean no, you didn't frighten me. Though you do look a bit odd in that hat.'

'Odd? You mean I look awful.' Sally sat down at the table and buried her face in her hands.

'It's just a hat,' said Claire, sitting down opposite her. 'Surely you can take it off?'

Sally looked up, her face miserable, and slowly took off the beret.

233

Claire gasped. 'Oh, Sally. What happened?'

'I know. It's awful, isn't it? How can I go out tonight?'

'It's not awful,' said Claire. 'It's just a bit . . .' She couldn't think of a tactful word.

'Clown-like?' Sally wailed.

'It's just a little bit . . . curly.' Sally's hair, which for the last three months had been styled into a lovely, silky, straight bob, was now in large ringlet curls tight to her head. She reminded Claire of Shirley Temple, though she didn't like to say so.

'What am I going to do?' wailed Sally. 'I wish I'd never gone to the hairdresser's.'

'Can't you wash it?'

'I have.' Sally pulled at one of the curls which pinged back into a tight blonde coil as soon as she let go. 'Twice. Now I think it's worse than when I left the salon!'

'Why did you . . . ?' Claire's voice trailed off as she tried to phrase the question.

'Why did I ask them to make me look like one of the Marx brothers?'

'Well, at least you haven't got a moustache and big cigar.'

'No, not Groucho,' said Sally exasperatedly. 'The other one with the curly hair; was it Chico or Harpo?'

'It's not that bad,' Claire tried to reassure her. 'But I still don't understand what happened. I only left you a few hours ago and your hair was . . .'

'Straight? Beautiful? Sophisticated?'

'Yes, all of those.'

'I went to the hairdresser's after I left you, so that I'd look gorgeous for tonight.'

'Yes, I know. You said you were going for a trim,' said Claire.

'The girl who cut it for me before had gone to collect her sick baby from nursery and so I had the only other person available – a man. Very handsome, very persuasive – very young. He said he could make it a bit wavy when he dried it.'

'Oh . . .'

'A bit like Kylie Minogue, he said – just a bit of a change for tonight. Well, you know, I've always wanted to look like Kylie. How could I resist? Then he suggested a light perm so that it could be a bit wavy for longer.'

'A light perm,' Claire repeated slowly.

'Yes,' said Sally, trying to smooth down her hair with her hands. 'It seemed like a good idea at the time, but I think he left the stuff on for too long. Turned out he's only a student – a first year on the hair and beauty course at my college, on work experience at the salon for the week. He didn't have a clue what he was doing.'

'What did he say when he saw how it turned out?' asked Claire.

'That the curls would drop and become waves later.'

'When later?' asked Claire.

'Over the next few weeks.'

Claire thought Sally's face was about to crumple into tears.

'What am I going to do? What will Josh say? He won't want to be seen in the student bar with a middle-aged poodle.'

Claire looked at her phone on the table. She longed to check her messages. She couldn't look at it in front of Sally. She knew she wouldn't approve.

'Right,' Claire said, standing up decisively and looking at her watch. 'We've got half an hour before we pick up the children. I'm going to get my straighteners and I'll see what I can do.'

Claire came back and plugged in the tongs.

Sally asked: 'What were you doing when I came in? Was I interrupting something?'

'Nothing much,' said Claire, starting to pull the metal straighteners through a curly strand of hair. 'Only opening some cards.'

'You looked very guilty.' Sally picked up the postcard. 'Ooo, Matisse – you went to see a Matisse exhibition with your photographer man, didn't you?' She turned it over.

Claire snatched it from her. The straighteners slipped.

'Ow!' cried Sally. 'You've burned my ear. Now I'll have clown hair and a red ear. Great!'

'Well, you shouldn't read other people's correspondence,' said Claire crossly. 'It's rude.'

She picked up the postcard and moved it to the dresser.

'Did I see you had your mobile in your hand when I came in?' Sally obviously wasn't going to let the subject drop.

'Maybe,' said Claire innocently.

'Were you sending a text?'

'No! Just remember who's holding the hot tongs,' said Claire.

'Thanking people for birthday cards?'

'No.'

Sally suddenly turned around and looked at Claire, her eyes narrowed.

'Careful!' said Claire, quickly moving the straighteners away.

'You're the one who needs to be careful,' Sally said pointedly.

The phone rang again and Claire quickly pushed it far away across the table with the end of the straighteners, into the pile of birthday cards. Sally tried to grab it and missed. They both laughed.

Sally looked suddenly serious. 'Don't play with fire, Claire.'

'*Voilà*!' said Claire, unplugging the tongs and ignoring Sally's warning. She didn't want to be having the Stefan conversation with her. She didn't want her friend's disapproval to spoil the euphoria that she had been feeling for the last few hours. 'I think your hair looks lovely now!' She had turned the curls into gently undulating waves around Sally's face. It really did look very pretty.

'Thank you,' said Sally, getting up and looking in the small mirror beside the door. 'What a relief. Now I can go to the ball!'

'But first we have five children to pick up from school, give tea, bath, put in pyjamas, get to bed . . .'

'And you've got a *husband* to feed.'

'OK,' Claire said. 'I get the message. Sending texts to other men is wrong.' She picked up the phone and put it in a drawer of the dresser.

'And dangerous,' Sally added. 'Don't do anything to jeopardise the girls' night out. Otherwise the wrath of the Oakwood Primary mothers will come down upon you and you'll be very sorry.' She picked up her car keys. 'Are you coming then, Birthday Babe?'

'You go on. I've just got to turn something off upstairs.'

As soon as Sally's car had disappeared down the driveway Claire retrieved the phone. No messages.

Maybe he had sent an email? Claire looked at the clock on the kitchen wall; she was going to be late anyway, a few more minutes wouldn't make any difference.

In the study she scrolled down the list of messages on the screen, her heart sinking as she realised there was no sign of Stefan's name. Just as she was about to shut the computer down another name on the list of emails caught her eye, the name of the beautiful department store in Central London that she dreamed of selling her work to. Emily Love Enquiry, the message title said. She opened it and read:

*We came across your lovely work in this month's* Idyllic Homes *magazine, it would look fabulous in our Home and Gift department, the quirky vintage feel is just what we're after for our last-minute Christmas Shopping promotion in the store. We'd like to order the following:*

*200 x Christmas stockings (as on the cover of* Idyllic Homes*)*

*100 x assorted aprons*

*150 x assorted shopping bags*

*50 x assorted tea cosies*

*50 x washing line peg bags*

*500 x lavender hearts*

*Delivery date December 1st.*

*Lance Monroe. Buying manager.*

Claire whooped out loud and jumped around the room as she imagined her work displayed in the shop's luxurious surroundings; sitting beside the work of other craftspeople and manufacturers she admired so much. She went back to the computer and read the message again, it was a lot of work to make, but it would be a lot

237

of money too. She did a little salsa dance. She read the message again – December 1st! That was less than a month away – how would she ever get the order done in that time – that would be a lot of sleep to do without, William would have to help her with the children at the weekends and his clean and tidy home would just have to go to hell until she'd finished.

Resigning herself to an entry in Mrs Wenham's *Tardy Parent* book, Claire typed a quick reply, her fingers tripping over the keys with excitement.

*Thank you for your order. December 1st is no problem.*

She smiled to herself; now this really was something worth celebrating tonight.

The children were so excited about the fireworks party that they wanted to get dressed for it hours before they had to go. It took Claire ages to find matching gloves and mittens and scarves and bobble hats.

'My scarf's too itchy,' whined Emily.

'My hat feels too tight,' complained Oliver.

Ben dropped a mitten in the toilet and they all refused to eat the lasagne Claire had made them for their tea.

'We'll have soup and baked potatoes at the bonfire,' said Emily. 'Like we always do.'

'Sparklers, sparklers, fizzy sparklers,' sang Ben.

At last they were all muffled up in clothes they were happy with and sitting in front of a DVD as they waited for William to come home.

Claire escaped upstairs to get ready. In her mind she had envisioned a leisurely soak in a bubble bath, maybe a scented candle on the side, a glass of wine, gentle music wafting in from the bedroom. In reality, it was a quick shower with just enough time to randomly slap on a bit of body lotion afterwards as a treat. She should have shaved her legs, she thought, but never mind, she'd be wearing tights.

She began combing tangles from her wet hair in front of the bathroom mirror, when Emily appeared.

'The DVD's finished and Oliver threw a cushion at Ben. He's crying.'

Claire went back downstairs, shivering in her damp towel, and tried to sort out a full-blown cushion fight that was going on between her sons.

William walked in. 'I've come home extra early so that you can go out.'

'Thank you. I really do appreciate it.' Claire gave him a hug and tried to sound as grateful as she could. 'Could you stay down here and sort out the children while I finish getting dressed? I've got some wonderful news to tell you.'

He followed her up the stairs. 'I think I'll have to go back to the office over the weekend to finish what I've been working on this week.'

'OK,' she said, sitting down at her dressing table.

'I've had a hell of a day,' he said, sitting down on the bed.

As Claire applied her make-up and quickly dried her hair – no time for glamorous styling now – William told her in great detail about the problems of his day. Claire put in as many *oh dear*s and *how awful*s as she could until he finished and she began to tell him her exiting news.

'I had a big order today.'

'I bought black paint to do the gate on the drive this weekend,' interrupted William.

'You know that gorgeous shop in London I've wanted to sell my work to for ages?'

'Have the children been swinging on the gate? It's very difficult to close – not that you ever bother to close it, anyone could walk right in and steal something.'

The sense of excitement leached out of Claire; she couldn't be bothered to tell him about the order now. She decided to wear her new underwear for the first time. She took the lacy bra and knickers from the back of her drawer and put them on; they felt luxuriously silky against her skin. William didn't seem to notice them.

She stepped into her new dress, smoothing down the green silk over her waist and hips. After she had put on her gold high heels, she stood in front of the mirror to see her reflection. She wished she still had the button necklace; it would have looked just right with the neckline of the dress.

'How do I look?' she asked, turning to face William.

'Fine,' he said, picking up a Screwfix catalogue from the bedside table and starting to read it.

'Just *fine?*'

'Very nice.'

'Do you think I look thirty-six?' Claire asked, looking back in the mirror at the fine lines around her eyes.

'Yes,' said William absent-mindedly.

'Do you think I'd look better if I went out with a paper bag over my head and wearing an old sack?'

'Mmm,' he said, engrossed in the magazine. 'There's a power drill here reduced to half price. It's much better than the one I've got.'

'You'd better get ready to go soon.'

'I'm not expected to come with you, am I?' William looked disgruntled. 'I thought it was just the coven on its own tonight?'

'No. I mean get ready to take the children to the fireworks party; they've been ready for hours.'

'Oh hell! I'd completely forgotten. Do you think they really want to go?'

Emily burst into their room. 'Sally's here to pick you up. She's got a big present for you.'

Claire picked up her handbag.

'You will look after the children, won't you?' she asked William. 'Don't let Ben have sparklers, and watch the soup, it's always piping hot, and you'll need to take charge of baked potatoes till they've cooled down.'

'OK,' he said, going back to the catalogue.

'Don't let any of them go anywhere near the bonfire.'

'Mmm.'

She kissed the top of his bent head. 'You'd better leave in five minutes; it's always a nightmare with the parking. I'll take a key. I don't know what time I'll be back.'

Claire left him on the bed.

'Tell Oliver to turn the telly off and get Ben ready to leave, will you, sweetheart?' she said to Emily as she ran down the stairs. 'Find everybody's wellington boots and then tell Daddy to get his coat on.'

'Wow, look at you,' said Sally, standing by the front door, holding a large glittery pink box. 'You look fantastic.'

'Thank you,' said Claire. 'You look beautiful too. Nice hair!' She took the box in her hands and shook it speculatively.

Sally started undoing the ribbon. 'Come on, I can't stand people who are into delayed gratification. Just open it now.' Inside was a beautiful red leather handbag that Claire had been admiring in the gallery where Sally still worked on Saturdays.

'You've mentioned how much you like it every time you come in,' said Sally. 'I thought you must be trying to give me a hint.'

'No,' laughed Claire. 'I never dreamed you'd get it for me. It cost a fortune.'

'Let's just say Anna hasn't paid me for the last few Saturdays. I just wanted to give you something for all the support you've given me since Gareth and I split up. You've been wonderful.' Sally moved forward to give Claire a hug.

'Don't make me cry,' Claire said, hugging her back. 'My mascara will smudge and I'll look like one of the living dead. Come on. Let's go out and have some fun.'

'Aren't you taking your new handbag?'

'Do you think it will go with my outfit?' asked Claire, looking down at her green dress and gold shoes. 'If I add red I might look a bit like a Christmas decoration.'

'You'll look like a lovely decoration – according to *Idyllic Homes* – it's nearly December after all. Come on, hurry up. I can hear a margarita calling to me from the bar.'

'It's a good job we're getting a taxi home,' said Claire, laughing as she started to transfer her things from her old bag to her new one.

Sally grabbed Claire's handbag from her and quickly tipped the contents into the red one. 'There, you're ready. Let's go.'

'Bye,' shouted Claire as she closed the front door behind her. The two women teetered down the gravel drive.

'Climb in, Madame,' said Sally, opening her car door and bowing like a chauffeur. 'I've managed to get most of the crushed Wotsits and half-sucked Haribo sweets off the seats.'

'You really know how to spoil a girl,' said Claire, getting in. She felt excited as Sally drove away, looking forward to a rare night out with her friends.

On the way to the restaurant she told Sally about her big order. Sally squealed with excitement, nearly crashing into a stone wall as she tried to give Claire a hug.

'Fantastic! This makes having your house photographed for Christmas in a heatwave and nearly leaving your husband for the photographer almost worth it!'

'It's such a lot of work. I'm worried I won't do it in the time.'

'I'll ask my Nana Needles, maybe she'd be able to do a bit of the sewing for you.'

'That's a great idea, if she'd give me a hand I'm sure I could do it.'

Fireworks were already exploding into the night sky as they approached the town and Claire felt as though they'd been laid on just for her.

In the hotel bar the sound of unleashed mothers filled the air – laughing and talking excitedly, unwinding from the pressures of children, jobs, and ill-tempered husbands. Everyone was dressed up and looking glamorous, out of the usual jeans and jumpers and office suits. Sequins and satin and lip gloss flashed and shimmered in the subdued lighting of the room.

They were escorted to a large table, in a corner away from the other diners. This proved to be a sensible decision on the part of the restaurant manager, as the noise level from their group rose steadily throughout the evening. The food was delicious – three courses and then a surprise birthday cake with sparkling candles.

'We wanted to get you a tower of fairy cakes from Patisserie Tremond,' said Sally as she sliced up the chocolate sponge. 'But it's closed down.'

'For good?'

'Yup, Trevor ran off with the man who has his fish van in the car park on a Friday and Edmond's moved to Spain to nurse his broken heart.'

'What a shame,' said Claire.

'It'll be a blessing for me,' laughed Sally, licking her chocolaty fingers. 'Imagine what it's been like being on a diet and knowing that all those huge meringues and pecan slices were waiting for me just down the road while I'd be trying to sort out displays and sell things in the gallery! I used to be drooling all over the hand-made jewellery and majolica dishes at the thought of all those delicious cakes.'

'It's such a lovely building,' said another mother. 'I've heard it's like a Tardis inside, a warren of little rooms and rickety stairs.'

Someone else told a funny story about an Abba night they'd been to in Trevor and Edmond's flat above the patisserie, and that led to singing and the singing led to the restaurant manager asking them to quieten down.

As Claire talked and laughed and ate and drank, she thought of Stefan – a constant presence in her mind, a precious secret from them all. Why had he suddenly got back in touch? What did the birthday postcard mean? Would she get an answer to her text? She longed to tell him about her big order; she knew he'd be so pleased for her. She longed to see Stefan again, so much it almost hurt. She had to force herself not to look at her phone throughout the meal.

In the ladies toilet, Claire applied a new coat of lipstick in the mirror. If she had a text from Stefan it would make it the most wonderful birthday ever – there was just time to have a quick look at her phone while she was on her own. As she started to rummage in the depths of her new handbag, Sally emerged, swaying, from a cubicle.

'Surely a gorgeous girl like you doesn't need any more make-up on.' She pulled Claire's arm. 'Come on, let's see if that grumpy manager will turn the music up and let us have a dance.'

# Chapter Twenty-seven

*'Oak floorboards, quarry tiles and slate flagstones
create a naturally rustic feel around the house.'*

When the taxi drew up outside the house it was shrouded in darkness. Sally had already got out in the village, accompanied by Josh, who had somehow materialised in the restaurant at the end of the evening. The taxi waited while Claire scrunched across the frosty gravel on the drive and unlocked the front door. As she opened it, she turned and waved, and the taxi pulled away.

The hall was inky dark. Claire fumbled for the light switch on the wall and turned it on. As the hallway lit up she jumped.

William was sitting on the stairs in front of her.

'What are you doing? You gave me a fright,' she said, putting down her handbag. 'How were the fireworks?' He stared directly at her but didn't speak. She noticed an empty whisky tumbler at his feet and then she saw the mobile phone in his hand. Her phone.

'Did you forget something?' William's words slurred slightly. He was drunk. She stepped forward to take the phone, but he snatched it back.

'*Finders keepers* we used to say at school,' he said and laughed. 'I found it on the floor. I was just locking up to go to bed when I heard it making a noise. I couldn't work out where it was at first but then I looked down and there it was, underneath the console table.'

She remembered Sally emptying the contents of her bag into

245

her new red one – her phone must have fallen on the floor in the rush.

Claire looked at him silently. She could hardly bear to hear what was coming next.

'I thought it might be important,' William continued. 'I thought it might be you trying to get through, maybe the taxi hadn't come, and maybe you needed a lift home. But no, it was a text. From someone else.'

Claire felt frozen to the spot.

'I was curious. Who would send you a text at ten o'clock on a Friday night? A special offer from your provider? Your mother needing to be rescued from that man she's run off with?' He stood up and slowly swayed towards her. 'No, those would be far too mundane, too hum-drum, too boring for my lovely wife. Do you want to see what it said?'

Claire shook her head mutely.

'Do you want to see it, Claire?' He thrust the phone in front of her face, too close to read it properly. The words *miss* and *want* and *must* were all she managed to make out.

'And I've seen all the other texts he sent,' said William. He didn't take his eyes from Claire. She hadn't deleted any of them; they went all the way back to the summer, all the way back to the beginning.

'Oh, God,' she said, stepping back, sinking down against the wall. She covered her face with her hands.

'What's going on?' William sounded unnervingly calm, almost as if he was talking to a child who'd scribbled on the furniture or thrown their food across the table.

'Who is he?' She heard the crack in his voice.

'I can't tell you,' she said, looking up. Their eyes met.

'I would very much like you to tell me, Claire.' She could tell he was trying very hard to keep control. 'S! It just says S on your contacts list and S at the end of the texts.' His voice rose. 'S for what? Is it a Steve, Sean, Simon? I can't think. I can't think of anyone we know whose name begins with S. What about Sally? Is it Sally?'

246

Claire laughed in disbelief, though inside all she felt was fear.

'Don't laugh at me!' William's voice was loud now.

'I'm sorry. It's not Sally.' She took a deep breath. 'The texts are from Stefan. The man who photographed the house for the magazine.'

William sat down again. 'The photographer,' he said, running his hands through his hair. 'The bloody photographer who photographed my house for an article that doesn't even mention me? I should have known. I should have worked that out!'

'It's not how it seems,' said Claire quietly.

'I bet it's not. I'm sure it's much worse.' It was William's turn to laugh now. 'You've been committing adultery with a man who photographed your lovely bloody life, the life I made for you. How many years of hard work, all hours of the day and night working on this place for you? And this is how you repay me?' He stood up. 'Well, thank you very bloody much.'

Claire put her hands to her face and shook her head.

'I'm sorry, William. I haven't even seen him since the summer.'

'I don't believe you,' he said, shaking the phone at her. He was shouting now. 'It sounds like you've been having some seedy little affair with a second-rate photographer behind my back for months.'

He threw the phone down on the floor and its plastic casing flew apart.

'Making a fool of me. Humiliating me. Contaminating everything we've ever had with your sordid, disgusting behaviour.'

He got up and stamped hard onto the pieces of her phone, grinding them with his foot and kicking the debris across the floor. Taking a step towards her he leant forward, his face inches from her own.

'Did you ever think about the children?'

She could smell the whisky on his breath.

'Did you ever think about our poor children when you were doing God-knows-what with him?' He leant in closer and hissed slowly in her ear. 'Did you ever think of me and what I've done for you? You selfish bitch.'

He moved back slightly and for a second Claire thought he was going to hit her, but instead he put his head in his hands and started to cry – huge sobs that shook his whole body.

'Just tell me why.' He looked up at her, his voice thick with tears. 'How could you do this to me? After everything we've been through, years of hard work on this house, losing Jack – you weren't the only one who grieved over him. You weren't the only one who felt pain.'

Claire knew she should do something, comfort him, put her arms around him, but she was unable to move.

'I didn't have an affair.'

'No? Then why was he sending you texts like that?'

'I only saw him a few times. I haven't had anything to do with him for months.' She kept looking at the floor; the uneven lines and cracks of the slate were like mountain ranges against a stormy sky. 'I didn't sleep with him.'

William suddenly sat back down, his head falling forward onto to his knees. It was the position of a small, frightened child. His voice shook. 'Do you want to leave me?'

'I don't know.'

She saw his shoulders shake with another huge sob.

'Do you love me?' he asked quietly.

Claire moved towards him and put her arms around him gently, rocking him as though he were one of the children. She kissed his hair and with one hand she lifted his head from his knees and kissed his wet face. 'I'm so sorry.'

'Don't do this to me.' His eyes pleaded with her.

'I can't think,' said Claire, tears beginning to fall from her own eyes. 'I can't think what I want.'

'I phoned him,' William said, still looking at her. 'I phoned him up when I saw the messages.'

'What did you say?'

'I don't want to tell you what I said.'

'OK.' At that moment, she didn't want to know.

'I can't believe you could do this,' he said, after they had been silent for a while. 'I thought I could trust you. I thought you were happy. Happy with all this.' His hand gestured around the room. 'I thought I'd made you the home you wanted. It has all been for you, Claire.'

'You've felt so detached for so long,' she said, sitting down beside him, her hand still touching his bent head. 'As soon as you come home from work there's always something that you're doing at home, on the house, making plans for the next thing you want to do. Last summer it was all about the summer house. Now you're busy making plans for the extension over the kitchen. It never stops. I only wanted us to be together, to be a family together. I don't care about new guest rooms or summer houses. I just want a house to live in, not some eternal project. I thought you didn't really care about me any more.'

William shook his head. 'You know how busy it is at work at the moment,' he said. 'That's why I have to work so late. I thought you understood that.'

'You're not listening,' Claire sighed. 'I'm not talking about your job. I'm talking about when you're here, when you're at home. You're obsessed with this house.'

A movement above them caught Claire's eye. Oliver and Emily stood at the top of the stairs looking down at their parents on the hall floor.

'What's the matter?' asked Oliver.

'What's wrong with Dad?' Emily sounded frightened.

'He's fine,' said Claire, getting up. 'Don't worry, everything's fine.'

She came up the stairs and gave them each a hug.

'Back into your beds now.'

Looking down, she saw that William still sat crouched on the floor, his head on his knees, oblivious to Emily and Oliver.

'Come on,' she said to the children. 'Don't wake up Ben.'

She got them back into bed. By the time she got back downstairs, William had disappeared from the hallway.

Claire went into the kitchen. He was sitting in the dark at the table, the whisky bottle and a full glass beside him. When she turned on the light, she could see the bottle was three-quarters empty; he must have drunk a lot of it before she came home. William gulped the whisky down in one go.

'Does that help?'

'Yes,' he said, and got up and retched into the sink. Claire turned on the kettle. William was sitting down again, sobbing into his hands.

'I think you need to go to bed now,' she said. 'We can talk in the morning. Everything will seem clearer in the morning.' She doubted this was true.

She helped him get up. He stumbled against the Aga and she steadied him and guided him, still sobbing, towards the stairs. He was too drunk to manage them, so she led him into the living room to lie down on the sofa.

'Just leave me alone,' he mumbled thickly as she sat down beside him. 'I don't want to look at you. I don't want to be with you. I hate you.'

Claire winced and left him on his own.

She made a cup of tea and sat at the kitchen table with it, trying to think. She couldn't believe that this had happened; could hardly bear to remember the texts William must have read. She knew how stupid she had been not to delete them, but she also knew why she hadn't.

'Stupid, stupid, stupid,' she said out loud. She had tried so hard not to look at her phone all evening that she'd never thought to check that she actually had it with her. 'Stupid,' she said out loud again; so stupid for making this whole mess in the first place.

She wondered what William had said to Stefan on the phone. Pressing her aching eyes with her fingers, she thought about Stefan. What would he be thinking now?

William was asleep when Claire went back into the living room. He lay along the length of the sofa, a loose arm hanging down to the floor. In the fireplace the flames cast shifting shadows onto his open-mouthed, unconscious face. Claire picked up a

250

wool throw from an armchair and put it over him. For a while she stood looking down at him, watching his chest move slowly up and down with each breath he took. She was numb and unable to move, unable to think what to do next. The grandfather clock in the hall struck three, the last chime echoing in Claire's ears as the house became silent once more.

Suddenly she knew that she must see Stefan as soon as possible, talk to him and ask him how he really felt. What did he want to do? She wished she knew what his text had said; it must have been something to make William suspicious enough to check back through her other texts.

Still looking at her sleeping husband, she quickly formed a plan in her head. She would drive to London. She could be there by dawn. But what about the children? William would be in no fit state to look after them when he woke up. Claire phoned Sally to see if she could come and take the children home with her in the morning. Her friend didn't answer; no doubt busy entertaining Josh. She would leave a note through her door and ask her to come round as soon as she woke up. In the kitchen she quickly wrote the note.

As she folded it in half she glanced at the *Idyllic Homes* magazine on the table beside her. Stefan's photograph of their decorated fireplace seemed to shine out at her from the cover. The scene looked fake and contrived. *Not such an idyllic home now*, she thought.

She crept upstairs and checked the children one by one. She longed to bend down to stroke their sleeping faces, but dared not risk waking them. She wondered what she was doing. Was she really going to tear their lives apart?

Glancing at William still sleeping heavily beside the dying embers of the fire, Claire quietly left the house.

# Chapter Twenty-eight

*'The family gather around the glowing fire to exchange presents
and wish each other a Happy Christmas.'*

Ice sparkled in the car's headlights as Claire drove carefully down
the steep hill to Sally's house. It was in darkness as she slipped the
note through the brass letterbox.

The larger roads had been gritted the night before and Claire
drove faster as she passed the town and headed for the motorway.
All she could think about was getting to Stefan, seeing him again.
She was nervous. Her heart thumping in her chest, she felt sick
with anticipation, her stomach tight beneath her seatbelt. She took
a deep breath, trying to calm down and control her nerves.

Suddenly she wondered if she was over the alcohol limit for
driving; it was only a few hours since she had left the restaurant.
Claire slowed down; maybe she should stop. A sign to the first
service station on the motorway loomed up in front of her. Coffee.
She needed strong coffee, food. And cigarettes.

Dawn started to spread towards her as she began to drive again. By
the time she approached the edge of London it was nearly light. A
grey sky gradually turned blue.

The traffic increased as Claire passed endless miles of low industrial units and out-of-town shops. Gradually Lego-like estates
of houses appeared, then pebble-dashed terraces and tall, dreary
tower blocks, giving way to the glass towers of city offices and

hotels. Claire had remembered Stefan's address by heart after she had sent him the apron for his sister; like a lovesick teenager she had even looked it up on a map. When she hit the South Circular she headed north, eventually turning into a high street lined with stalls setting up for a Saturday-morning market.

Everything looked bright and busy in the early-morning sun – primary colours, bold patterns, graffiti, music blaring and people everywhere. It was so different from the soft muted tones and quiet sounds of Claire's country life. Once she had been part of all this colour and pattern and noise. Now it seemed so strange and unfamiliar to her.

She knew she was getting close. She turned off the main street into a square of brown-bricked Victorian houses, pulled over and parked. This was near enough for her to collect her nerves and work out exactly where she was going. Turning on her satnav she found it was only a few streets away.

Back in the car she wished she still had her mobile phone and could call Sally to make sure that the children were all right. She glanced around for a phone box. Nothing. She would phone from Stefan's.

Claire drove off again, slowly turning down a succession of roads until she found Stefan's street. It was quiet. A hotchpotch of Victorian houses, a mixture of terraced and detached, stood on pavements lined with pollarded lime trees. It seemed too staid and solid for Stefan – too dull. Just as she was about to check the street name in the A–Z she saw the block of Art Deco flats, startlingly white against the blue winter sky. It stood apart from the other buildings, a strip of smooth green lawn in front. Huge metal-framed windows curved elegantly around each side of the building with long balconies climbing up above each other to the fifth floor. She knew this was it even before she saw the large silver number on a set of double doors and the beautiful convertible parked just up the road.

Claire found a gap between two cars directly opposite the building and managed to squeeze the cumbersome people carrier into it. She knew Stefan lived on the ground floor, he had told her that. The ground-floor window on the left looked dark and lifeless behind the sweep of shining glass. The window on the right was shrouded in heavy curtains, still drawn. Claire looked at her watch. Eight o'clock. Still early on a Saturday morning if you didn't have children to wake you up.

The double doors swung open and a man wearing Lycra and mirrored sunglasses came out pulling a bike alongside him. As he bumped it down the short flight of steps, he reminded Claire of an ant dragging a heavy object, concentrating hard on its challenging task. Once on the road the man cycled away and everything was quiet and still again. Claire took a deep breath. This was it; she couldn't sit here all day. She reached for the door handle of the car and stopped. She didn't even know if Stefan would be there; he could have sent his text from anywhere. For all she knew he could be away working, photographing seafront homes in California or ice houses in Greenland. She hadn't even thought about what she was going to say to him. Nothing she could think of sounded right. All she wanted to do was to feel his arms around her once more, touch him and be safe in his embrace again. He would know what to do. She felt sure he would.

She opened the car door and started to get out. Something made her glance across at the right-hand window. A movement – at first just slight. The curtains swayed then separated to leave a gap of a few feet. Claire hesitated and got back in the car. A figure appeared in the window. It was a woman, tall and thin, with long curls of tangled dark hair falling over her shoulders. She was wearing a large white T-shirt much too big for her, pale legs bare below it. She stood with her slender arms wrapped around herself as if she was cold. Claire realised that this couldn't be Stefan's flat. His must be the empty-looking flat on the other side of the front door, or maybe there were more flats at the back.

She watched the figure for a few seconds. The woman was very still. She looked deep in thought. Another figure moved towards her from the depths of the room. A man. He gently touched her shoulder and she turned into his opened arms. He hugged her, stroked her long hair. He was tall and dark too. He glanced up briefly before taking the woman's face in his hands and tenderly kissing her cheek.

Claire felt a stab of pain go through her as she realised that the man was Stefan. He was with another woman – embracing another woman – someone he was clearly intimate with. Someone he must have spent the night with. Claire looked away, sick with hurt and confusion. Why had he sent the card? What had his text actually said? When Claire looked back, the figures at the window were gone; only an empty gap between the curtains was left where they had stood.

Claire desperately hoped she had been wrong. Maybe she had imagined it? Could she be in the middle of a dream? In a minute she would wake up, in bed, William asleep beside her. Everything would return to normal. Maybe there had been no magazine, no photographer, no other man and she could go back to being the obedient wife and mother that she had been before. The good wife and mother who didn't leave her children in the middle of the night and didn't dream of being in the arms of another man; who didn't smoke and send adulterous texts. The good wife who didn't let herself get into situations where she felt her life was falling apart. But Claire knew it wasn't a dream. Stefan did exist and it had been him with a woman at the window.

She didn't know what to do. She wanted to cross the road, ring his doorbell, and confront him, but something inside her kept her sitting in the car. She felt too shocked to move, too humiliated. Inside, her hopes and fantasies were collapsing painfully into nothing. She sat motionless, her hands limp in her lap, her eyes still fixed on the dark gap between the curtains. She didn't know how long she sat like that. The road started to come to life around her. People jogged and rollerbladed, parents pushed prams, smartly dressed men and women hurried past – all oblivious to her. The bright sunshine seemed to make things worse, belying her mood of despair and hopelessness.

Just as she began to think about summoning the strength to drive away, the front doors of the flats swung open and Stefan and the woman appeared. Wrapped up in winter coats and long scarves, they began walking down the steps towards Claire's car. In panic, she slid down in her seat. With one hand she reached down onto the floor, scrabbling for any form of camouflage. Finding a red knitted hat of Oliver's she put it on, pulling it down hard, until she could only just see the road outside. She pushed back her hair and put on a pair of old sunglasses she found in the glove box. She silently prayed they wouldn't see her and that Stefan wouldn't recognise her car, but he never even glanced in her direction.

At the bottom of the steps Stefan put his arm around the woman and they turned and walked down the street. Claire saw him say something to her, his mouth close to her ear. She laughed affectionately and pushed him with her elbow. He seemed to squeeze her harder and she laughed again. Stefan turned his face towards the woman, and from his profile Claire could see he was smiling, and then all she could see were their backs, their coats swinging out behind them as they walked away and disappeared from view.

Claire sat up and took off the sunglasses. Anger started to rise inside her. How could she have been so stupid? She had meant nothing to him. She had only been a game to him. What a fool she had been to have ever thought it could have been anything else. She wondered how long he had been with the woman. They looked close, as if they had been a couple for some time. Maybe they had been together in the summer, even when Claire had first met him. Maybe they had been together for years. Maybe they were married. Maybe it was the woman from Australia. Claire felt sorry for her. She was probably completely unaware of how Stefan behaved; how he was with other women. He obviously didn't care about the consequences of his actions, for all his virtuous talk last summer. He had just destroyed her marriage, her family, her children's happiness, her life – yet he could walk away with someone else, oblivious to the pain he'd caused. Claire hit the steering wheel hard and she found herself crying, tears pouring down her face, dripping down her neck and onto the green silk dress she was still wearing from her birthday meal. She realised she hadn't even taken off her coat from the time she'd left the restaurant the night before.

Claire jumped at a sudden loud tap on the passenger-side window. She looked up to see a cross-faced elderly man wearing a tweed jacket and spotted blue cravat. Claire turned on the ignition and pushed the button to open the window.

'This is permit parking only,' he said, a grey moustache twitching above his thin lips. 'Have you not seen the signs?' He jabbed a finger towards a small sign on a pole just up the street.

'Oh,' she said, sniffing. 'Sorry, I didn't realise.'

'You seem to think you can just sit here for hours and it won't matter,' went on the man. 'Other people could be trying to park.'

'Sorry.' She reached up to brush the tears away and realised she was still wearing Oliver's hat. She whipped it off quickly and used it to wipe her eyes. The damp wool stung her face. She felt ridiculous.

'I've been watching you,' said the man, his voice raised. He seemed oblivious to Claire's distress. 'Sitting there, no permit visible. I'm sure you've been there for more than an hour. What about the proper residents? You could be prosecuted. I've every right to call the authorities, you know. You should be fined.'

'Oh, shut up,' said Claire suddenly and shut the window. The man was shouting at her, but she couldn't hear his words. She started the car and pulled away as quickly as she could.

As she looked in her rear-view mirror she could see the man still standing on the pavement, one hand cupped to his mouth. Two teenage girls walked past and stared at him and then at Claire's car as she manoeuvred over the series of speed bumps faster than she should have.

She had stopped crying by the time she was driving on the motorway. Her head seemed clearer, her pain already less, or at least more manageable. Now she knew the truth. At least she knew there was no point in hoping any more. Stefan wasn't worth it. He had never been worth it. She had made a terrible mistake, she only had herself to blame, and now it was up to her to try to sort out the mess she had made. The car clock said it was still only ten o'clock. This time yesterday she had been coming home to find the postcard. She couldn't believe that so much could happen in twenty-four hours.

She had a huge desire to be at home, to be sitting in her sunny kitchen with a cup of tea, to be with her children. She wanted to see William, to try and sort things out. To say she was so sorry.

The miles passed quickly but Claire longed for them to pass faster. William would be hungover she was sure, maybe still asleep. Would he ever forgive her? Maybe this was the chance they needed to start really communicating with each other. Maybe William would begin to understand what she had been trying to say about the house and his obsession with it. They could both try harder, try to change things, make things better.

The country roads were still white with a thick hoarfrost as she drove towards the village. The branches on the trees glittered around her like a Christmas card scene.

As she approached, a thin mist fell, turning the sun into a shrouded hazy ball. The mist grew thicker as she passed Sally's house, last night's bonfire was still smouldering on the village green, adding to the haze. Claire decided to go home before picking up the children so that she could talk to William without the threat of interruptions. She needed to see him as soon as possible.

As she turned the corner to start the climb up the hill she saw something out of place. At first she thought it was a cloud, a long black cloud, but then she realised that clouds were rarely vertical. Instead, a plume of thick black smoke stretched high into the sky and a spike of bright orange shot up through it, followed by another. Claire's heart clenched. Fear took over and she blindly accelerated upwards, desperately hoping it was just a farmer in a nearby field burning tyres.

By the time she was halfway up the hill she knew it was her home.

Flames leapt up from the thatched roof and burst out of the windows as they shattered. Smoke rolled out behind the flames and poured down the walls. Most of the village seemed to be gathered at the end of Claire's drive and three fire engines filled the front garden. Men in yellow uniforms ran around the house pointing hoses in all directions. The crowd beside the drive parted as Claire's car screeched to a halt.

As she opened the door, heat, smoke and noise hit her. Loud bangs and cracks like gunshots exploded out of the burning building and she could feel the intense heat on her face as she almost fell out of the car in her panic.

She could hear someone shouting hysterically, 'The children, the children, where are the children?' and then she realised it was her own voice.

Looking around she saw only horror and pity on her neighbours' faces. A fireman appeared and started to move back the throng of people.

'Is this your house?' he asked Claire.

'My children are in there,' Claire screamed above the noise. She tried to push him towards the house. 'Get them out! You've got to get them out!'

'It's all right,' he said, taking her gently by the arm. 'We've got them safe. They're up here.' He led her to the orchard where she could see Oliver and Emily huddled, frightened and shaking, next to Sally, who was holding a howling Ben. Beside her stood Josh, looking horrified, and on Sally's other side a soot-blackened Gareth, with his arms around the boys, who stood frozen and un-moving for once. They all looked grey as they stared at the burning scene.

With a surge of relief, Claire ran to them.

'Thank God. Thank God,' she said over and over again. She

gathered Emily and Oliver into her arms'and clung to them. They were all crying, including Sally and Gareth. She took Ben from Sally and hugged him, burying her face into his neck to try to find the smell of him she loved so much. All she could smell was smoke.

'You've got this chap here to thank for them being safe,' the fireman said, pointing with his thumb at Gareth. 'He saw them at an upstairs window and he somehow got them down. I can't think how – it's quite a drop. Climbed up the rosebush onto the porch, he said.'

'I didn't find your note till it was too late,' said Sally through her tears. 'I only found it when I came to the front door when I heard the fire engines go by. I don't know what would have happened if Gareth hadn't been driving past to bring the boys home. They'd been so dreadful with him that he decided to bring them back early.'

Claire's stomach heaved; she fought back the urge to be sick. She tried to force the thought of what could have happened into the back of her mind. It was too much to take in. The bad dream had turned into a nightmare now. When would she wake up? All she wanted to do was wake up.

She knew she'd brought this about herself, by her own selfish behaviour. How could she have left the children?

'Is Dad with you?' Emily shouted to her above the noise.

'William?' she said, frantically looking around her. 'Where's William? Have you seen him?'

Sally shook her head. 'We thought he was with you.'

Oliver lifted his face from the depths of Claire's coat.

'I couldn't find you, Mum,' he said. 'The smoke alarm was going off. It woke us up. I shouted and shouted. We looked in your bedroom but you weren't there. I thought Dad was with you. I thought you'd both gone out.'

'I wouldn't have left you on your own.' Claire could hardly bear to think of how the children must have felt, thinking they had been abandoned in a burning house. Nausea swept over her again with the realisation that William must still be inside. Her head swam, and she clung harder on to the children to stop herself from falling.

'Then Dad is still in there?' Oliver cried out. He tried to break away from Claire, as if to run towards the burning building. Sally held on to him. He struggled wildly, but Sally's arms were strong.

'There's someone in the building,' the fireman spoke urgently into his walkie-talkie.

'OK. We're going in,' came the crackled reply.

'The fire was well established by the time we got here,' the fireman said. 'We think it must have started on the ground floor. We had no idea anyone was still in there.'

'Dad!' Oliver was screaming again and again. 'Dad, Dad!'

Emily started screaming his name too: 'Daddy, Daddy!' Their cries cut through Claire like knives. She couldn't bear it.

'I know where he is,' she said. 'I'm going to get him out.' She kicked off her gold high heels, thrust Ben into the fireman's arms, and started to run.

'Claire, no!' Sally tried to grab her but she pulled away.

'Hey!' the fireman shouted behind her.

Suddenly everything was silent; smoky air rushed past her. She found herself moving across the grass towards the house, her legs running faster than they ever had. Heat seemed to swallow her up. The burning house sucked her inside and then it was dark – pitch black. Hot, thick, poisonous air was all around her. She pulled her coat up over her mouth as she pushed through splintered shards of glass left in the French windows. She knew her feet were being cut but she felt no pain. Orange lights glowed and shifted in the darkness. It was very quiet. Claire dropped to her knees, one hand over her mouth. She daren't take a breath. Her eyes burned and she closed them tightly, inching forward trying to get her bearings. How far to the sofa? Surely not so far? Her hand touched something soft on the floor, she groped out further. It was an arm, then a hand. It must be William. She managed to get to her feet and started to pull. He was heavy; much heavier than she had expected.

'Come on,' she said inside her head. 'You're not going to do this to me, William. You're getting out. I'm getting you out.' She heaved and he moved an inch or two in her direction.

'That's it,' she thought. 'You're coming with me. I'll not let you go like this.' She heaved again.

A huge blast broke the silence, a bright white flash lighting up the darkness. In an instant she was surrounded by crashing and cracking. Tiny hot red stars fell like confetti around her and then larger chunks of burning timber started cascading down on top of her. She inched William towards her again and then a colossal bang came from above. The ceiling was falling. Through squinted eyes she saw flames encircling her arm. Her coat was on fire. She heaved again and was filled with an overwhelming energy and strength.

She was at the door and dragging William's inert body over the threshold when a huge crash seemed to shake the entire structure of the house. She felt herself being pulled from behind. She wasn't holding William's arm any more, she was gliding weightless, floating above the ground, flying over the burning house, up above the children, the crowds, and fire engines above the smoke and flames. A man was talking to her, touching her face softly.

'Stefan,' she said and opened her eyes.

'No, I'm Mike. I'm a paramedic,' the man said. 'I'm going to try to get you into the ambulance now.'

Claire looked around. She was lying on the grass, her arm wrapped in something wet and cold. She tried to take a breath and immediately started coughing.

'Try to relax,' the man said. 'You've inhaled a lot of smoke.' He put a mask over her face.

'That was quite some stunt you pulled.' The fireman from before was squatting down beside her. 'I never expected you to do that. One minute you were beside me, the next I had a baby in my arms and you were in there.' He pointed in the direction of what had been the house. The thatched roof was completely gone, burning timbers caved into a gaping hole where the roof had been. 'I never had such a shock in my life. Anyway, you got him out. He's alive.' He smiled at her. 'But promise you'll never try anything like that again. Leave it to the professionals next time.' He looked down kindly at her.

Claire tried to say she hoped there would never be a next time but she was overwhelmed with another bout of coughing.

'Your husband's in the ambulance,' the paramedic said. 'He's in a bad way. We'll get him to the hospital and find out what the damage is.'

Claire tried to get up.

'Don't worry,' said the paramedic soothingly. 'We'll get you in there too. You can go to the hospital together.'

'You must really love him to have risked your life like that,' said the fireman, still smiling down at her. 'Good luck to both of you.' He got up and walked away.

In the ambulance, Claire sat beside William. The oxygen mask looked huge clamped over his smoke-blackened face. She didn't dare look out of the back window as they started to move slowly away down the hill. She couldn't stop shaking; her teeth chattered together, her arm throbbed.

William groaned and his hand pulled at the mask. Claire looked anxiously at the paramedic, but he was busy with a piece of apparatus.

'Don't worry,' said Claire, stroking William's arm. 'You're safe. The children are safe. They're going to Sally's house now.'

William managed to pull off the mask. His eyes opened; they looked wild and shining. He stared at her as if he didn't recognise her.

'It's all right,' she said. 'We'll be at the hospital soon. There was a fire in the house but everyone's all right.'

'The magazine,' he wheezed. 'I wanted to burn the magazine, to burn that article. It went up so quickly. Too much paraffin. Everything started to catch fire.' He took a deep rasping breath. 'I didn't care. I wanted to get rid of it all. I didn't want any of it any more.' He started to cough and splutter alarmingly. The paramedic got up and put the mask back on. William's eyes closed as he lost consciousness again.

Claire sat numb with shock. William had started the fire. William had destroyed their home – the home he loved. He could have killed the children.

It was all her fault.

# Chapter Twenty-nine

*'Original features and modern luxuries . . .'*

William was in intensive care; linked up to monitors and kept sedated, to stop him from moving; he looked older, smaller, as though the fire had wizened him up. The doctors said his lungs were damaged but they'd probably make a reasonable recovery in time, the most serious injury was to his back. The lintel from the doorway had fallen across him and fractured his spine. A doctor patiently explained to Claire, in detail that her horror-numbed brain found hard to follow, that with careful care, a back brace, rest, and physiotherapy he should be able to recover fully.

'But he could be paralysed?' Claire realised her hands were shaking in her lap and her heart was beating so fast she was sure the doctor could hear it.

'That would be the worst-case scenario. Let's try to think positively.'

Claire's arm was badly burned and her feet had been cut by splinters of glass from the French windows. She had to have twenty-two shards extracted under local anaesthetic. The doctors gave her painkillers for her arm and feet and tranquilisers for her tears and distress. She lay between the cold hospital sheets and tried to make sense of the series of hazy, horrific images that swam through her mind. Drifting in and out of a medicated sleep, she woke from nightmares only to realise that reality was just as bad.

The children had stayed with Sally. William's mother came and offered to take them home with her but they cried and begged to stay where they were. William's mother seemed relieved to have the time to stay at her son's bedside instead of taking care of three traumatised grandchildren.

'He'll be heartbroken, of course,' she said, as she stood beside Claire's hospital bed on a cursory visit to her daughter-in-law. 'He put everything into that house and now it's all gone.' She took a tissue from inside her cardigan pocket and sniffed loudly.

'He's still got his family,' Claire tried to say. 'He's lucky . . .'

'One careless act and his life destroyed,' her mother-in-law interrupted. 'You must have left the iron on or let something burn on top of the Aga. I expect it's easy to forget when you're struggling to look after so many children.'

Claire opened her mouth to protest but felt too weak. Anyway, the truth was so much worse and she was more culpable than if she had simply made a domestic slip.

Elizabeth and Brian arrived from France while Claire was still in hospital. Her mother held her hand and stroked her hair as if Claire was a little girl again. It made her feel guilty. She knew she didn't deserve sympathy or kindness.

Brian went to the house and found Macavity, frightened and hungry, hiding in the old wood shed. He left him there but took food and a box of blankets for him to sleep in.

'It's not a pretty sight up there,' Claire overheard him say to her mother when they thought she was asleep. 'There's not much left. The roof is gone and half of it is just a burned-out shell.'

'Come and stay with us in France until you sort yourselves out,' said her mother when Claire opened her eyes. 'We've room for all of you.'

Claire shook her head. She needed to be close to William, even though he turned away whenever she approached the hospital bed where he lay linked up to oxygen by plastic tubes.

*

266

After two blurred days the doctor told her she could go home. Home? She smiled and thanked him, but she knew she no longer had a home to go back to.

Claire swapped her hospital bed for Sally's spare one and held Oliver, Emily, and Ben tightly to her through the long, awful nights. She couldn't sleep for fear of nightmares, but the thoughts that filled her head as the children breathed quietly beside her were just as horrifying in themselves. Guilt, horror, fear of what could have happened, what still might happen to William if his spine didn't heal — it all seemed to pin her down like a heavy weight, crushing her, making her feel sick. When she closed her eyes she could see the fire, the burning house, the terror on the children's faces. She could still feel the heat on her face. The smell of smoke was inescapable, as if the thick, black, acrid air had got inside her permanently. She couldn't bear the dark and kept the bedside lamp on all through the endless nights.

She wouldn't let herself think of Stefan or the texts or re-member her early-morning drive to London or the woman with the long dark hair. She pushed the memories away into a painful corner of her mind.

Instead of school the children sat on Sally's sofa watching day-time television and wearing borrowed clothes. They were quiet; too quiet. Oliver and Emily's eyes looked empty and hollow, dark shadows underneath them. Claire couldn't bear to think of the terror they must have felt as they tried to get out of the burning house. They didn't talk about what had happened, though every now and then Emily would remember a toy or book or piece of clothing that was lost forever and start to cry and Oliver asked Claire repeatedly what they were going to do. Ben was confused; he wanted to go home. He clung to Claire, following her, climb-ing on her, crying when she disappeared from sight.

Gareth took the boys to stay with him in the room he rented above a newsagent's in town so that the cottage wouldn't be too crowded. Every day he came to check that Claire and the children were all right. He seemed nearly as traumatised as they were. It was as though he needed to reassure himself that the children were really there, that he really had succeeded in getting them out of the burning house.

Sally didn't ask too many questions about what had happened after their night out. Every day she drove her to the surgery to have the dressings on her cuts and burns re-dressed and to the hospital to visit William; conscious now, he refused to talk to Claire, or hold her hand or look at her. Claire had given Sally a brief outline of the events following her return from the restaurant, omitting to mention what William had told her in the ambulance. Only once did Sally chastise her.

'If only you could have just forgotten about that photographer. I told you not to play with fire.'

'Is that meant to be a joke?' said Claire, flatly.

'I'm sorry,' said Sally, changing gear as she approached the hospital car park. 'Bad choice of phrase. I meant I warned you not to get involved with Stefan again. I know the fire was an accident but if only you'd been there at the time it might not have been so bad.'

'I know.' Tears welled in Claire's eyes and she searched in her handbag for tissues. 'I know I was stupid.' Sally handed her a tissue from the glove box. 'And to make it worse, when I got to London to see him he was with another woman.'

Claire started to sob into the small white square. She couldn't stop, tears kept on coming. She wiped them away with her bandaged arm. It felt as if all the pain was pouring out, all the remorse, the shame, the loss; it kept coming out in heaving sobs.

Sally took her in her arms and rocked her as though she was a baby. She kissed her hair and stroked her back.

'It's all right. It's all right,' Sally repeated until Claire was able to sit up and compose herself enough to go and face William's silence again.

A fire officer phoned and made an appointment to discuss the results of their investigation into the cause of the fire. Claire could feel her hands shaking with fear as Sally showed him into the living room. They must have found out that it was started with paraffin. She hadn't told anyone about what William had told her in the ambulance, she could hardly bear to think it was true, maybe it was some sort of post-trauma hallucination, she hoped that she had just imagined it but in her heart she feared that it was true. What would she say when she was questioned? Would the police be involved? Could William go to prison for arson? How would he cope with prison if he couldn't walk? She couldn't bear it, it was all her fault, she had driven him to do it.

Claire could feel her heart beating fast. It seemed to bang in her ears as the fire officer exchanged comments on the weather with Sally and accepted her offer of a cup of coffee.

When Sally had gone he ruffled through a sheaf of papers on a clipboard, breathing loudly, his bulky frame perched uncomfortably on the edge of Sally's sofa. Claire stared at his plump, shiny cheeks; they were mottled red and purple. She wondered if they were discoloured from years of facing into flames and heat. The thought of fire made her want to be sick.

'Sorry to keep you,' he said, looking up at her. 'I'm just making sure I've got everything in order before I start.' Claire had a terrible feeling she really was going to be sick.

Sally returned with coffee and a plate of bourbon biscuits. The fire officer started talking to Sally about the diet he was meant to be on. Claire could hardly bear it and willed him to get on with what he had come for.

'Now then,' he said when Sally had finally left the room. 'We take cases like these extremely seriously and do everything we can to find the cause. We want to know how a fire has started and of course you want to know how it started.'

Claire nodded silently.

'My team, my very experienced and conscientious team, has searched the scene extensively, using all methods of investigation available to them.' He took a sip of coffee; the mug looked tiny in his large, fleshy hands.

*Get on with it*, thought Claire, *just tell me*.

The fire officer sighed. 'But I'm afraid in this particular case we couldn't find a definite cause.'

Claire could hardly believe it. She tried not to laugh.

'It was most likely a burning log that rolled out onto the rug in front of the fireplace,' the fire officer continued, helping himself to his third biscuit. 'It's very common with open fires. Leave them unattended and *whoosh*, the whole house gone in no time.'

He illustrated the 'whoosh' with his hands, spilling coffee onto his jacket. He didn't seem to notice.

'And then once a fire gets its teeth into a thatched roof . . .' He took another bite of biscuit. 'Well, you've seen for yourself what happens.'

He shook his head and grimaced, then he smiled. 'You can't beat a nice bourbon cream. Got to be in the top ten for biscuits, in my book.' Putting the mug down, he stood up, revealing a white shirt straining across a sagging stomach.

'We'll be passing our report on to your insurance company. There shouldn't be any problem there.' He cleared his throat and looked down at Claire, who was dumb with relief. 'I'd just like to express my condolences about the loss of your house,' he said. 'It must be a terrible time for you. My missus said she saw it in one of those fancy magazines – she reads them in the hairdresser's. Very pretty, she said it was. Such a shame. I know the insurance company will re-home you and then rebuild and repair the building, but it's the little things you can't replace, like photographs and all the knick-knacks you'll have collected over the years, it's always very sad.'

He held out his hand to Claire and she stood up to see him out.

As she closed the front door she felt almost ecstatic. She didn't know if she wanted to laugh or cry. For nights she had lain awake with worry that they would find the container or do some test that would reveal a trace of paraffin but the intense heat must have destroyed any evidence. Would they have been looking for it anyway? Who would suspect that a happy husband and father, living in the beautiful home he had worked so hard to create, would ever try to burn it down as his family slept upstairs? It could only have been a terrible accident. Claire suddenly slumped down against the hallway wall; could her betrayal really have pushed William so far?

A local newspaper ran a story on the fire and the irony that the house was being featured in an interiors magazine at the time. A national newspaper picked up on it and tried to interview Claire. When she refused to talk to them over the phone they came to Sally's house, camping outside on the village green, waiting for Claire to come out.

'How does it feel to have lost everything?' The reporter tried to shove a small microphone at Claire as she got into Sally's car. His cheap leather coat flapped around him in the wind. 'What's it like to have your beautiful home burned to the ground?'

'What do you think it's like, you stupid man?' shouted Sally. 'Piss off and leave her alone.'

A short photographer with greasy hair took pictures, pushing his camera against the car window as Sally drove away with a screech of tyres.

The next day the story appeared as a double-page spread with pictures of the burned-out shell beside the pictures from *Idyllic Homes*.

'Up In Flames. The Dream Destroyed', screamed the headline. 'Cushion-maker, 37, still in shock as her husband lies critically ill in hospital.'

There was an out-of-focus picture of Claire staring through the glass of the car window. She looked haggard and confused, her complexion ashen beneath her scraped-back hair, her bandaged arm raised as if to try to cover her face.

'"She is devastated," a close friend told us,' it said underneath.

Claire carefully folded up the newspaper and put it on the table in front of her.

'I told you not to look at it,' said Sally.

'I'm glad I saw it,' said Claire. 'At least I know what the house looks like now. It makes it easier to accept what has happened. It's made it real.'

'If I were you, I'd ask them to print an apology for saying that you're thirty-seven.'

A large bouquet of flowers arrived from Celia Howard. She sent her condolences for 'the terrible tragedy that you have suffered'.

Claire thought about Stefan. What must he be thinking? He must know about the fire; even if he hadn't seen the newspaper surely Celia would have told him. She kept thinking he might try to get in touch but days passed and she heard nothing. She told herself he was the last person she wanted to see, to even think about, but small bubbles of longing still seemed to burst through the disgust, anger and shame that covered her feelings for him.

# Chapter Thirty

*'An intriguing mix of old and new.'*

'I don't want to push you out,' said Sally, the first morning that Oliver and Emily went back to school. Ben still seemed too clingy to return to nursery and he sat on Claire's lap playing with Lego blocks while she tried to take sips from a steaming cup of tea. Sally reached out for Claire's hand across the table.

'You know you can stay here as long as you like, but have you thought about the future? Where you're going to live until the insurance claim is sorted out? What you're going to do?'

Claire tried to focus her mind. She had been trying to think about the future for days, to work out some sort of plan for herself, for the children, for William when he came out of hospital. But every time she tried to think about it her mind seemed to turn to fuzz.

'Have you let the department store know you can't do their order?' Sally asked. Claire shook her head; she couldn't bear to see that dream disappear but she knew there was no way she could fulfil the order now, she had no fabric, no sewing machine, and all the little bits of lace and ribbon and jars of buttons she'd spent so many years collecting had gone.

'I'll do it this afternoon,' she said with a sigh. 'And I need to let all my other stockists and customers know that Emily Love is, quite literally, no more.'

'There's something I haven't told you yet,' said Sally. 'Gareth and I are getting back together.'

'Oh, Sally, that's great news! I do like Gareth; he's been so kind since the fire and of course everything he did that morning was amazing.'

'I know,' Sally grinned. 'He's such a hero. It made me realise how much I miss him. How much I really love him. I know he messed things up with his cyber-flirtation stuff but everyone makes mistakes. You've made me realise that. I can see now that temptation can lead anyone astray in even the strongest marriages, like yours.'

Claire took a sip of her tea. 'I'm glad something good has come out of the whole fiasco. I'm really pleased for you both.'

'I can't wait to rekindle the old passion,' said Sally wistfully. 'It will be like when we first met.' She sighed happily. 'Though obviously not in the back of his dad's Ford Cortina.'

'Doesn't Gareth mind about you and Josh?'

'Josh is long gone now. Apparently it all got too "heavy" after the fire. It did me the world of good while it lasted, though, and jealousy was the best punishment for Gareth. Anyway, I've got some new tricks now that I'm longing to show him. He won't be interested in busty Betties any more!'

'Well, I can see you won't want us in your way when he comes back.' Claire felt panic rising. Where could they go?

'Could you find somewhere to rent in town?' asked Sally gently. 'I know there's probably not much to choose from but I could make enquiries for you. Anna did say you could stay in the rooms above the gallery but there isn't a proper kitchen and the heating is a bit hit and miss. What about those new houses they were building last summer by the river? Some of them are now for rent.'

*Modern monstrosities*, she remembered William calling them. Claire stared out of the window; it looked out at grey December fields and a leafless wood of oak trees that climbed the steep hill to where her home had been.

'What do you think?' said Sally. 'Shall I go and buy a local paper for you? Shall we see what rental properties they've got advertised?'

274

Claire turned and looked at her friend.

'I think I know what I need to do,' she said to Sally. 'I've thought of somewhere we could live.'

It was the first time Claire had driven since the fire. The cuts on her feet still hurt as she pressed down on the pedals and she was relieved that she only had to go a mile up the hill.

'I'll come with you,' Sally had said.

'No,' replied Claire. 'This is something I need to do myself.'

The air still smelled of charred wood as she opened the car door. Tentatively she got out into the grey winter rain and forced herself to look in front of her. Even though she'd seen the picture in the newspaper, the reality was hard to take in. She squinted her eyes so that the house became a hazy blur. That was easier. She could almost believe that the thatched roof was still there, glass still in the windows, walls still painted Dorset cream. Slowly she refocused and let herself take in the sagging blackened hole that gaped open, like a festered wound, where the roof had been. One chimney had partially collapsed and the walls were blackened and streaked with smoke stain. All around lay glass from the windows and bits of stone that had fallen from the chimney. One remaining black branch of rose bush outlined the doorless porch. Claire thought of Gareth climbing it to rescue the children and shuddered at the thought of what a close escape they'd had.

Charred and broken objects lay scattered around the perimeter of the house, twisted bits of plastic toys, blackened and water-warped books and papers, scorched furniture and everywhere little scraps of dirty, damp unrecognisable fabric.

She could hardly bear to look at the fabric; losing the vintage materials and buttons and ribbons that she'd collected for so many years seemed to upset her more than losing her personal possessions. If only she had had that order from the department store a few weeks before, she could have had it done and delivered it before the fire. Now she had no fabric to make things out of, no

275

sewing machine, and nowhere to make anything anyway. She shook herself, determined to try not to think about it and continued walking round the building.

Looking at the devastation around her she remembered the yew trees that William had got rid of last summer and wondered if the old folklore about cutting them down could be true.

No, she thought, it wasn't the yew trees taking revenge for what had happened to them, it was William taking revenge for what she'd done to him.

As she picked her way forward through the rubble she heard the crunch of glass under her boots. Looking down she saw a jewel-bright fragment in the ash; she picked it up and found it was a fragment of broken pottery, a jagged shard of pink camellia petal. With a strength she didn't know she any longer had she threw it, far away, into the hedge.

Walking around to the back garden she stumbled as her foot hit against a fallen beam. It lay across the path like a giant stick of charcoal. Claire put out her hand to steady herself on the wall beside her. When she took her hand away she saw each fingertip was black, as if she had been fingerprinted for a crime. She bent down and wiped her fingers on the damp grass before continuing on, away from the empty shell of the house, across the lawn towards the view, towards the summer house.

The summer house looked perfect, its pretty green exterior untouched by flames or smoke.

Claire pushed the door. She had thought it would have been locked; that William, always so fanatical about security, would have kept it locked. Surprisingly, it opened to her touch and so she went inside. William had laid an extravagant solid oak floor and, the weekend before the fire, had painted the wooden-panelled walls and ceiling white. It was empty apart from the little wood burner in one corner and a small enamel sink against a wall.

Claire flicked the light switch and the room lit up. It felt dry and warmer than the cold outside air. The smell of pine and paint was a welcome relief from the smell of burned house. It was clean and simple and full of possibilities, maybe?

She looked around the single room. It was large – much too large, she had thought, when it had been erected – but with all of them in it, it would be a little cramped.

Slowly she walked around. If they had a fold-out sofa bed at one end and three small mattresses that could be put away in the daytime, there would still be room for a table and chairs at the other end and some sort of a cupboard that could be used as a work surface. She could buy a microwave, a small fridge, a kettle, and a single electric ring would be enough to cook on. She would need shelves on the walls for storage. Surely it would be a start, a temporary home until the house was rebuilt.

Her eyes swept round the room again. *But it was just a shed; a chilly, empty, glorified garden shed.* She took a deep breath and looked around the room once more. Was this really somewhere she could live? Where she could force her children to live?

She felt an energy born of anger build inside her and she straightened herself to her full height. She would not let William's fire stop her; she would not let the consequences of her futile love affair with Stefan ruin all her hard work. She would not live here. For a start she needed somewhere bigger, somewhere more comfortable, somewhere away from what had been their home, and most importantly she needed somewhere she could set up Emily Love again; she had to get that order done in time.

Getting back into the car she drove into town and went straight to the estate agent's. A surge of happiness swept over Claire. She felt excited, determined, filled with a sense of purpose.

'I want to rent the patisserie,' she said to the sleek-suited youth with gelled hair behind the desk. He raised his eyebrows, surprised by her slightly manic enthusiasm.

'Do you mean the flat above it?' he asked. It was hard to rent out shops in the dismal economic climate.

'The whole thing,' said Claire.

He jumped up from his chair. 'I'll get the keys. You'll need to look round.'

'Just get the contract and I'll sign it. I'll look round afterwards.'

On the way to see the shop she stopped at Mrs Needles' neat white bungalow and explained she desperately needed her help. Mrs Needles made them both a cup of Lady Grey tea and listened while Claire told her what she wanted. She wrote a list of all the items the department store needed and the quantities beside them.

Mrs Needles sucked her teeth. 'That's a lot of sewing,' she said.

'What about the other ladies in the W.I.? Surely lots of them can sew?' said Claire. 'If I can find the fabric and set up work benches and people are kind enough to lend their sewing machines we could get a production line going by this weekend.'

Mrs Needles shook her head. 'I'd like to help you, Claire, my dear. I know you've been through a terrible ordeal but it's such a busy time coming up to Christmas, we've got cakes to make and mincemeat to mix and we have the market every day through December, and then there's the Christmas shopping and we've all got grandchildren who need costumes for their nativity plays.'

'We've got twenty days,' Claire interrupted. 'If we get this done by then there'll be plenty of time for Christmas cakes and the market and shepherd's tunics and you and all the other ladies will be well paid – I promise, and that should help with Christmas, shouldn't it?' Claire reached out and touched the old woman's blue-veined hand. 'This is my big chance, Mrs Needles. Please say you'll try and help me.'

'Let me see what I can do.'

The large bunch of keys felt heavy in Claire's hand as she surveyed the outside of what had been Patisserie Tremond. The little shop was wedged in between a wholefood café and a children's bookshop. The mullioned window bowed outwards as though as a result of being squeezed on either side by its neighbours, and the wooden sign that swung from a curved metal bracket beside it still bore the fancy French name that Trevor and Edmond had given their cake shop. At the threshold of the door, mosaic tiles spelt 'Taylor's Ironmongers' from an earlier Victorian incarnation. Claire looked up. The building was tall and crooked; a single sash window was set into the worn yellow stonework and above the window a little painted dormer was edged in scalloped weather board. The terracotta-tiled roof undulated in a way that suggested it hadn't been replaced for centuries and a wonky red-brick chimney stack tilted to one side.

Claire put the key into the solid front door, turned it, and then pushed. She felt nervous; had she been right to commit herself to the six-month lease before she had properly seen around? The thick oak door was heavier than it looked; it gave way and let Claire into a little vestibule with a pretty etched glass door leading inside. A bell jingled as she opened it, disturbing the silence of the empty shop. It smelled of cake and biscuits. A shaft of golden sunlight flooded through from a doorway at the back picking out the dust suspended in the still, warm air. Everything was gone; Trevor and Edmond had either taken or sold it all, the mahogany counter, the rows of shelves, the old pine dresser where Trevor and Edmond displayed their range of artisan jams and chutneys. Only the wide oak floorboards remained, the wood worn lower at the doorway where customers had walked in and out for hundreds of years.

Claire went into the back and found herself in what must have been the storeroom, as empty as the shop. This led into another room and then another with a large oven in it; beyond that was a tiny kitchenette and then an ancient toilet and enamel washbasin. Beside that small room an uneven wooden staircase led upwards in a spiral; the walls enclosing it were lined with painted panelling. The treads were high and Claire had to lift her legs up higher than she was used to in order to go upstairs. A warren of little rooms ran backwards from the landing; Claire's footsteps echoed as she opened door after door and the level of the floor went up and down with a succession of small steps and slopes.

Claire mentally allocated each room to a child. Towards the back she found a bathroom and simple kitchen made up of fitted white units, a sink, and a 1950s pale blue kitchen cabinet just like one her grandmother had once had.

The last room was big, with an ancient gas fire set amongst a surround of garish marble tiles. A large arched window looked down at a small overgrown garden and beyond the tumbledown garden wall, the river. Claire saw two swans glide past followed by a brightly painted barge with a well-wrapped-up couple on the deck. They looked up and waved, Claire waved back, and when they'd disappeared she turned and climbed the rickety set of open tread stairs which led up to the second floor.

This was the attic room; the low ceiling beams were dark against the fresh white paint on the walls and ceiling. A little dormer window at the back looked onto the river again and a little dormer window at the front looked down onto the high street. A single pale green Lloyd Loom chair stood, forgotten, in the middle of the room. Claire sat down in the chair and looked around her. This would be her room.

She smiled; she had been right, it would be perfect.

Her very first priority was to move into the flat as quickly as she could. Sally helped her clean the small white kitchen and the bathroom with its rose-coloured sink and toilet and chipped enamel bath. Then they swept out the big room with the large arched window to make a temporary bedroom for Claire and the children until Claire had time to sort out the other rooms.

Claire bought four blow-up mattresses plus a basic assortment of pillows, duvets and plain white bed linen.

'We'll get more furniture and rugs and curtains when I've finished the big order. I'll make it really cosy for us,' she told the children as they stood in the sunlit room. It was bare apart from four beds neatly made and lined up along the wall and a bin bag full of clothes that people had kindly given for the children.

She wasn't sure what their reaction would be to the empty shop and flat, it was so different from the pristinely decorated and furnished home they had been used to. There were no toys, no comfortable sofas, no large television; she hadn't had time to replace anything they had lost in the fire. The children were wide-eyed and silent, their expression giving nothing away. Claire held her breath, waiting for protests or even tears.

'It will be a bit like camping,' she said, trying to sound enthusiastic. 'It will be great being able to see the river, there are ducks and swans and boats and –'

Oliver interrupted her. 'It's really *cool*.' He let out the last word slowly as he looked around him.

'It's like a fairy's cottage,' said Emily, smiling. 'I like all the tiny rooms.'

'Yeah, like a hobbit's house.' Oliver was nodding with approval. 'Can I have that room that doesn't have a window?'

Ben ran a small toy car, which one of Sally's boys had given him, down the slanted floor. He laughed with delight when it gathered speed and crashed into the skirting board with a satisfying *thwack*.

'I'm afraid there isn't any television or computer,' said Claire. 'I'll get that sorted but it won't be for a few days.'

'No probs,' said Oliver, 'we can play hide and seek.'

'Can we do it now?' said Emily. 'It's the perfect place for hide and seek.'

'Of course,' said Claire with relief that they seemed so enthusiastic.

The children went in all directions, their feet noisy on the bare boards, their hands running down the bumpy walls. Claire smiled to see them enjoying themselves and she went into the kitchen to make jam sandwiches for tea.

Claire bought a power drill, followed by a box of screws, a tape measure, a spirit level, and several long packs of wooden shelving.

'We could find someone to do this for you,' said Sally as Claire marked out in pencil on the walls where the shelves would go, measuring between them and testing the straightness with the spirit level.

'No,' replied Claire, concentrating on the numbers on the tape measure. 'I'm determined to do this myself.'

'Do you want a glass of Cava to give you courage?' asked Sally, sitting cross-legged on the floor with a bottle and two plastic cups she had brought with her to toast Claire's first attempt at DIY.

'I'll wait until after I've finished,' Claire said, plugging in the drill. 'I think drinking and drilling may be a criminal offence.'

'Are you sure you know what you're doing?' Sally asked. 'It's not too late to find a man to –' Her words were drowned by the shriek of the electric drill. Sally put her hands over her ears.

'There!' Claire stood back to admire the triangular support she had just attached to the wall. 'It's easy. I don't know why I've never tried it before. Come on, Sally, I need your help to hold one end of the shelf.'

An hour and a half later three neat rows of shelves and several rows of pegs and hooks lined the room plus a large blackboard where Claire intended to write a list of things to be done every day. The two women sat in the middle of the wooden floor.

'To my new workshop,' Claire said, raising the cup in her hand. Sally raised hers and they laughed as the plastic dented as they tried to clink them together.

'It's a far cry from that cramped spare room you were forever having to tidy up when William's parents came to stay. How did you ever think you could get the department store order done in there?'

'I'm still anxious about getting it done in here; we've only got two weeks now.'

'Leave it to Nana Needles! When I was little we called her Super Nana because in a crisis she always seemed to save the day! I can't count the number of times she stepped in to stop my mum from going completely bonkers looking after me and my brothers.

★

282

She'd suddenly appear and clean up all the mess and feed us proper food and kick my dad off the sofa and make him go to work.'

'Well, she'd be my superhero if she can help me get this order out, it is even more important for me than it was before the fire. I feel as though it could really change my life.'

She took a sip of wine. 'I'm beginning to feel excited about this.' With her arm she gestured around the room. 'I think it's going to be lovely in here and upstairs in the flat. It's really cosy up there. When the big order is out of the way I'm going to sort out the front and open an Emily Love shop.'

'Brilliant!' Sally sloshed more Cava into their cups. 'Let me come to work for you on the days I'm not in college. I only work Saturdays for Anna now and I wouldn't expect you to pay me much – in the beginning anyway. Do you think you would keep the shop and workshop here when you go back to the house?'

Claire shrugged. 'We'll see. It's funny, but I don't miss the house nearly as much as I thought I would. I don't miss our things, the furniture, the ornaments, my clothes. I don't feel sad, in fact I feel quite liberated.'

For the next three days she worked like a woman possessed. She sat in Gareth and Sally's cramped study and trawled eBay for materials. She successfully bid on bales of vintage fabric and boxes of buttons and reels and reels of lace and ribbon – much of it cost hardly anything at all. She had Emily Love labels made up on an express delivery service and from a haberdasher's website bought cotton thread, silk thread, needles, five pairs of fabric scissors, pins, and three tape measures and she begged and borrowed as many trestle tables and picnic tables as she could; when she couldn't find any more tables she took planks of wood retrieved from a skip and put them on stacks of bricks to make makeshift work benches.

She was surprised how much sunlight poured into the workshop through the little skylight. As she swept out the room, flour and icing sugar dust blew up around her, she could taste the sweetness in her mouth; it was strangely comforting.

Emily and Oliver helped her clean out a huge pile of wooden crates she had found in the garden; they would be perfect for keeping the finished stock in. When the fabric started to arrive the children helped her open and unpack the boxes and stack the ginghams, paisleys, spots, and stripes neatly along the new shelves. They sorted the buttons into size and colour and poured them into huge glass sweet jars that she'd also found in the garden.

On Saturday morning the W.I. ladies started to arrive. Mrs Needles had done well. She'd found eleven other women and six sewing machines. Some women seemed quite young and sprightly, some seemed much older – thin-skinned and frail.

One tiny woman called Doris told her she was over ninety, though her eyes sparkled like a young girl's in her wizened-apple face.

'I wish I'd had the opportunity to have my own business when I was young,' she said to Claire in a husky voice which made Claire wonder if it was from age or the packet of Silk Cut that she could see in her cardigan pocket, 'instead of spending all my days serving my bastard of a husband.'

Claire's eyes had widened, taken aback by the ancient woman's language. Mrs Nettles laughed at Claire's shocked face.

'She's right, he was a bloody lazy philanderer and he never could get his fingers out of other women's knickers.'

'Even in the hospice they couldn't trust him having his bed bath,' Doris added.

'You're well rid of him now, aren't you, Doris?' said Mrs Nettles.

'Too right I am. Much better off with my young Colin now.'

'Is Colin your son?' Claire asked. The room burst into laughter.

'Colin is her toy boy,' said a well-padded lady with frizzy purple hair. 'Seventy-nine he is and you wouldn't think he was a day over seventy to look at him.'

'You're such a lucky tart, Doris,' said another lady.

Claire could see they were going to be in for a colourful time.

Claire had cut out stencils of her bird and flower and heart and house designs in tracing paper. She set up a line of ladies to cut them out from stacks of pre-cut squares of fabric, who then passed them on to be pinned onto the Christmas stockings, cushions, bags, or aprons. Other ladies were put to sewing, others to ironing, and one lady in particular liked to add the lace or ribbon to the pictures.

The purple-haired woman was very good at sewing on buttons and Doris had a real talent for embroidery despite the fact that her hands were twisted with arthritis. Claire was amazed at the speed at which the women worked. Mrs Nettles became a sort of fore-man, consulting Claire's list on the blackboard, allocating jobs, overseeing quality control, openly being in charge of her 'girls' as she liked to call the W.I. ladies (or The Dirty Dozen as Claire and Sally had taken to referring to them.)

When she wasn't at school, Emily sat at her own little table stuffing gingham hearts with lavender. Doris helped her when her embroidery techniques weren't needed elsewhere. The old lady and the little girl were soon chatting like old friends and Claire tried to make sure that all the women toned down their language when the children were around.

Even Oliver was keen to help and spent a whole weekend sitting cross-legged on the wooden floor pinning the Emily Love labels to the finished products.

Claire's days were so busy she sometimes forgot about the house and the fire and even William; sometimes time ran away and she'd arrive too late at the hospital for visiting hours and she'd have to beg the nurses to let her and the children see him.

He was out of intensive care now but though he seemed to chat to other patients on his ward he turned his head away whenever Claire approached the hospital bed. Sometimes the children could make him smile, but mostly he just stared at the ceiling. He didn't want to speak to Claire at all.

But his progress was good, he was no longer connected to oxygen and fluids by tubes and with physiotherapy and proper care the doctors felt sure his spine would mend and he'd regain full mobility.

'Have you heard back from the insurance company? When will they start to rebuild the house?'

William's mother phoned Claire for updates every day as though she was desperate to recreate the house as soon as possible and didn't quite trust her daughter-in-law to get it done.

'It's all in hand,' Claire soothed. 'I have a meeting with the builders next week.'

'You'll make sure it's put back just like it was?'

'Yes, I'll have it put back like it was before.'

'If you need to know what colours or finishes were used you will ask me, won't you?'

'Trust me. I'll make it perfect for William.'

A watery sun struggled through a grey winter sky as Claire's car made its way up the lane towards the house.

The builder's car was already parked in front of the soggy, sagging shell. As Claire opened the door the smell of charred timbers and thatch seemed worse than it had done before. She felt sick.

A stocky, square-faced man came towards her holding out his hand.

'Hi, I'm Neville Brady.' His accent had a vaguely Midlands twang. 'As I'm sure you're aware, my company has been contacted by your insurers to rebuild your home.'

Claire nodded and pulled her scarf up over her face to try and block the smell. She shivered in the cold early-morning air.

'I know this time is never easy for families whose lives have been ripped apart by the destructive power of fire,' he said as though he was reading from a script. 'Well, never fear, Brady and Sons is here.'

Despite the awfulness of the situation Claire wanted to laugh.

'For twenty years my company has been specialising in

repairing fire- and smoke-damaged buildings. We'll turn this tragedy around and make it into something positive for you.'

He stopped and looked at Claire as if requiring some sort of affirmation. She nodded again.

'Very good,' she said through her scarf.

He looked pleased and carried on with his speech. 'Like a phoenix from the flames, your dream will rise again.' He raised up his arms to illustrate what he was saying. 'And then your home will be returned to you,' his arms went higher 'and you and your loved ones can continue with your happy lives once more.' He raised his arms over his head in a triumphant finale.

Claire resisted the urge to give him a round of applause.

'How long will it take?' Claire asked.

Neville Brady turned around and looked at the home as though seeing it for the first time. He drew in his breath.

'It's quite bad damage you've got here.' His head looked left to right and up and down as though to size up the job, then he turned back to Claire and smiled. 'Six months,' he said. 'Give or take a few days.'

'Will it be like it was before?'

'Yes.'

'Exactly?'

'Well, the problem is we don't really know what it looked like before and you may think you know what it looked like but usually I find that people can't really remember the details.'

'I have photographs.'

'You do?'

'Well, they're in a magazine.'

'Do you have the magazine?'

'No, our copy went up in the fire but you can still buy that issue in the shops.' Any time Claire went to the supermarket, *Idyllic Homes* seemed to glare reproachfully out at her from the mass of publications lined up on the shelves.

Neville Brady looked at the house and back to Claire again. 'You're the family with the perfect house that went on fire. I read

287

about it in the newspaper. What a tragedy.' He tutted and shook his head. 'If you buy another copy of the magazine we can go over it together,' he went on, 'then I can get a good impression of what the house was like.'

'Can you buy it?' asked Claire. 'It's just –'

'Oh, I can imagine.' He put his hand onto his heart. 'It must be painful, too painful. I'll pick up a copy on my way back to the office now. Don't worry about a thing. We will give you back a house you'd be proud to show off in a magazine again.'

# Chapter Thirty-one

*'Filled to the brim with interesting ornaments, soft furnishings and*
*her children's art works – for Claire it is a dream come true.'*

Two weeks after Mrs Needles and her girls began, they finished.

The old wooden crates were stacked up in the store room, each one lined with calico and piled with beautifully crafted items waiting to be packed in cellophane, placed in cardboard boxes and delivered to the London store.

When the last box had been taped up and sent down the motorway in the back of the courier's transit van, Claire called everyone together. Then she went into the little kitchenette at the back of the shop and returned with several bottles of champagne. She set out the wine glasses she'd bought specially for the occasion and she and Sally filled each glass with the sparkling wine. Claire picked up Ben who had been trying to ride a sewing machine like a rocking horse and with one hand she banged a pair of steel shears on a work bench to silence the girls.

'I just want to say something to mark this very special occasion,' she began. 'Three weeks ago, getting that huge order together seemed an impossible task. I had no workshop, no sewing machine, no fabric, no home,' she smiled at the mass of smiling, wrinkled faces in front of her, 'and now thanks to all you fabulous girls it's actually done and on its way. I'm so grateful to you for all your hard work and dedication, I don't know what I'd have done without you, you've been so –'

'Oh, get on with it, for God's sake,' a croaky voice said from the back. 'I'm gagging for a bloody drink.'

'Well said, Doris,' laughed Sally. 'Quit being so sentimental and let's have a party.'

'OK then.' Claire raised her glass.

'Let's drink to a successful future for Emily Love and all those who've helped keep her sailing,' shouted Sally.

A cheer that must have been heard right down the high street went round the room and Mrs Nettles put Radio 2 on very loud and before long everyone was dancing to Steve Wright's Non-Stop Oldies. Sally and a group of women got on the sturdiest table and did the twist and Doris showed them that she still knew how to jive even though she did it sitting down. Claire hugged Mrs Nettles and Mrs Nettles had to dab her eyes with a little scrap of yellow gingham left on a table beside her.

'What's going on?'

Claire turned to see William's mother standing stiffly behind her. Claire smiled and stepped forward to give her a hug too but William's mother stepped back.

'Who are these people?' She looked around her with disdain. 'Is it some sort of old people's aerobic group?' She had to shout above the noise of the radio but her last few words had coincided with the end of a song and all eyes turned to look at her. She straightened the silk scarf at her neck and looked slightly uncomfortable. She pursed her lips.

'It's a pensioner's rave,' said Doris wickedly, 'and you look old enough to join in. Grab a glass of bubbly and have a bop, the male stripper will be here soon. You did order one, didn't you, Claire?'

William's mother's face started to turn dark purple. Claire hastily ushered her out of the store room into the shop where she found William's father hovering nervously near the door.

'That was just Doris; she's very lively for her age.'

'What is she doing here? What are all those old women doing here? I thought you'd rented this building to do some of your

290

sewing in. It looks as if you're hosting some sort of wild gathering for vulgar pensioners in the middle of the afternoon.'

'They're mostly very respectable members of the W.I.'

'They don't look like the W.I. members from my village!'

'I'm sure they don't,' sighed Claire. 'How's William? I presume you've been visiting him today.'

'Yes, we've been to visit my poor boy. Of course I find it very distressing to see him the way he is.'

'He's lucky, it could have been so much worse.'

'You do realise just how serious William's condition is, don't you, Claire?'

'Of course, it's awful for him and I'd imagine the next six months lying on his back in a body brace will be pure hell for him but the doctor does say he will get better.'

'And he's very miserable, Claire, his home is in ruins, he's desperately upset. I thought you might want to spend more time with him but all you seem able to think about is work and –' she indicated towards the doorway with one bony hand, 'having parties and drinking in the afternoon.'

'You make it sound like I'm having some sort of debauched drunken rave.'

'Nothing you did would surprise me.'

Claire picked up a piece of calico that had been left bundled on a makeshift table. She started to fold it. 'I'm trying to do my best for the future of my family; if I can keep building on the success of Emily Love it might not matter if William isn't well enough to go to work for a while. If I can get more orders from large stores I might be able to support us instead of William having to worry when his sick pay runs out.'

William's mother didn't comment on what Claire had said. Instead she glanced around her and gave a sniff.

'Look at this place. You've chosen to house your children in a ramshackle shop. The insurance company would have paid for you to rent somewhere much more suitable. I have to say that without William to guide you your choices seem a little odd.'

Claire opened her mouth to speak but fury seemed to prevent the words from coming out. She simply stared at the boorish woman in front of her and waited for her to speak again.

'I want to –' William's mother turned and looked at her husband. '*We* want you to promise that you are going to do everything to make sure that house will be rebuilt as soon as possible.'

'You behave as if you don't believe me. As if you don't trust me.'

'Trust?' William's mother's laugh was mocking. 'Maybe you should know that William's told me about your sordid little affair.'

'My sordid little affair, as you put it, is all in the past.' Claire held the folded calico against her body like a shield; as though it might provide protection from her mother-in-law's cruel words.

'It's not in the past for William. He's so distressed about it.'

'I know we've got a lot to sort out, but I'm determined to re-build our lives together. He's my husband, we've got the children to think of, and we'll get through this.' Claire squeezed the calico tighter.

'At least William has had the support of old friends. Vanessa has been wonderful. Do you remember the girl he was going to marry before you? I'm sure you know that she's been to visit him in hospital.'

Claire didn't know but she smiled brightly and said, 'I know, she's been so kind.'

William's mother only briefly looked disconcerted and then her eyes narrowed.

'I don't know why William's so surprised at your faithless behaviour.'

She casually flicked some sequins on a table in front of her onto the floor.

'From the minute I first saw you I knew you couldn't be trusted. I recognised you at once for the flighty tart that you have proved to be.'

Claire couldn't help laughing. 'Flighty tart! I like that.' She looked at the bony, hard-faced woman and kept smiling as she

292

spoke. 'I think you've said all you came to say. This is my home for the time being and I and the children are very happy here. The house you found behind my back and treated as though it was your own is gone. I no longer have to feel beholden to you. I no longer have to be your skivvy while you fawn all over your treasured son and find fault with me. William is not a little boy at prep school any more. He's forty-three and he can decide for himself what he wants for the future, but personally I'd rather you didn't visit us here again. Now, I'd really like you to leave.'

'Well!' William's mother looked as though she was about to explode. Her long camel-hair coat seemed to visibly swell with rage. 'I've never been spoken to so rudely. You are so ungrateful.' Behind her William's father gave Claire a weak smile. Claire turned back in the direction of the music and laughter of the workshop.

At the doorway she looked back and William's parents had vanished. The shop door had been left open, swinging on its hinges, letting in the icy winter air.

In the weeks leading up to Christmas, Claire concentrated on making the rambling upstairs flat as cosy as she possibly could.

The department store had paid their invoice and, after she had paid 'the girls', Claire had enough to live on for a little while. William's company was paying him sick pay but Claire felt determined to furnish the flat with her own money.

She made curtains for the windows and found a slightly saggy but pretty chintz-covered sofa in a junk shop. With the help of Oliver and Gareth she rescued a small stained table from a skip in the back lane along with five mismatched wooden chairs for the kitchen – she covered the table with a brightly patterned piece of oil cloth and she and Emily painted the chairs red.

At a local car boot sale she bought a box of assorted bone-handled knives and forks, a set of steel saucepans, a bag of wooden spoons, and a huge old colander. She also found a prewar Poole pottery jug, a pale green Denbigh teapot, and a box of plates and mugs of assorted colours and sizes, some chipped, some cracked, it didn't matter.

Mrs Nettles found out about a house sale in an old farm and Claire came home with three simple wrought-iron beds for the children and a big brass bed for herself as well as a battered leather armchair, three moth-eaten but beautiful oriental rugs, and an old-fashioned rocking horse that sat too wonkily on his rockers for anyone to want him. She strung brightly coloured bunting around the kitchen and fairy lights around the living room. She painted one entire wall of the corridor with blackboard paint and encouraged the children to draw and write and scribble on it as much as they liked.

The mantelpiece above the gas fire seemed to grow more cluttered every day. It displayed the growing collection of 1950s pottery that kept catching Claire's eye as she searched through charity shops for clothes that could be cut up and used for Emily Love. The children added bits of their artwork and piles of pebbles from the river. Claire found a beautiful Victorian lace blouse amongst a bundle of fabric and she hung it on the wall above the fireplace; it seemed as much a work of art as any painting.

One icy morning Claire had gone to the house to fetch Macavity. Thin and bewildered by the loss of his warm home, he cowered from her touch, but with the help of some little bits of cut-up chicken she lured him into a box and popped him in the back of the car.

When he emerged into the flat he immediately started to purr, he then curled up in front of the gas fire as though he'd lived there all his life.

'You've made it gorgeous in here,' Sally said as she filled Claire's chipped Denbigh teapot with boiling water. 'It would make a lovely feature for a magazine. Very shabby chic, I can see the title on the cover now – *Style on a Shoestring*, or would it be *Style from a Skip* – oh, I know, *Skipping with Style.*'

'Very funny. You are joking about ever doing another magazine feature, aren't you?' Claire joined her friend at the table.

'Sorry,' said Sally. 'I forgot. I was only trying to say how nice it is in here.'

'Thank you for the compliment, but I think I've had enough of showing off in magazines.'

'Been there, done that, got the burned-out shell and ruined marriage to prove it?' Sally gave a cheeky grin.

'Sally!' said Claire laughing. 'Though that just about sums it up. Now the house is being repaired I just need to work on the marriage.'

'How is William?' Sally asked, her face suddenly serious.

'He's being transferred to a spinal injuries unit next week. It's too far away to visit every day but I'll take the children at the weekends.'

'He'll be lonely.'

'It's five miles down the road from his parents.'

'Then he'll probably be desperate to be on his own soon. I'm sure his mother will be at his bedside night and day.'

'He'll go and stay with his parents when he comes out of hospital. Just until the house is finished.'

Sally looked around her. 'You have managed to pick a flat with the most steps and stairs and undulating floors I've ever seen, certainly not the most suitable of places for someone who's had a back injury.'

'It must have been subconscious.' Claire realised Sally was right.

'It will be odd when you're living back together again,' said Sally. 'When I look round here I realise how different your tastes are, how much William influenced the house. It makes me sad to think that you liked all this colour and pattern and clutter when William wanted everything so neat and tidy.' She paused. 'I always envied the perfect environment you lived in but when I look at all the interesting things you've got in this flat and how lovely you've made it already, I realise how dull your house was before.'

'I really feel myself here, I feel like I can breathe.'

'You will go back though, won't you, Claire?'

Claire didn't answer but ran her fingers through her hair and tried to sort out the confused feelings she felt every time she thought about the house.

'One thing's for sure,' she finally said. 'Things will have to change; William will have to let up on the DIY front for a start.'

'The house will be like brand new; surely there won't be anything to do?' said Sally.

'I wouldn't put it past William to decide to build a ginormous tree house in the old oak tree or put an Olympic pool on the lawn.'

'Ooo, a swimming pool, what a fab idea, Claire!'

Claire shook her head. 'It's not going to happen, Sally. And another thing I've decided is that I'm having a cleaner and if things aren't as spotless and tidy as William wants then he can complain to her.'

# Chapter Thirty-two

*'The perfect country Christmas.'*

The week before Christmas, Elizabeth and Brian arrived from France. Poor Buster had been left behind and his space in the side car was packed full with a wonderful collection of antique quilts and bedspreads that Elizabeth had found in a bric-a-brac market.

'I thought you must need all the vintage fabric you can get,' said Elizabeth.

'But these are much too lovely to cut up.' Claire held each one up in the living room to admire them. 'I'm going to use them in the flat; they'll look beautiful on our beds.' She threw a quilt of faded cabbage roses across the sofa, startling Macavity who lay curled up in one corner. 'And perfect as throws in here.'

For days the children had been decorating the flat with paper chains, arranging holly in vases, and trailing ivy over the windows and along the fireplace. Claire had strung up swathes of twinkling fairy lights and made a pretty wreath of winter foliage for the front door of the shop.

Claire and the children dragged a Christmas tree up the twisting stairs and put it up in front of the long arched window. They draped it in lights and together they sat on the floor and made brightly coloured hanging decorations – the resulting mess when

297

Ben tipped over a tub of glitter left the whole flat sparkling well into the New Year.

While Elizabeth spent time with the children in the flat, Claire and Brian started working on the shop downstairs. Now the big department store order was over, Mrs Needles and her girls came in on a rota: four of them a day sat in the warm workshop, singing along to the radio, gossiping and making up the orders. They were also working on building up stock in preparation for the grand opening of the Emily Love shop on New Year's Eve.

Claire had already started on the shop fittings before Brian had come to help. She'd painted the walls a soft dove grey and with her new-found drilling skills she'd put up lines of shelves and pegs which she painted white. Mrs Needles' neighbour had been throwing out a hideous orange pine dresser; Claire rescued it and soon transformed it by painting it white, picking out its carved swirls and twirls in grey, and replacing its ugly wooden handles with white china ones. As she showed Brian what she'd done she felt ridiculously proud.

'You've done well, Claire.' He put his hand on her shoulder and smiled at her. 'You've transformed your business, expanding it in ways you'd never have thought of before the fire, and you've made a fantastic home for those kids – you'd never think they'd been through all that trauma, they seem so happy now. And you've done it all without William. You're better off without him, you know.'

Claire looked at him, taken aback.

'As far as I'm concerned, we're still together. When the house is finished we'll go back. Of course I want to keep the shop and workshop, but the children will want to go home.'

'And you?' asked Brian gently. 'Do you want to go home?'

Claire felt confusion swirling in her head again. She closed her eyes and quickly opened them again as a sudden vision of the burning house flashed in front of her.

'I expect you're still in shock,' Brian said. 'Things will look clearer in time, you'll see.'

Claire and Brian sanded down the rough wooden floorboards and rubbed beeswax into them until they glowed a mellow amber. They painted the bow window inside and out and cleaned the pretty etched glass door. Brian went with Oliver, in a hired van, to collect a large Edwardian shop counter that Claire had bought on eBay and Claire found an old dressmaker's dummy in a skip and re-covered it in calico. Emily helped arrange the cushions and tea cosies on the dresser shelves and to hang the shopping bags from the painted wooden pegs. Claire dressed the dummy in an embroidered apron and pinned on a large ribbon corsage. From a piece of rope suspended across one wall she hung her peg bags and across the ceiling she strung strings of bunting in a medley of chintz and gingham and stripy flags. Brian helped her, holding each end of the bunting as Claire tried not to wobble on top of a rickety ladder borrowed from the café next door.

'How's Mum finding the Dordogne winter?' Claire asked.

'Colder than she expected. I think she's had such fantasies about living in France the reality has taken a little getting used to.'

'She seems very happy being there.'

'I'm certainly very happy having her living with me but I just wish she'd agree to make an honest man of me.'

'Are you still asking her to marry you?'

'Most days I have a go.'

Claire laughed. 'Maybe you should give it a rest for a while. She might start to miss your proposals and start to wonder if she was right to refuse you so often.'

'Ah-ha,' said Brian, 'reverse psychology. You women are so cunning.'

'Who's cunning?'

Claire's mother walked into the room with two cups of tea; Ben proudly followed behind with a plate of star-shaped biscuits he'd just made with his grandmother.

'You,' said Brian with a smile and gave her a kiss on the cheek.

The little shop bell jangled and a rosy-faced man poked his head around the front door with a cheerful grin.

'All done now. The signs are up. Do you want to come and have a look?'

Claire scooped up Ben and she and Elizabeth and Brian trooped outside into the fading light of the afternoon. Standing on the pavement they looked up at the shop front. Suspended where the patisserie sign had once been was a dove-grey sign with white letters spelling out *Emily Love*. A longer sign above the window also said *Emily Love* and had white silhouettes of hearts and birds decorating each end.

'Oh, love, it looks wonderful,' exclaimed Elizabeth.

'All you need now is the window display,' said Brian.

'You'll have to wait for New Years' Eve for that,' said Claire.


Christmas Day arrived with a low grey sky threatening snow. Claire had been too busy to even think how she'd make Christmas dinner. How different it was going to be to the day in July when they'd pretended to celebrate it for the magazine. Claire felt a huge relief that for the first time in her married life she wouldn't be spending Christmas with William's mother; she didn't care if they just opened up a tin of baked beans followed by a box of After Eights, but Brian insisted that he would make the meal and, after a boozy night sampling Brian's rhubarb wine (specially brought over from France to toast Claire's new home), Gareth also insisted he was going to help.

'I got into cooking those few months I lived on my own,' Gareth explained, following Claire's expression of surprise.

'He's fantastic,' said Sally, giving him a squeeze. 'You should taste his Thai green curry and the venison pie and potatoes dauphine we had for Sunday dinner. He's completely buggered up my diet.'

Brian and Gareth spent a long evening drawing up a menu and writing a shopping list. They bought the last goose in the butcher's shop and the cooking started on Christmas Eve. Claire and Brian brought up two of the trestle tables from downstairs and set them up together in the living room, so that they could fit all the adults

300

and children around them. Claire covered the tables in silver damask and trailed ivy in between little night lights in old jam jars.

As dusk fell, she lit candles all around the room and Brian and Gareth solemnly carried the enormous bird along with more trimmings than Claire had ever thought it possible to produce from the small kitchen. There were crackers and indoor fireworks and lots and lots of sparkling wine followed by a Christmas pudding and cheese and port and afterwards Mrs Needles and Doris appeared with a bottle of Bailey's Irish Cream. They all grew drowsy and Claire turned on the television and they watched *Doctor Who* until Oliver shouted that he could see snow falling outside the window and the party drew to a close.

On Boxing Day, Claire visited William. As she drove the children through the glittering white countryside she determined to start the dialogue with him that she hoped would end the uncomfortable limbo they were living in.

Claire took the children to William's parents' house to open their presents from their grandparents. William's father came out to the car to fetch them while William's mother stood, arms folded at the large front door. As the children walked reluctantly towards their grandmother, William's father bent his head and looked inside the car.

'Happy Christmas, Claire,' he said. 'Keep your chin up; I think you're doing a wonderful job.' Then he scampered back up the snowy drive to face the wrath of his wife for talking to Claire.

William lay on the narrow hospital bed, enclosed in a back brace. A television positioned high up by the ceiling was silently showing the *EastEnders* Christmas special, which Claire was sure he would hate. She couldn't find the remote control to turn it off and didn't want to disturb the nurses who she knew were short-staffed because of flu. She decided to try to ignore it and concentrate on trying to get William to speak to her.

'I'm so sorry,' she whispered for the hundredth time since the fire. 'I'm so sorry about everything that happened.'

William turned his head away.

'We'll begin again,' she said. 'The builders are starting to re-build the house tomorrow; everything will be like it was before.'

She reached out to try to hold his hand but he edged his arm away, wincing with the movement as if it caused him pain. Claire saw him glance down and followed his line of sight to her own arm. Beneath the pushed-up sleeve of her cardigan the ugly raised red scars of her burns were visible – a reminder of the horror of what had happened to them. She pulled her sleeve down and looked up at the television screen. The actors were mouthing mutely, anguished expressions suggested tragedies of their own unfolding in Albert Square. She hardly ever watched the pro-gramme but with a little smile she realised that an unconsummated extra-marital love affair and a house fire started in a jealous rage were the classic fodder of prime-time soap – in fact pretty minor compared to the turbulent lives many of the characters led.

She almost jumped when she felt a slight pressure on her hand and she realised that William had taken her hand in his own; the first time he'd acknowledged her since the fire. She placed her other hand on top of his and when she looked at his gaunt grey face she realised he was crying.

'Don't cry.' She stroked his head and with her fingers gently pushed his tears away. 'It's going to be all right. I've told you, it's going to be all right.'

She put her head on his pillow, leaning over from her seated position on the chair beside him. A long time passed and finally his tears stopped and he spoke.

'I'm sorry, Claire. I'm so sorry.'

'Hush,' she said, comforting him like she would one of the children. 'Let's forget about the past.'

'You will take me home, won't you?'

'I'll take you home, I promise. As soon as you get better and the builders have finished, I'll take you home.'

# Chapter Thirty-three

*'A beautiful antique mirror illuminates the space.'*

Claire put up muslin in Emily Love's shop window so that no one could see what she was creating. She worked late into the night the day before New Year's Eve; it was well past midnight when she stood back to look at what she had done. She longed to see it from the front but she too would have to wait until the unveiling at the grand opening of the shop the following lunchtime.

Gareth had designed flyers which Brian and Elizabeth had distributed around the town and Claire had sent out press releases to local radio and the newspaper. A breakfast DJ had phoned up the day before to ask if she'd do a live telephone interview with him about the new shop and two papers had promised to run articles about it, one on the front page.

Claire had bought several bottles of champagne, made up jugs of elderflower cordial, hired champagne flutes, and filled little bowls with sweets. She bought five dozen plain cupcakes, iced them with pale pink icing, and Brian and Elizabeth piped white icing outlines of hearts on each one.

By midday a small crowd had gathered outside the shop.

'How will they all fit in?' Elizabeth asked, peering down at the street through the upstairs window.

'They'll just have to squash up,' said Claire as she smoothed down her new crepe dress and put on a bright red apron which

Doris had embroidered specially with 'Emily Love' and had put little hearts and daisies all round its hem.

'Is it time to reveal the window?' Sally shouted up the stairs.

'Yes,' Claire shouted back, slipping her feet into black suede heels. 'Do it now so I can see the customers' reactions from up here and then open the door and I'll be straight down. Brian? Are you ready with the fizzy stuff?'

'Yep, all ready to go down here,' Brian shouted back. 'Oliver and Emily have the cakes on plates. Is Ben suitably restrained with you?'

'I have him firmly by the hand,' shouted back Elizabeth, 'make sure all sweets are above his eye level before we come down.'

'Sally's taking the muslin off now.'

Claire and Elizabeth looked down as the crowd suddenly noticed the shop window. They could hear the *oohs* and *aahs* and exclamations of delight as Claire's creation appeared.

Dozens of little embroidered birds hung down from sparkling painted branches. Each branch was festooned with pale pink fairy lights while white-ribbon flowers delicately threaded their way amongst the lights; strings of lacy lavender hearts were suspended at either side of the display and white crochet bunting made a delicately pretty backdrop to it all.

Claire ran down the stairs into the shop and was immediately greeted by enthusiastic customers giving their congratulations for her new shop and already picking things up off the shelves and queuing up in front of the till where Sally tried desperately to keep up with the sales.

'It's never like this in the gallery,' she cried as the shopping frenzy started to peak.

Afterwards, as the last customers reluctantly dwindled away, Claire turned the sign on the door to closed. Sally let out a great whoop from behind the till.

'You won't believe how much you've taken, Claire. This is fab. I'm definitely coming to work for you.'

'Yes, oh, Sally, please do. You'd be fantastic, you could be shop manager.'

'I've had enough experience working at Anna's gallery and by the time I've finished my course this summer I'll even be qualified to do it! We'll be a great team.'

'Oh, Sally, I can't believe all this has really happened.'

Sally hugged her. 'What a year you've had, like a bloody roller-coaster. Let's open another bottle of champagne and drink to the New Year and hope it's as successful but slightly less dramatic than the last one!'

Spring arrived in a burst of celandines along the hedgerows and daffodils swinging in large clumps beside the riverbank.

Brian and Elizabeth were long gone back to France. Claire was busy with orders and the shop. A large chain of department stores was asking for work and the original one in London wanted more and more.

As the air grew warmer and the days longer, Claire felt an exhilarating lightness inside. In the evenings the children played beside the river with their school friends, who often ended up coming back for tea in the flat. Claire loved the lively chaos and chatter, the requests for hot chocolate and her home-made flapjacks.

In the mornings she could walk Emily and Oliver to school in a matter of minutes – no more mad rushes down country lanes. No more late marks in Mrs Wenham's *Tardy Parent* book. Ben's nursery was just around the corner, and Claire enjoyed the bustle of the high street around her and the friendly gossip of her neighbours and the other shopkeepers.

Every few days she drove back to the house to see how the work was progressing. She had been amazed how quickly it all seemed to be reappearing, as if by magic, in front of her eyes. Soon the thatched roof would be finished; already the house had regained its reproachful expression as the thatcher neatly cut the willow around the windows. The porch had been rebuilt and as Claire pulled up on the drive on the first hot afternoon they had had in May she noted a haze of colour around it. The roses were in bloom. Despite the fire and smoke they had survived to flower again. The sight filled Claire with optimism.

'Come and see the living room,' said Neville Brady loudly so that she could hear him over the cacophony of hammering and chiselling coming from the house. He handed her a hard yellow hat to wear and held out the copy of *Idyllic Homes*.

'Look, I think the floor looks just the same and we've got the width of the lintel over the fireplace exactly right.' He walked over to the French windows. 'The window panes are a slightly different proportion in these doors but the joiner and I think it actually works better.'

Claire nodded, trying not to remember how she'd dragged William's inert body through the fire months before.

'The conservatory is being delivered next week so soon it should start to look like its old self at the back as well as the front. After that we'll have you back in here in no time at all.'

Every weekend Claire and the children visited William. He was walking now and would soon be well enough to leave the hospital. Claire dreaded the idea of having to visit him at his mother's house.

'Not much longer till the house is ready now,' she said as she sat beside him in the garden of the hospital, watching the children playing underneath the willow tree on the lawn. 'Neville Brady seems to think just a few weeks, six at the most.'

William nodded briefly, his face as immobile as a statue. She wondered if he was suffering from depression; it wouldn't be surprising; he'd been through major trauma in so many ways.

'The shop's doing really well,' she said, trying to sound cheery, 'and the girls are really busy with the orders I'm getting now. Three orders from America this week and a gift shop in Berlin has asked to see some samples.'

She wondered if William was listening.

'I want to keep the shop after we move back into the house.'

She looked at his face, searching for a reaction.

'Emily Love is making a good profit now. You know, if you don't want to go back to work for a while, I think we'd manage.'

She took his hand in hers and felt relieved when his fingers curled round hers and he held her hand back.

'We're going to be all right,' she told him. 'When we get back to the house we'll sort everything out and start again.'

William turned to her, his eyes searching her face.

'I'd like that,' he said. 'I'd like to try to start again.' His hand squeezed hers. 'I've had a lot of time to think while I've been lying on my back for months. I can see I made a lot of mistakes in the past, Claire.' It was Claire's turn to be still and silent, waiting to see what he had to say. 'I took you for granted,' he went on. 'I thought you'd always be there and that I never needed to worry about your needs. I thought the house and children would be enough to keep you happy and that my job was to make a home for us all to live in. I didn't realise you'd become so lonely.'

Claire remained silent.

'I can see now that I didn't spend enough time with you or the children. I know that often when I came home from work I'd be grumpy with you. I'd expect my dinner on the table. I'd expect a clean house, clean clothes, and well-behaved children. I think I can see now why you might have been unhappy. I don't know how I got to be the sort of husband I'd become. I was so excited when we first moved to the house together. Do you remember how we'd make toasted sandwiches every night and then start doing work on the house together?'

Claire nodded.

'At the time I thought I'd never been so happy, we had a dream and we were making it happen together and then you got pregnant and that was great, we weren't just doing the house for us, we were doing it for our children too.'

'I remember how excited you were,' said Claire. 'You wanted to start on the nursery as soon as we got home from my first scan.'

'I wanted to make the most wonderful house in the world for my family.' He stopped and watched Oliver racing across the grass in front of them; Emily and Ben were following, laughing as they tried to catch him. 'And then the boys were born.' William's voice

307

became quieter. 'That was such an awful time, Claire. I thought I was going to lose you all. The boys were so tiny in those incubators and you were so ill in the beginning too, and do you know what I thought?'

'What?'

'I thought it was all my fault.'

'How?'

'I thought I'd made you do too much, made you push too many wheelbarrows around, helped me carry too many planks of wood, lift rocks, hack at plaster –'

'I wasn't doing those sorts of things when I was pregnant. I was on to painting window frames and sanding down the front door by then.'

'Even then I thought maybe the paint fumes or the floor varnish had done you harm.'

'Why didn't you tell me this before? I could have told you it was nonsense. None of that contributed to having the babies so early; don't you remember what the doctors said? If you'd talked to me about this I could have made you realise it was nothing to do with you or the house.'

'I just tried to push those thoughts away and then Jack died and you became so sad and so wrapped up in looking after Oliver I couldn't talk to you, you didn't want me to.'

Claire looked at William and realised his eyes were wet with tears.

'I didn't know what to do. I felt powerless to help you. All I could do was carry on with the house, try to make it as lovely as possible to try to make you happy again but somewhere along the line I must have got it all wrong and then you –' his voice trailed away and the tears were pouring down his cheeks.

Claire got up and crouched down in front of him.

'It's all right,' she stroked his face. 'That's all in the past.'

'But the fire?'

His eyes looked into hers and anxiety swept across his face.

'You know it was an accident, don't you, Claire? You know I'd never have done anything to destroy our house like that, to put our children's lives at risk?'

Claire didn't reply.

'Tell me you know it was an accident, Claire. I need you to tell me that.'

'Yes,' she said after a few moments. 'It was just an accident. Like the fire officer said, a log falling from the fireplace, it was no one's fault. These things happen and it was just unfortunate it happened to us.'

# Chapter Thirty-four

*'Where the heart is . . .'*

At the end of May, Claire took the children to France to visit Elizabeth and Brian. It corresponded with William's move from the spinal unit to his parents'. Claire felt relieved that she could put off visiting his mother's house for another week. She wondered if his mother had ever told him of their encounter before Christmas. Somehow she doubted that she had.

After the longest journey Claire had ever done without William to share the driving, they finally arrived. At the end of a rutted concrete drive the flat, yellow house glowed warmly in the sun; faded green shutters were closed at the windows to protect it from the heat of the Dordogne summer. There seemed to be no one about. Claire and the children unfurled themselves from the car and the large house welcomed them into its cool, quiet interior. The ancient walls and limestone floors soothed her as soon as she walked in. Suddenly a heavy oak door opened and a beaming Brian and Elizabeth and a barking Buster tumbled into the hallway in a rush to greet them.

'We weren't expecting you so soon,' Elizabeth cried, flinging her arms around her daughter.

'We were in the kitchen preparing a feast for you,' said Brian, wiping his hands on a stripy apron before giving Claire a kiss and ruffling the children's hair.

'What a treat to have you here at last,' Elizabeth said, as she led them into a huge kitchen lined with pine cabinets and glass-fronted cupboards. Rustic pottery and copper saucepans were piled on the shelves and bunches of dried herbs hung from hooks on the walls. The most wonderful smell emanated from a huge cast-iron range; Brian took up position in front of it, stirring the bubbling pan of venison stew.

It felt good to be back in her mother's and Brian's easy company again. They insisted on Claire resting in the garden with white wine while Brian brought in the bags and Elizabeth showed the children all the special hidden places in the house with Buster following, his thick tail wagging in a frenzy of delight.

On her first morning, waking up in a wrought-iron bed under a crisp white quilt, Claire felt as though she'd had the best night's sleep she'd had since the fire.

Long, lazy days merged into one another. Her mother and Brian fussed around their visitors, cooking lingering al fresco meals which they ate in the dappled shade of a vine-covered trellis. Friendly neighbours came and went, joining meals, bringing produce from their gardens.

Claire marvelled at her mother's rapid French. She seemed to become more gregarious as she spoke the language that Claire could only partly understand, her eyes twinkling, her laughter easy. Like the French themselves, she used her hands as she spoke, gesticulating to get her point across. Claire felt sad that her mother had spent so many years only having bored adolescents to share her love of France with.

Buster was a constant presence, his coat as golden as the farmhouse. He followed the children in their games around the garden before collapsing with them, hot and panting, for afternoon naps in the shade. Dog and children tangled together in contented sleep.

Before lunch Claire liked to sketch or read on the patio while Brian taught the children how to fish in the stream that ran through the garden or look for fossils in the small quarry at the bottom of his land. In the late afternoon they walked to a nearby lake where they would swim from a little wooden jetty or drift around in Brian's dinghy – Buster at the helm – Claire and her mother reclined on cushions while the children trailed their hands in the water and took it in turns to try to row the boat with Brian.

They visited a Sunday-morning bric-a-brac market and Claire bought a bale of 1960s floral fabric, a green enamel jug, an art deco mirror, and a set of pre-war kitchen jars with Sucre, Café, Thé, and Epices written on them.

Sometimes her mother and Brian's easy companionship and obvious adoration of each other gave Claire a pang of envy.

Her mother seemed radiant. She was a different person to the bitter woman Claire had shared her teenage years with in the dark, cramped flat. She told Claire she'd started writing a novel at last and she had obviously developed a passion for gardening. Tall yellow sunflowers swayed above jewel-coloured geraniums and salvias.

'Brian laughs at me for planting sunflowers,' she said as she straightened a bamboo support.

Claire noticed how brown her mother's arms had become.

'The fields round here are full of them – they're crops like corn or barley – but I love them. They make me cheerful.'

'I don't think you need sunflowers to make you cheerful,' Claire said gently. 'Brian seems to do that very well himself.'

Her mother smiled. 'He's started asking me to marry him again. He'd stopped for a while after Christmas but now the silly man has started with it all over again.'

'Well, why not?'

'I don't want to go there again. I've been married and it was a disaster. All that pain for so many years. I just want to stay as we are. Why spoil it?'

'Oh, Mum.' Claire took her hand. 'It wasn't being married that spoilt it the last time, it was the man. Brian's so different from Dad. I'm sure he'd never hurt you. He loves you. For him marriage is a way of showing you how much.'

Her mother shrugged and bent down to pluck a weed from the

hot, dry soil. When she didn't get up Claire crouched down beside her and saw that her mother was crying.

'Mum, what's wrong?' Claire put her arms around her.

'I'm sorry, darling,' her mother spoke through muffled sobs. 'I just get overwhelmed by it all. I can't believe that this has happened to me: that I met Brian, that I've moved here to this beautiful house and that I can share it with you and the children.'

'But why are you crying?'

The older woman wiped her eyes and looked at her daughter with a smile.

'I'm crying because I'm just so happy.'

All too soon the week had gone; it was time to go home. Claire felt a sense of trepidation as she thought of William and the house which, no doubt, would be ever nearer to completion. As Elizabeth and Brian stood at the top of the drive and waved goodbye she wondered if she would ever be as happy as her mother seemed now; could she ever be that happy with William? Maybe moving back after this enforced break would bring them closer together again – closer than before the fire, maybe as close as they had once been long ago. As close as they had been before the house had come into their lives?

# Chapter Thirty-five

*'Claire has let the structural materials assert themselves
beautifully against the pure white walls.'*

'Do you mind if we don't have this on?'

'OK.'

Claire turned the radio off. William had turned the volume up
but with Radio 4 presenters blaring at her, Claire couldn't think
properly to drive. She felt hot. She lowered the window a little;
outside a fresh breeze kept the temperature cool despite the bright
sun shining down from the blue July sky.

The children were with Sally, she'd thought it best that they
weren't there the first time that William saw the house again.

Claire had spent weeks scouring shops and catalogues for the
right furniture and rugs and lamps and cutlery and children's toys
and everything exactly as they'd had before.

As Claire had walked through the rooms that morning, she'd
felt as though she was walking around a show home. Everything
was immaculate, no finger-prints, no sticky patches, no dust balls
nesting in the corners. It looked very similar to the way it had
been before the fire but it felt sterile; lifeless, as though it were a
soulless reflection of the family home it once had been.

Claire placed a vase of lilies on the console table in the hall.
Remembering William, she fetched a cork table mat and put it
under the patterned vase. The vase was almost identical to the
Moorcroft vase they'd had before; though the pattern was of

harebells not of snowdrops and the glaze was slightly duller, a little less intense. Claire shivered and went to turn the heating on despite the time of year. The house just needed people living in it to bring it properly back to life.

Claire stopped the car in the drive and walked round to help William out of the car. He still walked with a stick and the long journey had obviously left his back stiff and painful. He slowly pulled himself into a standing position. Claire fetched his bag from the boot and followed him to the front door. The roses were in the second flush of bloom and the newly planted lavender sent a heady scent into the air around them. Claire took a deep breath and prayed that William would like what he saw.

Walking into the hall, William was silent and remained silent as together they went from room to room. Claire kept glancing at his face for a reaction but she found she couldn't read his thoughts at all.

Finally they stood in the spotless kitchen. The dresser shelves were still empty. Claire hadn't managed to replace the Cornishware she had loved so much and the kitchen walls were free from the jumble of children's drawings that had filled them before. The new Aga gleamed, the wooden work surfaces were yet to be scratched and stained by knives and spills, and the paintwork on the units was fresh and clean. Claire could hardly recognise it as the room she'd once loved so much.

William leant his stick against a chair and ran his fingers over the shiny new fridge-freezer and touched the smooth unblemished pine table. He looked at Claire and smiled.

'It's perfect,' he said. 'It's all so perfect!'

He took her in his arms.

'It's just as I imagined it would be when we first moved here, just as I always wanted it to be. I can't wait to show it to my mother. Did I tell you that my parents are coming this afternoon to look round? I know my mother will be so pleased.'

He leant down and kissed her lips and then taking her face between his hands he looked into her eyes.

'You'll try and keep it just like this, won't you? You will look after it, don't let the children spoil it, will you, Claire?'

Claire felt as though cold water were running through her veins.

'We have to live in it, William. It's not going to stay quite this clean and immaculate for long.'

'But we can try to keep it like this, can't we?'

'William, we have three children; there'll be five of us living here. I don't think it's going to be possible to keep it like this all the time, that's not realistic.'

'You haven't changed,' he said to her, letting his hands drop to his sides.

'I haven't changed? I thought you were going to change?'

'All I'm asking is that you respect our home.'

Claire could hear anger in his voice and she looked behind her as though checking for a clear exit. He took hold of her arm and though his grip seemed gentle she could feel each fingertip exert a subtle pressure. Her heart began to beat faster. The walls of the flawless kitchen seemed to be closing in on her.

'Is that too much to ask?' William continued.

Suddenly she felt that everything was clear. She knew where she wanted her home to be and it wasn't here, it wasn't with William.

'I can't do this,' she said.

'What?'

'Live here with you.'

He looked as though she'd hit him, incredulity spreading over his face.

'But it's all so lovely now. You and the children can just move back in with me and we'll go on like before, won't we? You told me that's how it would be.'

The children. Claire thought of them and faltered. Then she thought of how happy they had seemed in the past few months, relaxed and full of life in the clutter of the higgledy flat. They never talked about coming home.

Claire picked up her keys from the work surface and detached the front-door key from her car keys and handed it to William.

'It's all yours now,' she said. 'I don't want this house any more. I've made a new home, somewhere that is really mine, somewhere that really feels like home.'

She turned to leave and, though she thought he would, William didn't try to stop her.

Outside Claire could hear a blackbird; it seemed to be pouring out its heart in euphoric song. As she got into her car Claire felt as though she'd been released and as she drove down the hill she wanted to sing with all her heart as loudly as the bird.

# Chapter Thirty-six

*'Exquisite taste and an eye for olde world charm.'*

Just after her second Christmas in the shop, Claire and Sally sat at the counter, sketching out plans for a New Year window display.

Claire had been delighted as she and Sally had unpacked the boxes from the pottery in Stoke on Trent, she had been developing designs with them for months and finally the first batch of Emily Love tableware had arrived. It was glazed in softest duck-egg blue with small white hearts and flowers and birds that ran around the rims and edges of the mugs and bowls and jugs, while teapots and plates were decorated in a delicate pattern of spots and stripes and wiggly lines.

'I thought cut-out silhouettes of cupcakes suspended above the display?' said Sally. 'It would be like a nod to good old Patisserie Tremond as well as in keeping with the simple designs on the pottery.'

'Great idea,' said Claire giving a little grey whippet, with velvet fur and chocolate eyes, a stroke on his long nose. She had found Napoleon wandering along a poplar-lined French road, skeletally thin and bearing the scars of having been repeatedly beaten. Claire had fallen in love immediately and, after treatment by the vet, had brought him back to England to nurse him back to health. Now Napoleon was happy to sit with Claire in the shop all day and run like a mad thing along the riverbank with the children, when they came home from school.

Every few months Claire, the children, and Napoleon piled into her new blue Emily Love-emblazoned van and went to see her mother and Brian in France. The children and Napoleon spent happy days in their old farmhouse romping around with Buster, while Claire went on tours of junk shops and old house sales, collecting pretty wrought-iron furniture, vintage floral quilts, scarves, and lace. She started buying enamel kitchen utensils and old tin storage jars which sold very well in the shop and complemented her own work.

'Can I tempt you to a tiny triangle?' Claire took a large bar of duty-free Toblerone from her stash under the counter and waved it enticingly at Sally. Sally shook her head and virtuously produced an apple to accompany her tea.

'Girls?' Claire called behind her into the workshop. 'Chocolate?'

The hum of sewing machines stopped and Claire could hear a murmur going round the room. After a few seconds a shuffling noise heralded Doris, who, with a 'don't mind if we do,' snatched up the whole bar from Claire's hand and disappeared back into the room and closed the door.

'Is it my overly active imagination, or does Doris remind you of some sort of naughty goblin who every now and then emerges from the Middle Earth that is the workshop to scavenge for anything that might be on offer?' said Sally.

'She has to keep her strength up for Young Colin,' replied Claire with a laugh. 'Especially now they're engaged.'

'Doesn't that give you hope, Claire? Maybe you could find a nice toy boy of your own?'

'Your cupcake idea for the window reminds me of something else I need to tell you.' Claire wanted to change the subject.

'Go on,' encouraged Sally through a mouthful of apple. 'Is it that you've got a date with a baker?'

'No!' With a huff Claire continued, 'You know the café next door is closing soon?'

'Yes, it's such a shame,' said Sally, taking a sip from a new Emily Love mug. 'This town needs a good café. It will probably end up

319

as another empty shop. It won't look good next to us, and where will I get my lunchtime salad now?'

'I've been thinking,' Claire said. 'I might take on the lease myself.'

Sally nodded slowly as she munched on a mouthful of apple. 'It is a bit bigger than this shop. More floor space for us. We could certainly do with it, but it seems a shame to have to move when we've got it looking so nice in here.'

'I don't mean we'd leave here,' said Claire. 'We'd keep this as the shop and keep next door as a café. We could have the café as part of the shop.'

'Knock through into next door, do you mean?'

'Yes,' said Claire. 'We could use the new Emily Love tableware and the matching napkins and tablecloths and then we could promote what we have to sell in here.'

'What sort of café?'

'Like a teashop really. Cakes and muffins, tarts, chocolate brownies, I'm sure you can imagine the sort of thing.'

Sally groaned. 'Too well!'

'Plus a simple lunchtime menu, home-made from seasonal local produce.'

'Claire, are you trying to torture me?' Sally wailed. 'I'll never be able to concentrate on my job, let alone stick to my diet.'

Claire ignored her; she knew Sally had developed a will of steel when it came to maintaining her hard-won slender figure.

'We could find a really good bakery to supply it. I was even thinking about our own range of fairy cakes with pretty Emily Love-inspired designs in icing on the top.'

'Coordinating cupcakes – now that is a fabulous idea.' Sally beamed at her. 'Cushions and cakes – everything a woman could possibly want all in one place! My tutors in college would have been so impressed with you, Claire.'

'But I'd need someone to run the café. We would never have enough time.'

Sally laughed. 'You definitely couldn't trust me. I might fall off the wagon and eat more than I'd sell.'

'What about Gareth?' asked Claire. 'He's so fantastic in the kitchen now and he's always saying he'd like to leave his IT job to work freelance as a web designer.'

Sally sat up straighter on her stool. 'It's sounding interesting but I can't see how the two things tie together.'

'If he could manage the café through the mornings and at lunchtime – make the quiches, soup, a few nice salads, maybe a selection of paninis – we could get a couple of waitresses to work with him and take over in the afternoon so that he could develop his web-designing business at home.'

'As long as the waitresses are elderly and toothless, I think it could be a very good idea. I wouldn't want Gareth working with any svelte young things in pinnies,' Sally warned. 'I still have to keep an eye on him, you know.'

'Don't be silly,' Claire laughed. 'Gareth only has eyes for you and no wonder – you look a million dollars in those tight jeans. Gareth wouldn't be interested in waitresses – young or old.'

Sally looked delighted at the compliment and at the idea of working with Gareth. 'What a team we could be!' she said. 'Like the Three Musketeers. One for all and all for Emily Love.'

Claire laughed. 'Shouldn't that be "cushions for all"?'

'Talking of slogans, what do you want to call the café bit? It ought to have its own separate name.'

'I have been thinking about a name,' said Claire.

'Claire's Cupcakes?'

'Nice,' she said, 'but I think I've already found the one I like.'

'I know, I know.' Sally bounced excitedly on her seat. 'What about "The Flighty Tart"? Your mother-in-law would love that.'

Claire had told her what William's mother had called her on the last occasion they had ever spoken. The two women burst out laughing. Claire laughed so much she spilt her tea on the credit card machine.

'That name is appealing,' said Claire, popping the plastic cover off the machine and mopping at its internal mass of wires and chip pads, 'but Emily has come up with a name for us. It's quite simple but it seems to say it all: "Emily Loves Cakes".'

'That sounds great,' said Sally. 'As the wife of the potential café manager I'd like to endorse that name and propose a toast.'

Sally raised her mug. 'To Emily Loves Cakes.'

The two women clinked their Emily Love mugs together with a cheer that made Napoleon jump.

# Chapter Thirty-seven

*'Teatime is always special in Claire's house.'*

The café had been an instant success. Claire's regular customers loved the excuse to have a cup of tea and a cake in lovely surroundings and those in search of refreshments alone were often lured into the shop to be tempted by the gorgeous stock after they had enjoyed their coffee and cakes.

When Claire had taken over the lease, the café had been decorated with hacienda-style swirls of shiny yellow plaster and heavily varnished orange pine panelling. Claire ordered builders to hack off the lumpy plaster and, over one weekend, with the help of Sally, she painted the walls a soft cream and covered the varnished wood with palest duck-egg blue. She furnished it with a mixture of comfortable sofas and painted chairs grouped around tables covered with spotty tablecloths. The effect was fresh and pretty, the perfect backdrop for her cushions, tea cosies and embroidered napkins.

Gareth had jumped at the chance of leaving his job and being able to cook every day. Two waitresses, vetted by Sally – not too young, too pretty, or too thin – wore brightly coloured Emily Love aprons over black tops and trousers as they served the pots of tea or freshly brewed coffee. Large glass domes on a wooden counter covered slices of moist sponge, rich fruit cake, lemon drizzle squares and chocolate brownies. But most popular of all were the little cupcakes iced with tiny pink hearts and pretty birds and flowers in the distinctive Emily Love style.

Gareth kept lunch simple: home-made soup or fresh rolls with assorted fillings, which were advertised on a large chalkboard on the wall. His one stipulation on accepting the job was that he wouldn't make quiche.

'Real men and all that,' he'd said. 'I don't care if you call it a tart or a flan or a galette – I'll know it's a quiche and I just won't do it.'

It had been Gareth's idea to clear the overgrown garden at the back to make it into an outdoor eating area for warmer weather. After he and a few friends from the pub had hacked back the nettles and brambles, Claire employed a builder to pave the area with reclaimed flagstones and make raised flower beds around the edge. She bought up a collection of pretty wrought-iron chairs and tables from a café in France that was closing down and hung old tin advertising signs and antique garden implements around the stone walls. Window boxes lined the windowsills and hanging baskets cascaded down either side of the doorway.

'Wow,' Sally said, as she and Claire looked around them at the finished effect. 'I know where I'll be spending my lunchtimes from now on.'

Claire smiled. 'It does look lovely. Well done Gareth for coming up with the idea!'

'Well done you.' Sally put her arm across Claire's shoulder. 'You've come a long way from making bits of bunting in your spare room.'

'I can hardly remember that time,' said Claire. 'It seems like someone else's life. I feel like a different person now.'

The warm bank-holiday sun shone down on Claire as she planted a selection of herbs in the new café garden. The children were all at birthday parties and Claire was enjoying a few free hours to get jobs done at work. She hummed an Aretha Franklin tune to herself as she dug down into the soft moist soil.

'Claire.'

Startled at the unexpected voice, she turned around to find William standing behind her.

'Sorry, I didn't mean to make you jump.'

He wore a pink shirt, something he would never have worn in the past but it suited him, complementing the deep suntan he'd acquired on a recent holiday abroad.

'I just wanted to have a word without the children being about.'

The only time Claire ever saw William was when he picked up the children to take them for weekends with him at the house.

Claire stood up, shaking the dirt from her gardening gloves before taking them off.

'Sit down then.'

She pulled out a chair from one of the tables, offered it to him, and sat down opposite, placing the gloves on the table in between them.

William looked around him at the little walled garden.

'You've made this really lovely.'

Surprised by the unexpected compliment, Claire smiled at her ex-husband.

'You're looking well,' she said.

'I am well.' He smiled back at her. 'I suppose that's what I want to talk to you about. I wanted you to hear this from me, not from the children, or from,' he hesitated and looked down at his hands, clenched together, on the table in front of him, 'or from my mother.'

'You've met someone,' Claire said; surely the only reason her ex-mother-in-law would ever get in touch with her would be to gloat.

'Yes,' said William, still looking at his hands.

'That's great,' said Claire, smiling. She felt genuinely pleased for him. 'I knew you wouldn't have gone on a Mediterranean holiday alone. Who is she?'

'Vanessa.'

'Vanessa.' Claire repeated the name slowly, suddenly feeling her congeniality sinking. 'Your old Vanessa or have you found a new one?'

William looked irritated. 'Please don't be flippant, Claire. I'm seeing Vanessa, my fiancée from before . . .' He paused.

'From before me,' prompted Claire.

'Yes.' His face turned slightly pink; Claire noticed that it clashed with his shirt. 'She was very good to me after the . . .' Again a pause; Claire resisted the urge to prompt him this time. 'After everything that happened,' William finally said.

A hundred questions flew around Claire's head but most seemed too futile to ask.

'My mother told her I was in hospital and she came to visit me a few times.' Claire raised her eyebrows. 'Nothing happened, Claire. She was just a good friend to me until you and I divorced. Since then she's helped me get myself together, to really sort myself out, and we've realised we still have feelings for each other.'

'I see,' said Claire.

'I've come to tell you that she's moving in with me. Moving in to the house.'

They were silent for a while as Claire tried to work out why this news had made her feel so unsettled.

'I'm hoping we'll get married next summer,' continued William. 'It's not as if you and I were ever going to get back together or anything like that,' his voice trailed away.

'I'm sure your mother is delighted.' Claire picked up a gardening glove and began to fiddle with its fingers, picking the crusty flakes of earth from the hardened suede. 'Isn't this what she always wanted, Vanessa as her daughter-in-law, Vanessa living in that house instead of me?'

'I don't care what my mother thinks. It's about what I want and what Vanessa wants. She makes me very happy and she loves the house – I'm just pleased we found each other again.'

'How romantic.'

'Are you being sarcastic?'

Claire smiled. 'No, I'm not. I'm glad you're happy and I wish you all the best for your future.' And suddenly she realised that she meant it.

He returned the smile with a look of relief, and shrugged his shoulders to indicate there was nothing more to say.

'Thank you for telling me,' said Claire.

William stood up. 'I must go. Vanessa and I are seeing an architect this afternoon about that extension I want to do above the kitchen.'

'Don't get too obsessive this time,' Claire said, standing up as well.

'What do you mean?'

'All I'm saying is that a house is only bricks and mortar. It's people that really make it a home.'

She reached up and gently kissed his cheek. He looked surprised and confused. As he walked out of the garden, Claire wondered if he would ever understand.

# Chapter Thirty-eight

*'The sun-drenched rooms provide the perfect setting for collections of treasured finds and vintage ephemera.'*

'Do you really not mind?' Sally asked, arranging a new display of cushions on a little painted dresser.

Claire leant against the counter, opening the morning's post.

'No, I don't. I'm pleased for William. The children met Vanessa at the weekend and they said she's nice. Ben loved her because she let him have two ice creams at the park but he says her bottom's not as big as mine – I'm not sure if he thought that was good or bad! Emily made things better by telling me that Vanessa's hair is grey at the roots and that she thinks she's got a face like a Shetland pony.'

'Good for Emily,' laughed Sally. 'I wish I had a daughter to be sensitive to my emotional needs. Now both the boys are at secondary school I think they've forgotten I even exist.'

'Oliver is just the same; I'm just the person who keeps the fridge stocked, as far as he's concerned.'

'But what about you?' Sally stopped midway through slotting a daisy cushion in beside a row of patchwork heart ones. 'When are you going to find yourself a man and start having a bit of fun?'

'I am having fun,' she said, a little annoyed. She enjoyed the shop and the café; she loved the flat, being with the children, the dog, and Macavity. 'I don't need a man to make my life complete.'

Sally raised her eyebrows and turned back to the cushions.

After a little while she said, 'I always hoped you'd get back together with William.'

Claire laughed. 'That was never very likely. I know you always thought that William was Mr Wonderful but looking back I realise how unhappy I had become. I felt like a little girl playing in the perfect doll's house, but I never seemed to get the rules of the game right. He thought he'd done it all for me, but in the end he'd boxed me in so much that I'd completely lost who I'd once been.'

Sally took all the cushions down and started rearranging them in a different order.

'Did you ever hear what happened to that photographer man?' she asked.

'No.' Claire ripped open an envelope and after staring at a brightly coloured piece of junk mail, scrunched it up and threw it in the bin.

'Don't you ever wonder where he is?'

'No,' said Claire again.

'But don't you ever think . . .'

'No, I don't.' Claire started tidying up around her. She picked up a pile of leaflets about their summer sale and banged them down hard on the counter. 'I don't know what happened to him. I don't know where he is. I don't think about him and, to be quite honest, I don't care.'

'OK,' said Sally, holding up a cushion in defence. 'I was only asking.'

The phone rang.

'I suppose, as you now seem to be in such a bad mood, I'd better answer that,' said Sally.

She picked up the receiver and Claire listened as Sally made little *uhhu* noises and said *I see* a lot, then she covered the phone with her hand and, unable to contain a grin, said to Claire, 'There's a journalist from a magazine on the phone, she wants to do a feature on your home.'

'Absolutely no way.' Claire shook her head to emphasise her refusal. 'Tell them they can do an article about my work or the shop but I will not let them come and take photographs of my home.'

329

Sally spoke into the phone again using her poshest voice. 'I'm afraid Claire will have to decline your request, she never allows the media access to her private domicile.'

Claire stifled a giggle and waited for Sally to put the phone down but she didn't, instead she started making the little *uhhu* noises again together with some added *ooo*s; after a few more seconds of this, she covered the receiver once more, 'The journalist says you know her, she says her name is Zoë and that you were at college together.'

Claire grabbed the phone. 'Zoë! How are you?'

'All the better for hearing your voice after all these years. Hey, did you get my birthday card that time?'

Claire thought back to how she had sat at the kitchen table reading Zoë's card just before she'd found the card from Stefan.

'Yes, I'm sorry that I never got back to you.'

'Don't worry, I read about the fire,' continued Zoë. 'That sounded terrible, I thought my number probably went up in flames. I've been meaning to get in touch for ages – I just love your work, I see it everywhere I go, you've done so well.'

'Thank you. Sally says that you're a journalist. I remember how you always enjoyed writing.'

'I've been given a brief to do a feature on a vintage-inspired home of an artist and I thought of you.'

'You haven't seen my flat,' said Claire. 'It's very different in style from the house that was photographed in *Idyllic Homes*. A lot messier, a lot more clutter.'

'Great, is it anything like your bedroom used to be in Clapham? Lots of quirky ornaments and antique clothes and pottery – that's the sort of look I'm after.'

'I suppose it is a bit, though without the underwear and ash trays lying about.'

'Can we come to have a look?'

'No, Zoë, I can't do it. I didn't have a good experience having this sort of thing done in the past.'

'I'd let you see what I've written before it's published. It would be fantastic for your business.'

'I really don't want to let a photographer take pictures of my home again.'

'It would be the best photographer I know,' Zoë said. 'In fact the photographer would be my absolutely gorgeous partner; actually we've just got married.'

Claire's heart lurched, it couldn't be, the coincidence would be too great; surely there were loads of gorgeous photographers working in interiors. She felt sick.

'What's his name,' she managed to ask.

'Her. Sienna. Sienna Crabtree, she's widely regarded as the best in the business.'

Claire felt flooded with relief, how stupid to have imagined it could have been Stefan. Then she thought about what Zoë had actually said.

'Sienna? Is Sienna a girl?'

'I'd say Sienna is more of a woman than a girl but she's definitely not a man.' Zoë was laughing on the other end of the phone.

'But you always had so many boyfriends,' said Claire, remembering how Zoë never seemed to spend a night alone.

'And they were never what I was looking for.' Zoë was still laughing. 'In fact it turned out I wasn't looking for a boyfriend at all.'

'Well, congratulations on your marriage, I hope you'll be very happy.'

'Come on,' coaxed Zoë. 'Why don't we both come and visit you and you can meet Sienna and you and I can have a good old catch-up and see how you feel then?'

Claire glanced at Sally, she was giving her encouraging nods and smiles and she'd written in capitals on a piece of paper: WHAT HAVE YOU GOT TO LOSE? Claire picked up a lavender heart and threw it at her.

'Claire? Are you still there?'

'All right,' said Claire. 'Come to lunch on Sunday, the children will be with William for the weekend.'

'Oh yes,' Zoë sounded intrigued. 'You can tell me what

331

happened with you and William and maybe I'll tell you the nickname I used to have for him.'

Zoë and Sienna were early, arriving well before the chicken, which Claire was roasting, was ready.

'Fantastic!' said Zoë, standing in the living room looking around her.

'What an eye you have for mixing patterns and colour and texture,' added Sienna. 'Everywhere I look I see a perfect picture for this piece. I love your collection of old straw hats on the wall and those paper Chinese lanterns above the fireplace are just inspired. This is going to look wonderful in the magazine.'

'I haven't agreed to do it yet,' said Claire, setting down a tray of glasses on top of the pile of old leather suitcases that she used as a coffee table. 'Sit down,' she gestured to the sofa and the two women sat down in front of her while she took the armchair and handed out the chilled white wine.

Sienna draped her svelte body across her seat laconically. Claire had to agree with Zoë. Sienna was gorgeous; honey hair cascaded over her shoulders in a mass of curls, her long legs, clad in skintight denim, seemed to go on forever and an oversized striped T-shirt emphasised her tiny hips. Zoë perched beside her, still the same, small and dark and pretty, though the long hair she'd always had at college had been cut into a gamine crop. She too wore skin-tight jeans but with a white silk blouse, a suede waistcoat, and long strings of coral beads that hung from her slender neck.

'You're much thinner than you used to be,' said Claire as she handed Zoë her drink.

'Now that I don't drink six pints of lager every night followed by a greasy kebab from that awful takeaway we used to live above.'

Claire laughed. 'I think we thought that was a balanced diet.'

'Yes, together with the twenty Marlboro Lights and the bowls of Frosties we lived on during the day – we thought we had all our major food groups covered.'

'Which allowed us to have Pop Tarts as a treat on Sundays.'

'You guys are lucky you survived on all that junk.'

Sienna's accent had a slightly trans-Atlantic drawl.

'We eat a very healthy diet now, don't we, Zoë? We only buy organic and we're both vegetarian.'

Claire thought about the chicken in the oven; could she rustle up a quick carrot risotto instead?

'Thank you for inviting us over,' Sienna said. 'I hope Zoë didn't push you into it too much. We understand you've got to think about having this place featured in the magazine.'

'The funny thing is,' said Zoë, 'that Sienna was actually meant to photograph your house before.'

'I thought your name was familiar,' Claire said. 'Now I remember, Celia Howard told me you were going to do the job and then in the end you couldn't.'

'I had an accident hang-gliding in the Rockies,' Sienna explained. 'I broke my leg in three places.'

Zoë put her hand on Sienna's thigh. 'Poor thing, you were out of action for weeks, weren't you? Hobbling around on crutches while I had to run round obeying your every command like some sort of manic minion.'

Sienna smiled at Zoë. 'Hey, don't gripe, babe, you know you loved it really.' The pair exchanged an intimate look.

'I do remember Celia telling me you were a very good photographer,' said Claire.

'Who did the shoot in the end?' asked Zoë.

Claire felt her stomach suddenly clench.

'Ummm,' she said as though trying to remember.

'Oh yeah, I know.' A row of silver bracelets jangled on Sienna's arm. 'Stefan, Stefan Kendrick, he did it instead of me, didn't he, Claire?'

'Yes, I think that was him.'

Everything around seemed to go a little hazy, she was sure the two woman would be able to see the agitation she was suddenly feeling at the mention of his name.

'Do I know him?' Zoë asked.

'You met him at Celia's fiftieth birthday bash,' Sienna told her. 'You must remember, afterwards I accused you of flirting with him and we had a row in the middle of Berkeley Square.'

'Oh yes.' Zoë raised her eyebrows. 'I remember him, he was absolutely divine.'

Sienna slapped Zoë's knee.

'There you go again, you did fancy him, didn't you?'

'You know I only have eyes for you, darling, but maybe I just had the tiniest bit of a crush on him when I met him that night.'

She looked at Claire. 'Lucky you then. But you told me you had a bad experience – how could that have been when you had someone so dishy to look at and he had such a great personality too; I remember that he made me laugh a lot when we were trying to eat those weird, wrapped prawns.'

'Zoë! I'm warning you.' Sienna slapped her knee again. 'I think it's a good job he disappeared the way he did.'

'Disappeared?' Claire's voice felt thick and croaky.

'He literally flew off one day without a word. Celia was furious, he had a pile of shoots he was booked in for, I had to mop up some of them.'

'Where did he go?' Claire asked.

Sienna shrugged. 'Haven't a clue. It was strange, he was a lovely bloke, it didn't seem in keeping that he'd just have gone off without good reason, but then he'd not long been back from Australia so maybe he was a bit of a wanderer who'd had enough of London.'

'I thought he had a girlfriend,' said Claire. She could feel her heart beating beneath her cotton blouse.

'No one special that I ever heard of,' said Sienna. 'He seemed like one of those people who was always searching for the elusive perfect partner.'

'When I met him at Celia's birthday party he told me he was in love,' said Zoë.

Sienna pulled a face. 'Just goes to show, you never can tell what's going on in other people's lives. Maybe he ran off to Vegas to get hitched like Zoë and I did and just never came back.'

'I knew he had a girlfriend all along.'

Claire hadn't realised that she had spoken out loud. The two women looked at her quizzically. She felt flustered.

'And so you've never heard anything about him again?' she asked, trying to sound only vaguely interested.

Sienna shook her head, then after a moment's pause, 'Come to think of it, I did see his name a few months ago; it was in the *National Geographic*, he was credited with the photography for a piece about the nomadic tribes of West Africa.'

'Oh, Claire.' Zoë clamped her hand over her mouth. 'I've just caught the most delicious whiff of roast chicken coming from your kitchen and realised that I completely forgot to mention that we're vegetarian when I spoke to you on the phone.'

'Don't worry,' said Claire, suddenly relieved to change the conversation. 'I'd already realised I might have to rush out and get something else for our Sunday lunch.' She paused and then she smiled. 'Would Pop Tarts be OK?'

Two weeks later Zoë and Sienna returned to take the pictures. Claire had only done the briefest of spring-cleaning jobs as both the women insisted that they liked the flat just the way it was.

Zoë put her arm around Claire's shoulder as Sienna packed her camera away.

'Are you pleased we talked you into it? It's going to be a lovely feature, especially now the editor's agreed to double the amount of pages it will cover.'

'Yes, if you manage to combine the shop and café and the flat then I can see it makes it very good advertising for Emily Love.'

'Those shots we did in the workshop should come out well. People always like to see pictures of things being made. I loved the one of Mrs Needles sewing miniature frilly knickers onto peg bags and the way that Doris played up to the camera was a scream; she should be on television!'

'I think she'd be too rude,' laughed Claire.

'I'll email you the article by the end of the week,' continued

Zoë. 'And I'll happily make any changes that you want. We'll email the pictures too so you and the kids can go through them and say if there are any you particularly don't want used. Is Oliver sure he really doesn't want to appear in any of the photographs?'

Zoë glanced at Oliver slouched on the sofa playing with his DS. Emily and Ben sat beside him eating a large packet of marshmallows that Sienna had given them for being in some of the shots.

'You know what it's like when you're thirteen,' Claire grimaced. 'The last thing you want is someone taking pictures of you.' She paused. 'In fact it's the last thing you want when you're nearly forty.'

'You'll look lovely,' Zoë reassured her. 'You still look as beautiful as you did when we were in college. You really were wasted on that anally retentive mummy's boy.'

Claire couldn't help smiling. 'You still haven't told me what you used to call William.'

Aware that the children were around, Zoë whispered in Claire's ear. Claire threw her head back and laughed.

'That's worthy of the kind of language Doris uses,' she said. 'You never told me at the time.'

'I did! But you were too blinded by love to hear me.'

Claire shrugged. 'Oh well, it's all turned out all right in the end, William's very happy with Vanessa, he should probably have never left her in the first place.'

'And what about you?' Zoë asked. 'Are there any handsome princes, or princesses, hanging around waiting to whisk you off your feet?'

# Chapter Thirty-nine

*'Everything has been chosen with love.'*

After persistent proposals from Brian, Claire's mother had finally said 'yes'. The wedding was to take place on a September Saturday in France with Claire and the children arriving two days early to help with the preparations and to make sure Elizabeth didn't get cold feet at the last minute.

The early-morning sky was clear and bright as Claire packed up her little van with things to take to the wedding. Sally helped her carry trays and boxes from the shop, filled with lace-edged tablecloths, embroidered napkins, and yards of floral bunting that she had made specially to decorate the garden. Claire had even had hundreds of tiny cupcakes made, all iced with red and pink hearts. Napoleon skittered excitedly between the two women as they went backwards and forwards between the shop and the van; he seemed to know a journey was imminent and kept trying to jump into the van, desperate not to be left behind.

Inside the café the children watched their mother and Sally through the window as Gareth made them bacon muffins and strawberry smoothies for breakfast. Emily and Ben could hardly contain their excitement as they waited for Claire to finish so that they could finally set off for France. Oliver was trying to look nonchalant and bored but Claire knew he was secretly just as excited as his siblings.

'I wish I could come with you,' Sally sighed. 'I love a wedding. Any excuse for dressing up and having a bit of a bop.'

She wiggled her hips in a little demonstration of her dancing skills.

'Sorry, Cinderella, you've got a shop to run,' said Claire, as she tried to squeeze the last box of bunting into the back of the van. Together the two women banged the doors shut and leant back against them for a rest.

'I'll just have to wait for yours then.' Sally grinned at Claire.

'Wait for my what?'

'Your wedding.'

'You'll be waiting a long time,' said Claire. 'Like forever.'

'Why don't you hitch up with that bloke from the butcher's?' Sally waved towards a shop on the other side of the street. 'I know he fancies you. He's always asking you to try his speciality sausages. You could do worse – though it is a bit of a shame about the wart on his chin and the dodgy comb-over. Look, I can see him now, arranging his chops in the window – shall I go over and tell him you're desperate for a nibble on his chipolata?'

'Sally, stop it.' Claire gave her friend a playful swipe.

'Or that man from the estate agent's who comes in for his lemon meringue slice every day? There are things you can do to cure halitosis, you know. Just a few hints on your first date and he'd have it all cleared up by the wedding day.'

'Sally! I'm not marrying the butcher or the estate agent just to give you the opportunity to show off your moves on the dance floor – I'm sure Oliver would get you a ticket to the next youth club disco if you're that desperate for a boogie.'

'Don't worry, our invite to William and Vanessa's wedding will be dropping through the letter box any day now.'

Claire laughed. 'Somehow I don't think you and Gareth will be top of the guest list and I doubt that the Cotswold String Quartet will be taking requests for "Dancing Queen".'

'Sounds like it's going to be a barrel of laughs,' said Sally making a face. 'Don't tell me – William's mother is in charge of the preparations.'

'Of course, and from what Emily tells me it's pretty much a

338

re-run of mine and William's wedding though with the right bride in the grotesque dress this time!'

'Are you sure you're all right about William getting married again?'

Sally touched Claire's arm, her face genuinely concerned.

'I keep telling you. I'm fine about it. Anyway William and Vanessa are made for each other, not to mention William's mother and Vanessa! William and I were never really meant to be. It's all in the past.'

'Have you got the copy of the magazine to show to your mum and Brian?' Sally made as though to run and fetch it.

'No, don't worry, my mum got it sent over especially last week, she couldn't wait this long to see it.'

'What did she think?'

'She was impressed. I'm very happy with it, it looks lovely and Zoë's written the article beautifully.'

'No made-up bits this time,' laughed Sally. 'And I look very nice in that picture where I'm hanging bunting from the dresser. My boobs look stupendous.'

'That'll be the reason that we've had so many more men coming in this week.'

'Have we?'

'No!' Claire laughed. 'I'm only joking, I don't think people looking in an interiors magazine are really going to notice a pair of big boobs, especially when the picture is only the size of a postage stamp.'

'Gareth wants to ask Sienna for the original so he can put it in a frame.'

'Ahhh,' smiled Claire. 'Isn't he lovely? Sienna certainly is a very good photographer. It's funny to think if she hadn't broken her leg she would have photographed the house that time.'

'How differently everything would have turned out then,' said Sally. 'You'd probably still be trying to make lavender bags in the spare room, William would probably have built a three-storey windmill in the garden, I'd still be working at Anna's, and Gareth

339

would have been stuck in his IT job, and Gareth and I would never have got back together, nor would William and Vanessa. In fact Sienna falling off her hang-glider started a whole chain of events that have ended up with us here, outside your lovely shop.'

Claire smiled. Sally was right, though she had omitted to mention the biggest catalyst of all in the chain of events – Stefan; though she tried hard not to think of him, Claire couldn't deny that after that moment when she set eyes on Stefan her life had never been the same again.

At last Claire piled the children into the little blue van, with Napoleon sitting between them and she pulled slowly away from the curb, waving from the open window.

'I hope it's a good wedding,' Gareth called from the café doorway.

'Maybe you'll find a man in France,' shouted Sally as Gareth placed his arm around her shoulder.

'I'm not interested,' Claire called back.

'If you found a man, Mummy, would you have another baby?' Emily asked from the seat beside her mother.

'No, darling,' smiled Claire, edging through the town's early morning traffic. 'I don't think I'll be providing you with any more brothers or sisters, man or no man.'

'You're too old for a man now, Mummy, aren't you?' said Ben.

'Yes, Ben, I'm too old and too busy. You lot are enough for me.'

The morning of the wedding was warm and cloudless. Claire got ready in the sun-drenched bedroom, carefully taking her dress down from its hanger on the hook behind the door. All the guests had been asked to dress in white and Claire had found a genuine Dior concoction of silk and satin and chiffon in an antiques market in Bergerac. It hung delicately from thin shoulder straps and as she slipped into it she felt as though she was being surrounded by a gentle breeze. Looking into the mirror, she gathered her hair up loosely in a mother-of-pearl clasp and put on a softly crocheted silk cardigan to hide the ugly scars on her arm.

There was a gentle tapping at the door and Claire's mother walked into the room. Claire smiled; her mother looked beautiful, almost regal, in flowing lavender with a lilac lace bolero jacket and a comb of yellow rosebuds in her hair. Her eyes shone brightly and her sun-browned skin looked radiant.

'Will I do?' Elizabeth asked.

'Oh, Mum, you will so much more than do! You look amazing.'

'So do you,' replied Elizabeth, taking her daughter's hand in hers. 'You should be the one getting married; you look like the perfect bride. I'm too old for all this nonsense; this should be your day.'

Claire laughed. 'You're worse than Sally; she's been trying to marry me off to all sorts of ghastly men lately. I'm perfectly happy being a wedding guest, thank you.'

Her mother picked up a pink camellia corsage from the little oak dressing table beside them and carefully pinned it to the bodice of Claire's dress.

'Your grandmother's favourite flower,' she said, adjusting the petals against the spray of green leaves behind. 'What is it they are meant to mean?'

'Longing,' answered Claire, trying to banish the image of a painted teacup from her mind.

The door opened again and Emily appeared, looking like an angel in a simple white lace tunic, a bunch of loosely tied pink roses in her hand. She stopped and gazed at her grandmother.

'Wow, Granny. I didn't know you were so pretty.'

Elizabeth raised her eyebrows and smiled. 'Thank you, darling – I think that was a compliment.'

Emily ceremoniously handed her grandmother the bouquet with a curtsy. 'Here are your flowers and a message from Brian, he says, "Don't be late and don't change your mind".'

'Do you know, I think I have changed my mind,' Elizabeth said as she took the flowers from Emily and let them hang limply by her side. 'I'm not sure this getting married thing is really such a good idea. I don't know why Brian wants to make such a fuss, let's just call the whole ceremony off and have a jolly good party instead.'

'Come on,' laughed Claire, taking her mother firmly by the arm. 'Emily, you take the other side and don't let go of her until we reach the town hall!'

Brian arrived at the ancient town hall by motorbike and sidecar, wearing a bright purple silk shirt, Buster and Napoleon beside him with large white bows tied onto their collars. The dogs were allowed in especially for the ceremony; Oliver and Emily kept them under control by bribing them with dog biscuits throughout the formalities. Elizabeth shakily got through her marriage vows while Brian anxiously waited for each response, but as the mayor pronounced them man and wife, Elizabeth's beaming smile betrayed her joy. Standing on the steps of the hall, as they were showered with rice and petals, a contagious happiness radiated from them both.

Afterwards it seemed as if the whole town gathered at the old farmhouse for the reception. They stood amid a mass of flowers that Claire's mother had grown in the garden. Her sunflowers swayed like extra guests surveying the scene from their lofty heights, and window boxes overflowed with red and pink geraniums along the front of the house.

A violinist friend of Brian's – the son of a gypsy, so he claimed – wandered around playing music to the crowd as they drank tall glasses of Pimm's floating with cucumber and wild borage flowers. The children helped themselves to cloudy home-made lemonade from earthenware jugs that sat on a table in the shade of the vine-covered trellis.

Long tables stretched across the grass, clothed in white and interspersed with jam jars filled with lavender and late roses. Claire had scattered pink petals in between the plates and cutlery.

Assorted pies and two cold poached salmon waited in the cool kitchen to be brought out, along with a selection of fresh salads piled into huge, honey-coloured bowls made by a local potter.

Neighbours brought large wheels of cheese, home-cured hams, breads, and wonderful desserts and pastries to add to the feast.

The lunch was long and leisurely. Bottle after bottle of champagne was opened, toasts drunk, and touching speeches made. Brian's speech had even reduced the men in the party to tears as he declared his happiness at finding someone that he loved so much to share his life. Then Claire's mother stood up and in French thanked everyone for coming and making the day so special, and then thanked Brian for transforming her life and bringing her such joy. As the newly married couple kissed to the guests' cheers, two local women appeared carrying a pyramid of choux buns covered with a delicate cobweb of spun sugar, a thick band of brightly coloured marigolds and chrysanthemums at its base. Claire explained to the children that this was a traditional French wedding cake called a *croquembouche*, and they were delighted when a large silver sword was produced for the bride and groom to hit the top with, showering the guests with shards of splintered caramel.

At last the light began to fade and the evening party began. A group of local musicians played accordions and violins and the guests danced, young and old alike, on a dance floor Brian had made from wooden pallets and old floorboards.

Claire sat on the steps of the kitchen, watching from a distance. She had danced with various men: the local doctor, the potter, the baker's teenage son. After that she had accepted a dance from the town's mayor, who had performed the wedding ceremony that morning. By the time Claire danced with him he was very drunk and his feet repeatedly stepped on hers as he spun her around enthusiastically. She didn't like the way he held her too close in his sweaty arms and she caught a glimpse of his wife watching them, her arms crossed over her large expanse of bosom.

At last Claire managed to escape. Leaving the dance floor she found a glass of wine and a quiet space to watch the magical scene. Fairy lights criss-crossed their way between the trees. Glass lanterns hung, suspended from branches, their candle flames reflected in the inky water of the river. All around her fireflies darted back and forth in the warm air as though they were part of the evening's decorations too.

Claire sipped her wine and marvelled at the complicated dance steps that the older local people seemed to know. She could see Oliver and Emily amongst a group of children at the river's edge, laughing and splashing their feet in the cool water as they tried, in their basic French, to join in with the children's conversations. They seemed almost luminous in their white clothes, bathed in the light of an enormous harvest moon that rose behind the wedding party, like a beautiful backdrop in a play.

Oliver and Emily were growing up so quickly. Claire felt a pang of sadness. She looked around for Ben; still her little boy. He was dancing in his typically exuberant style with an elderly lady. Her olive-skinned face revealed a bone structure that, even in old age, made her beautiful. She solemnly followed the steps of the dance, gracefully accommodating her partner's lack of stature and coordination.

Brian's son was there, dancing in a slightly embarrassed way on the edge of the dance floor, out of time to the music, with the glazed look of a man who had driven through the night and only just made it to his father's wedding on time. In his arms he jigged his daughter – the little girl that had been the baby that Brian had come to visit when Claire's mother had fatefully run him over. His wife sat on a nearby chair breastfeeding their second child, looking exhausted and hot. Claire thought she ought to offer her a glass of lemonade, but just as she was about to get up her mother appeared. Sitting down beside her, she took Claire's hand in hers and squeezed it.

'Are you enjoying yourself, darling?' her mother asked.

'Yes,' replied Claire. 'It's lovely.'

'You certainly had no shortage of men wanting to dance with you,' her mother said, nodding towards the dance floor.

'I'd no idea what I was meant to be doing. The dances are so complicated.'

'You looked like you were making a good job of it from where I was sitting.'

Her mother's eyes twinkled in amusement.

'I think François, the potter, rather likes you. He hasn't taken his eyes off you since you had your dance with him. I thought he was going to come over and punch the mayor when he was flinging you around.'

'Mum! Are you trying to play the matchmaker?' Claire asked in mock incredulity.

'No, I wouldn't dream of it. But it's been a while since you and William separated. Don't you ever think about finding someone else?'

'Look who's talking,' Claire smiled. 'You were on your own for twenty-five years before you met Brian.'

'I was just a miserable, bitter old grump of a woman. Don't be like me, darling. Don't leave it so long. You have so much to offer.' She put her arm around Claire's shoulder. 'My beautiful, clever daughter. I only want to see you happy.'

Claire sighed. 'I am happy, Mum. I have my gorgeous children, my own business, a lovely home, my garden. I don't need anyone else when I've got so much to make me happy.'

'It's just sometimes I see such sadness behind your eyes and I wonder if you've been hurt more than you let on. You're well rid of William and that stuck-up mother of his.' Elizabeth shuddered at the thought of her. 'I hope you don't regret your divorce.'

'I'm fine, Mum,' Claire said. 'I think I hurt William more than he hurt me.'

She looked into the distance, beyond the dancers and the twinkling lights, into the darkness.

'I can't imagine falling in love with anyone again, having those intense feelings for another man, the desire to share my life with anyone else. Maybe you only get one chance at love in your life and mine just slipped away.'

She took a sip of wine.

'I'm living proof that you *do* get another chance,' said her mother. 'This whole day is proof of that for me and for Brian.' She gently stroked her daughter's face. 'Go and ask François for another dance and make your old mother very happy.'

'Mum,' Claire warned. 'I don't want to encourage him, or any other man. Anyway, tonight isn't about me. It's about you.'

She stood up.

'Why don't you come and dance with me instead, and we can try to work out some of these mad dance steps together?'

Claire and her mother walked hand in hand towards the dance floor. The music had grown louder. A robustly built woman with red hair piled in curls on her head began to sing.

'I hope you know how lovely you look,' Claire said, above the sounds of the accordion and the woman's soulful voice.

'Yes,' replied her mother, smiling. 'I can't count the times Brian has told me today.'

'He's a lucky man to have you.'

'No, I'm the lucky one,' Elizabeth said as she put her hand lightly on her daughter's waist to begin the dance. 'And I believe that one day you'll be just as lucky too.'

'Can I cut in?'

The voice came from behind her, but Claire felt her heart lurch in recognition and she hardly dared to turn around. She registered her mother's curious face, her polite smile for the stranger.

'Yes, of course you can,' Elizabeth said and let go of her daughter, moving to one side to be swept up by Brian and waltzed away. Claire wondered if she was about to faint but suddenly she felt strong arms take hold of her, starting to gently move her across the dance floor to the rhythm of the music. She forced herself to look up into the face of her dancing partner. It swam in front of her as she tried to focus, tried to comprehend whom she was looking at.

'What are you doing here?' she whispered.

'Looking for you.'

Stefan bent his head and kissed her softly on the lips. She felt as though she was melting. *This must be a dream*, she thought, and found herself kissing him back. It felt so easy, so delicious.

346

She pulled away abruptly.

'How on earth did you get here? Why are you here?'

She stopped, motionless in the middle of all the moving couples on the dance floor and looked up at the face she had never expected to see again. His hair was shorter than she remembered and speckled with strands of grey. He wore a collarless white linen shirt and jeans. A fine layer of stubble covered the lower half of his tanned brown face.

'I'm sorry. I know this must be a total shock.'

He had to shout above the music. Other dance couples were staring at them, irritated that they were blocking the dance floor.

'And I'm sorry for kissing you like that. I couldn't help it. You look so beautiful in white, like the day I first saw you in your garden. Do you remember?'

He took her hand. 'Can we go somewhere quieter to talk?'

Claire started to let him lead her from the dance floor then suddenly reality came flooding back – what had happened, what Stefan had done to her, done to her life. Anger swelled inside and she stopped and snatched her hand away.

'No, we can't talk. I never want to see you again, let alone talk to you.'

Stefan moved towards her and she stepped back. He looked upset.

'I've driven for ten hours to get here. Couldn't you at least give me a few minutes?'

Claire desperately tried to decide what to do. Force him to leave and try to forget he'd been there, or let him stay to reopen old wounds and memories so painful she hadn't even dared to think about them for three years?

'You do realise that you're gate-crashing my mother's wedding?' she said.

'I know. Sally said it would be all right.'

Claire felt her head spinning; she wished she hadn't drunk so much wine.

'Sally told you where to find me? How do you know Sally? I'm sure she'd never have told you where I was.'

'Could we go somewhere more private?' Stefan reached out and touched her arm.

'Don't touch me,' she blurted out, pushing him away. 'Don't think you have any right to touch me, or any right to be here at all. What do you want? Why have you come here?'

Claire was shouting now. She was vaguely aware that the music and the singing had stopped, that the other guests were watching, listening; she could see Elizabeth and Brian, their faces alarmed. Claire didn't care.

'How dare you walk into my life again after everything that happened? How dare you just appear like this from nowhere and expect me to want to talk to you? You turned my life upside down, destroyed everything in it – my home, my family, my heart. You did that and look at you now: standing here like nothing happened at all, remembering how we first met, asking me if I remember it too. Of course I remember it and I wish it had never happened. I wish you'd never walked into my garden. I wish I'd never met you at all.

'You have no idea what I had to go through to get to where I am today – while you've been swanning around the world, no doubt seducing other naïve women in their idyllic homes and then going home to your girlfriend. Or is she your wife?'

'I don't have a girlfriend or a wife.'

'I saw you with her.' Claire's voice was getting louder. 'You lied to me. You led me on. You let me fall in love with you, risk everything for you, and all along you were seeing someone else.'

'Claire, I . . .'

She wouldn't let Stefan interrupt, tears were rolling down her cheeks; she tried to brush them away with her fingers.

'Do you know what happened? Do you know what William did to the house because of you – because of us?'

'I know,' said Stefan. 'Sally told me. It must have been terrible.'

'Terrible!' shouted Claire. 'Yes, of course it was terrible. The whole house up in flames, gone forever; all those rooms you photographed, gone, all our possessions destroyed. The children could have been killed.'

348

She pushed up the soft translucent sleeve of her cardigan and held up her arm in front of his face.

'Look at these scars. And these are only the scars on the outside. You hurt me, Stefan. You hurt me more than you'll ever know and the last thing I ever want to do is see you again.'

Brian stepped forward and put his arm protectively around her.

'Do you need help, Claire? Shall I ask this man to leave?'

Claire looked around her and suddenly felt embarrassed by her very public outburst.

'What's going on, darling?' her mother asked, coming to join Brian by Claire's side.

'If I could just have a chance to explain, to tell you what really happened.'

Stefan's dark eyes held Claire's own. Powerless to look away she remembered how he made her feel. Emotions buried long ago came flooding back. Suddenly someone was pushing through the crowd of people.

'Sally, what on earth are you doing here?'

Sally's face was flushed; she sounded out of breath. 'You've got to talk to him, Claire. Please give him a chance to explain what happened.'

Claire looked into Stefan's eyes again; they seemed to plead with her.

'Please, Claire, he needs to talk to you.' Sally gave her a hug and then a little shake. 'I wouldn't have come all this way with someone who drove like a maniac and talked about nothing else but you for seven hundred miles if I didn't think that it was important for you to hear what he's got to say.'

'I don't understand.'

'For God's sake, just talk to the man.' She practically pushed Claire and Stefan from the dance floor.

'OK,' Claire sighed.

Stefan followed as she led him away from the inquisitive eyes, out of sight, to the side of the house. An antique lantern cast a flickering light across the cobbled drive.

'Claudia!' Claire exclaimed, as she saw the car parked in front of her. The top was down. She reached out and touched the shiny bonnet; it felt hot.

'She's done really well,' said Stefan, putting his hand beside hers on the car. 'She's been locked up in a garage for years and then suddenly I'm driving her like a madman across France to get to see you. Do you want to get in?' he asked, opening the passenger door.

Wordlessly Claire slipped onto the smooth red seat. Stefan got into the other side and they sat in silence for a while. The music in the garden had started up again.

'Are we going anywhere?' Claire asked tentatively.

'Do you mean in the car?'

'Of course. What else would I mean?'

'Something more allegorical?'

Claire said nothing. Suddenly Napoleon jumped in and sat beside Claire as though ready to set off for a drive in the car.

'A friend of yours?' asked Stefan.

'My new man.'

'What's he called?'

'Napoleon.'

'I won't pick a fight with him then.'

He leant across Claire to scratch Napoleon's head, then sat back.

'I like your shop and café,' he said after a few moments. 'Nice fairy cakes.'

'Thank you,' she said, staring straight ahead of her, watching moths as they buffeted around the lantern, then realising what he'd said. 'You've been there?'

Stefan nodded. 'I wondered if you're still using locally sourced ants in your pies?'

'Sorry?'

'The squashed ants in your mincemeat. I never eat a mince pie without thinking of you.'

Claire laughed; she couldn't help it. She stopped laughing and looked at him.

'What do you want, Stefan?'

'I'm so sorry about everything,' he said, holding her gaze. 'I've been abroad. I had no idea about what happened. I'm so sorry,' he repeated. 'It's all been such a mess.'

Suddenly tears were falling from Claire's eyes again. Stefan reached across her and produced a large white handkerchief from the glove box. She wiped her eyes with it and she could smell Stefan on the cotton – lemons, sandalwood. It filled her with a longing to touch him. She resisted and tightly scrunched the damp handkerchief between both her hands.

'I don't know why you've come back,' she said, looking out across the garden. 'I've spent so long trying not to think about you.'

'I've spent so long thinking of little else but you,' he said.

He took a deep breath and sighed. After a few moments' silence he said, 'You were wrong. She wasn't my girlfriend, or my wife – the woman you saw me with. She was my sister.'

Claire looked at him.

'She came to see me that night after your husband had found my texts and phoned me up.'

'William told me that he had. I couldn't bear to ask him what he said.'

'He told me that he loved you, that you were the most precious thing in his life.' Stefan sighed before going on. 'He said he'd made mistakes, that he hadn't appreciated you and that you'd been working on your marriage since the summer, I think he even mentioned counselling. He said you were very happy together and he begged me to leave you alone, to give him a chance to keep his marriage and family together. He was sobbing; it was heartbreaking to listen to. He told me he was going to show you just how much he loved you.'

'Is that what he was trying to do when he set fire to the house?' said Claire grimly.

Stefan looked at Claire with a shocked expression.

'I didn't realise he set fire to the house.'

Claire nodded and Stefan ran his fingers through his hair and let out a deep breath.

'He was in a terrible state. I promised him you wouldn't hear from me again. I'd already decided I would leave the country if you didn't want to see me. I'd already started packing because I doubted very much you'd say yes. After I spoke to William I phoned my sister to say goodbye, she came over and we had a bottle of wine and in the end she stayed the night. There was so much to arrange, the flat to sort out, I wanted to put Claudia in a lock-up, I needed my sister's help. That was who you must have seen at my flat, it couldn't have been anyone else.'

Claire looked at him; she thought about the woman that she'd seen at the window, she had been tall like Stefan, dark like Stefan, wavy hair, just like Stefan's would be if he let it grow. Claire felt her head spinning again. If she had known that was his sister she would have got out of the car and rung the doorbell and everything would have been so very different.

'What did you say in your text?' Claire asked.

'I said that I missed you, that I wanted to see you, I asked you to meet me. If I'd seen you face to face I would have told you I'd spent months regretting what I said that afternoon at the hotel, I'd have begged you to leave William, begged you to come and live with me, you and the children, I had it all planned, I wanted us to find a house together with enough space for you to work, enough space for the kids, I didn't care where, anywhere that you were happy would have been enough for me.'

'And you let William change your mind?'

'He was your husband, Claire. I wanted to believe he made your life miserable but the way he talked sounded as though you'd sorted things out, that you were happy. He sounded as though he adored you. I remember picking up my copy of *Idyllic Homes* and thinking that perhaps it all really was as wonderful as we'd made it seem in the photographs, perhaps your life really was perfect and you'd never been serious about me.'

'Oh Stefan, how could you have doubted I was serious, after everything I said to you?'

He put his head in his hands.

'I know, now I can see how stupid I was to think that. I never would have dreamed that William would go on to do what he did that night. How could he have done that to his home, his family? I know I shouldn't have believed what he said on the phone, I should have come to find you, talked to you before I gave up hope.'

He sat up and stared ahead of him as though remembering.

'In fact I did try one more time, I sent another text from outside the Heathrow terminus but when you didn't answer I got on the plane.'

'William destroyed my phone; he smashed it up and ground it into the floor. I never could have got that message.'

She put her hand on his arm and kept it there. 'Where did you go?'

'I spent a few months in the States working for different magazines over there. Then I started just aimlessly travelling around the world, taking random pictures, having adventures that seemed pointless to be having alone but mostly trying to forget you.'

He paused and looked straight at her and then laughed.

'I wasn't very good at that, I'm afraid, but I started selling my pictures to travel publications instead of interiors magazines.'

'Isn't that what you wanted?' Claire asked. 'To be a travel photographer?'

'Yes. It's funny the way things happen. Life can end up going the way you wanted it to but not necessarily by the most direct route, or the smoothest.'

'I know what you mean,' she said.

'I only came back to England yesterday morning.'

'What brought you back?' Claire asked.

'Oh, you know,' said Stefan, 'frosty mornings.'

'Marmite,' she said, with a small smile, remembering their long-ago conversation in the heat of a July afternoon.

'And you,' he said.

'Why now?'

'I saw an article about you in a magazine. I was waiting in an airport lounge for a flight from New York to Tokyo and there was a rack of British magazines on a newsstand. I picked one up to pass the time, started to half-heartedly flick through it when suddenly there you were, smiling out at me, surrounded by a completely different home from the one I thought you were happily living in with William. Your flat, the shop, I immediately recognised your taste – Sienna's pictures were really lovely. I skimmed through the article, it said you were divorced, it mentioned the fire though of course I needed Sally to put all that into context, and it didn't seem to suggest any other men in your life, though now I do seem to remember there was a picture of a dog a lot like him.'

He stroked Napoleon's head again.

'I had to see you straight away. I nearly got arrested because I walked off with the magazine and forgot to pay; the newspaper vendor got me chased by a great big, gun-toting airport guard who didn't seem to understand I'd just rediscovered the love of my life. After I'd got out of that awkward situation I changed my flight from Tokyo to Heathrow and as soon as the plane landed set off to find your shop. I had flowers for you and everything. I was devastated when I met Sally and she told me you were away.'

He laughed.

'She's a feisty woman. She gave me quite a piece of her mind when I told her who I was.'

'I can imagine,' Claire said with a small smile.

'I explained everything to her, told her about the texts and William, told her how I feel about you, how important it was that I saw you, and before I knew it she'd agreed to bring me to you here.'

'She'd use any excuse to get to a wedding,' Claire said, smiling.

'On the way she told me everything that had happened to you. It's true what you said. I really did ruin your life.'

'Maybe it's not really ruined,' she said. 'Just changed. I'm much happier now than I ever was in that house with William and his endless home improvements.'

'If I had known, Claire, if I had known about the fire, about your divorce, I would have come to find you long ago. I wish I'd known, I wish you'd never had to go through all that on your own.'

'Things haven't worked out so badly for me after all.'

'What about us?' he asked.

Claire didn't reply. Stefan reached into the pocket of his shirt and brought out a length of silver chain interspersed with small pearl buttons. Claire remained silent as she stared at the familiar necklace.

'I've kept it with me wherever I've gone. I've always wanted to give it back to you one day.'

He reached out and took her hand and let the chain coil into her palm. He gently closed her fingers over it, let go of her hand and sat back in his seat.

Claire looked straight ahead at the shifting shadows of the lantern-lit drive. She noticed pale pink roses scrambling over a trellis in front of them. According to her grandmother, pale pink roses meant perfect happiness to come. She turned to Stefan.

'I vowed I'd never get involved with anyone again. I'm used to being on my own, and I've got the children to think of and . . .'

Her voice trailed off. She looked into his soft brown eyes and found it hard to look away.

'We could take it very slowly,' he said, looking back at her.

She had to fight an urge to touch his face.

'Just one day at a time. We could make a lovely home together.'

'Please don't say it could be perfect,' said Claire. She thought she saw a glimpse of Sally and her mother peeping round the corner of the house. Stefan was gradually moving towards her.

'OK,' he said. 'It definitely won't be perfect.'

And he leant across the red leather seat and gently kissed her lips.

**Read on for an extract from Kate Glanville's**
*The Peacock House . . .*

# EVELYN

## December 1943
## Vaughan Court, North Wales

*Dismal.* It was the only word that Evelyn could think of.

*Dismal, dismal, dismal* – it ricocheted around her head as she stared out of the bay window. The rain ran in unrelenting tears down the diamonds of glass and the wind moaned through the gaps around the ancient frame.

Outside there was a world of nothing. The garden had completely disappeared into the thick, grey mist. It was hard to imagine the view; the sea in the distance, the mountains that swept down to the shore, the rooftops of the houses that clustered around the crescent bay.

Evelyn turned and looked around the enormous bedroom; it was much too big for the mean little fire that crackled in the grate.

Flopping down onto the eiderdown she stared at the ornately plastered ceiling. Its Jacobean swirls reminded her of a wedding cake. There had been no cake at her wedding to Howard, rationing had made sure of that. The war had also made sure there had been no white satin dress, or trailing bouquet, though she wasn't sure the war could be blamed for the lack of other things a bride expected.

It had been two years since her wedding day, nearly two years since she had been banished to the land of rain and rocks and shrouding cloud. *Two years*, Evelyn whispered and saw a chilly puff of air escape between her lips.

This would be her second Christmas in Wales, in the huge house, with only her mother-in-law for company at the dinner table. So different from the boisterous Christmas dinners at Wilton Terrace where there had been jokes and riddles, and indoor fireworks, and endless bottles of champagne from the cellar. There had always been a huge fir tree in the hall, soaring up through the stairwell; Evelyn and her brother and sister had to stand on ladders to decorate it. At Vaughan Court they didn't have a tree.

'They are unpatriotic!' Lady Vaughan had declared when Evelyn had dared to suggest they put one up in the drawing room. 'We will take no part in Germanic traditions at Vaughan Court.'

She wondered if Howard would come to visit this year. She doubted it. His work in Whitehall was much more important than a wife, especially when he had everything he wanted in London. She tried not to think of the letter; the swirling writing, the sickening scent of violets, the words that had suggested an intimacy Evelyn had no experience of. Instead she glanced over at the jumper she'd been knitting; her mother-in-law had suggested it as a gift for Howard.

'It will give you something to do,' Lady Vaughan had said.

The colour of the wool was hideous, it was all that they had in the town.

Evelyn closed her eyes and wished for something to happen, anything, anything at all, as long as it was something more exciting than the life she had.

She opened her eyes at the sound of the rain beating harder against the windows. The moaning of the wind grew louder, more like a howl, and then a roar. She sat up. The windowpanes started to rattle in their leaden frames and for a moment everything seemed to darken, as though the shadow of some colossal beast had passed by outside. Then there was a bang, an explosion. The whole room seemed to shake; Evelyn thought the windowpanes might shatter. Jumping up from the bed she tried to crane her neck to see from the window, but everything was fog. She heard shouting below her. The boys.

*A crash, there's been a crash on the mountain.*

Without even stopping to think she wrenched open the bedroom door and ran. Racing down the long corridor, she had no time to scowl at the beastly portraits, the Persian rugs slipping beneath her feet. She almost tripped as she took the steps of the marble stair case two at a time. With an ungraceful skid she crossed the black-and-white-tiled hall and pulled at the heavy oak door until it opened and she was outside.

The rain had turned to sleet, slivers of ice pricking at her cheeks; her hands were already turning numb. Ignoring the cold, Evelyn ran around the side of the house. The boys were smudges ahead of her, already scrambling up the steep path.

*Peter, Billy.*

She called their names and set off as fast as she could, following them upwards, clambering over rocks and boulders. The smell of smoke was thick on the wind and high above her on the mountainside something was giving off a ghostly glow.

**Available to order**

ACCENT

## Discover more unforgettable stories
## by Kate Glanville . . .

**It's hard to run away from your deepest secrets . . .**

When Phoebe's lover dies in a car accident, their hushed
affair goes with him to the grave.

Heartbroken, she abandons her life in England and searches
out the old boathouse on the west coast of Ireland left to her
by her grandmother. Soon she is embraced by the villagers
of nearby Carraigmore and slowly begins to heal.

But when Phoebe discovers a collection of old diaries hidden
under the floor of the boathouse, she finds herself immersed
in a story of family scandal and a passionate affair between
her grandmother and a young Irish artist.

With so many unanswered questions, Phoebe turns to the locals who
knew her late grandmother best. But when she is met by silence, she
realises she's not the only one (in her family) with something to hide . . .

**Available to order**

**ACCENT**

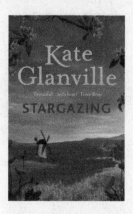

*Three women connected by one man.*

Daniel is father to Seren, husband to Nesta and lover to Frankie.
When he leaves Nesta and their beautiful home in the middle
of a party celebrating their fortieth wedding anniversary, Seren's
world begins to crumble. Only the continuation of the family
ideal can make things right. But Nesta isn't so sure.

And for Frankie, Daniel offers hope of a safe and secure future.
But all three women are carrying secrets that they've
kept hidden, even from those closest to them. Secrets
that might threaten a life . . .

**Available to order**

**ACCENT**

**A warm, inviting story of love and family secrets set
in the beautiful French countryside.**

Twenty-five years ago, Martha Morgan lost everything. Once a
member of a prestigious band, she now lives in solitude in the heart of
the Dordogne, surrounded by an ancient cherry orchard.

Attempting to piece her life back together, Martha decides to
rent her idyllic French farmhouse *Le Couvent des Cerises*
to holidaymakers for the summer, hiring the mysterious
Ben to help reconstruct the dishevelled B&B.

But when a vicious storm makes its way across the village, tensions
begin to rise. Martha, Ben and the guests are forced to pull together and
they're about to find out that they have more in common than they
realise – but it might mean jeopardising the secret of Martha's past . . .

**Available to order**

**ACCENT**